BUCKETS OF DIAMONDS

BUCKETS OF DIAMONDS

AND OTHER STORIES

The Complete Short Fiction
of Clifford D. Simak,
Volume Thirteen

Introduction by David W. Wixon

OPEN ROAD

INTEGRATED MEDIA
NEW YORK

"Horrible Example" © 1961 by Street & Smith Publications, Inc. © 1989 by the Estate of Clifford D. Simak. Originally published in *Analog Science Fact/Science Fiction*, v. 67, no. 1, March, 1961. Reprinted by permission of the Estate of Clifford D. Simak.

"Lobby" © 1944 by Street & Smith Publications, Inc. © 1972 by Clifford D. Simak. Originally published in *Astounding Science Fiction*, v. 33, no. 2, April, 1944. Reprinted by permission of the Estate of Clifford D. Simak.

"The Trouble with Ants" © 1950 by Ziff-Davis Publishing Company. © 1978 by Clifford D. Simak. Originally published in *Fantastic Adventures*, v. 13, no. 1, January, 1951. Reprinted by permission of the Estate of Clifford D. Simak.

"Buckets of Diamonds" © 1969 by Galaxy Publishing Corporation. © 1997 by the Estate of Clifford D. Simak. Originally published in *Galaxy Magazine*, v. 28, no. 3, April, 1969. Reprinted by permission of the Estate of Clifford D. Simak.

"The Fighting Doc of Bushwhack Basin" © 1944 by Popular Publications, Inc. © 1972 by Clifford D. Simak. Originally published in *.44 Western Magazine*, v. 11, no. 4, November, 1944. Reprinted by permission of the Estate of Clifford D. Simak.

". . . And the Truth Shall Make You Free" © 1953 by Columbia Publications, Inc. © 1981 by Clifford D. Simak. Originally published in *Future Science Fiction*, v. 3, no. 6, March, 1953. Reprinted by permission of the Estate of Clifford D. Simak.

"Clerical Error" © 1940 by Street & Smith Publications, Inc. © 1968 by Clifford D. Simak. Originally published in *Astounding Science-Fiction*, August, 1940, vol. 25, no. 6. Reprinted by permission of the Estate of Clifford D. Simak.

"Shadow of Life" © 1943 by Street & Smith Publications, Inc. © 1971 by Clifford D. Simak. Originally published in *Astounding Science-Fiction*, v. 31, no. 1, March, 1943. Reprinted by permission of the Estate of Clifford D. Simak.

"Infiltration" © 1943 by Columbia Publications, Inc. © 1971 by Clifford D. Simak. Originally published in *Science Fiction Stories*, v. 3, no. 5, July, 1943. Reprinted by permission of the Estate of Clifford D. Simak.

"The Marathon Photograph" © 1974 by Clifford D. Simak. © 2002 by the Estate of Clifford D. Simak. Originally appeared in *Threads of Time: Three Original Novellas of Science Fiction*, ed. Robert Silverberg, published by Thomas Nelson & Son, Nashville, 1974. Reprinted by permission of the Estate of Clifford D. Simak.

Introduction © 2023 by David W. Wixon

ISBN: 978-1-5040-8311-9

This edition published in 2023 by Open Road Integrated Media, Inc.
180 Maiden Lane
New York, NY 10038
www.openroadmedia.com

CONTENTS

INTRODUCTION:
CLIFFORD D. SIMAK:
HIGH ANXIETY?

"It was dark and lonely and unending in the depths of space with no Companion."

—*Clifford D. Simak, in "A Death in the House"*

Something about space travel, as we envision it, did not appeal to the writer Clifford D. Simak; and I have come to believe that there is a reason for this that may be rooted in that author's psyche.

In his long career Clifford D. Simak wrote more than 150 science fiction stories (the exact number is unclear, since records show that some of his stories have been lost); but it may be surprising to learn that a relatively small number of those stories revolved around that mainstay motif of science fiction—space travel.

It is true that some of Cliff Simak's science fiction involved the actual portrayal of that classic mode of travel; but close examination of both his novels and shorter fiction reveals that most mentioned spaceships only in passing, focusing on the story of what happened after the ship landed. (I will not argue the issue of whether "Target Generation" (see Volume 7 of this series, *The*

Complete Short Fiction of Clifford D. Simak) counts as such a tale, since although most of the action did in fact take place during interstellar travel, the story was a "generation ship" story, and most of the ship's passengers were unaware that they were on a spaceship until the end of the story.)

It is also true that Cliff Simak's fiction tended to focus more on personalities than on technology. Still, I find in his work a puzzling sort of aversion to space travel. In, for instance, "The Shipshape Miracle" (see Volume 10 of this series, *The Complete Short Fiction of Clifford D. Simak*), a marooned criminal, seeking to evade law enforcement, is offered a ride in a spaceship—only to find himself locked inside it . . . for life. And in "Lulu," (see Volume 14), three Earthmen struggle to gain control of their ship which, having been created to have its own robotic personality, is making life very difficult for the passengers . . .

And then there is the novel *Time is the Simplest Thing*, in which the entire plot revolves around the fact that space travel is impossibly deadly for human beings; other ways to explore the universe must be used.

In fact, a number of Cliff's stories revolved around ways to travel off-Earth by means other than ships. In the novel *Shakespeare's Planet*, an Earthman who has been in suspended animation on an interstellar voyage awakens on a distant world, only to discover that humankind has learned, since his ship left Earth, to travel farther and faster than his ship could, through the use of mysterious "tunnels" through space—thus passing him by while he slept. And in "The Spaceman's Van Gogh" (see Volume 12), people travel by means of something called "polting," which is never really explained, perhaps because it is irrelevant to the plot.

And yet, despite such evidence, Simak wrote an entire astronomy-popularization book entitled *Wonder and Glory: The Story of the Universe* (St. Martin's Press, 1969)—a title that also happens to contain a phrase he used a number of times in his fiction: wonder and glory. In it he wrote enthusiastically of the "glory" of the stars, of the Universe. That makes me sure that he really liked the idea of being Out There—but that he preferred some form of travel that would not require a ship.

What might have caused Simak to find some aspects, at least, of space travel unappealing? If he liked the idea of being Out There, but did not want to be in a ship—was it that he did not want to be confined? Was he indulging some secret fantasy, in "All the Traps of Earth" (see Volume 1) when his character, the robot Richard Daniel, rode on the outside of a ship in interstellar space, and received thereby an extraordinary gift? Or consider the story "Brother" (see Volume 8), in which Phil, an "extension" of the stay-at-home writer Edward Lambert, travels in or on ships. In what might have been Cliff's Simak's most autobiographical piece of fiction, did his point-of-view character find another way to see the Universe without having to get into a ship?

In "Condition of Employment" (see Volume 3), humans have to be drugged and brainwashed to make them willing to endure a space voyage. And in "A Death in the House" (Volume 7), an alien being who has crash-landed on Earth survives and is able to return to space due to the aid of a lonely, ignorant Earthman. In thanks, the alien makes a gift to the Earthman of the device that helps it endure the awfulness of space travel.

Did Cliff Simak have some sort of phobia about space travel? He told me, when his wife died, that he had chosen to have them both interred in an above-ground vault rather than buried in a conventional grave; he explained to me that he did not like the idea of being put underground. I drew a line from that comment to his great story "Huddling Place" (Volume 5), in which the point-of-view character tragically fails to board a ship that was to take him to Mars to save a friend's life. The character diagnoses himself as having agoraphobia, but he is unable to deal with the disabling condition.

Please note that I am not suggesting that Cliff Simak suffered from agoraphobia—or, for that matter, from claustrophobia; and in fact Cliff's daughter has told me that she knows nothing about her father having either such phobia. (Interestingly, she added that she was under the impression that the vault was her mother's idea; and knowing Cliff, I would not put it past him to have taken upon himself the responsibility for such a decision. . . .)

I have come to the conclusion that although Cliff Simak liked the idea of being Out There, he did not want to be in a ship, did not want to be confined. His idea might have been best expressed, albeit ambivalently, by Richard Daniel, the robot who, in "All the Traps of Earth," rode on the outside of a ship that entered hyperspace and was transformed. Richard Daniel, Cliff wrote, "felt the mystery and delight and the loneliness and the color and the great uncaring . . ."

In fact, Cliff, on several occasions, spoke of the cold darkness between the stars, and of the "great uncaringness" Out There. But I would suggest that despite the negative feelings displayed in such words, he made it clear on many occasions that he felt a strong attraction to the wonderfulness of the Universe.

David W. Wixon

HORRIBLE EXAMPLE

One of the reasons Clifford D. Simak would come to be described as the "pastoralist of science fiction" was because so many of his most endearing stories were set in small towns—towns often much like those in the Middle America of Cliff's boyhood. And many of those small towns bore the name "Millville"—which happened to be the name of the closest town to the Wisconsin farm on which Cliff Simak was raised. But don't be misled: the actual Millville was very little like the Millvilles of Cliff's stories. Cliff often remarked that his memories of his home area frequently turned out to be different, on those occasions when he returned; the valleys were deeper, he said, the ridges steeper and higher—and the woods darker and more mysterious.

This particular story, though, is concerned less with the countryside than with the people of the small town—their attitudes and mores, their very human strengths and failings . . . Cliff Simak could portray that kind of thing better than most.

"Horrible Example" first appeared in the March 1961 issue of Analog Science Fiction/Science Fact.

—dww

Tobias staggered down the street and thought how tough it was.

He hadn't any money and Joe, the barkeep, had hurled him out of Happy Hollow tavern before he'd much more than wet his whistle and now all that was left for him was the cold and lonely shack that he called a home and no one gave a damn, no matter what might happen. For, he told himself, with maudlin self-pity, he was nothing but a bum and a drunken one at that and it was a wonder the town put up with him at all.

It was getting dusk, but there still were people on the street and he could sense that they were trying, very consciously, not to look at him.

And that was all right, he told himself. If they didn't want to look, that was all right with him. They didn't have to look. If it helped them any, there was no reason they should look.

He was the town's disgrace. He was its people's social cross. He was their public shame. He was the horrible example. And he was unique, for there never was more than one of him in any little town—there simply wasn't room for more than one like him.

He reeled forlornly down the sidewalk and he saw that Elmer Clark, the village cop, was standing on the corner. Not doing anything. Just standing there and watching. But it was all right. Elmer was a good guy. Elmer knew exactly how it was.

Tobias stood for a moment to get his bearings and finally he had them; he set a dead sight for the corner where Elmer waited for him. He navigated well. He finally reached the corner.

"Tobe," said Elmer, "maybe you should let me take you home. The car's just over there."

Tobias drew himself erect with fly-blown dignity.

"Couldn't think of it," he announced, every inch a gentleman. "Cannot let you do it. Very kindly of you."

Elmer grinned. "Take it easy, then. Sure that you can make it?"

"Poshitive," said Tobias, wobbling quickly off.

He did fairly well. He managed several blocks without incident.

But on the corner of Third and Maple, disaster overtook him. He fell flat upon his face and Mrs. Frobisher was standing on her porch where she could see him fall. Tomorrow, he was full aware, she would tell all the women at the Ladies Aid Society what a shameful thing it was. They all would quietly cluck among themselves, pursing up their mouths and feeling extra holy. For Mrs. Frobisher was their leader; she could do nothing wrong. Her husband was the banker and her son the star of Millville's football team, which was headed for the Conference championship. And that, without a doubt, was a thing of pride and wonder. It had been years since Millville High had won the Conference crown.

Tobias got up and dusted himself off, none too quietly and rather awkwardly, then managed to make his way to the corner of Third and Oak, where he sat down on the low stone wall that ran along the front of the Baptist church. The pastor, he knew, when he came from his basement study, would be sure to see him there. And it might do the pastor, he told himself, a world of good to see him. It might buck him up no end.

The pastor, he feared, was taking it too easy lately. Everything was going just a bit too smoothly and he might be getting smug, with his wife the president of the local DAR and his leggy daughter making such good progress with her music.

Tobias was sitting there and waiting for the pastor to come out when he heard the footsteps shuffling down the walk. It was fairly dark by now and it was not until the man got closer that he saw it was Andy Donovan, the janitor at the school.

Tobias chided himself a bit. He should have recognized the shuffle.

"Good evening, Andy," he said. "How are things tonight?"

Andy stopped and looked at him. Andy brushed his drooping mustache and spat upon the sidewalk so that if anyone were looking they'd be convinced of his disgust.

"If you're waiting for Mr. Halvorsen to come out," he said, "it's a dreadful waste of time. He is out of town."

"I didn't know," Tobias said, contritely.

"You've done quite enough tonight," said Andy, tartly. "You might just as well go home. Mrs. Frobisher stopped me as I was going past. She said we simply have to do something firm about you."

"Mrs. Frobisher," said Tobias, staggering to his feet, "is an old busybody."

"She's all of that," said Andy. "She's likewise a decent woman."

He scraped around abruptly and went shuffling down the street, moving, it seemed, a trifle more rapidly than was his usual pace.

Tobias wobbled solemnly down the street behind him, with the wobble somewhat less pronounced, and he felt the bitterness and the question grew inside of him.

For it was unfair.

Unfair that he should be as he was when he could just as well be something else entirely—when the whole conglomerate of emotion and desire that spelled the total of himself cried out for something else.

He should not, he told himself, be compelled to be the conscience of this town. He was made for better things, he assured himself, hiccuping solemnly.

The houses became more scattered and infrequent and the sidewalk ended and he went stumbling down the unpaved road, heading for his shack at the edge of town.

His shack stood on a hill set above a swamp just beyond the intersection of this road on which he walked with Highway 49 and it was a friendly place to live, he thought. Often he just sat outside and watched the cars stream past.

But there was no traffic now and the moon was coming up above a distant copse and its light was turning the countryside to a black and silver etching.

He went down the road, his feet plopping in the dust and every now and then something set a bird to twitter and there was the smell of burning autumn leaves.

It was beautiful, Tobias thought—beautiful and lonely. But what the hell, he thought, he was always lonely.

Far off he heard the sound of the car, running hard and fast, and he grumbled to himself at how some people drove.

He went stumbling down the dusty stretch and now, some distance to the east, he saw the headlights of the car, traveling rapidly.

He watched it as he walked and as it neared the intersection there was a squeal of brakes and the headlights swung toward him as the car made a sudden turn into his road.

Then the headlight beams knifed into the sky and swept across it in a rapid arc and he caught the dash of glowing taillights as the car skidded with the scream of rubber grinding into pavement.

Slowly, almost ponderously, the car was going over, toppling as it plunged toward the ditch.

Tobias found that he was running, legs pumping desperately and no wobble in them now.

Ahead of him the car hit on its side and skidded with a shrill, harsh grinding, then nosed easily, almost deliberately down into the roadside ditch. He heard the gentle splash of water as it slid to a halt and hung there, canted on its side, with its wheels still spinning.

He leaped from the road down onto the side of the car that lay uppermost and wrenched savagely at the door, using both his hands. But the door was a stubborn thing that creaked and groaned, but still refused to stir. He braced himself as best he could and yanked; it came open by an inch or so. He bent and got his fingers hooked beneath the door edge and even as he did he smelled the acrid odor of burning insulation and he knew the time was short. He became aware as well of the trapped and frightened desperation underneath the door.

A pair of hands from inside was helping with the door and he slowly straightened, pulling with every ounce of strength he had within his body and the door came open, but protestingly.

There were sounds now from inside the car, a soft, insistent whimpering, and the smell of burning sharper, and he caught the flare of flame running underneath the hood.

Something snapped and the door came upward, then stuck tight again, but now there was room enough and Tobias reached down into the opening and found an arm and hauled. A man came out.

"She's still in there," gasped the man. "She's still—"

But already Tobias was reaching down blindly into the darkness of the car's interior and now there was smoke as well as smell and the area beneath the hood was a gushing redness.

He found something alive and soft and struggling and somehow got a hold on it and hauled. A girl came out; a limp, bedraggled thing she was and scared out of her wits.

"Get out of here!" Tobias yelled and pushed the man so that he tumbled off the car and scrambled up the ditchside until he reached the road.

Tobias jumped, half carrying, half dragging the girl, and behind him the car went up in a gush of flame.

They staggered up the road, the three of them, driven by the heat of the burning car. Somewhere, somehow, the man got the girl out of Tobias' grasp and stood her on her feet. She seemed to be all right except for the trickle of darkness that ran out of her hairline, down across her face.

There were people running down the road now. Doors were banging far away and there was shouting back and forth, while the three of them stood in the road and waited, all of them just a little dazed.

And now, for the first time, Tobias saw the faces of those other two. The man, he saw, was Randy Frobisher, Millville's football hero, and the girl was Betty Halvorsen, the musical daughter of the Baptist minister.

Those who were running down the road were getting close by now and the pillar of flame from the burning car was dying down a bit. There was no further need, Tobias told himself, for him to stick around. For it had been a great mistake, he told himself; he never should have done it.

He abruptly turned around and went humping down the road, as rapidly as he could manage short of actual running. He thought he heard one of the two standing in the road call out after him, but he paid them no attention and kept on moving, getting out of there as fast as he was able.

He reached the intersection and crossed it and left the road and went up the path to where his shack perched in all its loneliness on the hill above the swamp.

And he forgot to stagger.

But it didn't matter now, for there was no one watching.

He felt all cold and shivery and there was a sense of panic in him. For this might spoil everything; this might jeopardize his job.

There was a whiteness sticking out of the rusty, battered mail box nailed beside the door and he stared at it with wonder, for it was very seldom that he got a piece of mail.

He took the letter from the box and went inside. He found the lamp and lit it and sat down in the rickety chair beside the table in the center of the room.

And now his time was his, he thought, to do with as he wished.

He was off the job—although, technically, that was not entirely true, for he was never off the job entirely.

He rose and took off his tattered jacket and hung it on the chair back, then opened up his shirt to reveal a hairless chest. He sought the panel in his chest and pushed against it and it slid open underneath his hand. At the sink, he took out the container and emptied the beer that he had swallowed. Then he put the container back into his chest again and slid the panel shut. He buttoned up his shirt.

He let his breathing die.

He became comfortably himself.

He sat quietly in the chair and let his brain run down, wiping out his day. Then, slowly, he started up his brain again and made it a different kind of brain—a brain oriented to this private life of his, when he no longer was a drunken bum or a village conscience or a horrible example.

But tonight the day failed to be wiped out entirely and there was bitterness again—the old and acid bitterness that he should be used to protect the humans in the village against their human viciousness.

For there could be no more than one human derelict in any single village—through some strange social law there was never room for more than one of them. Old Bill or Old Charlie or Old Tobe—the pity of the people, regarded with a mingled sentiment of tolerance and disgust. And just as surely as there could not be more than one of them, there always was that one.

But take a robot, a Class One humanoid robot that under ordinary scrutiny would pass as a human being—take that robot and make him the village bum or the village idiot and you beat that social law. And it was perfectly all right for a manlike robot to be the village bum. Because in making him the bum, you spared the village a truly human bum, you spared the human race one blot against itself, you forced that potential human bum, edged out by the robot, to be acceptable. Not too good a citizen, per-haps, but at least marginally respectable.

To be a drunken bum was terrible for a human, but it was all right for a robot. Because robots had no souls. Robots didn't count.

And the most horrible thing about it, Tobias told himself, was that you must stay in character—you must not step out of it except for that little moment, such as now, when you were absolutely sure no one could be watching.

But he'd stepped out of it this night. For a few isolated moments he'd been forced to step out of it. With two human lives at stake, there had been no choice.

Although, he told himself, there might be little harm. The two kids had been so shaken up that there was a chance they'd not known who he was. In the shock of the moment, he might have gone unrecognized.

But the terrible thing about it, he admitted to himself, was that he yearned for that recognition. For there was within himself a certain humanness that called for recognition, for any recognition, for anything at all that would lift him above the drunken bum.

And that was unworthy of himself, he scolded—unworthy of the tradition of the robot.

He forced himself to sit quietly in the chair, not breathing, not doing anything but thinking—being honest with himself, being what he was, not play-acting any more.

It would not be so bad, he thought, if it was all that he was good for—if, in being Millville's horrible example he was working at the limit of his talent.

That, he realized, had been true at one time. It had been true when he'd signed the contract for the job. But it was true no longer. He was ready now for a bigger job.

For he had grown, in that subtle, inexplicable, curious way that robots grew.

And it wasn't right that he should be stuck with this job when there were other, bigger jobs that he could handle easily.

But there was no remedy. There was no way out of it. There was no one he could go to. There was no way he could quit.

For in order to be effective in this job of his, it was basic that no one—no one, except a single contact, who in turn must keep the secret—know he was a robot. He must be accepted as a human. For if it should be known that he was not a human, then the effectiveness of his work would collapse entirely. As a drunken human bum he was a shield held between the town and petty, vulgar vice; as a drunken, lousy, no-good robot he would not count at all.

So no one knew, not even the village council which paid the annual fee, grumblingly, perhaps, to the Society for the Advancement and Betterment of the Human Race, not knowing for what specific purpose it might pay the fee, but fearful not to pay it. For it was not every municipality that was offered the unique and distinctive service of SABHR. Once the fee should be refused, it might be a long, long time before Millville could get on the list again.

So here he sat, he thought, with a contract to this town which would run another decade—a contract of which the town knew nothing, but binding just the same.

There was no recourse, he realized. There was no one he could go to. There was none he could explain to, for once he had explained he'd have wiped out his total sum of service. He would have cheaply tricked the town. And that was something no robot could ever bring himself to do. It would not be the proper thing.

He tried to find within himself some logic for this consuming passion to do the proper thing, for the bond of honor involved within a contract. But there was no clear-cut logic; it was just the way it was. It was the robot way, one of the many conditioning factors which went into a robot's makeup.

So there was no way out of it. He faced another decade of carrying out the contract, of getting drunk, of stumbling down the street, of acting out the besotted, ambitionless, degraded human being—and all to the end that there should be no such actual human.

And being all of this, he thought, choked with bitterness, while knowing he was fit for better things, fit under his present rating for sociological engineering at the supervisor level.

He put out his arm and leaned it on the table and heard the rustle underneath his arm.

The letter. He'd forgotten it.

He picked up the envelope and looked at it and there was no return address and he was fairly certain who it might be from.

He tore it open and took out the folded sheet of paper and he had been right. The letterhead was that of the Society for the Advancement and Betterment of the Human Race.

The letter read:

Dear Associate:

You will be glad to know that your recent rating has been analyzed and that the final computation shows you to be best fitted as a co-ordinator and expediter with a beginning human colony. We feel that you have a great deal to offer in this type of employment and would be able to place you immediately if there were no other consideration.

But we know that you are under a contractual obligation and perhaps do not feel free to consider other employment at the moment.

If there should be a change in this situation, please let us know at once.

The letter was signed with an undecipherable scrawl.

Carefully, he folded the sheet and stuffed it in his pocket.

He could see it now: Out to another planet that claimed another star for sun, helping to establish a human colony, working with the colonists, not as a robot—for in sociology, one never was a robot—but as another human being, a normal human being, a member of the colony.

It would be a brand-new job and a brand-new group of people and a brand-new situation.

And it would be a straight role. No more comedy, no more tragedy. No more clowning, ever.

He got up and paced the floor.

It wasn't right, he told himself. He shouldn't waste another ten years here. He owed this village nothing—nothing but his contract, a sacred obligation. Sacred to a robot.

And here he was, tied to this tiny dot upon the map, when he might go among the stars, when he might play a part in planting among those stars the roots of human culture.

It would not be a large group that would be going out. There was no longer any massive colonizing being done. It had been tried in the early days and failed. Now the groups were small and closely tied together by common interests and old associations.

It was more, he told himself, like homesteading than colonizing. Groups from home communities went out to try their luck, even little villages sending out their bands as in the ancient past the eastern communities had sent their wagon trains into the virgin west.

And he could be in on this great adventure if he could only break his contract, if he could walk out on this village, if he could quit this petty job.

But he couldn't. There was nothing he could do. He'd reached the bare and bitter end of ultimate frustration.

There was a knocking on the door and he stopped his pacing, stricken, for it had been years since there'd been a knock upon the door. A knock upon the door, he told himself, could mean nothing else but trouble. It could only mean that he'd been recognized back there on the road—just when he'd been beginning to believe that he'd gone unrecognized.

He went slowly to the door and opened it and there stood the four of them—the village banker, Herman Frobisher; Mrs. Halvorsen, the wife of the Baptist minister; Bud Anderson, the football coach; and Chris Lambert, the editor of the weekly paper.

And he knew by the looks of them that the trouble would be big—that here was something he could not brush lightly to one side. They had a dedicated and an earnest look about them—and as well the baffled look of people who had been very wrong and had made up their minds most resolutely to do what they could about it.

Herman held out his pudgy hand with a friendly forcefulness so overdone it was ridiculous.

"Tobe," he said, "I don't know how to thank you, I don't have the words to thank you for what you did tonight."

Tobias took his hand and gave it a quick clasp, then tried to let go of it, but the banker's hand held on almost tearfully.

"And running off," shrilled Mrs. Halvorsen, "without waiting to take any credit for how wonderful you were. I can't, for the life of me, know what got into you."

"Oh," Tobias said uncomfortably, "it really wasn't nothing."

The banker let go of Tobias' hand and the coach grabbed hold of it, almost as if he had been waiting for the chance to do so.

"Randy will be all right, thanks to you," he said. "I don't know what we'd have done without him, Tobe, in the game tomorrow night."

"I'll want a picture of you, Tobe," said the editor. "Have you got a picture? No, I suppose you haven't. We'll take one tomorrow."

"But first," the banker said, "we'll get you out of here."

"Out of here?" asked Tobias, really frightened now. "But, Mr. Frobisher, this place is my home!"

"Not any more, it isn't," shrilled Mrs. Halvorsen. "We're going to see that you get the chance that you never had. We're going to talk to AA about you."

"AA?" Tobias asked in a burst of desperation.

"Alcoholics Anonymous," the pastor's wife said primly. "They will help you stop your drinking."

"But suppose," the editor suggested, "that Tobe here doesn't want to."

Mrs. Halvorsen clicked her teeth, exasperated. "Of course he does," she said. "There never was a man—"

"Now, now," said Herman, "I think we may be going just a bit too fast. We'll talk to Tobe tomorrow—"

"Yeah," said Tobias, reaching for the door, "talk to me tomorrow."

"No, you don't," said Herman. "You're coming home with me. The wife's got a supper waiting and we have a room for you and you can stay with us until we get this straightened out."

"I don't see," protested Tobias, "there's much to straighten out."

"But there is," said Mrs. Halvorsen. "This town has never done a thing for you. We've all stood calmly by and watched you stagger past. And it isn't right. I'll talk to Mr. Halvorsen about it."

The banker put a companionable arm around Tobias's shoulder.

"Come on, Tobe," he said. "We never can repay you, but we'll do the best we can."

He lay in bed, with a crisp white sheet beneath him and a crisp white sheet on top and now he had the job, when everyone was asleep, of sneaking to the bathroom and flushing all the food they'd insisted he should eat down the toilet bowl.

And he didn't need white sheets. He didn't need a bed. He had one in his shack, but it was just for the looks of things. But here he had to lie between white sheets and Herman even had insisted that he take a bath and he had needed one, all right, but it had been quite a shock.

His whole life was all loused up, he told himself. His job was down the drain. He'd failed, he thought, and failed most miserably. And now he'd never get a chance to go on a colonizing venture—even after his present job was all wrapped up and done, he'd never have a chance at a really good job. He'd just get another piddling one and he'd spend another twenty years at it and he'd maybe fail in that one, too—for if you had a weakness, it would seek you out.

And he had a weakness. Tonight he'd found it out.

But what should he have done, he asked himself. Should he have hurried past and leave the kids to die inside the flaming car?

He lay between the clean white sheets and looked at the clean, white moonlight streaming through the window and asked himself the question for which there was no answer.

Although there was a hope and he thought about the hope and it became a brighter hope and he felt a good deal better.

He could beat this thing, he told himself—all he had to do was get drunk again, or pretend to get drunk again, for he was never really drunk. He could go on a binge that would be an epic in the history of the village. He could irretrievably disgrace himself. He could publicly and willfully throw away the chance that had been offered him to become a decent citizen. He could slap the good intentions of all these worthy people right smack in the puss and he'd become, because of that, a bigger stinker than he'd ever been before.

He lay there and thought about it. It was a good idea and he would have to do it—but perhaps not right away.

It might look a little better if he waited for a while. It might have more effect if he played at being decent for a week or so. Then when he fell out of grace, the shock might be the greater. Let them wallow for a while in all the holiness of feeling that they had rescued him from a vicious life, let them build up hope before he, laughing in their faces, staggered back to the shack above the swamp.

And when he did that it would be all right. He'd be back on the job again, better than before.

A week or two, perhaps. Or maybe more than that.

And suddenly he knew. He fought against the knowing, but it stood out plain and clear.

He wasn't being honest.

He didn't want to go back to the person he had been.

This was what he'd wanted, he admitted to himself. It was something he had wanted for a long time now—to live in the respect of his fellow villagers, to win some acceptance from them, to win contentment with himself.

Henry had talked after supper about a job for him—an honest, steady job. And lying there, he knew that he yearned to have that job, to become in all reality a humble, worthy citizen of Millville.

But it was impossible and he knew it was and the entire situation was worse than ever now. For he was no longer a simple fumbler, but a traitor, self-confessed.

It was ironical, he told himself, that in failure he should find his heart's desire, a fulfillment he could not consider keeping.

If he'd been a man, he'd have wept.

But he couldn't weep. He lay cold and rigid in the crisp white bed with the crisp white moonlight pouring through the window.

He needed help. For the first time in his life, he was in need of friendly help.

There was one place that he could go, one place of last resort.

Moving softly, he got into his clothes and eased out of the door and went on tiptoe down the stairs.

A block from the house he figured that it was safe to run and he ran in slobbering haste, with the wild horsemen of fear running at his heels.

Tomorrow was the game—the big game that Randy Frobisher was still alive to play in—and Andy Donovan would work late tonight so that he'd have time off from his janitoring to take in the game.

He wondered what the time was and he knew it must be late. But, he told himself, Andy must still be there at his chores of janitoring—he simply must be there.

He reached the school and ran up the curving walk toward the building, looming in all its massive darkness. He wondered, with a sinking feeling, if he had come in vain, if he'd run all this way for nothing.

Then he saw the dim light shining in one of the basement windows—down in the storage room—and he knew it was all right.

The door was locked and he raised a fist and hammered on it, then waited for a while, then hammered once again.

Finally he heard the shuffling footsteps come scuffing up the stairs and a moment later saw the wavering of a shadow just beyond the door.

There was a fumbling of the keys and the snicking of the lock and the door came open.

A hand reached out and dragged him quickly in. The door sighed to behind him.

"Tobe!" cried Andy Donovan. "I am glad you came."

"Andy, I made a mess of it!"

"Yes," Andy said impatiently. "Yes, I know you did."

"I couldn't let them die. I couldn't stand there and do nothing for them. It wouldn't have been human."

"It would have been all right," said Andy. "For you aren't human."

He led the way down the stairs, clinging to the rail and shuffling warily.

And all around them, silence echoing in emptiness, Tobias sensed the eerie terror of a school waiting through the night.

They turned right at the foot of the stairs into the storage room.

The janitor sat down on an empty crate and waved the robot to another.

Tobias did not sit immediately. He had quick amends to make.

"Andy," he said, "I've got it figured out. I'll go on the biggest drunk—"

Andy shook his head, "It would do no good," he said. "You have shown a spark of goodness, a certain sense of greatness. Remembering what you've done, they'd make excuses for you. They'd say there was some good in you, no matter what you did. You couldn't do enough, you couldn't be big enough a louse for them ever to forget."

"Then," said Tobias, and it was half a question.

"You are all washed up," said Andy. "You are useless here."

He sat silently for a moment, staring at the stricken robot.

"You've done a good job here," Andy finally said. "It's time that someone told you. You've been conscientious and unsparing of yourself. You've had a fine influence on the town. No one else could have forced himself to be so low-down and despicable and disgusting—"

"Andy," said Tobias bitterly, "don't go pinning medals on me."

"I wish," said the janitor, "you wouldn't feel like that."

Out of the bitterness, Tobias felt a snicker—a very ghastly snicker—rising in his brain.

And the snicker kept on growing—a snicker at this village if it could only know that it was being engineered by two nondescripts, by a shuffling janitor and a filthy bum.

And with him, Tobias, robot, it probably didn't matter, but the human factor would. Not the banker, nor the merchant, nor the pastor, but the janitor—the cleaner of the windows, the mopper of the floors, the tender of the fires. To him had been assigned the keeping of the secret; it was he who had been appointed the engineering contact. Of all the humans in the village, he was the most important.

But the villagers would never know, neither their debt nor their humiliation. They'd patronize the janitor. They'd tolerate the bum—or whatever might succeed the bum.

For there'd be a bum no longer. He was all washed up. Andy Donovan had said so.

And they were not alone. He could sense they weren't.

He spun swiftly on his heel and there stood another man.

He was young and polished and most efficient-looking. His hair was black and smooth and he had an eager look about him that made one ill at ease.

"Your replacement," said Andy, chuckling just a little. "This one, let me tell you, is a really dirty trick."

"But he doesn't look—"

"Don't let his appearance fool you," Andy warned. "He is worse than you are. He's the latest gimmick. He is the dirtiest of all. They'll despise him more than they ever despised you. He'll earn an honest hatred that will raise the moral tone of Millville to a degree as yet undreamed of. They'll work so hard to be unlike him that we'll make honest men out of every one of them—even Frobisher."

"I don't understand," Tobias told him weakly.

"He'll set up an office, a very proper office for an alert young business man. Insurance and real estate and property management and anything else where he can earn a dollar. He'll skin them blind, but legal. He'll be very sanctimonious, but there's no friendship in him. He'll gyp them one by one and he'll smile most prettily and sincerely while he robs them by the letter of the law. There'll be no trick so low he'll not employ it, no subterfuge so vile that he'll hesitate to use it."

"But it's unfair," Tobias cried. "At least I was an honest bum."

"We must," Andy told him unctuously, "act for the good of all humanity. Surely it would be a shame for Millville to ever have an actual human such as he."

"All right, then," Tobias said. "I wash my hands of it. How about myself?"

"Why, nothing at the moment," Andy told him. "You go back to Herman's place and let nature take its course. Take the job he hunts up for you and be a decent citizen."

Tobias got cold all over. "You mean you're ditching me entirely? You mean you have no further use for me at all? I only did my best. There was nothing else I could have done tonight. You can't just throw me out!"

Andy shook his head. "There's something I should tell you. It's just a little early to be saying anything—but there's quiet talk in the village of sending out a colony."

Tobias stood stiff and straight and hope went pounding through him, then the hope died out.

"But me," he said. "Not me. Not a bum like me!"

"Worse than a bum," said Andy. "Much worse than a bum. As a bum you were a known quantity. They knew what to expect from you. They could sit down at any time and plot a behavior curve for you. As a reformed bum, you'll be something else again. You'll be unpredictable. They'll be watching you, wondering what will happen next. You'll make them nervous and uneasy. They'll be wondering all the time if what they did was right. You'll be a burden on their conscience and a rasp across their nerves and they'll be afraid that you'll somehow prove some day that they were awfully stupid."

"Feeling that way," Tobias said, with no final shred of hope, "they'd never let me go out to the colony."

"I think you're wrong," said Andy. "I am sure that you will go. The good and nervous people of this village couldn't pass up a chance like that of getting rid of you."

LOBBY

If, having recognized that this was one of several science fiction stories that made use of the concept of atomic bombs before one had ever been exploded ("Lobby" was sold to John W. Campbell, Jr., in August of 1943, and was published in Astounding Science Fiction's *April 1944 issue), you wonder why the story was named "Lobby," the answer may be found in the fact that the real villain, the real danger that Cliff Simak was pointing out in this story, was the danger humanity faced from the perfidy of big business.*

In that, Cliff was, in this story, reprising some of the attitude that informed his "City" stories, which also began from a vision of the way greed and power had led the world into the biggest war ever.

As it happened, Cliff got some details about atomic explosions wrong. But he got the people right—and all this in a story for which he was paid only $60.

—dww

The lettering on the door read:

ATOMIC POWER, INC.

Felix Jones, reporter for the *Daily Messenger,* opened it.
"Hi," he said to the stenographer-receptionist. "Cobb in?"

"Not to you," she told him.

"I'll see him, anyhow."

Miss Joyce Lane shrugged her eyebrows. "I shall hold the door open," she said, "when he throws you out."

"*Tsk, tsk,*" commented Felix. "What a temper!"

He moved toward the inner door.

"Do you bounce easy?" asked Miss Lane.

"I'm an expert at it," he assured her.

"So is Mr. Cobb," she said.

He opened the door and Bill Cobb looked up from his desk.

"It's you again," he said, unenthusiastically.

"You heard about Walker this afternoon?" asked Felix.

"I heard Walker," said Cobb. "I turned on the 'visor and there he was. Senator Walker is a doddering old fool and a rascally politician. You can quote me."

Felix walked across the room and perched on the desk. "You going to take it lying down?" he asked.

"I'm not taking it any way," said Cobb. "I didn't even think about it until you came in. You're wasting your time."

"You're not talking?" asked Felix, trying to sound surprised but not doing very well.

"Why should I?" Cobb demanded. "Would you give me a break? Not in a million years. But you'll print all the lies Walker and the power lobby and the Primitives shout against atomic power. If you want to take the words of a foul-ball politician and a half-baked sect, that's O.K. with me. go ahead and make a fool out of your paper. Couple of years from now I'll come in and cram all those lousy stories down Mann's neck. You can tell him that."

"But Walker said atomics were dangerous—"

"Sure he said they were dangerous. He's been saying it for a year now. And he's right. They are dangerous. That's why we're not offering anything for sale. If some of the pure and holy power outfits that are fighting us had half as good a set-up as we have, they'd be selling right and left. Maybe a few people would get hurt, but what would they care."

He rapped the desk viciously with his pencil.

"When we have means to control atomic power, we'll put it on the market. Not before then. What do you think we put our experimental plant out in Montana for? Simply so that if it should blow fewer people would get killed."

"You're bitter," Felix said.

"Not bitter," Cobb told him. "Just astounded at what fools the people are. For years they've dreamed about atomic power. Reams of speculation have been written about it. Men have planned for it and banked on it, built future worlds on it. And now that it's within their grasp, what do people do? Now that they can practically reach out and touch power so ridiculously cheap it would be almost free, what do they say and think? They allow a power lobby and a bunch of crooked politicians to scare them silly with bogey stories about the terrible menace of atomics. They listen to yelping preachers on the street corner who tell them it's sacrilege to destroy God-created matter, that it's tempting Providence, asking the lightning to strike."

Felix hoisted himself off the desk.

"Scram," said Cobb.

"Now I know why Walker hates you," Felix said.

"So do I," said Cobb. "A million bucks a year."

He watched the reporter walk toward the door, called to him as he reached it. Felix swung around.

"Just one thing," warned Cobb. "If you write a line with my name in it . . . ever again . . . I'll come down to your office, personally, and break your neck."

"You're vicious," Felix told him and went out, shutting the door behind him.

Cobb tapped his teeth with the pencil, eyes still on the door.

"I should have plastered him," he told himself.

Through the open window came the droning of the New York sky lanes, the mutter of bank teller and shoe clerk and café waitress going home.

Rousing himself, he walked to the wall safe, twirled the combination and swung out the door. From a small box he took a sheet of paper, and carried it back to the desk. There he ran his finger down the left-hand margin, stopped at the notation—3 to 6 p.m. September 6th. Opposite it was a short-wave logging.

A nuisance, he told himself. And illegal, too. But the only way in which he and Ramsey could keep their wave length from being tapped.

He set the 'visor call dial, snapped up the toggle and punched the signal key. The screen lighted up and Scott Ramsey looked out at him.

"I've been expecting you," said Ramsey. "You listened to Walker?"

Cobb nodded. "I liked that part where he practically bawled over how the poor widows and orphans with their savings all tucked away in power securities would want for a crust of bread."

"It may sound laughable to us," said Ramsey, soberly, "but it got the senators. Mostly, I suppose, because they're the orphans who have their money socked away in power stocks. It's dirty politics, but we haven't seen the worst yet. We've got them scared, Bill, and when they get scared, they're dangerous. There's a rumor around we're ready to pop."

"Walker and his gang will be around with a proposition before long," predicted Cobb. "You know what to do."

"Sure. There was someone around this morning. But I don't think he was connected with the power lobby. Wanted to know how he could help us. I laughed at him. Said his name was Ford Adams. Mean anything to you?"

"Never heard of him," said Cobb. "Probably just a screwball."

"I'm afraid of something happening at the plant," declared Ramsey. "You better get hold of Butler. If you got time, it might be a good idea to go out and see him rather than just calling him. Impress on him the necessity to be on guard all the time. He's so tied up in his research he doesn't know half what's going on."

"They wouldn't try anything at the plant," said Cobb.

"That's what you think," Ramsey told him. "This gang is all steamed up, I tell you. They're scared. They figure we're about due to go on the market any day now and they're half nuts. They know that once a successful atomic plant is developed they're dead ducks. To compete with us they'd have to sell their stuff for less than half of actual cost, probably even less than that. There are financial empires at stake, not only here, but all over the world. Men fighting for financial empires won't stop at anything."

"How about the Department of the Interior?" asked Cobb. "You going to be able to hold that off?"

"I wish I could tell you yes," said Ramsey, "but I'm not too sure. Sullivan is getting budget jitters. If he doesn't play ball the power crowd can cut his budget to a shadow and leave him out on a long, bare limb. And he's not too happy about those nice, big dams he's got. Once atomic power comes in, the dams are shot. All they'll be good for is irrigation then and with this tank farming business, there isn't going to be too much need for irrigation.

"Then, too, he can slap an order on us to shut down until we can show we have developed adequate safety measures. It won't hold, of course, for we can prove we're doing experimental work and there's always some danger in that type of development. It's just a recognized fact. But he could hold us up a while."

"Do the best you can, Scott," urged Cobb. "No danger of Walker's law going through, is there?"

"Not this session. Most of them aren't too sure how the folks back home feel. Maybe it'll have a chance next session. Especially if the Primitives keep going to town. This town is plastered with soap boxes and spouting preachers. They say it's sacrilege—"

"Yes, I know. I've heard them. Any chance of proving the power gang is behind them?"

"Not a ghost," said Ramsey.

"O.K., then, I'll go see Butler tonight. Good luck with Sullivan."

The screen dimmed and Cobb clicked the toggle, carefully reset the dial to its legal wave length.

The intercommunicator buzzed at him and he flipped it open. "Yes."

"A Mr. Adams here to see you," said Miss Lane. "A Mr. Ford Adams."

"I don't know any Ford Adams."

"He insists that it's important."

Ford Adams? Ford—

Yes, that was the name of Ramsey's screwball.

"I'll see Mr. Adams in a minute," Cobb said.

He picked up the slip of paper with the dial settings, put it back in the safe and locked it. Back at the intercommunicator he said:

"Send him in."

Ford Adams was tall, almost wraithlike. He walked with a limp and carried a heavy cane. He laid it on the desk, saw Cobb look at it for a second.

"Sicily," he explained.

"I missed that one," said Cobb.

"You probably know I saw Mr. Ramsey this morning."

Cobb nodded and motioned to a chair.

"I offered my help," said Adams. "Mr. Ramsey didn't seem to take me seriously."

"What makes you think we need your help?"

"It's obvious," said Adams. "Here you are, a handful of you, fighting what amounts to a world combine. I've looked into the matter quite thoroughly and know much of the background. You offered your developments to the power corporations on condition they would form a world compact among themselves to hold their earnings to no more than their present earnings and, for a period of the next twenty years, would divert the greater portions of those earnings to converting the entire world to atomic power. They refused."

"Sure they did," said Cobb. "We expected they would, although we went to them in all good faith. They saw a chance to make a killing and they turned us down. They figured their own technicians could find the answers before we could begin operating. They guessed wrong. Butler is the only man in the field who found the answers and he had them when we talked to them. All the rest of the researchers are a million miles off base."

"You threatened you would ruin them," said Adams and he didn't make it an accusation or a question. It was simply a statement.

Cobb grinned crookedly. "As I remember it, we did. If they'd been decent, we'd gone in with them. Believe it or not, we aren't out to make a fortune. We probably won't. Butler is the head man with us and he doesn't even know there is such a thing as money. You've seen his kind. Had one ruling passion. The only thing that counts with him is atomic power. Not atomic power as a theory or as something to play around with, but power that will turn wheels—cheap. Power that will free the world, that will help develop the world. Power so cheap and plentiful and safe to handle that no man is so poor he can't afford to use it."

Adams fumbled with a cigarette. "What you've said, Cobb, may go for Butler," he declared, "but it doesn't go for you. You've lost sight of Butler's goal. It's become a game for you. A game in which either you or the power lobby wins. You're out to break the power gang."

"I hate their guts," said Cobb.

"You aren't a scientist," said Adams.

"No, I'm not. I'm a business man. Butler would be lost in the business end. So I'm here. He's out in Montana. It works O.K."

"But you aren't the only atomic company in the field."

Cobb laughed shortly. "You're thinking of Atomic Development. Forget it, Adams. You know as well as I do Development is another power lobby trick. All it's done is sell stock. They've peddled it all over the world. Store clerks and stenographers are loaded with it."

Adams nodded. "At the psychological moment, it blows."

"And blows us with it," said Cobb. "The people, in their blind panic, won't be able to distinguish between one atomic company and another. To them, we'll all be crooks."

"It isn't a pretty picture," said Adams.

Cobb leaned across the desk. "Just what do you mean by that?"

"It's sordid."

"The power gang asked for it that way," said Cobb. "They've bought off the papers with advertising campaigns. They've elected their men to Congress. They have organized a so-called religious sect to preach against us. They're bringing all the pressure they can in Washington. They've established a phony stock company for no other reason than to stir up a scandal that will smear us, too, when it busts wide open."

He smashed his fist on the desk. "If they want to play rough, it's O.K. with us. Before we're through with this we'll have them begging in the street. Those newspaper publishers who are bucking us now will come through that door over there on hands and knees and blow three times—and then we'll give them power to turn their presses."

"How about the world committee?" asked Adams. "You could appeal to it. Have it declare you an international project. No one could touch you then. You'd be free to work out atomic power without all the annoyance to which you are now subjected. Some arrangement could be worked out with the power companies. They'd see reason if the committee took a hand."

"We applied," said Cobb, "but apparently the committee can't be bothered. They're up to their necks in Europe and Asia. Figure the Americas should stagger along as best they can until some of the squabbles over there are ironed out."

"But it's not a question of the Americas," insisted Adams. "It's a question of the world. The whole world is concerned with atomic power."

"They wouldn't touch it with a ten-foot pole," declared Cobb. "It's too hot for them. Their powers are limited. The only reason they have lasted this long is that the little people of the world are determined there's never going to be another war, yell their heads off when anybody makes a move toward the world committee. But something like this—"

"Don't you see where this is leading?" demanded Adams. "If you let atomic power loose upon the world the way you propose to do, you're letting loose economic chaos. You'll absolutely iron out vast companies that employ hundreds of thousands of men and women. You'll create a securities panic, which will have repercussions throughout the world, upsetting trade schedules which just now are beginning to have some influence toward a structure for enduring peace. You're not too young to remember what 1929 was like. That was just a ripple in comparison to the sort of chaos you can bring about."

"Adams," Cobb told him coldly, "you came in here and asked to help us. I didn't know who you were and I didn't ask. Isn't it about time to climb out of the tree?"

"I'm really no one," Adams said. "Just a private citizen with certain . . . well, you might call them eccentricities."

"Walker sent you," declared Cobb. "Walker or one of the power mob."

"I can assure you that is not so."

"Who did then? And what is the proposition?"

"There is no proposition," declared Adams. "Not now, at least. I did have something in mind, but there is no use in wasting time outlining it to you. When the power gang licks you, I'll drop around again."

"The power gang won't lick us," snapped Cobb.

Adams reached for his cane, pulled himself out of the chair, his fantastically tall, slender body towering over Cobb's desk.

"But they will," he said.

"Get out," said Cobb.

"Good-by, Mr. Cobb," said Adams. He limped toward the door.

"And don't come back," Cobb told him.

Cobb sat in his chair, cold with rage. If Walker thought such a thin deception would work—

The door opened and Miss Lane stood there, a newspaper clutched in her hand.

"Mr. Cobb," she said.

"What is it?"

She walked across the room and laid the paper down in front of him.

It was the *Messenger* and the screaming type of the headline smacked him in the face:

ATOMIC DANGEROUS, COBB FINALLY ADMITS

The peaks of the Absoraka range shone with white, ghostly light under the pale whiteness of a sickle moon that hung just above the jagged mountain saw-tooth.

The 'copter muttered, driving ahead, while below the darkness that was Montana slid away like a black and flowing river.

Cobb, pipe clenched between his teeth, leaned back comfortably in his seat, taking it easy, trying to relax, trying to think.

It had been clumsy of the power mob to send Adams. But it was possible that back of that clumsiness there might be some purpose. Perhaps they had meant him to detect Adams as their emissary, using him as a deliberate decoy against some other move that might be underway.

Adams, of course, had denied he had any connection with the

power lobby, but that was to be expected. Unless the power crowd was more desperate than he had reason to suspect, they probably wouldn't come out openly with a compromise at this stage of the game.

Cobb bent forward and stared out of the window of the machine, but all was darkness. Not even an isolated ranchhouse light. He glanced at his watch. Midnight.

His pipe went out and he lighted it again, watching the peaks swing nearer, still keeping their ghostly character. He noted the reading on his course and corrected it slightly.

Suddenly the sky above the peak flashed.

That was the word that best described it—flashed. There was no consciousness of fire, no flame, no glow—just a sudden, blinding flash, like a photographer's bulb popping—a million bulbs popping. A flash that came and lasted for one split second, then was gone, leaving a blackness that for a moment blotted out the moon and the snowy peaks—a blackness that persisted until one's eyes could readjust themselves.

The ship plowed on, while Cobb, blinded, reached out for something to clutch, instinctively reacting to the bewilderment of blackness.

Sound came. A sudden clap of sound that was vicious and nerve-wrenching. Like one short gasp of a million thunders rolled together.

The 'copter bucked and plunged and Cobb reached out blind hands, hauled back on the wheel to send it rocketing skyward. Beneath him the ship jerked and trembled, wallowing in tortured air.

Cold realization chilled Cobb's brain, tensed his body as he fought the bucking ship.

There was only one thing on Earth that could make a flash like that—a disintegrating atomic power plant!

The ship quieted and Cobb's eyes cleared. The moon still hung above the peaks. There was no glow above the range.

There wouldn't be, Cobb knew. There'd be no fire . . . unless . . . unless—

He narrowed his eyes, trying to project his sight deeper into the night. There was no glow, no hint of fire. Just the night blue of the sky, the silver of the mountain snow, the whiteness of the moon.

His breath came in gasps.

The blast apparently had been a blast and that was all. it had not set off a progressive disintegration. Probably all the fears that had been held on that account were groundless. Perhaps the blasting atoms destroyed themselves utterly, expended all their power in one vicious flare of energy.

He pushed the machine down in a long, steep glide above the peaks, steeling himself for what he knew he'd see.

From far off he saw it, the jagged scar that snaked across the valley, the powdery gleam of riven rock, polished by the blast.

He held his breath as he swung above the scar. There was no sign of buildings, no sign of life, no smoke, not even the wavering of dancing motes of dust hanging in the air. There would be no dust, he knew. An atomic explosion would leave no dust. The dust itself would be a part of that bursting energy which had gouged out the hole across the valley.

He glided the ship toward the mountain spur that ran into the valley, brought it down on idling vanes. The spur, he saw, had been chopped off, cut off as a knife might slice through cheese, sheared in a straight and vicious line. A black hole gaped in the face of the spur and Cobb felt a surge of thankfulness.

At the end of that tunnel was the vault where Butler kept the records. If the blast had smashed the vault, blown it into nothingness, it would have wiped out the work of many years. But with the vault apparently intact—

The wheels touched the rock and rolled forward slowly. Cobb applied the brakes and cut the motor, flung open the door and jumped out.

Swiftly he headed for the tunnel, running up the slope.

Something moved in the tunnel's mouth, a weaving, staggering something. A man walking on wobbly legs, gripping a portfolio under one arm.

The man looked up and the pale moonlight slanted across his face.

"Butler!" Cobb cried.

Butler stopped, reached out a hand to steady himself. The portfolio fell to the ground and slid along the rock.

"Butler," yelled Cobb. "Butler, thank God!"

Butler's right hand came up and the moonlight gleamed on dull metal.

Butler's voice croaked at him. "Stay where you are!"

Cobb took another step forward.

"I'll shoot," croaked Butler. "I'll shoot, so help me—"

The gun barked, its muzzle flash throwing a swift red shadow on the man who held it.

"Butler, it's Cobb! Bill Cobb!"

The gun roared again and a bullet whined close.

"For the love of Mike," yelled Cobb.

The gun wavered and Butler's knees gave way. Cobb leaped forward, but he was too late to catch the falling man. When he reached Butler, the scientist had tumbled forward, across the portfolio, guarding it even as he clawed feebly to regain his feet.

Cobb knelt and lifted him, bent low to hear the whisper.

"Got to get away," it ran. "Get into the hills. Got to—"

Cobb shook him and Butler's eyes flicked open.

"Bill," he said.

"Yes," said Cobb.

"Let's get out of here," Butler whispered. "The power mob. Spies. One of them . . . one of them—"

Cobb nodded grimly.

"The papers?" he asked.

Half croak, half whisper, Butler told him: "All here. All we need. The rest . . . mean nothing."

Swiftly, Cobb picked Butler up, cradling him in his arms, staggering toward the ship.

"Blast . . . knocked me . . . out," Butler said. "Came to after . . . while. Shaky . . . can't talk good—"

"Shock," said Cobb.

It was a miracle, he knew, that the man hadn't been killed outright by the pressure and the flare of radioactive particles. The downward turn of the tunnel and the depth of the vault, he knew, was all that saved him.

With Butler in the ship, he sprinted back to pick up the portfolio and revolver, then raced to the plane and took it up, vanes whirring wildly, sent it fleeing across the mountaintops.

"Doctor," croaked Butler.

"I'm taking you to one," said Cobb. "Sit back and take it easy. Keep yourself covered up."

Butler's hand reached out and plucked at his sleeve.

"What is it, Glenn?" Cobb asked.

"Maybe it . . . would be . . . better—"

"Take your time," cautioned Cobb. "Don't try too hard."

"—If they thought . . . I . . . was dead."

Cobb grunted. "Maybe it would, at that."

"Work in . . . secret . . . then."

"Sure, sure," said Cobb. "That's the idea."

He stared straight ahead into the blackness.

Work in secret. Underground. Skulking like criminals. Hiding from powerful men who saw in them a threat to empire.

And even if they did, where would they get the money? Atomic research took money, a lot of money. There had been trouble scraping together enough to build the plant—the plant that now was gone. Millions of dollars for a flash in the sky and a scar gouged in the ground.

Atomic Power Inc., he knew, was beaten, cleaned out. It was

no more than a gilt name on an office door back in New York. And after tomorrow, after the newspapers and Primitives got through with them, it wouldn't even be that. It would be nothing—absolutely nothing.

There was, he told himself, bitterly, just one thing to do. Come morning and he would go down to the *Messenger* office and beat up Felix Jones. He'd told Jones he would do that. Although Jones wasn't really to blame. He was just a newspaperman, one of many, doing the best he knew, writing what his boss wanted him to write at so many bucks a week.

The men he wanted to beat couldn't be reached—not now. There was only one way to beat them, take away the things they owned, smash the things they'd built, hold them up to pity and to ridicule. And now that couldn't be done.

Tomorrow those men would sit and gloat. Tomorrow—

He twisted his head around and looked back toward the misty peaks. The moon was sinking, the lower horn just touching the mountains.

Something floated across its face, a tiny thing with tiny spinning vanes. He watched it, fascinated, saw the moon-glint strike like hidden fire against the blades.

Another helicopter!

Butler mumbled at him.

"Yes, what is it?"

"Doctor—"

"It's O.K.," said Cobb. "I'll take you to a friend of mine. He won't say a thing. Won't even know who you are. He won't ask and I won't tell him."

"Best way," said Butler.

Pale morning light was filtering through the windows when Cobb let himself into the office and hurried to the wall safe. Swiftly he spun the combination and thrust the portfolio inside.

"Good morning, Mr. Cobb," said a voice from the doorway.

Cobb swung about.

The man who stood there was tall and thin and carried a heavy cane.

"It was most fortunate about Butler," Ford Adams said.

"You are just too late," said Cobb. "If you'd caught up with me a minute sooner, you could have brained me with that stick. The portfolio would have been yours."

"I could have caught up with you any time," Adams told him. "But I wasn't interested in the portfolio. I wanted to talk to you again. Remember I said I would."

Cobb thrust his hands into his coat pockets, felt the hardness of the revolver he'd picked up back at the tunnel. Slowly his fingers curled around it.

"Come in," he said.

Adams limped across the room, laid his cane on the desk and sat down.

"There was a certain proposition—" he started to say, but Cobb stopped him with a gesture.

"Forget the proposition, Adams," Cobb said. "A hundred men died out in Montana tonight. Most of them friends of mine. Three or four million dollars of equipment and years of labor went up in a flash. You were out there. I saw a 'copter as I was leaving."

Adams nodded. "I was there. I followed you."

"Then," said Cobb, "it's time for you to talk."

His hand came out of his pocket and he laid the revolver on the desk.

"There is," said Adams, "no need for melodrama."

"There's no melodrama involved," Cobb told him. "If your explanation isn't good, I'm going to shoot you deader than a mackerel. If for no other reason than you know Butler is alive. What's simpler than that?"

"I see," said Adams.

"No one," said Cobb, "is going to ruin his chance again. Nor the world's chance, either. He's the only man today who can give the world workable atomic power. If something happened to him, no one knows how long the world would have to wait."

"You mean the power people would hunt him down if they knew he were alive?"

Cobb nodded. "They won't touch Ramsey or me. We don't count. We don't have the brain that Butler has."

The radio on the desk flashed a green light, chirped persuasively.

Cobb stared at it. The green light flashed again. The chirp seemed more insistent.

"It might be about Butler," Adams said.

Cobb reached out for the gun, swiveled it on Adams, then bent over the radio.

"One move," he warned.

"You needn't worry," said Adams. "My life is something I value very highly."

Cobb snapped on the radio. A puffy face came in the plate, a red face with tousled white hair and small, close set, green eyes. It was the face of Senator Jay Walker.

"You!" snapped Walker.

"You called my wave length," Cobb declared.

Walker snarled. "I wasn't calling you. I didn't even know it was your length. Is there a man named Adams with you?"

Adams sat rigid in his chair.

"He asked me to call this wave length," the senator sputtered. "Said I'd learn something interesting."

"He's here," said Cobb.

Cobb backed away from the radio, motioned Adams forward with the gun. His lips formed soundless words. "What I said still goes."

"Naturally," said Adams. He spoke into the radio. "How are you, senator?"

"What do you want?" growled Walker.

"An atomic plant exploded in Montana tonight," said Adams. "More than one hundred men were killed."

"So," said the senator, and one could hear the breath whistling through his lips. "So. Too bad."

"I have evidence," said Adams, "that would convict the men who planned it. Quite complete evidence."

"Men don't have to be involved in an atomic explosion," purred the senator. "The stuff's unstable, dangerous, hard to handle. *Pouf,* it goes like that."

"Men were involved in this one," declared Adams. "A lot of men. I thought you might know some of them."

"Mr. Adams, will you tell me who you are?" And the way the senator said it was an insult.

"I was formerly a member of the war guilt commission," Adams said. "At the moment I'm on the legal staff of the world committee at Geneva, Switzerland."

"And you—" said the senator. "And you—"

"I have evidence enough to hang about a dozen of you. You're one of the dozen, Walker."

"You'll never make it stick," stormed the senator. "It's blackmail. Bare-faced blackmail. We'll fight you—"

"You won't do any fighting," Adams told him. "You'll appear before a court of justice, the world court at Geneva. A lot different than other courts. You'll submit your defense and arguments in writing. There'll be no legal trickery or delay. There'll be no jury to talk into feeling sorry for you. This issue will be decided solely on merit. And there's no court of appeal."

"You have no jurisdiction," sputtered Walker.

"You won't be tried for murder alone," said Adams. "The entire history of your attempt to impede the development of atomic power, a factor vital to world development and mankind's welfare, will be clearly shown. That is something clearly within our jurisdiction. And we can show that murder was one of the methods that you used."

"You'll never get away with it," snapped Walker.

"You're positively archaic," said Adams. "The day is gone forever when a million dollars can't be convicted. It went out the day the last Axis solider died in the last fox hole of Japan. A lot of things went out that day, never to return. You're living in a new world, Walker, and you don't even know it."

Walker choked, wiped his face with a pudgy hand. "But you called me. You had a reason. What do you want?"

"All existing power installations in the world today," said Adams. "Complete restitution on all stock sold by Atomic Development. Full confessions for the record."

"But that—" gasped Walker. "That—"

"That's justice," Adams snapped. "No one would gain a thing by hanging you. This way you contribute to the world's welfare."

"But you haven't got atomic power," shrieked Walker. "Butler's dead and he's—"

Adams purred at him. "Why, senator, how did you know that?"

Walker said nothing. His lips moved, but no words came. His face sagged and he was an old, old man.

"Cobb and I will see you this afternoon," Adams told him.

He snapped the toggle and turned around.

Cobb had laid the revolver on the desk.

"How close are you to working power?"

"A month," said Cobb. "Two months. No more. They got wind of it. Blasting the plant was the ace card they didn't want to use."

He found a cigarette, lit it with a shaking hand.

"You going to let them get away with it?" he asked.

"Get away?"

"Sure," said Cobb, and his voice was hard. "They've committed murder. The law says death or life imprisonment, depending upon what court you face. It was murder, Adams, premeditated, cold-blooded murder. Done for profit."

"You want justice done?"

"Yes," said Cobb.

"Justice is an ideal," declared Adams, "very rarely arrived at. We have thought our courts signified and typified justice and in theory they did, but too often they failed in practice. Take Walker and his gang before any court in this land or any other land and what is the answer? You know it as well as I do. They'd wiggle out of it. They'd be represented by an array of legal talent that would confuse and becloud the issue, would get the jury so tangled up that it didn't know whether it was coming or going. Result: not guilty for lack of evidence."

"But a deal," protested Cobb. "A deal with criminals, with murderers."

"We have to be realistic," Adams said. "After all, we're doing no more than any other court would do. We're turning them loose, letting them go free, but we, in this case, will accomplish something at least. Something in the way of justice, something in the way of advancement for the world. No court, not even the international court, could confiscate a criminal's property. But let us say the criminal is conscience-stricken, that he wants to make restitution for the crime he has committed—"

"The people won't believe you," declared Cobb. "They'll know you made the deal."

"They won't mind," said Adams. "For one thing, they'd enjoy it too much."

Cobb frowned. "But a hundred lives—"

"Don't you see, Cobb, that this is bigger than a hundred men, any hundred men. For the first time the world is on the path to a balanced scientific government. This is the stroke of work that will entrench it. Until this moment the world committee has been weak, faced by all the hatreds of nationalism, all the greed of private enterprise, all the feudalistic ideas that have persisted through the years. It had to play safe and grab its chances as they came. And atomic power, international control and administration of atomic power, is the first step to real authority.

"Give the committee another hundred years and government by demagoguery will be gone. Little men with a talent for grabbing votes will have given way to men who make a profession of good government. Men who are trained for government just as doctors are trained for medicine or attorneys are trained for law. Men of science will govern, running the world scientifically in the interest of the stockholders—the little people of the world."

Cobb crushed out his cigarette. "If they hadn't blasted the plant, what then? If they hadn't handed you the club you used on them?"

"They would have won," said Adams. "We would have had to let them win. For we couldn't move until we had a club that would make them cower. We couldn't come out in the open. It had to be an undercover job. We've been working on this thing ever since you filed your application for international status, but we had to keep it quiet. If the power gang had known we were interested, there'd be no world committee now. They would have smashed us flat—just as they smashed you. But in smashing you, they played into our hands.

"And that would have been too bad. For they—and many others—have no place in this new world. Their mentality doesn't fit them for a place in it. It's an old mentality, stemming from the Dark Ages and before, the idea of top dog eat underdog, of grab and hold."

Banners of light in the east were pushing away the grayness of the dawn.

From far below came the first cry of a newsboy. From somewhere far off came the drone of an early worker's flier.

The city was awakening to a new day.

THE TROUBLE WITH ANTS

First published under the title "The Trouble with Ants," when it appeared in the January 1951 issue of the magazine Fantastic Adventures, *this story would appear in subsequent publications (including in the volume edition of* City) *under the title "The Simple Way"; from that, I infer that "The Simple Way" was Cliff Simak's preferred title. There is no other information in his files that bears on that question. But I present the story here in its magazine version, and so I will keep the first title.*

This was the only one of the original eight City *stories that did not appear in John W. Campbell's* Astounding Science Fiction *(see volume 14 of this collection for "Epilog," the later-added* City *story). This has led to uncorroborated suspicions that Simak and Campbell, after a long and intense partnership, were drifting apart—and it is certainly true that within a few years of this story's publication, more Simak stories would be going first to* Galaxy *rather than to* Astounding.

You will see from this story how Cliff Simak planned for the City *stories to come to a close—but events would lead to a change of plans.*

—dww

Archie, the little renegade raccoon, crouched on the hillside, trying to catch one of the tiny, scurrying things running in the grass. Rufus, Archie's robot, tried to talk to Archie, but the raccoon was too busy and he did not answer.

Homer did a thing no Dog had ever done before. He crossed the river and trotted into the wild robots' camp and he was scared, for there was no telling what the wild robots might do to him when they turned around and saw him. But he was worried worse than he was scared, so he trotted on.

Deep in a secret nest, ants dreamed and planned for a world they could not understand. And pushed into that world, hoping for the best, aiming at a thing no Dog, or robot, or man could understand.

In Geneva, Jon Webster rounded out his ten-thousandth year of suspended animation and slept on, not stirring. In the street outside, a wandering breeze rustled the leaves along the boulevard, but no one heard and no one saw.

Jenkins strode across the hill and did not look to either left or right, for there were things he did not wish to see. There was a tree that stood where another tree had stood in another world. There was the lay of ground that had been imprinted on his brain with a billion footsteps across ten thousand years.

And, if one listened closely, one might have heard laughter echoing down the ages . . . the sardonic laughter of a man named Joe.

Archie caught one of the scurrying things and held it clutched within his tight-shut paw. Carefully he lifted the paw and opened it and the thing was there, running madly, trying to escape.

"Archie," said Rufus, "you aren't listening to me."

The scurrying thing dived into Archie's fur, streaked swiftly up his forearm.

"Might have been a flea," said Archie. He sat up and scratched his belly.

"New kind of flea," he said. "Although I hope it wasn't. Just the ordinary kind are bad enough."

"You aren't listening," said Rufus.

"I'm busy," said Archie. "The grass is full of them things. Got to find out what they are."

"I'm leaving you, Archie."

"You're what!"

"Leaving you," said Rufus. "I'm going to the Building."

"You're crazy," fumed Archie. "You can't do a thing like that to me. You've been tetched ever since you fell into that ant hill . . ."

"I've had the Call," said Rufus. "I just got to go."

"I've been good to you," the raccoon pleaded. "I've never overworked you. You've been like a pal of mine instead of like a robot. I've always treated you just like an animal."

Rufus shook his head stubbornly. "You can't make me stay," he said. "I couldn't stay, no matter what you did. I got the Call and I got to go."

"It isn't like I could get another robot," Archie argued. "They drew my number and I ran away. I'm a deserter and you know I am. You know I can't get another robot with the wardens watching for me."

Rufus just stood there.

"I need you," Archie told him. "You got to stay and help me rustle grub. I can't go near none of the feeding places or the wardens will nab me and drag me up to Webster Hill. You got to help me dig a den. Winter's coming on and I will need a den. It won't have heat or light, but I got to have one. And you've got to . . ."

Rufus had turned around and was walking down the hill, heading for the river trail. Down the river trail . . . travelling toward the dark smudge above the far horizon.

Archie sat hunched against the wind that ruffled through his fur, tucked his tail around his feet. The wind had a chill about it, a chill it had not held an hour or so before. And it was not the chill of weather, but the chill of other things.

His bright, beady eyes searched the hillside and there was no sign of Rufus.

No food, no den, no robot. Hunted by the wardens. Eaten up by fleas.

And the Building, a smudge against the farther hills across the river valley.

A hundred years ago, so the records said, the Building had been no bigger than the Webster House.

But it had grown since . . . a place that never was completed. First it had covered an acre. And then a square mile. Now finally a township. And still it grew, sprawling out and towering up.

A smudge above the hills and a cloudy terror for the little, superstitious forest folks who watched it. A word to frighten kit and whelp and cub into sudden quiet.

For there was evil in it . . . the evil of the unknown, an understood evil, an evil sensed and attributed rather than seen or heard or smelled. A sensed evil, especially in the dark of night, when the lights were out and the wind keened in the den's mouth and the other animals were sleeping, while one lay awake and listened to the pulsing *otherness* that sang between the worlds.

Archie blinked in the autumn sunlight, scratched furtively at his side.

Maybe someday, he told himself, someone will find a way to handle fleas. Something to rub on one's fur so they will stay away. Or a way to reason with them, to reach them and talk things over with them. Maybe set up a reservation for them, a place where they could stay and be fed and not bother animals. Or something of the sort.

As it was, there wasn't much that could be done. You scratched yourself. You had your robot pick them off, although the robot usually got more fur than fleas. You rolled in the sand or dust. You went for a swim and drowned some of them . . . well, you really didn't drown them; you just washed them off and if some of them drowned that was their own tough luck.

You had your robot pick them off . . . but now there was no robot.

No robot to pick off fleas.

No robot to help him hunt for food.

But, Archie remembered, there was a black haw tree down in the river bottom and last night's frost would have touched the fruit. He smacked his lips, thinking of the haws. And there was a cornfield just over the ridge. If one was fast enough and bided his time and was sneaky about it, it was no trouble at all to get an ear of corn. And if worse came to worse there always would be roots and wild acorns and that patch of wild grapes over on the sand bar.

Let Rufus go, said Archie, mumbling to himself. Let the Dogs keep their feeding stations. Let the wardens go on watching.

He would live his own life. He would eat fruit and grub for roots and raid the cornfields, even as his remote ancestors had eaten fruit and grubbed for roots and raided fields.

He would live as the other raccoons had lived before the Dogs had come along with their ideas about the Brotherhood of Beasts. Like animals had lived before they could talk with words, before they could read the printed books that the Dogs provided, before they had robots that served in lieu of hands, before there was warmth and light for dens.

Yes, and before there was a drawing that told you if you stayed on Earth or went to another world.

The Dogs, Archie remembered, had been quite persuasive about it, very reasonable and suave. Some animals, they said, had to go to the other worlds or there would be too many animals on Earth. Earth wasn't big enough, they said, to hold everyone. And a drawing, they pointed out, was the fair way to decide which of them would go to the other worlds.

And, after all, they said, the other worlds would be almost like the Earth. For they were just extensions of the Earth. Just other worlds following in the track of Earth. Not quite like it, perhaps, but very close. Just a minor difference here and there. Maybe no tree where there was a tree on Earth. Maybe an oak tree where Earth had a walnut tree. Maybe a spring of fresh, cold water where there was no such spring on Earth.

Maybe, Homer had told him, growing very enthusiastic . . . maybe the world he would be assigned to would be a better world than Earth.

Archie hunched against the hillside, felt the warmish sun of autumn cutting through the cold chill of autumn's wind. He thought about the black haws. They would be soft and mushy and there would be some of them lying on the ground. He would eat those that were on the ground, then he'd climb the tree and pick some more and then he'd climb down again and finish off the ones he had shaken loose with his climbing of the tree.

He'd eat them and take them in his paws and smear them on his face. He might even roll in them.

Out of the corner of one eye, he saw the scurrying things running in the grass. Like ants, he thought, only they weren't ants. At least, not like any ants he'd ever seen before.

Fleas, maybe. A new kind of flea.

His paw darted out and snatched one up. He felt it running in his palm. He opened the paw and saw it running there and closed the paw again.

He raised his paw to his ear and listened.

The thing he'd caught was ticking!

The wild robot camp was not at all the way Homer had imagined it would be. It was not a camp and it was not a city. It was scarcely anything. There were no buildings and there were no streets. Just launching ramps and three spaceships and half a dozen robots working on one of the ships.

Although, come to think of it, Homer told himself, one should have known there would be no buildings in a robot camp. For the robots would have no use of shelter and that was all a building was.

Homer was scared, but he tried hard not to show it. He curled his tail over his back and carried his head high and his ears well forward and trotted toward the little group of robots, never hesitating. When he reached them, he sat down and lolled out his tongue and waited for one of them to speak.

But when none of them did, he screwed up his courage and spoke to them, himself.

"My name is Homer," he said, "and I represent the Dogs. If you have a head robot, I would like to talk to him."

The robots kept on working for a minute, but finally one of them turned around and came over and squatted down beside Homer so that his head was level with the dog's head. All the other robots kept on working as if nothing had happened.

"I am a robot called Andrew," said the robot squatting next to Homer, "and I am not what you would call the head robot, for we have no such thing among us. But I can speak with you."

"I came to you about the Building," Homer told him.

"I take it," said the robot called Andrew, "that you are speaking of the structure to the northeast of us. The one you can see from here if you just turn around."

"That's the one," said Homer. "I came to ask why you are building it."

"But we aren't building it," said Andrew.

"We have seen robots working on it."

"Yes, there are robots working there. But we are not building it."

"You are helping someone else?"

Andrew shook his head. "Some of us get a call . . . a call to go and work there. The rest of us do not try to stop them, for we are all free agents."

"But who is building it?" asked Homer.

"The ants," said Andrew.

Homer's jaw dropped slack.

"Ants? You mean the insects. The little things that live in ant hills?"

"Precisely," said Andrew. He made the fingers of one hand run across the sand like a harried ant.

"But they couldn't build a place like that," protested Homer. "They are stupid."

"Not any more," said Andrew.

Homer sat stock still, frozen to the sand, felt chilly feet of terror run along his nerves.

"Not any more," said Andrew, talking to himself. "Not stupid any more. You see, once upon a time, there was a man named Joe . . ."

"A man? What's that?" asked Homer.

The robot made a clucking noise, as if gently chiding Homer.

"Men were animals," he said. "Animals that went on two legs. They looked very much like us except they were flesh and we are metal."

"You must mean the websters," said Homer. "We know about things like that, but we call them websters."

The robot nodded slowly. "Yes, the websters could be men. There was a family of them by that name. Lived just across the river."

"There's a place called Webster House," said Homer. "It stands on Webster Hill."

"That's the place," said Andrew.

"We keep it up," said Homer. "It's a shrine to us, but we don't understand just why. It is the word that has been passed down to us . . . we must keep Webster House."

"The Websters," Andrew told him, "were the ones that taught you Dogs to speak."

Homer stiffened. "No one taught us to speak. We taught ourselves. We developed in the course of many years. And we taught the other animals."

Andrew, the robot, sat hunched in the sun, nodding his head as if he might be thinking to himself.

"Ten thousand years," he said. "No, I guess it's nearer twelve. Around eleven, maybe."

Homer waited, and as he waited he sensed the weight of years that pressed against the hills . . . the years of river and of sun, of sand and wind and sky.

And the years of Andrew.

"You are old," he said. "You can remember that far back?"

"Yes," said Andrew. "Although I am one of the last of the man-made robots. I was made just a few years before they went to Jupiter."

Homer sat silently, tumult stirring in his brain.

Man . . . a new word.

An animal that went on two legs.

An animal that made the robots, that taught the Dogs to talk.

And, as if he might be reading Homer's mind, Andrew spoke to him.

"You should not have stayed away from us," he said. "We should have worked together. We worked together once. We both would have gained if we had worked together."

"We were afraid of you," said Homer. "I am still afraid of you."

"Yes," said Andrew. "Yes, I suppose you would be. I suppose Jenkins kept you afraid of us. For Jenkins was a smart one. He knew that you must start afresh. He knew that you must not carry the memory of Man as a dead weight on your necks."

Homer sat silently.

"And we," the robot said, "are nothing more than the memory of Man. We do the things he did, although more scientifically, for, since we are machines, we must be scientific. More patiently than Man, because we have forever and he had a few short years."

Andrew drew two lines in the sand, crossed them with two other lines. He made an X in the open square in the upper left hand corner.

"You think I'm crazy," he said. "You think I'm talking through my hat."

Homer wriggled his haunches deeper into the sand.

"I don't know what to think," he said. "All these years . . ."

Andrew drew an O with his finger in the center square of the cross-hatch he had drawn in the sand.

"I know," he said. "All these years you have lived with a dream. The idea that the Dogs were the prime movers. And the facts are hard to understand, hard to reconcile. Maybe it would be just as well if you forgot what I said. Facts are painful things at times. A robot has to work with them, for they are the only things he has to work with. We can't dream, you know. Facts are all we have."

"We passed fact long ago," Homer told him. "Not that we don't use it, for there are times we do. But we work in other ways. Intuition and cobblying and listening."

"You aren't mechanical," said Andrew. "For you, two and two are not always four, but for us it must be four. And sometimes I wonder if tradition doesn't blind us. I wonder sometimes if two and two may not be something more or less than four."

They squatted in silence, watching the river, a flood of molten silver tumbling down a colored land.

Andrew made an X in the upper right hand corner of the cross-hatch, an O in the center upper space, and an X in the center lower space. With the flat of his hand, he rubbed the sand smooth.

"I never win," he said. "I'm too smart for myself."

"You were telling me about the ants," said Homer. "About them not being stupid any more."

"Oh, yes," said Andrew. "I was telling you about a man named Joe . . ."

Jenkins strode across the hill and did not look to either left or right, for there were things he did not wish to see, things that struck too deeply into memory. There was a tree that stood where another tree had stood in another world. There was the lay of ground that had been imprinted on his brain with a billion foot-steps across ten thousand years.

The weak winter sun of afternoon flickered in the sky, flick-ered like a candle guttering in the wind, and when it steadied and there was no flicker it was moonlight and not sunlight at all.

Jenkins checked his stride and swung around and the house was there . . . low-set against the ground, sprawled across the hill, like a sleepy young thing that clung close to mother earth.

Jenkins took a hesitant step and as he moved his metal body glowed and sparkled in the moonlight that had been sunlight a short heartbeat ago.

From the river valley came the sound of a night bird crying and a raccoon was whimpering in a cornfield just below the ridge.

Jenkins took another step and prayed the house would stay . . . although he knew it couldn't because it wasn't there.

For this was an empty hilltop that had never known a house. This was another world in which no house existed. The house remained, dark and silent, no smoke from the chimneys, no light from the windows, but with remembered lines that one could not mistake.

Jenkins moved slowly, carefully, afraid the house would leave, afraid that he would startle it and it would disappear.

But the house stayed put. And there were other things. The tree at the corner had been an elm and now it was an oak, as it had been before. And it was autumn moon instead of winter sun. The breeze was blowing from the west and not out of the north.

Something happened, thought Jenkins. The thing that has been growing on me. The thing I felt and could not understand. An ability developing? Or a new sense finally reaching light? Or a power I never dreamed I had.

A power to walk between the worlds at will. A power to go anywhere I choose by the shortest route that the twisting lines of force and happenstance can conjure up for me.

He walked less carefully and the house still stayed, unfright-ened, solid and substantial.

He crossed the grass-grown patio and stood before the door.

Hesitantly, he put out a hand and laid it on the latch. And the latch was there. No phantom thing, but substantial metal.

Slowly he lifted it and the door swung in and he stepped across the threshold.

After five thousand years, Jenkins had come home . . . back to Webster House.

So there was a man named Joe. Not a webster, but a man. For a webster was a man. And the Dogs had not been first.

Homer lay before the fire, a limp pile of fur and bone and muscle, with his paws stretched out in front of him and his head resting on his paws. Through half-closed eyes he saw the fire and shadow, felt the heat of the blazing logs reach out and fluff his fur.

But inside his brain he saw the sand and the squatting robot and the hills with the years upon them.

Andrew had squatted in the sand and talked, with the autumn sun shining on his shoulders . . . had talked of men and dogs and ants. Of a thing that had happened when Nathaniel was alive, and that was a time long gone, for Nathaniel was the first Dog.

There had been a man named Joe . . . a mutant-man, a more-than-man . . . who had wondered about ants twelve thousand years ago. Wondered why they had progressed so far and then no farther, why they had reached the dead end of destiny.

Hunger, perhaps, Joe had reasoned . . . the ever-pressing need to garner food so that they might live. Hibernation, perhaps, the stagnation of the winter sleep, the broken memory chain, the starting over once again, each year a genesis for ants.

So, Andrew said, his bald pate gleaming in the sun, Joe had picked one hill, had set himself up as a god to change the destiny of ants. He had fed them, so that they need not strive with hunger. He had enclosed their hill in a dome of glassite and had heated it so they need not hibernate.

And the thing had worked. The ants advanced. They fashioned carts and they smelted ore. This much one could know, for the carts were on the surface and acrid smelting smoke came from the chimneys that thrust up from the hill. What other things they did, what other things they learned, deep down in their tunnels, there was no way of knowing.

Joe was crazy, Andrew said. Crazy . . . and yet, maybe not so crazy either.

For one day he broke the dome of glassite and tore the hill asunder with his foot, then turned and walked away, not caring any more what happened to the ants.

But the ants had cared.

The hand that broke the dome, the foot that ripped the hill had put the ants on the road to greatness. It had made them fight . . . fight to keep the things they had, fight to keep the bottleneck of destiny from closing once again.

A kick in the pants, said Andrew. A kick in the pants for ants. A kick in the right direction.

Twelve thousand years ago a broken, trampled hill. Today a mighty building that grew with each passing year. A building that had covered a township in one short century, that would cover a hundred townships in the next. A building that would push out and take the land. Land that belonged, not to ants, but animals.

A building . . . and that was not quite right, although it had been called the Building from the very start. For a building was a shelter, a place to hide from storm and cold. The ants would have no need of that, for they had their tunnels and their hills.

Why would an ant build a place that sprawled across a township in a hundred years and yet that kept on growing? What possible use could an ant have for a place like that?

Homer nuzzled his chin deep into his paws, growled inside his throat.

There was no way of knowing. For first you had to know how an ant would think. You would have to know her ambition and her goal. You would have to probe her knowledge.

Twelve thousand years of knowledge. Twelve thousand years from a starting point that itself was unknowable.

But one had to know. There must be a way to know.

For, year after year, the Building would push out. A mile across, and then six miles and after that a hundred. A hundred miles and then another hundred and after that the world.

Retreat, thought Homer. Yes, we could retreat. We could migrate to those other worlds, the worlds that follow us in the stream of time, the worlds that tread on one another's heels. We could give the Earth to ants and there still would be space for us.

But this is home. This is where the Dogs arose. This is where we taught the animals to talk and think and act together. This is the place where we created the Brotherhood of Beasts.

For it does not matter who came first . . . the webster or the dog. This place is home. Our home as well as webster's home. Our home as well as ants'.

And we must stop the ants.

There must be a way to stop them. A way to talk to them, find out what they want. A way to reason with them. Some basis for negotiation. Some agreement to be reached.

Homer lay motionless on the hearth and listened to the whisperings that ran through the house, the soft, far-off padding of robots on their rounds of duties, the muted talk of Dogs in a room upstairs, the crackling of the flames as they ate along the log.

A good life, said Homer, muttering to himself. A good life and we thought we were the ones who made it. Although Andrew says it wasn't us. Andrew says we have not added one iota to the mechanical skill and mechanical logic that was our heritage . . . and that we have lost a lot. He spoke of chemistry and he tried to explain, but I couldn't understand. The study of elements, he said, and things like molecules and atoms. And electronics . . . although he said we did certain things without the benefit of electronics more wonderfully than man could have done with all his knowledge. You might study electronics for a million years, he said, and not reach those other worlds, not even know they're there . . . and we did it, we did a thing a webster could not do.

Because we think differently than a webster does. No, it's man, not webster.

And our robots. Our robots are no better than the ones that were left to us by man. A minor modification here and there . . . an obvious modification, but no real improvement.

Whoever would have dreamed there could be a better robot?

A better ear of corn, yes. Or a better walnut tree. Or a wild rice that would grow a fuller head. A better way to make the yeast that substitutes for meat.

But a better robot . . . why, a robot does everything we might wish that it could do. Why should it be better?

And yet . . . the robots receive a call and go off to work on the Building, to build a thing that will push us off the Earth.

We do not understand. Of course, we cannot understand. If we knew our robots better, we might understand. Understanding, we might fix it so that the robots would not receive the call, or, receiving it, would pay it no attention.

And that, of course, would be the answer. If the robots did not work, there would be no building. For the ants, without the aid of robots, could not go on with their building.

A flea ran along Homer's scalp and he twitched his ear.

Although Andrew might be wrong, he told himself. We have our legend of the rise of the Brotherhood of Beasts and the wild robots have their legend of the fall of man. At this date, who is there to tell which of the two is right?

But Andrew's story does tie in. There were Dogs and there were robots and when man fell they went their separate ways . . . although we kept some of the robots to serve as hands for us. Some robots stayed with us, but no dogs stayed with the robots.

A late autumn fly buzzed out of a corner, bewildered in the fire-light. It buzzed around Homer's head and settled on his nose. Homer glared at it and it lifted its legs and insolently brushed its wings. Homer dabbed at it with a paw and it flew away.

A knock came at the door.

Homer lifted his head and blinked at the knocking sound.

"Come in," he finally said.

It was the robot, Hezekiah.

"They caught Archie," Hezekiah said.

"Archie?"

"Archie, the raccoon."

"Oh, yes," said Homer. "He was the one that ran away."

"They have him out here now," said Hezekiah. "Do you want to see him?"

"Send them in," said Homer.

Hezekiah beckoned with his finger and Archie ambled through the door. His fur was matted with burrs and his tail was dragging. Behind him stalked two robot wardens.

"He tried to steal some corn," one of the wardens said, "and we spotted him, but he led us quite a chase."

Homer sat up ponderously and stared at Archie. Archie stared straight back.

"They never would have caught me," Archie said, "if I'd still had Rufus. Rufus was my robot and he would have warned me."

"And where is Rufus now?"

"He got the call today," said Archie, "and left me for the Building."

"Tell me," said Homer. "Did anything happen to Rufus before he left? Anything unusual? Out of the ordinary?"

"Nothing," Archie told him. "Except that he fell into an ant hill. He was a clumsy robot. A regular stumblebum. Always tripping himself, getting tangled up. He wasn't coordinated just the way he should be. He had a screw loose someplace."

Something black and tiny jumped off of Archie's nose, raced along the floor. Archie's paw went out in a lightning stroke and scooped it up.

"You better move back a ways," Hezekiah warned Homer. "He's simply dripping fleas."

"It's not a flea," said Archie, puffing up in anger. "It is something else. I caught it this afternoon. It ticks and it looks like an ant, but it isn't one."

The thing that ticked oozed between Archie's claws and tumbled to the floor. It landed right side up and was off again. Archie made a stab at it, but it zig-zagged out of reach. Like a flash it reached Hezekiah and streaked up his leg.

Homer came to his feet in a sudden flash of knowledge.

"Quick!" he shouted. "Get it! Catch it! Don't let it . . ."

But the thing was gone.

Slowly Homer sat down again. His voice was quiet now, quiet and almost deadly.

"Wardens," he said, "take Hezekiah into custody. Don't leave his side, don't let him get away. Report to me everything he does."

Hezekiah backed away.

"But I haven't done a thing."

"No," said Homer, softly. "No, you haven't yet. But you will. You'll get the Call and you'll try to desert us for the Building. And before we let you go, we'll find out what it is that made you do it. What it is and how it works."

Homer turned around, a doggish grin wrinkling up his face.

"And, now, Archie . . ."

But there was no Archie.

There was an open window. And there was no Archie.

Homer stirred on his bed of hay, unwilling to awake, a growl gurgling in his throat.

Getting old, he thought. Too many years upon me, like the years upon the hills. There was a time when I'd be out of bed at the first sound of something at the door, on my feet, with hay sticking in my fur, barking my head off to let the robots know.

The knock came again and Homer staggered to his feet.

"Come in," he yelled. "Cut out the racket and come in."

The door opened and it was a robot, but a bigger robot than Homer had ever seen before. A gleaming robot, huge and massive, with a polished body that shone like slow fire even in the dark. And riding on the robot's shoulder was Archie, the raccoon.

"I am Jenkins," said the robot. "I came back tonight."

Homer gulped and sat down very slowly.

"Jenkins," he said. "There are stories . . . legends . . . from the long ago."

"No more than a legend?" Jenkins asked.

"That's all," said Homer. "A legend of a robot that looked after us. Although Andrew spoke of Jenkins this afternoon as if he might have known him. And there is a story of how the Dogs gave you a body on your seven thousandth birthday and it was a marvelous body that . . ."

His voice ran down . . . for the body of the robot that stood before him with the raccoon perched on his shoulder . . . that body could be none other than the birthday gift.

"And Webster House?" asked Jenkins. "You still keep Webster House?"

"We still keep Webster House," said Homer. "We keep it as it is. It's a thing we have to do."

"The websters?"

"There aren't any websters."

Jenkins nodded at that. His body's hair-trigger sense had told him there were no websters. There were no webster vibrations. There was no thought of websters in the minds of things he'd touched.

And that was as it should be.

He came slowly across the room, soft-footed as a cat despite his mighty weight, and Homer felt him moving, felt the friendliness and kindness of the metal creature, the protectiveness of the ponderous strength within him.

Jenkins squatted down beside him.

"You are in trouble," Jenkins said.

Homer stared at him.

"The ants," said Jenkins. "Archie told me. Said you were troubled by the ants."

"I went to Webster House to hide," said Archie. "I was scared you would hunt me down again and I thought that Webster House . . ."

"Hush, Archie," Jenkins told him. "You don't know a thing about it. You told me that you didn't. You just said the Dogs were having trouble with the ants."

He looked at Homer.

"I suppose they are Joe's ants," he said.

"So you know about Joe," said Homer. "So there was a man called Joe."

Jenkins chuckled. "Yes, a troublemaker. But likeable at times. He had the devil in him."

Homer said: "They're building. They get the robots to work for them and they are putting up a building."

"Surely," said Jenkins, "even ants have the right to build."

"But they're building too fast. They'll push us off the Earth. Another thousand years or so and they'll cover the whole Earth if they keep on building at the rate they've been."

"And you have no place to go? That's what worries you."

"Yes, we have a place to go. Many places. All the other worlds. The cobbly worlds."

Jenkins nodded gravely. "I was in a cobbly world. The first world after this. I took some websters there five thousand years ago. I just came back tonight. And I know the way you feel. No other world is home. I've hungered for the Earth for almost every one of those five thousand years. I came back to Webster House and I found Archie there. He told me about the ants and so I came up here. I hope you do not mind."

"We are glad you came," said Homer, softly.

"These ants," said Jenkins. "I suppose you want to stop them." Homer nodded his head.

"There is a way," said Jenkins. "I know there is a way. The websters had a way if I could just remember. But it's so long ago. And it's a simple way, I know. A very simple way."

His hand came up and scraped back and forth across his chin.

"What are you doing that for?" Archie asked.

"Eh?"

"Rubbing your face that way. What do you do it for?"

Jenkins dropped his hand. "Just a habit, Archie. A webster gesture. A way they had of thinking. I picked it up from them."

"Does it help you think?"

"Well, maybe. Maybe not. It seemed to help the websters. Now what would a webster do in a case like this? The websters could help us. I know they could . . ."

"The websters in the cobbly world," said Homer.

Jenkins shook his head. "There aren't any websters there."

"But you said you took some there."

"I know. But they aren't there now. I've been alone in the cobbly world for almost four thousand years."

"Then there aren't websters anywhere. The rest went to Jupiter. Andrew told me that. Jenkins, where is Jupiter?"

"Yes, there are," said Jenkins. "There are some websters left, I mean. Or there used to be. A few left at Geneva."

"It won't be easy," Homer said. "Not even for a webster. Those ants are smart. Archie told you about the flea he found."

"It wasn't any flea," said Archie.

"Yes, he told me," Jenkins said. "Said it got onto Hezekiah."

"Not onto," Homer told them. "Into is the word. It wasn't a

flea . . . It was a robot, a tiny robot. It drilled a hole in Hezekiah's skull and got into his brain. It sealed the hole behind it."

"And what is Hezekiah doing now?"

"Nothing," said Homer. "But we are pretty sure what will do as soon as the ant robot gets the setup fixed. He'll get the Call. He'll get the call to go and work on the Building."

Jenkins nodded. "Taking over," he said. "They can't do a job like that themselves, so they take control of things that can."

He lifted his hand again and scraped it across his chin.

"I wonder if Joe knew," he mumbled. "When he played god to the ants. I wonder if he knew."

But that was ridiculous. Joe never could have known. Even a mutation like Joe could not have looked twelve thousand years ahead.

So long ago, thought Jenkins. So many things have happened. Bruce Webster was just starting to experiment with dogs, had no more than dreamed his dream of talking, thinking dogs that would go down the path of destiny paw in hand with Man . . . not knowing then that Man within a few short centuries would scatter to the four winds of eternity and leave the Earth to robot and to dog. Not knowing then that even the name of Man would be forgotten in the dust of years, that the race would come to be known by the name of a single family.

And yet, thought Jenkins, if it was to be any family, the Websters were the ones. I can remember them as if it were yesterday. Those were the days when I thought of myself as a Webster, too.

Lord knows, I tried to be. I did the best I could. I stood by the Webster dogs when the race of men had gone and finally I took the last bothersome survivors of that madcap race into another world to clear the way for Dogs . . . so that the Dogs could fashion the Earth in the way they planned.

And now even those last bothersome survivors have gone . . . some place, somewhere . . . I wish that I could know. Escaped into some fantasy of the human mind. And the men on Jupiter are not even men, but something else. And Geneva is shut off . . . blocked off from the world.

Although it can't be farther away or blocked more tightly than the world from which I came. If only I could learn how it was I travelled from the exile cobbly world back to Webster House . . . then, maybe, perhaps, somehow or other, I could reach Geneva.

A new power, he told himself. A new ability. A thing that grew upon me without my knowing that it grew. A thing that every man and every robot . . . and perhaps every dog . . . could have if he but knew the way.

Although it may be my body that made it possible . . . this body that the Dogs gave me on my seven thousandth birthday. A body that has more than any body of flesh and blood has ever quite attained. A body that can know what a bear is thinking or a fox is dreaming, that can feel the happy little mouse thoughts running in the grass.

Wish fulfillment. That might be it. The answer to the strange, illogical yearnings for things that seldom are and often cannot be. But all of which are possible if one knows the way, if one can grow or develop or graft onto oneself the new ability that directs the mind and body to the fulfillment of the wish.

I walked the hill each day, he remembered. Walked there because I could not stay away, because the longing was so strong, steeling myself against looking too closely, for there were differences I did not wish to see.

I walked there a million times and it took that many times before the power within me was strong enough to take me back.

For I was trapped. The word, the thought, the concept that took me into the cobbly world was a one way ticket and while it took me there it could not take me back. But there was another way, a way I did not know. That even now I do not know.

"You said there was a way," urged Homer.

"A way?"

"Yes, a way to stop the ants?"

Jenkins nodded. "I am going to find out. I'm going to Geneva."

Jon Webster awoke.

And this is strange, he thought, for I said eternity.

I was to sleep forever and forever has no end.

All else was mist and the grayness of sleep forgetfulness, but this much stood out with mind-sharp clarity. Eternity, and this was not eternity.

A word ticked at his mind, like feeble tapping on a door that was far away.

He lay and listened to the tapping and the word became two words . . . words that spoke his name:

"Jon Webster. Jon Webster." On and on, on and on. Two words tapping at his brain.

"Jon Webster."

"Jon Webster."

"Yes," said Webster's brain, and the words stopped and did not come again.

Silence and the thinning of the mists of forgetfulness. And the trickling back of memory. One thing at a time.

There was a city and the name of the city was Geneva.

Men lived in the city, but men without a purpose.

The Dogs lived outside the city . . . in the whole world outside the city. The Dogs had purpose and a dream.

Sara climbed the hill to take a century of dreams.

And I . . . I, thought Jon Webster, climbed the hill and asked for eternity. This is not eternity.

"This is Jenkins, Jon Webster."

"Yes, Jenkins," said Jon Webster, and yet he did not say it, not with lip and tongue and throat, for he felt the fluid that pressed around his body inside its cylinder, fluid that fed him and kept him from dehydrating. Fluid that sealed his lips and eyes and ears.

"Yes, Jenkins," said Webster, speaking with his mind. "I remember you. I remember you now. You were with the family from the very first. You helped us teach the Dogs. You stayed with them when the family was no more."

"I am still with them," said Jenkins.

"I sought eternity," said Webster. "I closed the city and sought eternity."

"We often wondered," Jenkins told him. "Why did you close the city?"

"The Dogs," said Webster's mind. "The Dogs had to have their chance. Man would have spoiled their chance."

"The dogs are doing well," said Jenkins.

"But the city is open now?"

"No, the city still is closed."

"But you are here."

"Yes, but I'm the only one who knows the way. And there will be no others. Not for a long time, anyway."

"Time," said Webster. "I had forgotten time. How long is it, Jenkins?"

"Since you closed the city? Ten thousand years or so."

"And there are others?"

"Yes, but they are sleeping."

"And the robots? The robots still keep watch?"

"The robots still keep watch."

Webster lay quietly and a peace came upon his mind. The city still was closed and the last of men were sleeping. The Dogs were doing well and the robots stayed on watch.

"You should not have wakened me," he said. "You should have let me sleep."

"There was a thing I had to know. I knew it once, but I have forgotten and it is very simple. Simple and yet terribly important."

Webster chuckled in his brain. "What is it, Jenkins?"

"It's about ants," said Jenkins. "Ants used to trouble men. What did you do about it?"

"Why, we poisoned them," said Webster.

Jenkins gasped. "Poisoned them!"

"Yes," said Webster. "A very simple thing. We used a base of syrup, sweet, to attract the ants. And we put poison in it, a poison that was deadly to ants. But we did not put in enough of it to kill them right away. A slow poison, you see, so they would have time to carry it to the nest. That way we killed many instead of just two or three."

Silence hummed in Webster's head . . . the silence of no thought, no word.

"Jenkins," he said. "Jenkins, are you . . ."

"Yes, Jon Webster, I am here."

"That is all you want?"

"That is all I want."

"I can go to sleep again."

"Yes, Jon Webster. Go to sleep again."

Jenkins stood upon the hilltop and felt the first rough forerunning wind of winter whine across the land. Below him the slope that ran down to the river was etched in black and gray with the leafless skeletons of trees.

To the northeast rose the shadow-shape, the cloud of evil omen that was called the Building. A growing thing spawned in the mind of ants, built for what purpose and to what end nothing but an ant could even closely guess.

But there was a way to deal with ants.

The human way.

The way Jon Webster had told him after ten thousand years of sleep. A simple way and a fundamental way, a brutal, but efficient way. You took some syrup, sweet, so the ants would like it, and you put some poison in it . . . slow poison so it wouldn't work too fast.

The simple way of poison, Jenkins said. The very simple way.

Except it called for chemistry and the Dogs knew no chemistry.

Except it called for killing and there was no killing.

Not even fleas, and the Dogs were pestered plenty by the fleas. Not even ants . . . and the ants threatened to dispossess the animals of the world they called their birthplace.

There had been no killing for five thousand years or more. The idea of killing had been swept from the minds of things.

And it is better that way, Jenkins told himself. Better that one should lose a world than go back to killing.

He turned slowly and went down the hill.

Homer would be disappointed, he told himself.

Terribly disappointed when he found the websters had no way of dealing with the ants . . .

BUCKETS OF DIAMONDS

The number of ways in which the alien—or at least, the weird—can come to a Midwestern American town, in the middle of the twentieth century, is apparently endless; and Clifford D. Simak could imagine enough of them to create his own subgenre. And the resulting stories were instantly recognizable to Simak fans as arising in "Simak country."

This story originally appeared in the April, 1969, issue of Galaxy Magazine, *and I read it when that issue came out; I was starting to learn what "Simak country" was all about, and I remember thinking that my home town—which was even smaller than Willow Grove— would not have handled this situation any better. . . .*

—dww

I

The police picked up Uncle George walking west on Elm Street at 3 o'clock in the morning. He was shuffling along, muttering to himself, and his clothes were soaked, as if he'd been out in the rain—and Cottonwood County for the past three months had been suffering a drought, with the corn withering in the field and day after day not a cloud in sight. He was carrying a good-sized painting underneath one arm and in the other hand he carried a pail filled to the brim with diamonds. He was in his stocking feet; he'd lost his shoes somewhere. When Officer Alvin Saunders picked him up, he asked Uncle George what was going on, and George mumbled something that Alvin couldn't quite make out. He seemed to be befuddled.

So Alvin took him to the station, and it wasn't until then they saw that his pockets bulged. So they emptied his pockets and laid all the stuff out on a table, and when they'd had a good look at it, Sergeant Steve O'Donnell phoned Chief Chet Burnside to ask him what to do. The chief, sore at being hauled out of bed, said to throw George into pokey. So that is what they did. You couldn't really blame the chief, of course. Off and on, for years, Uncle George had given the police force of Willow Grove a fair amount of trouble.

But as soon as Uncle George had a chance to look around and realize where he was, he grabbed up a stool and beat upon the bars, yelling that the dirty fuzz had framed him once again and declaring very loudly that his constitutional rights as a free and upright citizen were being trampled on. "I know my rights," he yelled. "You owe me at least one phone call and when I get out of here I'm going to sue all of you on the grounds of false arrest."

So they unlocked the cell and let him make his call. As usual he made the call to me.

"Who is it?" Elsie asked, sitting up in bed.

"It's your Uncle George," I said.

"I knew it!" she exclaimed. "Aunt Myrt is off to California to visit relatives. And he's running loose again."

"All right," I said to George, "what could it be this time?"

"You needn't take that tone of voice, John," he said. "It's only once or twice a year I call you. And what's the use of having a lawyer in the family . . ."

"You can skip that part of it," I told him, "and get down to what is going on."

"This time," he said, triumphantly, "I got them dead to rights. This time you get paid off. I'll split the judgment with you. I wasn't doing nothing. I was walking down the street when the fuzz pulled up and hauled me in. I wasn't staggering and I wasn't singing. I was creating no disturbance. I tell you, John, a man has the right to walk the streets, no matter at what hour . . ."

"I'll be right down," I said.

"Don't be too long," said Elsie, "You have a hard day coming up in the court."

"Are you kidding?" I asked. "With Uncle George, the day's already lost."

When I got down to the station, they all were waiting for me. George was sitting beside a table, and on the table stood the pail of diamonds with the junk they'd taken from his pockets and the painting was leaning up against it. The police chief had gotten there, just a few minutes ahead of me.

"Okay," I said, "let's get down to business. What's the charge?"

The chief still was pretty sore. "We don't need no charge right yet."

"I'll tell you, Chet," I said, "you'll need one badly before the day is over, so you better start to thinking."

"I'm going to wait," said Chet, "to see what Charley says."

He meant Charley Nevins, the county attorney.

"All right, then," I said, "if there is no charge as yet, what are the circumstances?"

"Well," said the chief, "George here was carrying a pail of diamonds. And you tell me just how he came by a pail of diamonds."

"Maybe they aren't diamonds," I suggested. "How come you're so sure that they are diamonds?"

"Soon as he opens up, we'll get Harry in to have a look at them."

Harry was the jeweler, who had a shop across the square.

I went over to the table and picked up some of the diamonds. They surely looked like diamonds, but I am no jeweler. They were cut and faceted and shot fire in the light. Some of them were bigger than my fist.

"Even if they should be diamonds," I demanded, "what has that to do with it? There's no law I know of says a man can't carry diamonds."

"That's telling them!" cheered George.

"You shut up," I told him, "and keep out of this. Let me handle it."

"But George here hasn't got no diamonds," said the chief. "These must be stolen diamonds."

"Are you charging him with theft?" I asked.

"Well, not right now," said the chief. "I ain't got no evidence as yet."

"And there's that painting, too," said Alvin Saunders. "It looks to me just like one of them old masters."

"There's one thing," I told them, "that puzzles me exceedingly. Would you tell me where, in Willow Grove, anyone bent on thievery could find an old master or a pail of diamonds?"

That stopped them, of course. There isn't anyone in Willow Grove who has an honest-to-God painting except Banker Amos Stevens, who brought one back from a visit to Chicago; and knowing as little as he does about the world of art he was probably taken.

"You'll have to admit, though," said the chief, "there's something funny going on."

"Maybe so," I said, "but I doubt that that alone is sufficient ground to hold a man in jail."

"It ain't the diamonds or the painting so much as this other stuff," declared the chief, "that makes me think there are shenanigans afoot. Look at this, will you!"

He picked up a gadget from the table and held it out to me.

"Watch out," he warned. "One end of it's hot, and the other end is cold."

It was about a foot in length and shaped something like an hourglass. The hourglass part of it was some sort of transparent plastic, pinched in at the middle and flaring at both ends, and the ends were open. Through the center of it ran a rod that looked like metal. One end of the metal glowed redly, and when I held my hand down opposite the open end a blast of heat came out. The other end was white, covered by crystals. I turned it around to look.

"Keep away from it," warned the chief. "That end of it is colder than a witch's spit. Them's big ice crystals hanging onto it."

I laid it back upon the table, carefully.

"Well," the chief demanded, "what do you make of it?"

"I don't know," I said.

I never took any more physics in school than had been necessary and I'd long since forgotten all I'd ever known about it. But I knew damn well that the gadget on the table was impossible. But impossible or not, there it was, one end of the rod glowing with its heat, the other frosted by its cold.

"And this," said the chief, picking up a little triangle formed by a thin rod of metal or of plastic. "What do you think of this?"

"What should I think of it?" I asked. "It's just . . ."

"Stick your finger through it," said the police chief triumphantly.

I tried to stick my finger through it and I couldn't. There was nothing there to stop me. My finger didn't hit anything, there was no pressure on it and I couldn't feel a thing, but I couldn't put my finger through the center of that triangle. It was as if I'd hit a solid wall that I couldn't see or feel.

"Let me see that thing," I said.

The chief handed it to me, and I held it up to the ceiling light and I twisted it and turned it, and so help me, there wasn't anything there. I could see right through it and I could see there was nothing there, but when I tried to put my finger through the center, there was something there to stop it.

I laid it back on the table beside the hourglass thing.

"You want to see more?" asked the chief.

I shook my head. "I'll grant you, Chet, that I don't know what this is all about, but I don't see a thing here that justifies you in holding George."

"I'm holding him," said the chief, "until I can talk to Charley."

"You know, of course, that as soon as court opens, I'll be back here with an order for his release."

"I know that, John," said the chief. "You're a real good lawyer. But I can't let him go."

"If that's the case," I said, "I want a signed inventory of all this stuff you took off of him, and then I want you to lock it up."

"But . . ."

"Theoretically," I said, "it's George's property . . ."

"It couldn't be. You know it couldn't, John. Where would he have gotten . . ."

"Until you can prove that he has stolen it from some specific person, I imagine the law would say that it was his. A man doesn't have to prove where he obtained such property."

"Oh, all right," said the chief. "I'll make out the inventory, but I don't know just what we'll call some of this stuff."

"And now," I said, "I'd like to have a moment to confer with my client."

After balking and stalling around a bit, the chief opened up the city council chamber for us.

"Now, George," I said, "I want you to tell me exactly how it was. Tell me everything that happened and tell it from the start."

George knew I wasn't fooling, and he knew better than to lie to me. I always caught him in his lies.

"You know, of course," said George, "that Myrt is gone."

"I know that," I said.

"And you know that every time she's gone, I go out and get drunk and get into some sort of trouble. But this time I promised myself I wouldn't do any drinking and wouldn't get into any kind of trouble. Myrt's put up with a lot from me, and this time I was set to show her I could behave myself. So last night I was sitting in the living room, with my shoes off, in my stocking feet, with the TV turned on, watching a ball game. You know, John, if them Twins could get a shortstop they might stand a chance next year. A shortstop and a little better pitching and some left-handed batters and . . ."

"Get on with it," I said.

"I was just sitting there," said George, "watching this here ball game and drinking beer. I had got a six-pack and I guess I was on the last bottle of it . . ."

"I thought you said you had promised yourself you would do no drinking."

"Ah, John, this was only beer. I can drink beer all day and never . . ."

"All right, go on," I said.

"Well, I was just sitting there, drinking that last bottle of beer and the game was in the seventh inning and the Yanks had two men on and Mantle coming up . . ."

"Damn it, not the game!" I yelled at him. "Tell me what happened to you. You're the one in trouble."

"That's about all there was to it," said George. "It was the seventh inning and Mantle coming up, and the next thing I knew I was walking on the street and a police car pulling up."

"You mean you don't know what happened in between? You don't know where you got the pail of diamonds or the painting or all the other junk?"

George shook his head, "I'm telling you just the way it was. I don't remember anything. I wouldn't lie to you. It doesn't pay to lie to you. You always trip me up."

I sat there for a while, looking at him, and I knew it was no use to ask him any more. He probably had told me the truth, but perhaps not all of it, and it would take more time than I had right then to sweat it out of him.

"O.K.," I said, "we'll let it go at that. You go back and get into that cell and don't let out a whimper. Just behave yourself. I'll be down by nine o'clock or so and get you out. Don't talk to anyone. Don't answer any questions. Volunteer no information. If anyone asks you anything, tell them I've told you not to talk."

"Do I get to keep the diamonds?"

"I don't know," I said. "They may not be diamonds."

"But you asked for an inventory."

"Sure I did," I said, "but I don't know if I can make it stick."

"One thing, John. I got an awful thirst . . ."

"No," I said.

"Three or four bottles of beer. That couldn't hurt much. A man can't get drunk on only three or four. I wasn't drunk last night. I swear to you I wasn't."

"Where would I get beer at this time in the morning?"

"You always have a few tucked away in your refrigerator. And that's only six blocks or so away."

"Oh, all right," I said. "I'll ask the chief about it."

The chief said yes, he guessed it would be all right, so I left to get the beer.

II

The moon was setting behind the courthouse cupola, and in the courthouse square the Soldier's Monument was alternately lighted and darkened by a street lamp swaying in a little breeze. I had a look at the sky, and it seemed entirely clear. There were no clouds in sight and no chance of rain. The sun, in a few hours more, would blaze down again and the corn would dry a little more and the farmers would watch their wells anxiously as the pumps brought up lessening streams of water for their bawling cattle.

A pack of five or six dogs came running across the courthouse lawn. There was a dog-leashing ordinance, but everyone turned their dogs loose at night and hoped they would come home for breakfast before Virgil Thompson, the city dog catcher, could get wind of them.

I got into the car and drove home and found four bottles of beer in the refrigerator. I took it back to the station, then drove home again.

By this time it was 4:30, and I decided it wasn't worth my while to go back to bed, so I made some coffee and started to fry some eggs. Elsie heard me and came down, and I fried some eggs for her and we sat and talked.

Her Uncle George had been in a lot of scrapes, none of them serious, and I had always managed to get him out of them one way or another. He wasn't a vicious character and he was an honest man, liked by most everyone in town. He ran a junkyard out at the edge of town, charging people for dumping trash, most of which he used to fill in a swampy stretch of ground, salvaging some of the more usable junk and selling it cheap to people who might need it. It wasn't a very elevating kind of business, but he made an honest living at it and in a little town like ours if you made an honest living it counts for quite a lot.

But this scrape was just a little different, and it bothered me. It wasn't exactly the kind of situation that was covered in a law book. The thing that bothered me the most was where George could have gotten the stuff they found on him.

"Do you think we should phone Aunt Myrt?" asked Elsie.

"Not right now," I told her. "Having her here wouldn't help at all. All she'd do would be to scream and wring her hands."

"What are you going to do first of all?" she asked.

"First of all," I said, "I'm going to find Judge Benson and get a writ to spring him out of jail. Unless Charley Nivens can find some grounds for holding him and I don't think he can. Not right away, at least."

But I never got the writ. I was about to leave my office to go over to the courthouse to hunt up the judge when Dorothy Ingles, my old-maid secretary, told me I had a call from Charley.

I picked up the phone, and he didn't even wait for me to say hello. He just started shouting.

"All right," he yelled, "you can start explaining. Tell me how you did it."

"How I did what?" I asked.

"How George broke out of jail."

"But he isn't out of jail. When I left he was locked up and I was just now going over to the courthouse . . ."

"He's not locked up now," yelled Charley. "The cell door still is locked, but he isn't there. All that's left is four empty beer bottles, standing in a row."

"Look, Charley," I said, "I don't know a thing about this. You know me well enough . . ."

"Yeah," yelled Charley, "I know you well enough. There isn't any dirty trick . . ."

He strangled on his words, and it was only justice. Of all the tricky lawyers in the state, Charley is the trickiest.

"If you are thinking," I said, "of swearing out a fugitive warrant for him, you might give a thought to the lack of grounds for his incarceration."

"Grounds!" yelled Charley. "There is that pail of diamonds."

"If they are really diamonds."

"They are diamonds, that's for sure. Harry Johnson had a look at them this morning and he says that they are diamonds. There is just one thing wrong. Harry says there are no diamonds in the world as big as those. And very few as perfect."

He paused for a moment and then he whispered, hoarsely, "Tell me John, what is going on? Let me in on it."

"I don't know," I said.

"But you talked with him and he told the chief you had told him not to answer any questions."

"That's good legal procedure," I told him. "You can have no quarrel with that. And another thing, I'll hold you responsible for seeing that those diamonds don't disappear somehow. I have an inventory signed by Chet and there is no charge . . ."

"What about busting jail?"

"Not unless you can show cause for his being arrested in the first place."

He slammed down the receiver, and I hung up the phone and sat there trying to get the facts straight inside my mind. But they were too fantastic for me to make them spell out any sense.

"Dorothy," I yelled.

She poked her head around the door, her face prissy with her disapproval. Somehow, apparently, she had heard about what had been going on—as, no doubt, had everyone in town—and she was one of the few who held George in very ill-repute. She thought he was a slob. She resented my relationship to him and she often pointed out that he cost me, over the years, a lot of time and cash, with no money ever coming back. Which was true, of course, but you can't expect a junkyard operator to afford fancy legal fees and, in any case, he was Elsie's uncle.

"Put in a call to Calvin Ross," I told her, "at the Institute of Arts in Minneapolis. He is an old friend of mine and . . ."

Banker Amos Stevens came bursting through the door. He crossed the outer office and brushed past Dorothy as if she weren't there.

"John, do you know what you have got—what you've got down there!"

"No," I said. "Please tell me."

"You have got a Rembrandt!"

"Oh, you mean the painting."

"Where do you think George found a Rembrandt? There aren't any Rembrandts except in museums and such."

"We'll soon find out more about it," I told Banker Stevens, Willow Grove's one and only expert in the arts. "I've got a call in now and . . ."

Dorothy stuck her head around the door. "Mr. Ross is on the phone," she said.

I picked up the phone and I felt a little funny about it, because Cal Ross and I hadn't seen each other for a good fifteen years or more, and I wasn't even sure he would remember me. But I told him who I was and acted as if we'd had lunch together just the day before, and he did the same to me.

Then I got down to business. "Cal, we have a painting out here that maybe you should have a look at. Some people think it might be old and perhaps by one of the old masters. I know that it sounds crazy, but . . ."

"Where did you say this painting is?" he asked.

"Here in Willow Grove."

"Have you had a look at it?"

"Well, yes," I said, "a glance, but I wouldn't know . . ."

"Tell him," Stevens whispered, fiercely, "that it is a Rembrandt."

"Who owns it?"

"Not really anyone," I said. "It's down at the city jail."

"John, are you trying to suck me into something? As an expert witness, maybe."

"Nothing like that," I said, "but it does have a bearing on a case of mine and I suppose I could dig up a fee . . ."

"Tell him," Stevens insisted, "that it is a Rembrandt."

"Did I hear someone talking about a Rembrandt?" Cal asked.

"No," I said. "No one knows what it is."

"Maybe I could get away," he said.

He was getting interested—well, maybe interested isn't the word; intrigued might be more like it.

"I could arrange a charter to fly you out," I said.

"It's that important, is it?"

"To tell you the truth, Cal, I don't know if it is or not. I'd just like your opinion."

"Fix up the charter, then," he said, "and call me back. I can be at the airport to be picked up within an hour."

"Thanks, Cal," I said. "I'll be seeing you."

Elsie would be sore at me, I knew, and Dorothy would be furious. Chartering a plane, for a small-town lawyer in a place like Willow Grove, is downright extravagance. But if we could hang onto those diamonds, or even a part of them, the bill for the charter would be peanuts. If they were diamonds. I wasn't absolutely sure Harry Johnson would know a diamond if he saw one. He sold them in his store, of course, but I suspected that he just took some wholesaler's word that what he had were diamonds.

"Who was that you were talking to?" demanded Banker Stevens.

I told him who it was.

"Then why didn't you tell him it was a Rembrandt?" Stevens raged at me. "Don't you think that I would know a Rembrandt?"

I almost told him no, that I didn't think he would, and then thought better of it. Some day I might have to ask him for a loan.

"Look, Amos," I said, "I didn't want to do anything that would prejudice his judgment. Nothing that would sway him one way or the other. Once he gets here he will no doubt see right away that it is a Rembrandt."

That mollified him a bit, and then I called in Dorothy and asked her to fix up arrangements for Cal to be flown out, and her mouth got grimmer and her face more prissy at every word I said. If Amos hadn't been there, she'd have had something to say about throwing away my money.

Looking at her, I could understand the vast enjoyment she got out of the revival meetings that blossomed out in Willow Grove and other nearby towns each summer. She went to all of them, no matter what the sect, and sat on the hard benches in the summer heat and dropped in her quarter when the collection plate was passed and sucked out of the fire-and-brimstone preaching a vast amount of comfort. She was always urging me to go to them, but I never went. I always had the feeling she thought they might do me a world of good.

"You're going to be late in court," she told me curtly, "and the case this morning is one you've spent a lot of time on."

Which was her way of telling me I shouldn't be wasting any of my time on George.

So I went off to court.

At noon recess, I phoned the jail, and there'd been no sign of George. At three o'clock, Dorothy came across the square to tell me Calvin Ross would be coming in at five. I asked her to phone Elsie to be expecting a guest for dinner and maybe one for overnight; and she didn't say anything, but from her face I knew she thought I was a brute and she'd not blame Elsie any if she up and left me. Such inconsideration!

At five o'clock I picked Cal up at our little airport and a fair crowd was on hand. Somehow the word had got around that an art expert was flying out to have a look at the painting George Wetmore had picked up somewhere.

Cal was somewhat older than I had remembered him and age had served to emphasize and sharpen up the dignity that he'd had even in his youth. But he was kind and affable and as enthusiastic about his art as he had ever been. And I realized, with a start, that he was excited. The possibility of finding a long-lost painting of some significance must be, I realized, a dream that is dear to everyone in the field.

I drove him down to the square and we went into the station and I introduced him round. Chet told me there was no sign of George. After a little argument, he got out the painting and laid it on the table underneath the ceiling light.

Cal walked over to look down at it and suddenly he froze, like a bird dog on the point. For a long time he stood there, not moving, looking down at it, while the rest of us stood around and tried not to breathe too hard.

Then he took a folding magnifier out of his pocket and unfolded it. He bent above the painting and moved the glass from spot to spot, staring at each spot over which he held the glass for long seconds.

Finally he straightened up.

"John," he said, "would you please tilt it up for me."

I tilted it up on the table and he walked back a ways and had a long look at it from several angles and then came back and examined it with the glass again.

Finally he straightened up again and nodded to Chet.

"Thanks very much," he said. "If I were you, I'd guard that canvas very carefully."

Chet was dying to know what Cal might think, but I didn't give him a chance to ask. I doubt Cal would have told him anything even if he'd asked.

I hustled Cal out of there and got him in the car and we sat there for a moment without either of us saying anything at all.

Then Cal said, "Unless my critical faculties and my knowledge of art have deserted me entirely, that canvas in there is Toulouse-Lautrec's *Quadrille at the Moulin Rouge.*"

So it wasn't Rembrandt! I'd known damn well it wasn't. So much for Amos Stevens!

"I'd stake my life on it," said Cal. "I can't be mistaken. No one could copy the canvas as faithfully as that. There is only one thing wrong."

"What is that?" I asked.

"*Quadrille at the Moulin Rouge* is in Washington at the National Gallery of Art."

I experienced a sinking feeling in my gizzard. If George somehow had managed to rifle the National Gallery both of us were sunk.

"It's possible the painting is missing," said Cal, "and the National Gallery people are keeping quiet about it for a day or two. Although ordinarily, they'd notify other large museums and some of the dealers."

He shook his head, perplexed. "But why anyone should steal it is more than I would know. There's always the possibility that it could be sold to some collector who would keep it hidden. But that would require prior negotiations, and few collectors would be so insane as to buy a painting as famous as the *Moulin Rouge*."

I took some hope from that. "Then there isn't any possibility George could have stolen it."

He looked at me, funny. "From what you tell me," he said, "this George of yours wouldn't know one painting from another."

"I don't think he would."

"Well, that lets him out. He must have just picked it up somewhere. But where—that's the question."

I couldn't help him there.

"I think," said Cal, "I had better make a phone call."

We drove down to the office and climbed the stairs.

Dorothy was waiting for me to come back, and she still was sore at me. "There is a Colonel Sheldon Reynolds in your office," she told me. "He is from the Air Force."

"I can phone out here," said Cal.

"Colonel Reynolds has been waiting for some time," said Dorothy, "and he strikes me as a most patient man."

I could see she didn't approve of me associating with people from the world of art and that she highly disapproved of me meeting with the Air Force and she still was sore at me for giving Elsie such a short notice we were to have a dinner guest. She was very properly outraged, although she was too much of a lady and too loyal an employee to bawl me out in front of Cal.

I went into my office, and sure enough, Colonel Reynolds was there, acting most impatient, sitting on the edge of a chair and drumming his fingers on its arms.

He quit his drumming and stood up as soon as I came in.

"Mr. Page," he said.

"I'm sorry you had to wait," I said. "What can I do for you?"

We shook hands, and he sat down in the chair and I perched uneasily on the edge of the desk, waiting.

"It has come to my attention," he told me, "that there have been some extraordinary occurrences in town and that there are certain artifacts involved. I've spoken with the county attorney, and he says you are the man I have to talk with. It appears there is some question about the ownership of the artifacts."

"If you're talking about what I think you are," I told him, "there is no question whatsoever. All the articles in question are the property of my client."

"I understand your client has escaped from jail."

"Disappeared," I said. "And he was placed in custody originally in an illegal manner. The man was doing nothing except walking on the street."

"Mr. Page," said the colonel, "you do not have to convince me. I have no interest in the merits of the case. All the Air Force is concerned about are certain gadgets found in the possession of your client."

"You have seen these gadgets?"

He shook his head. "No. The county attorney told me you'd probably crucify him in court if he let me see them. But he said you were a reasonable man and if properly appealed to . . ."

"Colonel," I said, "I'm never a reasonable man where the welfare of my client could be jeopardized."

"You don't know where your client is?"

"I have no idea."

"He must have told you where he found the stuff."

"I don't think he knows himself," I said.

The colonel, I could see, didn't believe a word I told him, for which I couldn't very well blame him.

"Didn't your client tell you he'd contacted a UFO?"

I shook my head, bewildered. That was a new one on me. I'd never thought of it.

"Mr. Page," the colonel said, "I don't mind telling you that these gadgets might mean a lot to us. Not to the Air Force alone, but to the entire nation. If the other side should get hold of some of them before we did and . . ."

"Now wait a minute," I interrupted. "Are you trying to tell me there are such things as UFO's?"

He stiffened. "I'm not trying to tell you anything at all," he said. "I am simply asking . . ."

The door opened, and Cal stuck in his head. "Sorry for breaking in like this," he said, "but I have to leave."

"You can't do that," I protested. "Elsie is expecting you for dinner."

"I have to go to Washington," he said. "Your secretary says she will run me to the airport. If the pilot can get me home within an hour or so, I can catch a plane."

"You talked with the National Gallery?"

"The painting still is there," he said. "There is a remote possibility there may have been a substitution, but with the tight security that seems impossible. I don't suppose there would be any chance . . ."

"Not a ghost," I said. "The painting stays right here."

"But it belongs in Washington!"

"Not if there are two of them," I shouted.

"But there can't be."

"There appear to be," I told him.

"I'd feel a whole lot better, John, if it were in a safer place."

"The police are guarding it."

"A bank vault would be a whole lot better."

"I'll look into it," I promised. "What did the National Gallery say about it?"

"Not much of anything," said Cal. "They are flabbergasted. You may have them out here."

"I might as well," I said. "I have the Pentagon."

We shook hands, and he left, and I went back and perched upon the desk.

"You're a hard man to deal with," said the colonel. "How do I reach you? Patriotism, perhaps?"

"I'm not a patriotic man," I told him, "and I'll instruct my client not to be."

"Money?"

"If there were a lot of it."

"The public interest?"

"You've got to show me it's in the public interest."

We glared at one another. I didn't like this Colonel Sheldon Reynolds, and he reciprocated.

The phone banged at me.

It was Chet down at the police station. His words started tumbling over one another as soon as I picked up the phone.

"George is back!" he shouted. "This time he has got someone with him and he's driving something that looks like a car, but it hasn't got no wheels . . ."

I slammed down the phone and ran for the door. Out of the tail of my eye I saw that Reynolds had jumped up and was running after me.

Chet had been right. It looked like a car, but it had no wheels. It was standing in front of the police station, hanging there about two feet off the ground and a gentle thrumming indicated there was some mechanism somewhere inside of it that was running smoothly.

Quite a crowd had gathered and I forced my way through it and got up beside the car.

George was sitting in what appeared to be the driver's seat and sitting beside him was a scarecrow of a fellow with the sourest face I've ever seen on any man.

He wore a black robe that buttoned up the front and up close around his throat and a black skull cap that came down hard against his ears and across his forehead; his hands and face, all of him that showed, were fishbelly white.

"What happened to you?" I demanded of George. "What are you sitting here for?"

"I tell you, John," he said, "I am somewhat apprehensive that Chet will try to throw me into the pokey once again. If he makes a move I'm all ready to go shooting out of here. This here vehicle is the slickest thing there is.

"It'll go along the ground or it will shoot up in the air and make just like a plane. I ain't rightly got the hang of it yet, having hardly driven it, but it handles smooth and easy and it ain't no trick at all to drive it."

"You can tell him," said Charley Nevins, "that he need not fear arrest. There is something most peculiar going on here, but I'm not sure at all there is violation of the law involved."

I looked around in some surprise. I hadn't noticed Charley standing there when I'd pushed through the crowd.

Reynolds shoved in ahead of me and reached up to grab George by the arm.

"I am Colonel Reynolds," he said, "and I am from the Air Force and it's terribly important that I know what this is all about. Where did you get this vehicle?"

"Why," George said, "it was standing there with a pile of other junk, so I took it. Someone threw it away and didn't seem to want it. There were a lot of people there throwing things away that they didn't want."

"And I suppose," yelled Chet, "that someone threw away the painting and the pail of diamonds."

"I wouldn't know about that," George told him. "I don't seem to remember much about that other trip. Except there was this big pile of stuff and that it was raining . . ."

"Shut up, George," I said. He hadn't told me anything about a pile of stuff. Either his memory was improving or he had lied to me.

"I think," said Charley, getting edgy, "that we all better sit down together and see if we can make some sense out of these proceedings."

"That's all right with me," I said, "always remembering that this machine remains, technically, the property of my client."

"It seems to me," Charley said to me, "that you're being somewhat unreasonable and high-handed in this whole affair."

"Charley," I said, "you know I have to be. If I let down my guard a minute, you and Chet and the Pentagon will tramp all over me."

"Let's get on with it," said Charley. "George, you put that machine down on the ground and come along with us. Chet will stand guard over it and see no one touches it."

"And while you're doing that," I said, "don't take your eyes off the painting and the diamonds. The painting just might be worth an awful lot of money."

"Right now," said Chet, disgusted, "would be a swell time for someone to rob the bank. I'd have the entire force tied up watching all this junk of George's."

"I think, too," said Charley, "we better include this passenger of George's in our little talk. He might be able to add some enlightenment."

III

George's passenger didn't pay any attention. He'd been paying no attention all along. He had just been sitting there, bolt upright in his seat, with his face pointing straight ahead.

Chet walked officiously around the car. The passenger said something, at some length, in a high, chittering voice. I didn't recognize a word of it but crazy as it sounds, I knew exactly what he said.

"Don't touch me!" he said. "Get away from me. Don't interfere with me."

And, having said this, he opened the door and let himself to the ground. Chet stepped back from him and so did all the others. Silence fell upon the gathering which had been buzzing up until this moment. As he advanced down the street, the crowd parted and pressed back to make way for him. Charley and the colonel stepped backward, bumping into me, pinning me against the car, to get out of his way. He passed not more than ten feet from me and I got a good look at his face. There was no expression on it and it was set in a natural grimness—the way, I imagined, that a judge of the Inquisition might have looked. And there was something else that is very hard to say, an impression that translated itself into a sense of smell, although I am sure there was no actual odor. The odor of sanctity is as close as I can come to it, I guess. Some sort of vibration radiating from the man that impinged upon the senses in the same manner, perhaps, as ultrasonics will impinge without actual hearing upon the senses of a dog.

And then he was past me and gone, walking down the street through the lane of human bodies that stepped aside for him, walking slowly, unconcernedly, almost strolling—walking as if he might have been all alone, apparently unaware of a single one of us.

All of us watched him until he was free of the crowd and had turned a corner into another street. And even for a moment after that we stood uncertain and unmoving until finally someone spoke a whisper and someone answered him and the buzz of the crowd took up again, although now a quieter buzz.

Someone's fingers were digging hard into the muscles of my upper arm and when I looked around, I saw that it was Charley who had fastened onto me.

Ahead of me, the colonel turned his head to look at me. His face was white and tight and little drops of perspiration stood out along his hairline.

"John," said Charley, quietly, "I think it is important that we all sit down together."

I turned around toward the car and saw that it was now resting on the ground and that George was getting out of it.

"Come along," I said to George.

Charley led, pushing his way through the crowd, with the colonel following and George and me bringing up the rear. We went down the street, without a word among us, to the square and walked across the lawn to the courthouse steps.

When we got in Charley's office, Charley shut the door and dug down into a desk drawer and come up with a jug. He got out four paper cups and poured them almost full.

"No ice," he said, "but what the hell, it's the liquor that we need."

Each of us took a cup and found a place to sit and worked on the booze a while without saying anything.

"Colonel," Charley finally asked, "what do you make of it?"

"It might be a help," the colonel said, "if we could talk with the passenger. I assume some attempt will be made to apprehend the man."

"I suppose we should," said Charley. "Although how one apprehends a bird like that, I don't really know."

"He caught us by surprise," the colonel pointed out. "Next time we'll be ready for him. Plug your ears with cotton, so you cannot hear him . . ."

"It may take more than that," said Charley. "Did anyone actually hear him speak?"

"He spoke, all right," I said. "He uttered words, but there was none I recognized. Just a sort of chirping gibberish."

"But we knew what he meant," said Charley. "Every single one of us knew that. Telepathy, perhaps?"

"I doubt it," the colonel said. "Telepathy is not the simple thing so many people think."

"A new language," I suggested. "A language scientifically constructed. Sounds that are designed to trigger certain understandings. If one dug deep enough into semantics . . ."

Charley interrupted me; apparently he took no stock in my semantics talk.

"George," he asked, "what do you know of him?"

George was sunk back deep into a chair, with his shoeless feet stuck out in front of him. He had his big mitt wrapped around the paper cup and was wriggling his toes and he was content. It did not take an awful lot to make George content.

"I don't know a thing," said George.

"But he was riding with you. He must have told you something."

"He never told me a thing," said George. "He never said a word. I was just driving off and he came running up and jumped into the seat and then . . ."

"You were driving off from where?"

"Well," said George, "there was this big pile of stuff. It must have covered several acres and it was piled up high. It seemed to be in a sort of square, like the courthouse and no lawn, but just a sort of paving that might have been concrete and all around it, everywhere you looked, but quite a distance off, there were big high buildings."

Charley asked, exasperated, "Did you recognize the place?"

"I never saw the place before," said George, "nor no pictures of it, even."

"Perhaps it would be best," suggested Charley, "if you told it from the start."

So George told it the way he had told it to me.

"That first time it was raining pretty hard," he said, "and it was sort of dark, as if evening might be coming on, and all I saw was this pile of junk. I didn't see no buildings."

He hadn't told me he'd seen anything at all. He had claimed he hadn't known a thing until he was back in Willow Grove, walking on the street, with the police car pulling up. But I let it go and kept on listening.

"Then," said George, "after Chet threw me into pokey . . ."

"Now, wait a minute there," said Charley. "I think you skipped a bit. Where did you get the diamonds and the painting and all the other stuff?"

"Why, off the pile of junk," said George. "There was a lot of other stuff and if I'd had the time I might have done some better. But something seemed to warn me that I didn't have much time and it was raining and the rain was cold and the place was sort of spooky. So I grabbed what I could and put it in my pockets and I took the pail of diamonds, although I wasn't sure they were really diamonds, and then I took the painting because Myrt has been yelling that she wants a high class picture to hang in the dining room . . ."

"And then you were back home again?"

"That is it," said George, "and I am walking down the street, minding my own business and not doing anything illegal . . ."

"And how about the second time?"

"You mean going back again?"

"That's what I mean," said Charley.

"That first time," said George, "it was unintentional. I was just sitting in the living room with my shoes off and a can of beer, watching television and in the seventh inning the Yankees had two on and Mantle coming up to bat—say, I never did find out what Mantle did. Did he hit a homer?"

"He struck out," said Charley.

George nodded sadly; Mickey is his hero.

"The second time," said George, "I sort of worked at it. I don't mind a cell so much, you understand, as the injustice of being there when you ain't done nothing wrong. So I talked John into bringing me some beer and I sat down and started drinking it. There wasn't any television, but I imagined television. I imagined it real hard and I put two men on bases and had Mantle coming up—all in my mind, of course—and I guess it must have worked. I was back again, in the place where there was this pile of junk. Only you must understand it wasn't really junk. It was all good stuff. Some of it didn't make any sense at all, but a good part of it did; and it was just setting there and no one touching it and every now and then someone would come walking out from some of those tall buildings—and it was quite a walk, I tell you, for those buildings were a long ways off—and they'd be carrying something and they'd throw it on the pile of junk and go walking back."

"I take it," said the colonel, "that you spent more time there on your second trip."

"It was daytime," George explained, "and it wasn't raining and it didn't seem so spooky, although it did seem lonesome. There weren't any people—just the few who came walking to throw something on the pile, and they didn't pay much attention to me; they acted almost as if they didn't see me. You understand, I didn't know if I'd ever get back there again and there was a limit to how much I could carry, so this time I figured I'd do a job of it. I'd look over the pile and figure exactly what I wanted. Maybe I should say that a little differently. There was a lot of it I wanted, but I had to decide what I wanted most. So I started walking around the pile, picking up stuff I thought I wanted until I saw something I took a special liking to then I'd decide between it and something else I had picked up. Sometimes I'd discard the new thing I had picked up and sometimes I'd keep it and drop something else. Because, you see, I could carry just so much, and by this time I was loaded with about all that I could carry. There was a lot of nice items up on the sides of the pile, and once I tried climbing the pile to get a funny-looking sort of gadget, but that stuff was piled loose, just tossed up there, you know; and when I started to climb, the stuff started to shift and I was afraid it might all come down on top of me. So I climbed down again, real careful. After that I had to satisfy myself with whatever I could pick up at the bottom of the pile."

The colonel had become greatly interested, leaning forward in his chair so he wouldn't miss a word. "Some of this junk," he asked. "Could you tell what it was?"

"There was a pair of spectacles," said George, "with some sort of gadget on them and I tried them on and I got so happy that it scared me, so I took them off and I quit being happy; then I put them on again and I was happy right away . . ."

"Happy?" asked Charley. "Do you mean they made you drunk?"

"Not drunk happy," said George. "Just plain happy, that is all. No troubles and no worries and the world looked good and a man enjoyed living. Then there was another thing, a big square piece of glass. I suppose you'd call it a cube of glass. Like these fortune tellers have, but it was square instead of round. It was a pretty thing, all by itself, but when you looked into it—well, it didn't reflect your face, like a mirror does, but there seemed to be some sort of picture in it, deep inside of it. It looked to me, that first time, like maybe it was a tree and when I looked closer I could see it was a tree. A big, high elm tree like the one that used to stand in my grandfather's yard, the one that had the bobolink's nest way up at the top, and this one, too, I saw, had a bobolink's nest and there was the bobolink, himself, sitting on a limb beside the nest. And then I saw it was the very tree that I remembered, for there was my grandfather's house and the picket fence and the old man sitting in the battered lawn swing, smoking his corncob pipe. You see, that piece of glass showed you anything that you wanted to see. First there was just the tree, then I thought about the nest and the nest was there and then the house showed up and the picket fence and I was all right until I saw the old man himself—and him dead for twenty years or more. I looked at him for a while and then I made myself look away, because I had thought a lot of the old man and seeing him there made me remember too much, so I looked away. By then I thought I knew what this glass was all about and so I thought of a pumpkin pie and the pie was there, with gobs of whipped cream piled on it and then I thought of a stein of beer and the beer was there . . ."

"I don't believe," said Charley, "a single word of this."

"Go on," urged the colonel. "Tell us the rest of it."

"Well," said George, "I guess I must have walked almost all the way around that pile, picking one thing up and throwing another away and I was loaded, I can tell you. I had my arms full and my pockets full and stuff hung around my neck. And suddenly, driving out from those tall buildings came this car, floating about three feet off the ground . . ."

"You mean the vehicle that you have out there?"

"The very one," said George. "There was a sad-looking old geezer driving it, and he ran it up alongside the pile and set it down, then got out of it and started walking back, sort of hobbling. So I went up to it and I dumped all the stuff I had been carrying into the back seat and it occurred to me that with it I could carry away more than I could in my arms. But I thought that first, perhaps, I had ought to see if I could operate it, so I climbed in the driver's seat and there was no trick to it at all. I started it up and began to drive it, slow, around the pile, trying to remember where I had discarded some of the stuff I had picked up earlier—intending to go back and get it and put it in the back seat. I heard the sound of running feet behind me and when I looked around there was this gent all dressed in black. He reached the car and put one hand upon it and vaulted into the seat beside me. The next instant we were in Willow Grove."

"You mean to tell us," cried the colonel, leaping to his feet, "that you have the back seat of that car loaded with some of these things you have been telling us about?"

"Colonel, please sit down," said Charley. "You can't possibly believe any of the things he has been telling us. On the face of them, they are all impossible and . . ."

"Charley," I said, "let me cite a few more impossibilities, like a painting being in the National Gallery of Art and also in Willow

Grove, like that car out there without any wheels, like a gadget that is hot at one end and cold at the other."

"God, I don't know," said Charley, desperately. "And I am the guy that has it in his lap."

"Charley," I said, "I don't believe you have anything in your lap, at all. I don't think there is a single legal question involved in this whole mess. Taking a car, you might say, being of the particular turn of legal mind you are, without the permission of the owner, only it is not a car . . ."

"It's a vehicle!" Charley yelled.

"But the owner had junked it. He'd junked it and walked away and . . ."

"What I want to know," the colonel said, "is where this place is and why the people were discarding their possessions."

"And you'd also," I said, "love to get your hands on some of those possessions."

"You're damned right I would," said the colonel, grimly. "And I'm going to. Do you realize what some of them might mean to this nation of ours? Why, they might spell the margin of difference between us and the other side, and I don't intend . . ."

"Colonel," I said, "haul down the flag. There is no use of screaming. I am sure that George would be willing to discuss terms with you."

Feet came pounding up the stairs and down the hall. The door flew open and a deputy sheriff came skidding to a halt.

"Charley," he panted, "I don't know what to do. There's been a crazy-looking coot preaching to a crowd out by the Soldier's Monument. The sheriff, I am told, went out to stop it, him not having any license to be preaching anywhere, let alone the courthouse square, and then came charging back. I came in the back way, without knowing anything about what was going on, and I found the sheriff collecting up the guns and ammunition and when I asked him what was going on, he wouldn't talk to me, but went walking out the front door and he threw all of them guns and all that ammunition down at the base of the monument. And there are a lot of other people bringing other things and throwing them there, too . . ."

IV

I didn't wait to hear the rest of it. I dodged past the deputy and through the door and down the stairs, heading for the building's front.

The pile had grown to a size that was big enough to cover the base of the monument; and there were, I saw, such things as bicycles, radios, typewriters and sewing machines, electric razors and lawn mowers; and there was a car or two, jammed up against the monument. Dusk had fallen and the farmers were coming into town to trade and people were coming across the square, dark, muffled figures, lugging stuff to throw upon the pile.

There was no sign of the passenger. He had done his dirty work and gone. Standing there in the courthouse square, with the street lamps swinging in the tiny breeze and all those dark-enshrouded figures toiling up the lawn toward the monument, I had the vision of many other towns throughout the country with growing piles of discarded objects bearing testimony to the gull-ibility of the human race.

My God, I thought, they never understood a word of what he said, not a single syllable of that clacking tongue of his. But the message, as had been the case which we'd pushed back to clear the path for him, had been plain and clear. Thinking about it, I knew I'd been right up there in Charley's office when I'd said it was a matter of semantics.

We had words, of course, lots of words, perhaps more than an ordinary man would ever need, but intellectual words, tailored for their precise statement of one peculiar piece of understanding;

and we'd become so accustomed to them, to their endless ebb and flow, that many of them—perhaps the most of them—had lost the depth and the precision of their meaning. There had been a time when great orators could catch and hold the public ear with the pure poetry of their speech and men such as these had at times turned the tide of national opinion. Now, however, in large part, spoken words had lost their power to move. But the laugh, I thought, would never lose its meaning. The merry laugh that, even if one were not included in it, could lift the human spirits; the belly laugh that spelled out unthinking fellowship; the quiet laugh of superior, supercilious intellect that could cut the ground beneath one.

Sounds, I thought—sounds, not words—sounds that could trigger basic human reaction. Was it something such as this that the passenger had used? Sounds so laboriously put together, probing so deeply into the human psyche, that they said almost as much as the most carefully constructed sentence of intellectual speech, but with the one advantage that they were convincing as words could never be. Far back in man's prehistory there had been the grunt of warning, the cry of rage, the food-call, the little clucking recognition signals.

Was this strange language of the passenger's no more than a sophisticated extension of these primal sounds?

Old Con Weatherby came tramping stolidly across the lawn to fling his portable television set upon the pile, and behind him came a young housewife I didn't recognize who threw a toaster and a blender and a vacuum cleaner beside Con's television set.

My heart cried out to them in my pity of what was happening, and I suppose I should have hurried forth and spoken to them— Old Con at least—trying to stop them, to show them this was all damn foolishness. I knew Old Con had saved dollars here and there, going without the drinks he wanted, smoking only three cigars a day instead of his usual five, so that he and his old lady could have that television set. But, somehow, I knew how useless it would be to stop them, to do anything about it.

I went down across the lawn, feeling beat and all played out. Coming up the lawn toward me, staggering under a heavy load, came a familiar figure.

"Dorothy!" I yelled.

Dorothy stopped and some of the books that she was carrying up toward the monument came unstuck from the load and went thumping to the ground. In a flash I knew exactly what they were—my law books.

"Hey," I yelled, "take those back. Hey, what is going on!"

I didn't need to ask, of course. Of all the people in Willow Grove, she would have been the one most certain to be on hand to listen to the passenger and the most avid to believe. She could smell out an evangelist twenty miles away and the high moments of her life were those spent with her scrawny little bottom planted on the hardness of a bench in the suffocating air of a tent meeting and listening to some jackleg preacher spout about his hellfire and brimstone. She'd believe anything at all and subscribe to it whole-heartedly so long as it was evangelistic.

I started down the lawn toward her but was distracted.

From the other side of the square came a snarling, yipping sound; out of the dusk came a running figure, with a pack of dogs snapping at his heels. The man had shucked up his robe to give him extra leg room, and he was making exceptionally good time. Every once in a while one of the dogs would get a mouthful of the robe that flowed out behind him, snapping in the wind of his rapid movement, but it didn't slow him down.

It was the passenger, of course, and while he'd done right well with humans, it was quite evident he was doing not so well with dogs. They had just been let loose with the dusk, after being tied up for the day, and they were spoiling for a bit of fun. They didn't understand the talk of the passenger perhaps, or there was something so different about him that they immediately had pegged him as some sort of outlander to be hunted down.

He went across the lawn below me in a rush with the dogs very close behind, and out into the street, and it wasn't until then that I realized where he would be heading.

I let out a whoop and set out after him. He was heading for that car to make his getaway and I couldn't let him do it. That car belonged to George.

I knew I could never catch him, but I pinned my hopes on Chet. Chet would have a man or two guarding the car; and while the passenger would probably talk them out of it, they might slow him a bit, enough for me to catch up with him before he had taken off. He might try, of course, to talk me out of it as well with his chittering gibberish, but I told myself I'd have to do my best to resist whatever he might tell me.

We went whipping down the street, the passenger with the dogs close to his heels, and me close to the dogs; and there, up ahead, stood the car out in front of the station. There still was a fair-sized crowd around it, but the passenger yelled some outlandish sounds at them and they began to scatter.

He didn't even break his stride, and I'll say this much for him—he was quite an athlete. Ten feet or so from the car, he jumped and sailed up through the air and landed in the driver's seat. He was plenty scared of those mutts, of course, and that may have helped him some; under certain crisis circumstances a man can accomplish feats that ordinarily would be impossible. But even so, he had to be fairly athletic to manage what he did.

He landed in the driver's seat and immediately the car took off upward at a slant, and in a couple of seconds had soared up above the buildings and was out of sight. The two cops that Chet had detailed to guard the car just stood there with their jaws hanging down, looking up at where the car had gone. The crowd that had been there and scattered when the passenger yelled his gibberish at them now turned about and stared as vacantly, while the dogs circled around, puzzled, sniffing at the ground and every now and then pointing up a nose to bay.

I was standing there like the rest of them when someone came running up behind me and grabbed my arm. It was Colonel Sheldon Reynolds.

"What happened?"

I told him, somewhat bitterly and profanely, exactly what had happened.

"He's gone futureward," the colonel said. "We'll never see him or the car again."

"Futureward?" I asked stupidly.

"That must be it," the colonel said. "There's no other way to explain it. George wasn't in contact with any UFO, as I had thought to be the case. He must have travelled futureward. You probably were right about the way the passenger talked. That was a new semantics. A sort of speech shorthand, made up of basic sounds. I suppose it would be possible, but it would take a long time to develop. Maybe it developed, or was borrowed, when the race went to the stars—a sort of universal language, a vocal version of the sign language used by the Great Plains Indians . . ."

"But that would be time travel," I protested. "Hell, George doesn't know enough . . ."

"Look," said the colonel, "you maybe don't need to know anything to travel in time. You maybe have to feel something; you may have to be in tune. There might be only one man in the entire world today who can feel that way . . ."

"But, colonel," I said, "it makes no sense at all. Let's say George did go into the future—just for the sake of argument, let us say he did. Why should people up in the future be throwing away their things, why should there be the big pile of junk?"

"I don't know," the colonel said. "That is, I couldn't say for sure, but I have a theory."

He waited for me to ask about his theory, but when I didn't ask, he went ahead and told me.

"We've talked a lot," he said, "about contact with other intelligences that live on other stars and we've done some listening in the hope of picking up some signals sent out by peoples many light years distant. We haven't heard any signals yet and we may never hear any because the time span during which any race is technologically oriented may be very short."

I shook my head. "I don't see what you're driving at," I told him. "What has all that has happened here got to do with signals from the stars?"

"Perhaps not very much," he admitted, "except that if contact is ever made it must be made with a technological race very much like ours. And there are sociologists who tell us that the technological phase of any society finds ways and means of destroying itself or it creates stresses and pressures against which the people rebel or it becomes interested in something other than technology and . . . "

"Now hold up a minute," I said. "You are trying to tell me that this junk heap of George's is the result of the human race, in some future day, rejecting a technological society—throwing away technological items? It wouldn't work that way. It would be a gradual rejection, a gradual dying out of technology. People wouldn't just decide they wanted no more of it and go out and throw all their beautiful, comfortable gadgets . . ."

"That could happen," the colonel argued. "It could happen if the rejection was the result of a religious or evangelistic movement. The passenger may have been one of their evangelists. Look at what he did right here in a few minutes time. Typewriters, radios, television sets, vacuum cleaners in that pile on the courthouse lawn—all technological items."

"But a painting isn't technological," I protested. "A pail of diamonds isn't."

Both of us stopped talking and looked at one another in the deepening dusk. Both of us realized, I guess, that there wasn't too much sense of us standing there and arguing over a speculation.

The colonel shrugged. "I don't know," he said. "It was only an idea. The car is lost for good, of course, and all the stuff George had thrown into the back seat. But we have the other stuff . . ."

One of the cops who had been set to guard the car had been standing close and listening to us and now he broke in on us.

"I am sorry, sir," he said, gulping a little, "but we ain't got none of it. All of it is gone."

"All of it!" I yelled. "The painting and the diamonds. I told Chet . . ."

"Chet, he couldn't do nothing else," said the man. "He had two of us here and he had two inside guarding that other stuff and when the ruckus started up at the courthouse, he needed men and he didn't have them . . ."

"And so he brought the painting and the diamonds and the other stuff out here and put them in the car," I yelled. I knew Chet. I knew how he would think.

"That way he figured we could guard them all," said the man. "And we could have, but . . ."

I turned and started to walk away. I didn't want to hear another word. If Chet had been there, I would have strangled him.

I was walking down the sidewalk, clear of the crowd, and there was someone walking close beside me, just a little ways behind. I looked around, it was the colonel.

His mouth shaped a single word as I looked around at him. "George," he said.

We both of us must have had the same idea.

"Are the Yankees and Twins on TV tonight?" I asked.

He nodded.

"For the love of God," I said, "let us get some beer."

We made it in record time, each of us lugging a couple of six-packs.

George had beat us to it.

He was sitting in front of the TV set, in his stocking feet, watching the ball game with a can of beer in hand.

We didn't say a word. We just put the beer down beside him so there'd be no danger of his running out of it and went into the dining room and waited in the dark, keeping very quiet.

In the sixth, the Yanks had two men on and Mantle up to bat and Mantle hit a double. But nothing happened. George just went on drinking beer, wriggling his toes and watching television.

"Maybe," said the colonel, "it has to be the seventh."

"And maybe," I said, "a double doesn't count. It may take a strike-out."

We keep on trying, of course, but our hopes are fading. There are only four more Twin and Yankee games on television before the season ends. And someone wrote the other day that next year, for sure, Mantle will retire.

THE FIGHTING DOC
OF BUSHWHACK BASIN

As was often the case with Clifford D. Simak's Western stories, it appears that the title under which he sold this story was not the one under which it was published—but in this case it seems rather easy to conclude that the Simak story called, on submission, "Powdersmoke Prescription," which strongly hinted at a medical element in the story, turned into "The Fighting Doc of Bushwhack Basin." Moreover, Cliff's journal shows that after he sent "Powdersmoke Prescription" off to Popular Publications in July of 1944, he received $150 for the story, and it subsequently appeared in the November 1944 issue of .44 Western Magazine, which was one of Popular Publications' titles. (I have no idea why the magazine did not give the name of its editor, but that seems to have occurred now and then in the pulp magazines.)

Although the word was misspelled "Bushwack" on the cover, it was the longest story of the eight in the magazine, and it led off the issue (which carried a cover price of fifteen cents).

—dww

Chapter One
A Taste of Law and Order

Doctor Stephen Carter sat on a rickety chair beside the bed and watched Jake McCord die. There was nothing Carter could do about it. The bullet had struck the man in the chest and angled downward, lodging in his back, no more than an inch from the spinal column.

Just a little to one side, it would have struck the heart. And that, Carter told himself, would have been far more merciful, far better for everyone concerned, especially for Jake.

A smoky lantern on the table by the bed flickered in the gusty wind of dawn that crept coldly through a broken pane. A pane that had been stuffed with a gunny sack, but the sack had worked loose and now no one thought to fix it.

The face upon the pillow was a rugged face, like something chopped out of granite with a blunted axe. The high cheekbones stood out gauntly in the lantern light and the grizzled three day beard lent the man an age that must have been far beyond his years. The usually tight mouth was slack, gasping desperately for breath and the hair was tousled into an alarming salt and pepper rat's nest.

Jake McCord was fighting for his life, fighting as he had fought through many years. As he had fought heartbreak and disappointment, drought and blizzard, insects, lack of water and the guns of those who coveted the few acres that he had held for a few years.

But this was his last fight. This was the one that he would not win. Carter closed his hands into fists and then relaxed them, spreading the fingers, telling himself there was nothing anyone might have done. There was no cure for a bullet that smashed into a man's chest and coursed down through his body.

From somewhere outside, in the murky dawn, a lark awoke and sang and the song was a strange thing to be heard within the little cabin. A strange thing when a man lay dying.

In the dark corner by the foot of the bed, Mrs. McCord stirred in her chair and for a moment bent forward so the pale light from the window fell across her face . . . a face grey in the dawn, with eyes that were deep pools of black and a mouth strained tight against the hour.

"He ain't sufferin' none now, is he, doctor?"

Carter shook his head. "He probably never suffered, Mrs. McCord."

Through the thin partition he heard Mary McCord poking up the fire, setting on the coffee pot. The door opened and footsteps went to the woodbox. The armload of wood thumped gently. One stick fell on the floor. That, Carter knew, was Walker, the McCords' oldest son.

"He was a good man," said Mrs. McCord, speaking to no one in particular, probably not even realizing that she spoke of the man upon the bed as already dead. "He never asked a thing except a place to live. A place to make his home and raise his family and drive his plow. A place he could call his own. We went from place to place and it always was the same. . . ."

Walker McCord came into the room, tiptoeing noisily, came to a halt behind Carter's chair. In the silence, the doctor could hear the youth's breath whistling in his nostrils.

Jake McCord's breath faltered and stopped, took up again, stopped for a long moment and did not resume. Carter reached out for the man's wrist, held it for a moment, fingers feeling for a pulse beat. None came and he slowly laid the hand back on the bed, rose and pulled up the quilt to cover the face.

Mrs. McCord was sobbing in her dark corner and Walker moved toward the end of the bed, stooping awkwardly to comfort her. Carter lifted his bag from the floor, put it on the chair, closed it.

Moments like this, he decided, were the worst part of being a doctor. Doctors were supposed to heal, to make well, to save lives . . . not to sit by and watch life slip away, unable to raise a hand to stop it.

The McCords, he knew, had every right to hate him, every right to think that he had failed his duty, that he had failed in their faith of him. And yet, he knew equally as well, there had been nothing that he could have done, nothing that anyone could have done.

There wasn't even anything that he could say. "I'm sorry" was about all and that wasn't enough. It was at once inadequate and apologetic, as if anyone could apologize for death.

Heavily he paced out of the room and into the kitchen.

The morning light seeped through the windows and the fire in the stove threw a ruddy glow from the fire-box draft. Mary McCord stood in front of the stove, hands clasped in front of her, head bowed.

Carter set his bag on the lopsided table and moved slowly toward her. She lifted her head and in the glow of the fire he saw the shine of tears in her eyes.

"He's gone, isn't he?" she whispered, and he nodded.

Sobs shook her shoulders, but she still held up her head.

"I won't cry," she told Carter, fiercely. "I simply won't. He wouldn't have wanted me to cry. We have to go on living, the rest of us, no matter what the Plimptons do."

"You're sure, Mary, that it was the Plimptons?"

"Who else would it be?" she asked him. "They came in the dark, when Dad was coming in from the barn. They shot him and when Clyde ran at their horses one of them hit him with a whip."

Carter strode across the room to a small bed standing in the corner, looked down at the boy who lay there. His head and face were swathed in bandages, but he was asleep. Carter, looking at him, felt dull anger stir within him as he remembered the savage cuts that criss-crossed the face of Clyde McCord. A loaded whip could have been the only thing that could have inflicted punishment like that. A loaded whip and a brutal, pitiless arm.

His eyes traced the pitifully small outline of the body that lay huddled beneath the quilt. A tiny fellow. Small even for his age. Ten, perhaps. Maybe a bit more. Not more than twelve, at most.

He had not told the family, but he knew that Clyde McCord would bear facial scars for life, the savage mark of something that had happened short hours ago. A drum of hoofs across the barnyard, the snarling crash of a six-gun, the whistle of a striking whip.

He turned from the bed and walked back to the stove. Mary still stood there, head still up, as if she were gazing at the growing light that came from the window.

"I'm leaving salve for Clyde," he said. "Keep plenty of it on and keep the wounds clean. Change the bandages before they start to get dirty. I'll be around to see him again as soon as I can get away. Tonight, perhaps."

"We won't leave," said Mary. "They can't drive us out. Dad said, when we settled here, that we'd been driven far enough. Here we stay, he said, and there ain't guns enough in all the west to make us pull up stakes."

Walker McCord came into the kitchen.

"I left Ma in there with him," he said. "She said she just wanted to sit there alone for a little while."

The lad's face was haggard, and there were tear marks down his cheeks and his voice was a little shaky.

"See that she gets some sleep before the day is over," Carter told him.

Walker nodded. "Want me to get your horse?"

"Don't bother," Carter declared. "I'll get him myself. You put him in the barn?"

"Fed him, too," said Walker.

"You go and get him, Walker," said the girl. "I'll pour the doctor a cup of coffee and cook him up some eggs. Our hens are laying now."

"Just some coffee," said Carter. "If you have it ready."

He wanted to get away, but he could not seem to rush away. There were so many hard moments at a time like this. Like walking away and leaving a place. A place where one had failed and through one's failure left sorrow. Already the cabin held a sense of desolation, the queer and empty feeling that always comes on the heels of death.

"I don't know how we'll ever pay you," Mary said.

"Don't think about that now," Carter told her. "Don't think about it ever unless you feel that you're more than able to."

He drank the coffee standing and then Walker was at the door to say the horse was ready.

Outside he stood for a moment with the youth before getting into the saddle.

"Perhaps you'll want me to do something in town for you," he suggested.

Walker gulped. "Sure, doctor, if you will. You might tell Preacher Slocum to come up."

Carter nodded. "I'll see the sheriff, too."

"There ain't no need of that," said Walker. "No need at all. There ain't a blessed thing that can be done, lawful-like. I can't nohow prove who done it, but I know. And I sure aim to go on the warpath as soon as the funeral's over."

Carter gripped the boy's shoulder. "Don't do anything foolish, Walker. You can't match guns with Plimpton's riders. You'll only go out and get yourself killed, too. Just when your mother needs you most. You're the head man now, Walker, and you can't go off getting yourself killed."

The doctor swung into the saddle.

"They burned our hay," said Walker, fiercely. "And they shot our dog and run off our cattle. We stood it all. We didn't even try to fight back. But now they killed my Dad and they're going to pay for that. They're going to pay for everything they done."

"Wait for just a while," the doctor counseled. "Something's

bound to happen. Things like this have got to stop somewhere. They can't go on forever. After all, there's such a thing as law and order and someday soon this country is going to get a taste of it."

He wheeled his horse and headed down the trail.

The sun was not up yet, although the east was swiftly brightening with its coming. Before him, as he rode, the valley land of the Tumbling K spread like a great green carpet, cupped between the mountain spurs that ran out like spreading fingers.

The air was sharp with the lingering chill of night and heavy with the smell of pine. Birds whistled from the grass that grew beside the trail and others sang from the thickets and patches of forest that clung to the rolling hills.

The brown blotch at the far end of the green valley marked the ranch buildings of Bob Plimpton's Tumbling K and as Carter watched them he saw the pale plumes of smoke that rose from the distant chimneys.

"It's about time," he told himself, "that I dropped in on Plimpton."

Chapter Two
Mealy-Mouthed Tenderfoot

The Tumbling K had a look of sleek prosperity about it. The buildings were in good repair and the ranch house, unlike most others, was surrounded by a fenced yard that enclosed a lawn and a few beds of flowers which later in the year would bloom in colorful profusion.

Riding up to the hitching post before the yard gate, Carter took note of this, saw the corral with its shining horses, the neat stacks of hay that stood between two stables, heard the laughter that came from the cookhouse and the screech that the windmill made in the rising wind.

A fat dog came out leisurely to greet him, tail wagging, as he opened the gate and went up the steps of the wide front porch.

The door opened before he reached it and Bob Plimpton stood there, hand outstretched.

"Just in time for breakfast, doc," said Plimpton. "We've eaten, but there's plenty left. I'll have the cook—"

Carter shook his head. "Have to hurry back to town. Just stopped in for a word or two."

"Somebody sick out this way?" asked Plimpton, holding open the door so that Carter could step in.

Carter nodded. "Been up to the McCords."

"You're sure about that breakfast?" asked Plimpton. "No trouble at all to hustle you a bite."

"Yes, I'm sure. Just wanted to tell you something."

Plimpton led the way to the cubby off the living room that he used for an office, shoved out a chair for his visitor and sat down in the battered armed affair that stood before a littered rolltop desk.

The rancher stroked his drooping mustaches and looked hard at Carter. "Got something on your mind, doc?"

Plimpton, Carter reflected, was a man that you could like. A man one couldn't very well help liking. He was just beginning to grizzle at the temples, but his face still held the hint of youth. A broad shouldered man, he sat foursquare in the chair, filling it with his massiveness.

"Jake McCord died this morning," Carter told him flatly.

Plimpton's face twisted a little. "I'm sorry to hear that, doc. Jake was a right good neighbor."

"Someone shot him," Carter said. "Jake was coming in from the barn where he'd been doing chores. The little fellow was with him. Clyde, his name is. Two men rode up to them and without saying a word one of them shot Jake. Then, when Clyde ran at them, yelling, the other one cut him across the face with his whip."

Plimpton sat stolidly in the chair, face unchanging. His big hands, held across his lap, knitted fingers carefully together.

"That's too bad," said Plimpton. "Hits me mighty hard. Had some trouble with McCord, off and on, but we were neighbors just the same. Anything that I can do for them?"

Carter shook his head. "There's nothing anyone can do for them now. Except, perhaps, to leave them alone."

"I might ride up," said Plimpton.

"I wouldn't if I were you," said Carter.

Plimpton's eyes narrowed just a fraction. "Why not?"

"Because they figure it was your riders that shot him," Carter said.

Plimpton's hands unfolded, moved to the chair arms, gripped them.

"You came to tell me that?" There was threat in the booming voice.

"I came to tell you," said Carter, "that I'm getting sick and tired of so many gunshot cases. Scarcely a week goes by that I'm not called out on one."

Plimpton did not speak, but he gripped the chair arms so hard that Carter was surprised the wood stood up to the pressure.

"You see," said Carter, speaking slowly so he would pick the right words, "it's a doctor's business to eliminate the cause of sickness. First to find it, determine what it is, and then get rid of it. These shootings around here, Plimpton, are assuming the nature of a disease. Almost an epidemic, one might say."

"You figure," inquired the rancher, quietly, all too quietly, "there are too many of them."

Carter nodded. "Far too many. A dozen a year . . . well, maybe that would be about right. Normal probably for this country. But there are more than that. A lot more than that."

"And you're blaming me," snapped Plimpton. "You're blaming my outfit."

"No, I'm not blaming you," said Carter. "Just telling you. Wondering maybe if there isn't something you might do to bring down the incidence. Something you could do or say that would fix it so there wouldn't be quite so many of them. A little bloodshed now and then, Plimpton, is all right. I suppose it's just one of those things we have to expect when a country's new and wild, not quite settled yet. It's something we have to get along with. But the bloodshed should be slacking off a bit by now. But it isn't. In the last two years or so it's been getting worse than ever."

Plimpton leaned forward and tapped Carter on the knee. "Let me tell you a story, doc. A story that maybe you never heard. About how someone staked him out a ranch and had some tough sledding to get started, what with bad snows that sometime wiped out half the herd and Indians popping up every so often to run off whatever they would find. But finally, after long years he got on his feet and was just settling down to take it easy—"

"I've heard the story before," Carter interrupted him. "And just about then the nesters began showing up. They settled on land he felt belonged to him. They took up the spring holes and threw fences around them and they plowed up ground that was never meant for anything but grass and when they wanted meat they just went out and knocked over the first cow they happened to run up against. The usual story."

"Only," said Plimpton, "they aren't satisfied with just knocking over a beef now and then. Not any more, they aren't. I've lost more than a thousand cattle in the last year."

"You have something on your side, of course," agreed Carter, "but you can't settle it with guns."

"I'm still gunning any rustler I catch out in the open," snarled Plimpton.

"Jake didn't rustle any of your cattle," said Carter.

"And there ain't anybody saying, leastwise out loud, that I gunned Jake," warned Plimpton.

Carter disregarded the challenge. "You've got to realize," he told the rancher, "that things have changed. The old days of free range are over. It's too bad, perhaps, from your point of view, but it's the truth, and something you must face. Go out and kill all the nesters that are bothering you and there'll be more six months from now. Wagon wheels are rumbling all through the west and they're something men like you can't stop."

"At least," said Plimpton, and there was a deadly tone in his voice, "I can stop rustling of my own herd and I don't have to listen to any mealy-mouthed tenderfoot who doesn't like the way I run things."

Carter rose slowly from his chair. "I hoped you'd take this differently," he said.

"Get out," snarled Plimpton.

"And the killings keep on?" asked Carter.

"I said get out!"

"Because," said Carter, "you want to remember what I told you, about how a doctor's job is to find the root of trouble—"

With a roar, Plimpton heaved from the chair. Carter saw his fist coming, a bone-crushing blow that started from the knee and whistled toward his head.

Carter took one quick step backward, tilted his head, felt the blow go past with killing power.

Another step backward and another and there was Plimpton in front of him, caught off balance by the violence of the punch that missed. The man's head was twisted at an angle and his body was leaning forward, following through the blow that never landed.

If he had stopped to think, Carter might not have done what he did. In a sober moment, he knew later that he never would. But there was no time to think . . . and there was that outthrust chin, the turned head.

Carter pivoted on his right toe to bring his whole body into play and his fist smacked with brutal precision on the jaw just back on the chin. A scientific blow, placed with what amounted to detached interest rather than anger.

For a single second dull wonder shone in Plimpton's eyes, even as his huge body was crashing backward . . . backward to catch the chair and carry it with him into the corner.

The chair splintered under the weight of the falling man and Plimpton came to rest against its wreckage, half propped against the wall, sprawled like a dirty rag someone had thrown away.

Carter rubbed the knuckles of his right hand, wondering at the smart that was in them.

He stared at Plimpton and was surprised that he felt no regret.

The man stirred and moaned, tried to sit up, groaned and fell back again.

From where he stood, Carter made swift diagnosis. Not badly hurt. Knocked out. He'd have a sore jaw for a day or two.

Deliberately he turned, strode across the living room to the front door, let himself out. In the rear of the house he heard scurrying feet and someone calling.

The fat dog, tail still waving happily, escorted him sedately to the gate and stood watching as he rode away.

Chapter Three
"Land Ain't Worth Dyin' For!"

By the time he reached Basin City, Carter's right hand was noticeably swollen and he knew he'd have to do something about it. Ice pack to reduce the swelling, he told himself, and then remembered there was no place one could get ice in all of Basin City.

He was hungry and worn out, tired from the night long vigil, a bit shaken by his experience with Plimpton. He needed a shave and a change of clothes and he decided that would come before breakfast.

He rode past the town's lone restaurant, hailed the Chinese who professed to run it.

"Plate of ham and eggs in about half an hour, Charlie," he said.

The Chinese ducked his head in a quick bow that denoted he understood, smiled broadly. "Can do," he decided.

Carter left the horse at the livery barn, walked through the almost deserted street to his combined office-living quarters above the bank.

In the four years that he had been there, he decided, Basin City had changed but little. Clearly he remembered that day four years ago when he had ridden in with Chet Saunders, the stage driver and livery man, from Antelope Springs, the nearest rail town, forty miles to the south.

He smiled grimly at the memory. Fresh from Ohio, with its ordered farms and neat towns, he had been appalled at Basin City. He was not certain he still was not a bit appalled by it. But, he had told himself, it was a place to get a start, a new town that would grow, a town that had no doctor. A place where a young man, provided he tended strictly to business and got around a bit so the people knew him, might establish a solid practice.

With the memory of Ohio still in him, he shivered a bit as he looked at the weathered false fronts, the few languid ponies lounging three legged at the hitching rails. Inside the Gilded Lily saloon someone laughed and from down the street came the thumping of hammer on anvil as the blacksmith got in some early morning work.

He climbed the stairs to the office wearily. A shave, fresh clothes, and then that plate of ham and eggs. After that he'd try to get in an hour or two of sleep.

As he opened the door, a man rose from a chair and faced him. "Good mornin', doc," he said.

Carter felt surprised. It wasn't often that he had a patient so early in the morning.

The man, he saw, was Matt Denby, one of the nesters to the north of the Tumbling K.

"In early, aren't you, Matt?" asked Carter.

Matt agreed with him. "Middlin' early. Got up at the crack of dawn. Had some business in town."

"Been out all night myself," said Carter. "Just got in. Hope you didn't have to wait too long."

"Just an hour or so," said Matt. "Dozed off for a spell, sittin' in the chair. Woke up just a while ago."

"What can I do for you?" asked Carter. "Hope the wife's all right."

"She's fine," said Matt. "Ain't nothin' wrong with none of us. Just come in to see what I owed you."

"I'll have to look it up," said Carter.

He pulled open a desk drawer, brought out a dog-eared ledger, flipped the pages.

"Makes out to twenty dollars, Matt."

"Ain't got that much," said Matt.

"Why, that's all right. You can pay me any time."

Matt pulled out his pocketbook, fumbled at it with awkward fingers.

"Pay you somethin' on account right now," he said. "You see, we're pullin' out."

"Pulling out? Leaving the country, you mean?"

"Yep, that's it. But you don't need to worry, doc. I'll pay you five dollars now and send the rest to you by mail. Can't nohow pass up what I owe you, doc. You saved Jenny, and that's worth more than I ever can pay you."

He laid three ones and a two down on the desk, restored the pocketbook to his hip pocket.

"I'll write you a receipt," said Carter.

As he wrote he asked: "Where you going, Matt? Got a better thing somewhere?"

Matt shuffled awkwardly. "Not exactly a better thing. Just pullin' stakes, that's all. Itchy foot, I guess. Going farther west."

"Any place in particular?"

"Nope. Just west. Lots of land still to be had."

Carter stopped writing, laid down the pencil.

"You mean you're running out," he said. "You're clearing out because you're scared of Plimpton."

Matt wriggled. "Not exactly scared, doc. But I don't like it, nohow. Didn't mind it so much, the hellin' around the regular hands used to do. Could seem to put up with that. But since Plimpton's took to runnin' in them gun slingers of his'n I can't somehow feel comfortable."

Carter picked up the pencil again, started to write.

"Jake McCord died this morning," he said. "Somebody gunned him down."

"I told you," said Matt. "It ain't the same as it used to be. Not just a little private feudin'. Plimpton's plumb declared war on us fellers. Got a gang of gunslicks in to run us out."

"I hate to see you go, Matt," said Carter. "You fellows start pulling out and Plimpton wins. Just prolongs the situation. If he does it to one of you, he'll figure he can do it to all of you."

"You mean you figure we ought to stand up to him?" asked Denby. "Oil up our own irons and go after him."

Carter shook his head. "I wouldn't know," he said. "It's something I can't advise you on. I'm not a fighting man myself. I'm new here. I don't actually know what I'd do. All I know is I hate to see you leave."

"Plimpton's got everythin' fixed," said Denby bitterly. "That big valley of his'n. You've seen it."

"Sure I have."

"That ain't Plimpton's, legal-like," said Matt. "He grabbed holt of it, years back, under that Swamp Land act. You know. All you got to do is swear the land is under water and you can file on as big a hunk as you have a mind to."

"That law was repealed," Carter told him. "Too many valleys were turning up as swamp."

"Sure," agreed Matt. "Sure, it was repealed. But that don't mean that Plimpton gave up the valley. He got it fixed so he could hang onto it."

"I don't understand," protested Carter. "How could he do a thing like that?"

"In cahoots with the land office register," said Matt. "Paid him something, more than likely. Maybe still payin' him for all I know. Tried to file on a quarter section at the upper end of the valley when I come here but Grant said it wasn't open to entry. Said all was left was the foothill claims."

Carter tapped the pencil on the desk top. "I see," he said. "I see."

"Stands to reason must be lots of valley land out farther west," Matt told him. "Land a man can file on. Land that you can drive a plow in."

Carter rose from the desk, shaking himself mentally, held out the receipt.

Matt took it. "You say they got Jake?"

Carter nodded, not speaking.

"Ain't worth it," Matt declared. "Not even land. Ain't worth dyin' for."

He folded the receipt carefully and tucked it in his shirt pocket, clumped out of the door.

Chapter Four
Right Between the Eyes

One man had died and another man was quitting. All in one day's time. But they were not the first, nor would they be the last.

Carter found that he had trouble holding his fork. His knuckles were sore and the hand was swollen more than ever now, although he knew that in a few hours time it might start to go down and probably by tomorrow would be as good as new.

He speared a cut of ham and smeared it in some egg yolk, chewed the mouthful hungrily. He tried to feel a bit contrite about hitting Plimpton so hard, but he couldn't. It was a thing, perhaps, he had wanted to do for many months.

He stared about the restaurant. Small and clean and almost cheerful. As cheerful, anyhow, as a room ever got to be in Basin City. The sunlight spewed through the window, engulfed the yellow cat that lay on the window ledge.

Carter, he told himself, you're a fool to get so stirred up about this. It's no concern of yours. No concern of yours how many men get shot or how many up and leave. No skin off your nose that Plimpton stole the valley years ago and either bribed or blackmailed a dishonest land office man into allowing him to keep it. None of your business that men who come to make their homes are hounded by men who ride with skittish trigger fingers.

But, perhaps, he said, contradicting himself, it may be your business after all. For a doctor looks after his people. Almost like a minister looks after his people. Watches over them and guards them against sickness and against death. A friend ready to come at the moment of their call. A friend who pretends he doesn't need the fee if they are hard pushed.

He grimaced at his thoughts, reached for a slice of bread to sop up the plate.

In his absorption he did not hear the door click open and shut again and it was not until a shadow fell across the table, cutting out the sun that streamed in from the window, that he became aware someone stood before him.

He glanced up and saw the lanky, wiry form. For a moment he did not know the rawhide face and then he remembered the eyes. Stony eyes that glittered even when the man's back was against the sun. A pair of eyes that one could not forget. Plimpton's foreman.

"Hello, Mapes," he said. "Sit down."

"I didn't come in to sit down," said Mapes and his voice was flat and toneless.

"Plimpton send you?" asked Carter.

Ernie Mapes hooked his thumbs in the armpits of his vest, spat on the floor without moving his head.

"No one sent me," he announced. "I came on my own hook."

Carter dropped his eyes back to the plate, carefully mopped up the last bit of egg, reached out for the coffee cup.

"Start talking," said Mapes and the voice still was toneless and just a pitch above a whisper.

Carter let go of the coffee cup, looked up at the man again.

"I haven't anything to talk about with you."

"You better have," said Mapes.

"You mean about the ruckus this morning?"

Mapes nodded, his eyes still flinty bright.

"I haven't got a thing to say about it," Carter said. "If Plimpton wants to talk about it, tell him to come himself and not send a hired hand."

Mapes put his hands on the table top and leaned down so that his eyes were almost on a level with Carter's. "I'm tryin' real hard to be patient with you," he declared. "If you wasn't a sawbones I'd gun you where you sit."

"Look here, Mapes," said Carter, "it's all quite simple if you consider it. Plimpton swung at me and missed. I swung at him and didn't miss. That's the story. What could be simpler than that?"

"Doc," declared Mapes, "you're sticking your snoot in where it don't belong. You're getting too damn curious. We sort of like you out at the ranch and we'd hate to have anything happen to you, sudden-like, let's say."

"Like a bullet, perhaps?"

"Right between the eyes," said Mapes.

Carter shrugged. "That's all you have to say?"

He eyed Mapes and Mapes didn't speak, just stared back with those stony eyes.

"Because if it is," said Carter, "I have business to attend to. I'm going down to the land office and ask Grant about filing on a quarter section right smack in the center of Plimpton's valley land."

Mapes started, but the steady eyes held. "You're loco," he finally said. "You can't file on that land."

"That's what I'm going to find out," Carter declared. "Whether I can file on it or not. Grant may be able to bluff these poor kicked-around nesters who come in here, but he can't bluff me. If the land's open for entry, I'm finding out about it."

Mapes hunched forward, pushed his face closer. "If I were you, doc, I wouldn't do that. You might find out too much."

"I see," said Carter, soberly. "Then the land really doesn't belong to Plimpton."

Mapes' right hand left the table, deliberately reached back to his belt. Carter's hand shot out, grasped the coffee cup, hurled the steaming contents into Mapes' face.

With almost the same motion he was on his feet, grasping the chair back, lifting it from the floor. Mapes was staggering backwards, gun dangling from one hand, other hand clawing at his face.

With effortless ease, Carter swung the chair, brought it down with vicious force. Too late, Mapes tried to duck.

The chair smashed against his head. Rungs, sprung out of place, sprayed on the floor. Mapes went down as if he had been axed. The gun spun from his hand and clattered on the floor.

Carter dropped the few sticks of chair that still remained, bent over to pick up the fallen gun.

Charlie stood in the door that led into the kitchen, yellow face squeezed with dismay.

"How much do I owe you, Charlie?" asked Carter.

Charlie took in the situation. "Ham and eggs, six bits. Chair, five dollar."

"Little high on the chair, aren't you?" asked Carter.

"Good chair," said Charlie. "Lots of fun."

Carter paid, swung back to the room. Mapes was stirring, sitting up, groaning.

"I'll kill you for this, doc," he declared and it was a calm statement, almost as if he were talking about the weather.

Carter flipped the gun. "I'll leave this at the Gilded Lily," he said. "You can pick it up."

Chapter Five
Night Call—To Death!

The first thunderstorm of spring was threatening. Through the window beside his bed, Carter could see the play of lightning across the western horizon, heard the dull mutter of thunder rumble across the land.

Carter drew the blanket up around his shoulder, shut his eyes. Sleep rolled in a black wave to engulf him and he thought, foggily, that it was funny he had awakened. Never had a storm shook him out of sleep before.

Then he was sitting up, tensed and listening. Listening for the tiny sound that had crept into his brain between the rolls of distant thunder.

It came again, a muffled rapping.

Carter swung his feet out on the floor, cautiously stood erect, eyes trying to pierce the darkness of the room. The window glowed momentarily with a distant lightning streak and for a second the room flickered and he could see that there was nothing there. Nothing that would have made a noise.

The rapping came once more and for the first time, Carter recognized it for what it was. Someone was knocking at the door.

Reaching for his dressing robe, he grimaced in the dark, berating himself for his jumpiness. A doctor should get used to being routed out of bed at all hours, he told himself.

"I'm coming," he shouted.

He found the lamp and fumbling in the dark, located the tumbler of matches that stood beside it. Lighted, he carried it into the office, swung open the door.

A stranger blinked at the light.

"You the doctor?"

Carter nodded. "What can I do for you?"

"My partner's awful sick," the man told him. "I'm plumb scared he won't make it."

"Where is your partner?"

"Up on Snow mountain."

"That's a long ways."

"Sure is. But you're the nearest doctor. We trap in the winter and do some prospectin' when we can't trap."

"What's the matter with your partner?"

"It must have been them peaches, doc."

Carter nodded grimly. "Stood around in the can for a day or two."

The man agreed with him. "That's right. Opened a can and figured we'd eaten 'em all. Then Ted found there was one left in the can and guzzled it. Made me madder'n hell. I wanted that peach, my own self."

The trapper-prospector, Carter saw, was a small man, scarcely more than a kid. He had freckles on his nose and untrimmed blond hair stuck out under his battered broad-brimmed hat. His shirt was torn and his jeans muddy. His hands were none too clean. The cartridge belt around his middle was a plain strip of leather with cartridge loops—no fancy trimmings. The six-gun matched it. Plain handle.

"We got to hurry, Doc," he said.

"I guess we do," Carter agreed. "You go to the livery barn and get my horse. You know where it is?"

The man nodded. "Been in town once or twice," he said.

Back in his living quarters, Carter dressed hurriedly, took the heavy riding cloak off the nail. He was waiting at the foot of the stairs, bag in hand, when the man came down the street, leading his horse.

The night was pitch dark, except for the lightning flashes and the air was muggy. One could almost smell the brewing storm.

The town was silent and the hoof-beats of their horses echoed hollowly as they trotted down the street. A dog ran out, snarling at them, and then went back toward the darkness of the buildings. A windmill clattered in the rising wind.

"What is your name?" Carter asked.

"Becker," the other told him, and added: "We better get these ponies movin'."

Following the trail that skirted Plimpton's valley, Carter strained his eyes toward the spot where the buildings stood. But there was no light. From somewhere far at the upper end of the valley a cow bellowed, a shuddery sound in the blackness.

A few drops of rain spattered out of the west, huge, cold drops, and the wind whistled through the trail-side grass.

After the first few drops, the rain held off. The lightning marched higher in the sky—no longer mere snakes that streaked and flickered along the horizon, but livid bolts of blue that quivered and hung shivering in the air above one's head.

The horses kept at a dogged lope and Carter, still drugged with sleep, caught himself again and again on the verge of drowsing.

They took the trail that led past the McCord place and as they were passing the house a blazing streak of lightning hissed across the sky, lighting the nester's place with a brilliance that was in startling contrast to the blackness that had gripped it before.

In the vivid, eye-punishing glare that held the cluster of buildings for a moment, Carter saw the place in clear detail, the rickety barn, the lopsided haystack, the horse that stood hunched against it. And as the windows of the house shimmered for a moment, Carter thought he saw a movement behind one of them, as if someone might have been standing there, looking out at them.

Then the flare of lightning was gone and darkness came again, closing down black and tight even before the incredible blue of the flash had vanished from one's brain.

Darkness and a growing growl of thunder that came nearer and nearer, like a train rushing across the sky, until it split the air wide open with a tearing sound that made the horses shy off and fight the bit in terror.

The trail led up and up until they crossed a spur where the wind tore at them in fury, a wind filled with sharp warning, a wind that seemed to be a live thing. And yet the rain held off.

Carter spurred his horse abreast of Becker's, shouted at him through the wind. "How much farther?"

"Just a ways," the man howled back.

But it was more than just a ways. It was another half hour at least, Carter figured, before they swung around an abrupt cliff and into a canyon mouth where a campfire glowed.

Alarm bells rang inside Carter's head and he stiffened in his saddle, gathering the reins tightly in his fist. But before he could do anything the horse had taken the half dozen paces that brought him inside the ring of light. A dozen men sat around the fire and one stood beside it, not more than three paces from where Carter checked his horse.

A tall man, with a gun in hand and his hat tilted back so the firelight flickered across his face.

A man whose face was thin and hard, with eyes that glittered in the light.

"Glad to see you, doc," said Ernie Mapes.

Chapter Six
Back to the Wall

Time hesitated for a second, as if staggering from one watch tick to the next—a hesitation that held the breathless lull of the coming storm, the cold anger that knifed through Carter's brain.

Rain slashed down, an almost solid sheet of rain, as if someone, angered with the waiting, hurled it with wrathful violence out of the blackness that crouched all round the campfire.

Carter's horse reared at the impact of the storm, front feet clawing the air almost in front of Mapes' face. The campfire and the men around it dissolved and dimmed in a flare of violet brilliance as a bolt of lightning ripped across the night.

Red fire washed from the mouth of Mapes' gun and then Carter's horse was wheeling, rushing back along the trail, terrified by the sudden blasts of water tumbling from the sky, by the blinding flash that had filled the world.

Carter crouched low, blinded, groping. Beneath him the horse lurched, fought frantically to keep its feet. Carter felt himself rising in the air, made a desperate grab at the saddlehorn, felt the slick, wet leather slide through his clutching fingers.

Then the horse was not beneath him. He was floating in a sea of blackness. There was no sensation of being thrown or falling, no idea of disaster.

His body thudded against a tree, scraped against a sheer rock wall, thumped with a bone-cracking crunch upon the ground.

The breath gushed out of his lungs with a belching gurgle and it seemed that some great hand had spread itself above him, was slowly and inexorably pressing him into the soaking earth. His stomach came up and hit him in the face, and all the energy had been wrung from his body and left him a wilted thing.

For long minutes Carter lay there, huddled against the earth, with the rain beating in his face and rivulets pouring around him. Strength came back by bits. A feeble strength at first that let him claw at the ground with shaking fingers. Then strength enough to slowly raise himself until he sat upright. Finally strength enough to get on his knees and crawl, to clutch at the tree he found in the darkness and hand himself erect.

He leaned against the tree, one arm around its shaggy trunk, clinging to it while his stomach churned and he gasped for breath and little red pains chased in an endless dance through his aching head.

The storm roared down, the storm that had held back, that had seemed so reluctant to burst, but now was making up lost time. The tree moaned and behind it the cliff wall whined as the wind struck and slid along it.

Somewhere, as if from far off, came a shout and then another sound, a sound that was not of the storm, a sound that swept upon him. A purposeful sound with cadence to it—the splashing beat of horses' hoofs sweeping up the trail.

Carter hauled himself unsteadily around the tree until he stood between it and the rock wall.

Thunder talked along the cliff top and lightning flickered, lighting the dripping night with unsubstantial ghostly flares.

The horsemen came around a bend in the trail—four of them, hunched against the rain.

Carter flattened himself against the tree, tried to still his breathing, hoped fiercely that the lightning would not betray him.

The four went past, the horses trotting.

They're after me, Carter told himself. They're hunting me down, just like a man would hunt down a mad dog or beef-hungry bear. And when they get me they'll ask no questions, say no words. They'll shoot to kill and when the light comes there'll be eating for the buzzards.

He gripped the tree hard with both his hands and tried to calm his mind, tried to reason with himself, to fight down the blind, hunted panic that rose within him.

No horse, no gun. Not even a hat. He'd lost his hat when he'd been thrown from the horse. Only a vague idea where he was.

From his refuge behind the tree, he stared out unseeing into the storm, the rain awash against his face, the lightning almost a steady flicker against his eyes.

He had to get a gun. He had to fight. He. . . .

His wet shoes squished with every step he took and he slid and fell a dozen times when he tripped against stones and fallen branches. One of the branches he picked up and carried with him. It was heavy, but about the right length, easy to grip, easy to handle. It was a club.

When he saw the flicker of the campfire through the darkness he left the trail and went cautiously.

The fire was low and sputtering, but built against the bare rock wall, still successfully defying the rain. Huddled against the rock, blankets pulled around them, squatted three men.

From the brush where he crouched Carter tried to make out their faces. One was huge-boned, but the other two were smaller.

One of the smaller ones, he felt sure, was Becker, the one who had led him here.

He clutched his club and measured the distance that lay between himself and the blanket wrapped figures. He shuffled forward slowly, silently, parting the bushes with his free hand.

The rain was slacking off, but the lightning still weaved across the sky. Soon the four who had ridden up the trail would be coming back.

And when they came back. . . .

Carter rose carefully, tensed himself.

Without a word, he charged, was upon the three almost before they realized anyone was near.

One of them half arose and Carter swung his club, swung it with madness singing in his blood, with a bellow in his throat. The man went down like a stricken ox.

The other two were on their feet, shucking off the blankets, going for their guns. Carter rushed in, his club a streak that whistled in the air. The big man tried to duck, lifting his arm to ward off the blow. The club crashed down across the arm and the man screamed in sudden pain, staggered forward, falling on his knees.

Across his kneeling form, Carter stared into the eyes of the third man, and knew that he had failed. Knew the third man knew it too, for there was a twisted grin upon his lips and his eyes were steely bright, narrowed, already squinting for the shot.

With a wild yell, Carter heaved the club. The third man ducked and it whistled above his head, but even as he did, Carter was rushing for him, reached him in a leap that crashed into the man, drove him back against the rocky wall, slamming his body against it hard.

Off balance, Carter skidded on the slippery ground, fought desperately to keep his footing, felt himself going down and even as he fell, tensed himself against the bullet that he knew would come.

A gun barked and a bullet ricocheted off the cliff, screaming out into the rainy night.

Carter landed on the ground and rolled, tried to keep on rolling. Maybe, his numbed brain said . . . maybe, if he kept on rolling the bullets would not find him.

The gun crashed again and then another gun, a different gun—a gun that coughed as if it might be trying to attract someone's attention.

A voice said: "Get them up, boys. Drop the guns and reach for sky."

A voice that was clear and sharp . . . and yet funny, somehow.

Carter leaped to his feet, stared at the scene before him.

The first man he had hit was still sprawled upon the ground, half covered by the blanket, one arm doubled under him, the other reaching out ahead of him, fingers clenched, as if he might have been trying to pull himself along.

The second man still was on his knees. One arm dangled, but the other was above his head, very far above his head. A gun, smoke still trickling from its barrel, lay just in front of him. The third man was standing, back against the wall, but with both hands high.

"Doctor," said Mary McCord, "you better get their guns."

Carter stared at the girl who stood just inside the ring of firelight, a girl with skirts pinned up and packing a rifle that seemed twice too big for her.

"Go ahead," she urged. "Take away their guns."

He tried to speak, stammering, but she jerked her head at the men before her.

"We have to get away from here," she told him.

Swiftly, Carter moved forward, toward the man who stood against the wall. It was Becker.

"I'd ought to bust you one," said Carter. Quickly he stripped the gun belt off the youth, stepped back and picked up the gun that lay in front of the kneeling man.

From up the trail came the splashing clop of hoofs.

Carter took a step toward the man who lay sprawled upon the ground, then wheeled back. There wasn't time. There wasn't time to get that other gun.

"Run!" he shouted at Mary, and in a leap was by her side.

Wet branches slapped at them in the darkness and stones and broken branches lay underfoot to trip them.

In the darkness, Carter found the girl's hand, gripped it in his own.

"This way," she shouted at him. "I know a trail."

They had rounded the outjutting of rock that had formed the cliff, were plunging up a slope.

From behind them came angry shouts. The horsemen had reached the camp.

The slope rose until they practically crawled on hands and knees, groping in the darkness for saplings, trees, anything to help them up the path.

Lightning still flickered occasionally, lighting the way.

"We can't stay on the path," Carter wheezed.

In answer, the girl jerked at his hand, almost angrily.

"They'll find us," he gasped, protesting.

She did not answer and they climbed on, breath jerky with exertion, bodies aching.

From below came a shot. Then another shot and this time, Carter heard the bullet chug soggily into the hill above them.

With a yell, he swung around, saw the men in the path below as lightning raced across the sky. He lifted the gun he'd taken from the man who had been on his knees, surprised to realize for the first time that he had carried it all the time. Somehow or other he'd gotten the other gun belt strapped around his waist.

Red mouths twinkled from below and bullets hissed in the underbrush.

Then the gun in Carter's hand was jumping, jumping as he pulled the trigger. The sound of the shots were a dull hammer in his ears and the licking fire that belched from the muzzle painted his face with an angry glow.

The shots ran out, the hammer clicking on empty cases. Carter spun about and ran up the path, bumped into the girl.

She grasped his hand again. "Quick," she urged.

A hundred yards farther up the slope, she left the path and Carter followed. The brush thinned out and they climbed an almost bare, rock strewn slope, came to a thicket of scrub cedar.

Mary McCord sat down, leaned her back against a boulder, cradled the rifle across her lap.

"I wanted to get to my horse," she said, "but there wasn't a chance to make it."

She put both hands to her face and tried to push back her rain-soaked hair.

"This is the next best place," she said.

Chapter Seven
Wait Till The Day

The rain had stopped and the clouds were broken, scudding before the wind, thinning occasionally to allow a watery moon to shine, flooding the ground with a ghostly pallor.

Carter, sprawled on the soaking ground behind a low growing cedar, gun clutched in his fist, stared out over the land. They were at the top of an old rock slide backed against a towering cliff. On all sides the rocky rubble swept down to the shadowy valley. The slopes were dotted with boulders and with here and there a low-growing shrub, but nothing that afforded too much cover. Only here, at the top, in a small area, was there anything approaching adequate cover. Here the stunted cedars, wedging footholds among the scattered boulders, had found a secure place to root, to fight out their destiny against the everlasting wind.

Staring at the slopes below them, he realized that, given enough light, even two guns could hold their position against no matter how desperate a charge. He and the girl, he knew, never would have been able to make it except for the darkness.

"You must know this country pretty well," he said to Mary McCord.

The cedar rustled as she turned her head toward him. "I do," she said, and that was all. No other explanation. Perhaps, Carter reflected, she had ridden this way often. Life for a girl in a nester's cabin, he told himself, must become monotonous at times.

The night was quiet. There was no sign of motion, no rustling to betray the presence of anyone creeping up toward the rock slide. No shouts, no hoof beats.

Carter stared out over the valley, squinting his eyes to make out the dark mass that seemed to swim in the valley's shadows. But he could make out no shape, could hear no sound. Something was down there, he was sure and yet. . . .

"What I can't understand," he said, "is how you found me or why you came."

"I saw you riding by," Mary told him. "I had just gotten up to look at Clyde's face and Clyde wanted to look out the window and see the lightning. You know, the way a kid will do. The funny notions they will get."

"Yes, I know," said Carter. "How is Clyde's face?"

She didn't answer the question, but went on: "When we looked out the window a big flash came and we saw you riding past. Clyde yelled at me, told me the man who was with you was the one who hit him with the whip."

Carter sucked in a deep breath, held it. "You shouldn't have done it, Mary. I don't see—"

Her voice was flat and dead. "We buried Dad just before sunset, doctor. I helped Walker build the coffin. I sawed the boards for it and he nailed them together. We padded it with some old blankets so it wouldn't seem so bare. Some men came and dug the grave. Matt Denby, you told him about it. He brought some others with him. But it might have been we'd had to dig the grave, too."

Carter shivered, shivered in the cold of the night and the utter coldness that lay in the girl's flat words.

She wasn't crying. She talked about her father and there wasn't a sob in her voice. And he remembered how she hadn't cried when he had died, although her eyes had shone with tears. How she had held her chin so high and talked about not being driven out. It was something her father had said, he remembered. "There ain't guns enough in all the west to make us pull up stakes."

And what she had just said now probably wasn't really an explanation. Not, leastways, explaining like a person would sit down and tell why they did a thing. But there was an explanation in it.

"I had to come," said Mary. "I heard that you went to Plimpton's and what happened there. And when I saw you riding with one of Plimpton's men—"

Something whistled through the cedars, smashed against the wall of rock beyond and yowled away. From below came the flat cough of a rifle.

Carter huddled tight against the ground, forgetful now that it was cold and wet.

Another whiplike thing smashed through the boughs above his head, struck the cliff and screamed. Again the rifle coughed.

"Doctor!" said Mary.

"Yes?"

"Can you shoot a rifle?"

"Some," Carter told her. "I used to practice with one back in Ohio. Shot a lot of squirrels and rabbits and did some target shooting."

He heard her crawling toward him, wriggling through the low hanging branches.

She thrust the rifle at him.

"Here, you take it. I'm not too good a shot and we can't waste cartridges. We haven't many of them."

He reached out and took the gun.

"We never had much money to buy cartridges," she told him. "They are so expensive."

Wordlessly, he took the rifle, handed her the six-gun.

"Get behind one of those boulders," he told her. "Maybe they'll quit. Maybe they don't know we're up here. Just taking a chance we are and trying to smoke us out."

In the dim light, he saw her shake her head. "They found our tracks where we left the trail. Ain't no doubt about it. They know where we are. There wasn't anywhere else that we could have gone."

A bullet chugged into the ground just ahead of Carter, threw mud and gravel in his face. Another ripped across a boulder beside the cedar tree, throwing rock splinters in the moonlight.

Crawling inch by inch, Carter hunched himself forward, burrowing under the cedar boughs until he could see over the lip of the slide. Slowly, he thrust the rifle forward, eyes busy on the slope below.

A shadowy figure sprang from a thicket near the base and ran up the slope, flopped behind a boulder. From another clump of bushes at the base flame suddenly licked forth and the cedar rustled eerily. A severed twig fell on Carter's hand.

Fire, many points of it, flickered along the base of the slide and the cedars thrashed as if in a high gale while behind him the bullets screamed and shrieked as they slid off the rock face and tumbled into space.

The man behind the boulder was up again and running up the slope.

Carter brought the rifle up smoothly, saw the glint of moonlight shine along its barrel, cuddled his cheek against the stock and started to squeeze the trigger.

Easy, his mind told him. Easy does it. Hold it steady and squeeze, don't jerk. Take your time and make sure. That was the way he'd done it in those bright afternoons shooting at a target with his brother back in Ohio. That was the way to do it here, with the target a living man rushing up the slope.

Then suddenly he was jerking the rifle away, jerking it off the target even as it roared in his ears, even as fire gushed from out the muzzle.

The man on the slope ducked for cover, disappearing in a swift dive behind another boulder flanked by a scrawny bush.

For long seconds, Carter lay sick. Revulsion rose in his throat and his stomach bucked. He'd been about to kill a man. He'd had a bead upon a fellow human being and had been squeezing the trigger.

It's your job to save life, not to take it, said a voice in his brain. Your job to cure, not to destroy.

A bullet sang above his head, mushed into the growth behind him. Another chugged into the drop of ground beneath him. Something struck and jarred him, shook him as if a giant hand had struck a crushing blow.

His left shoulder suddenly grew numb and cautiously he moved his arm to see if there were any broken bones. Apparently there weren't. A flesh wound, he told himself, as coolly, as somberly as if he were diagnosing someone else. A bullet through the fleshy part of his upper arm.

He crouched lower against the ground as a storm of bullets raked the branches above his head. That shot he'd fired, he knew, had given the gunmen his position. And now they were raking the place in an attempt to get him. To get him and Mary McCord. To wipe out the two lives that huddled here on top of the rock slide.

A red spot of anger came to life within his brain, grew and spread until it frightened him. He felt a tenseness come upon him, knew that his left hand had an iron clutch on the rifle grip, was surprised when a tiny drip of perspiration tricked down his cheek.

The man who had huddled behind the boulder had jumped up again, was coming up the slope, leaping like a goat, rifle flung above his head.

Swiftly, Carter bent his head against the stock and once again his brain told him: "Easy . . . steady!"

The rifle bucked against his shoulder and the man was tumbling backward, as if a mighty hand had slapped him down the slope. Tumbling backward, turning a somersault, rolling over on his shoulders, flopping spread-eagled on the ground and sliding . . . slowly sliding.

Methodically, Carter worked the lever action, heard the satisfying click as the spent cartridge was ejected and a fresh one slid into place.

Silence smote his ears . . . an eerie silence. There were no guns, no whiplash song of bullets, no scream of lead whistling off the rock behind him.

"Mary," he called softly and in the low growing branches he heard a rustle.

"You all right?" he asked.

"Yes," she told him, but her voice was a little shaky, "and you? They didn't hit you?"

"No," he lied. No use of letting her know about the shoulder. No use in scaring her.

She crawled until she lay close beside him. Turning his head, he could see the white shine of moonlight upon her frozen face.

Her lips moved. "Maybe it wasn't so smart to come here. We're trapped. We can't get out. By morning they'll have guns up above us and light to shoot by. . . ."

A gun crashed below, but the shot was wide, missing the cedars entirely.

"I got one of them," he told her, almost bragging.

"I'm going to stay up here by you," she declared. "Maybe I can't hit anything, but I can make them duck. There's plenty of cartridges for the six-gun."

He did not answer. There would be, he told himself, no use in arguing. A bullet could find her almost as easily back there under the cedar branches as up here on the rim.

"It's cold," she said. "I wish we could have a fire."

It was cold, Carter agreed. Cold and wet and miserable. A rock was drilling itself into his hip and he shifted his body, trying to find a more comfortable position.

He stared down at the valley toward the dark mass that was milling there. From it came strange clicks and scrapings.

"There's something down there," he said.

The girl crawled closer until she could look over the rim.

"It's cattle!" she told him. "Don't you hear their hoofs? That clicking noise. They're milling around."

Cattle! That explained a lot of things. Helped explain the situation.

"What is it, doctor?" she asked.

"Don't you see," he told her. "It's a herd they've been gathering for the trail—a rustled herd. Plimpton told me he had lost over a thousand head of cattle and he blamed the nesters for it. Only—only—"

Mary finished the thought for him. "Only it's his own men who have been stealing from him. The gunmen he brought in to run us nesters out."

Carter nodded. "And Mapes is in on it. Mapes was Plimpton's foreman before the gunmen came. Maybe he was the one who hatched the whole thing. He talked Plimpton into it."

Carter wrested his gaze off the valley, examined the slope before him.

The rifles had fallen silent, had remained silent for a long time now. And that wasn't good. It meant something else was up. The Tumbling K gang had failed in their first attempt to get them with fire from the base of the slope, had lost one man. Now they would try something else.

Off to the left he heard a rustle, stared intently. But it was hard to see. The moonlight mottled the land with a tricky glow that made it impossible to distinguish any object. For a fleeting instant he thought he saw a moving figure, climbing up the slope to the left just beyond the slide.

By morning, Mary had said, they'll be above us. And that, Carter felt sure, was what was happening now. Getting above them, waiting for daylight. Able to shoot down onto the top of the slide, it would be like picking off a pair of rabbits.

A gun cracked, a vicious snarl . . . and snarled again. Off to the left a man screamed . . . a high pitched scream of pain. Rifles barked and six-guns hammered. Again the gun with the snarl talked back.

Mary grasped Carter's arm. "That's Walker!" she whispered harshly. "That's Walker. I'd know that gun anywhere. It was my father's and we used to joke about the way it sounded . . . the wicked way it sounded. . . ."

Rifles coughed sullenly and there was a long silence. The girl's grip tightened on Carter's arm until it was almost painful.

Then the gun that snarled ripped through the night again . . . farther away this time . . . and once again a man screamed, a scream that was chopped off as if death had stepped in and choked him.

Chapter Eight
Hostage—or Ally?

The moon was far down the west. Soon the east would be lighting with the coming dawn. The pre-dawn hush already had settled over the land and birds were stirring, twittering sleepily, restless for the day.

Carter stared up at the blackness of the spur that hung above the rock slide. Just a hump of darkness, like the spine of some prehistoric beast . . . black and dead and quiet.

But there were rifles there, he was almost sure of that. Rifles that would spit death with the coming of the light.

Sprawled under the cedar boughs, he gripped his rifle tighter. Beside him the girl moved slightly.

"It's been an awful long time," she said. "Wonder if Walker. . . ."

"Walker is all right," Carter assured her. "He must have been all right when we heard that last shot of his. And his was the last shot. There wasn't any shooting after that."

It wasn't quite so simple, he told himself. Walker, for all they knew, might have fired that last shot after being hit himself. He might be up there on the trail that led up the spur, sprawled on the wet earth, gun still clutched in his hand.

Dully, Carter turned his thoughts over once more, searching for that one thing which could get them out of there . . . some little thing he might have overlooked before, some factor he had not considered.

But there wasn't any factor. There simply was no chance. They were trapped, here on top of the rock slide. The only way they could get away was down the slide, racing in plain sight for the rifles to mow down. There were rifles above, and no doubt, others still lurking down below. Guns that were waiting. . . .

It was impossible, he told himself. It was a wild dream that he would awaken from. Such things simply couldn't happen—not to a man like him. To the nesters, perhaps, or to the gunslicks Plimpton had imported, but not to a doctor whose only mission in life was to cure and not to kill.

And still the hard fact remained. The situation did exist. This was war . . . a little war, perhaps, but war just the same. Ruthless war that would have no pity. A question of killing or be killed. For the men who lurked on the spur above, who waited in the thickets at the base of the slide, couldn't let them go, couldn't let him and Mary McCord ever leave their hiding place. For between the two of them, they knew too much. They knew about the cattle milling in the valley. Mary knew about the man who had slashed Clyde's face with a whip. He had seen and recognized the men who had tried to kill him.

And, perhaps over and above it all, was the way he had treated Mapes back in the restaurant. Mapes had lost face back there. A man doesn't let an unarmed man take a gun away from him and leave it at a public bar for him to pick up later. At least, not a man like Mapes.

That, he knew, was the reason he had been picked up in the first place. That had been why Mapes had sent Becker in to get him. Mapes, he knew had intended to gun him down. Only the sudden breaking of the storm, the flash of lightning, the terror of the horse had saved him.

And now, having failed to kill him then, Mapes couldn't let him get away.

"Doc," said Mary.

"What is it, Mary?"

"I been wondering. Why did you get mixed up in this? You ain't the shootin' kind. You haven't got a thing to gain."

Carter lay silent, thinking, trying to marshal words. It wasn't an easy question to answer. He had explained some of it to Plimpton, but not all of it. There were some deeper, bigger reasons. He shook his head.

"I just got sucked in," he finally said. "I just. . . . ah, hell, I can't tell you why. I don't know why myself, you see."

She touched his arm, gently. "You're fine," she said.

So that was it, he told himself. That was his epitaph. She knew as well as he knew what would happen when the light came.

Just two bodies. Two bodies with the vacant look that the dead have upon their faces.

He fought to erase the thought. It wasn't the way a man should think. Better not to think at all, if that was the way it went.

He reached out, found the girl's hand, held it tight.

"It's all right, doc," she told him, and her voice quavered just a bit. "It's all right."

Two human beings, his mind told him. Two human beings who were about to die, huddling against one another like frightened rabbits. And Mary was too young to die, too full of life, too proud and unspoiled to become no more than a body with a vacant face.

"I'm sorry, Mary," he said, gently. "If you hadn't come to help me—"

Her hand came up against his lips, stopped his words. "No," she said, "not that. That's no way for us to be."

He slid his arm around her, held her close.

From below came the half-heard noise of the herd out in the valley. A tiny wind came rustling through the cedars. From the distant prairie a wolf howled with nose pointed to the moon.

On the slope a rock thudded and thumped, skittered down the slide. Carter tensed, listening. For long moments silence held. Then came a scurrying sound, the sound of rolling dirt and gravel.

Someone was crawling up the slope, hugging the shadows of the wall.

Mary had drawn away from Carter, stared at him with rounded eyes.

He nodded. "Someone out there," his lips said without a sound.

Cautiously he wriggled his way to the rim, stared down. A dark shadow moved there, stealthily, like a wraith of dawn.

Slowly he raised the rifle, centered the sights on the crouching figure, his finger crooking around the trigger.

Easy, his mind told him. So easy to kill a man once you've done it. Easy to kill when you're backed into a hole and there's no way to get out.

The figure moved and Carter's finger tightened. Then suddenly the finger froze, loosened gently. Carefully, Carter slid the rifle back to Mary, reached out for the six-gun.

He felt the metal of it in his fist and his head whirled with the idea that had come to him, whirled and quieted, became as cold as ice, clear-cut as steel.

That man out there, edging up the slide, crouching in the shadow of the wall, might mean more alive than dead. Held as a hostage, he might spell life itself.

Swiftly, silently, Carter skulked through the cedars, knees bent, head held low. He reached the cliff wall, slid along it, flattened himself against it behind a cedar that was wedged against the rock.

His fist tightened on the gun and his ears seemed ready to pop with straining for the sound that would tell him his man was coming.

A pebble clicked faintly, and that was all. And then, long seconds after, another sound that might have been the crunch of a cautious footstep on the talus.

Carter held his breath and waited, pressing his body tight against the wall, huddling against the cedar. A foot came into view beyond the cedar and Carter tensed. A body followed, a massive body.

Carter leaned forward, shoved the gun into the paunchy belly. The man stopped, frozen, rifle hanging in his hand, head unturning, step unfinished with toe touching the ground and the heel still raised.

Slowly, almost inch by inch, he turned.

"All right, Plimpton," said Carter. "You can drop the gun. And get the hands up."

He punched the gun hard into Plimpton's ribs.

Plimpton growled at him, a growl that was scarcely more than a hoarse whisper. "Get that damned gun out of my belly, doc. I'm on your side."

"What's that?"

"I'm on your side. Ain't I makin' it plain enough? Them cattle out there are mine and them damn double-crossin' varmints I had working for me are fixin' to run them off."

* * *

Carter stared at him. What the man said was obviously true. It clicked. It made a lot of sense. And Plimpton was another gun.

He eyed Carter curiously. "How come you're mixed up in this?"

"Mapes sent Becker in to get me with a cock-and-bull story about someone being sick. Mapes was fixing to gun me, but I got away. Or rather Mary McCord came along and helped me get away."

Plimpton choked in exasperation. "Mary McCord? She's old Jake's girl, ain't she. She here, too?"

"Right here," said Mary.

Plimpton stared from one to the other of them. "Well, I be damned," he said. "Well, I be damned."

For a moment the three of them stood in silence, listening to the cheep of birds, the rustle of the cedars.

Plimpton shrugged his shoulders. "This hog-ties it," he finally said. "I figured maybe some of the hands were sticking with me. Heard the shooting and looked over the situation and figured maybe some of the boys had tried to argue with Mapes and holed up here. So I sneaked up to lend them a hand."

"And found us," said Mary, tartly.

"Yes, miss," agreed Plimpton, "I reckon that's about it. They all run out on me, whole kit and caboodle of them. I should of suspicioned it before, but I never did. I trusted Mapes, you see. I let him talk me into hirin' gunslingers to help scare off the nesters and he run in men of his own on me. I never meant for them to go as far as killin' anyone. And then there was all that rustling. Mapes claimed the nesters were doing it."

Carter nodded. "His own men were rustling and building up the herd out here. Cleaning you out a few hundred at a time. And blaming the nesters so as to keep you sore at them and keep you from firing the gun-slingers Mapes had hired."

"You got it about right, doc," said Plimpton. He spoke to Mary McCord. "I'm plumb sorry about your pa."

"You should be," Mary told him bluntly.

"I know," said Plimpton. "You got a right to feel that way, but it's something we can't argue about right now. It's something we can try to rectify—"

"Nothing you can do will rectify it," snapped Mary. "You think you can go around killing people and burning their places and—"

Carter stepped close to Mary, put an arm around her shoulders. "Plimpton's right," he said. "We can't argue about it here."

He felt sobs shaking the girl's body. . . . sobs after all these hours. There had been none back in the kitchen when Jake McCord had died, there had been none later when she told how she and Walker had made the casket. But now she clung to him and sobbed.

Carter looked across her head at Plimpton. "You came up the slope," he said. "Maybe we can get back that way. This place is a rat-trap."

Plimpton grunted. "Should have tried it before," he said.

"We didn't dare," Carter told him. "We figured Mapes had the whole slope covered."

Plimpton moved impatiently. "Let's get going, then. All this blabbin' around ain't getting us—"

Rifles crashed in a ripple of fire from the flanking timber and whistling lead tore into the cedar thicket, whipping the boughs, plowing up the earth, screaming off the rock wall and tumbled boulders.

Carter hurled himself to the ground, dragging the girl with him. Out of the corner of his eye, he saw Plimpton execute a lightning belly flop.

The rifles crashed again and winged, screeching death hummed above their heads.

Swiftly, Carter pushed Mary toward a boulder, crawled behind another one nearby.

To his left, Plimpton hugged the ground. The ranchman shoved his rifle forward, looked toward Carter.

"Doc," he croaked, "we sure as hell are in for it now."

Chapter Nine
The Doc Makes Death

On the ridge above the rifles chortled with what seemed like fiendish laughter, chunking lead into the tiny cedar patch. Pressed flat on the ground behind the boulder, Carter became aware that his left shoulder was stiff, almost as if it wasn't there, and suddenly remembered the bullet that had chewed through it an hour or so before. He had almost forgotten it, he realized, in the rush of events that had tumbled upon them.

Twisting his head, he saw Mary hugging the boulder behind which she crouched, like a puppy curled in some protecting corner. Plimpton was flat upon the ground, wedged against the rock wall on one side and a shielding cedar on the other. As Carter watched, he saw the twigs of the cedar twitch to the impact of crashing bullets.

It was foolish, he told himself, this blind shooting. Sooner or later some of the lead would find them, of course, but it seemed an unscientific way to fight . . . a shotgun method, a theory that enough lead poured into a certain area was almost certain to find the target that it sought.

Cautiously, Carter inched his body around the boulder, thrust the barrel of the six-gun beyond the protecting rock, slowly poked his head out to stare at the ridge above.

In the half dawn he could see the puffs of smoke that drifted above the hidden rifles, saw the red spitting fire that gushed from the muzzles.

A bullet struck the boulder just above his head, howled its way through a clump of cedar.

Carter lifted the six-gun, slanted it upwards at a thicket where at least one rifleman was nested, pressed the trigger, felt the weapon pounding in his hand.

A rifle bellowed almost in his ear and he switched his head around. Mary was on her knees, rifle rested across the boulder. Even as he looked the rifle spouted flame and the girl worked the lever. The empty casing spun out on the ground, a glittering brass thing that rolled and bounced.

Above them there was motion in a thicket, a half seen form of a man running, stooped over. Swiftly Carter snapped a shot at him, knew even as he fired that he had missed. Then Plimpton's gun bellowed and the running figure tumbled, rolled into sight, arms flopping grotesquely, came to rest against a slanting tree.

A hurtling thing chunked into the ground at Carter's elbow, a thing that fell from almost straight above, that did not have the angry hum that a bullet had. A rock! A piece of rock!

The cliff ledge above you, Carter's brain screamed at him and Carter swung around, staring up—straight into the muzzle of a rifle that seemed to hang from the rim of the cliff. And behind the rifle was a face—a freckled face, with untrimmed hair sticking out from beneath a hat.

The gun in Carter's hand exploded and the rifle fell, fell slowly, it seemed, almost as if it floated, whirling end over end, barrel glinting in the first rays of the sun.

Behind the rifle the man hunched forward, slid with fascinating slowness, his face a bloody ruin. Slid and caught and dangled.

Becker! The freckled face in the lamplight, telling that lie about his partner who had eaten a peach and gotten sick. . . .

A bullet twitched the front of Carter's shirt, knifing across his belly but not touching flesh. Mary's rifle slammed with throaty coughing. . . . coughed again.

On the ridge above someone shouted and men were rising out of the thickets, plunging down the slope toward them. On one knee, Plimpton churned his rifle steadily.

On the slope, one man threw up his arms and plunged face forward, skidding on his chest. Another went down as his knee gave way beneath him.

Carter charged forward through the cedars to meet the wave of running men, six-gun growling in his fist.

This is the end, said the back part of his brain. . . . the part that stood off to one side and watched. This is the last stand. . . .

In front of him loomed a man. . . . a tall wiry man with stony eyes that glittered as he ran. The same eyes that had glared at him across the table back at the restaurant, that had shone above the six-gun sights down there at the campfire.

Mapes' gun spat smoke and flame and Carter felt the wind of the bullet as it spun past his cheek. The man still was coming on, stride unchecked, gun still at his waist, leveled, ready for another shot. And suddenly Carter was aware that he was pulling the trigger of his own gun and nothing was happening. . . . only hollow clicks.

With a bellow or rage he flung the empty gun, a vicious throw that made the weapon a spinning wheel of light—a wheel of light that smashed into Mapes' chest and staggered him even as his gun belched redly.

Carter charged, head lowered, smashed into the reeling Mapes, felt himself going down on top of the falling man.

From the ridge above came the yells of men, the rapid crash of gunfire and then he and Mapes were on the ground. Carter's left hand lashed out, caught the other's gun wrist, twisted savagely, but the man held on. Mapes' knee came up and slammed into Carter's stomach, twisting him with nauseating pain. Carter gritted his teeth and chopped down viciously with his right fist against the forearm that held the gun. The fingers loosened and the gun dropped free, rolled down the slope.

Still sick from the stomach blow, Carter staggered to his feet, stood staring for a moment at what was happening behind him.

The slope above the slide swarmed with men, men with blasting guns. Men he knew! Mary's brother, Walker, with the gun that snarled. And Matt Denby, who'd come in to pay something on his bill before he left the country. The Jones kid from up north of Tumbling K.

Feet grated on the rubble and Carter swung around. Mapes was getting to his feet, was starting to charge.

With a growl in his throat, Carter swung to meet him, read the wild hatred and insanity in the glittering eyes as Mapes leaped forward. Carter swung, slammed home a blow that rocked the attacker on his feet, bored in—and ran into hard, brutal fists that slashed across his cheek, smashed into his mouth, that rocked his head with brain-jarring power.

Ducking his head, Carter pistoned jabs into the other's stomach, drove him back.

Suddenly Mapes slipped, staggered, fell away, was sliding down the rubble of the slope. On half-dead legs, Carter followed, plunging down after him.

Mapes had stopped sliding, was crawling to his hands and knees. And as he raised himself, he held something in his hand—a thing that glittered in the morning sun.

"Damn you, Carter," he croaked, "this time I got you. . . . got you. . . ."

He lifted the gun and as he did, Carter saw the trick that Mapes had played. . . . sliding down the slope until he reached the gun that he had lost.

Mapes' face was savage, a grinning face of death—it shone in the white-toothed grin, the steely eyes.

Carter staggered forward, stomach tensed against the lead that he knew would pour into it from the flaming gun.

Mapes' eyes changed. The grin came off, a startled look crept into the eyes and he was staring at his right hand as if he were wondering what could be the matter with it.

"Jammed," said Carter, softly. "All jammed up with sand. You better throw it away, Mapes."

With a scream of fury, Mapes leaped up the slope, gun raised and striking down. Carter ducked, felt the gun-barrel crash into his injured shoulder with paralyzing pain.

Pain that brought a haze of red. . . . red that swirled around and targeted a face. He smashed at the face, smashed with all the fury that was in him, with all the pain that ran through his body. Smashed with savage deliberation . . . right—left—right—

The face was falling away, falling out of sight and he raced to keep up with it, chopping viciously, right hand, left hand.

And suddenly it was gone.

Carter stood swaying, lifted a hand to wipe away the fog that swirled before his eyes, dimly saw the outstretched body of the man lying at his feet. . . . Mapes—with his neck twisted at a funny angle.

A hoarse voice croaked at him.

"Good Lord, man, you killed him with your fists."

"He isn't dead," protested Carter.

"The hell he ain't," said Plimpton. "No man ever lived with his neck in that shape."

Slowly, Carter swung around, saw Plimpton standing there, rifle under one arm, the other arm a bloody, dripping ruin.

Plimpton grimaced. "Slug caught me," he said.

"Mary?" asked Carter, terror welling in him.

"She's all right," said Plimpton. "The boys showed up in time."

"Boys?"

"Sure, the nesters. Mary's brother rounded them up. Said he was here last night, but couldn't do a thing alone. So he went for help."

Plimpton's face twisted. "Just in time, if you ask me."

Matt Denby was striding down the slide, six-gun in hand. He came to a halt above them.

"You all right, doc?" he asked.

Carter nodded.

Denby flipped his gun at Plimpton. "What about him?"

"He's O.K.," said Carter. "Came in and fought alongside of us."

Denby looked at Plimpton. "That right?" he challenged.

"Exactly right," said Plimpton. "Might as well. From the looks of it, you fellows didn't leave me no hands to run a ranch."

"Two or three of them got away," said Denby.

He swung back to Carter. "Think you can fix up some of the boys, doc? Some of them got plugged. Not fatal or nothin', but sort of inconvenient-like."

Carter nodded. "Plimpton, too," he said.

"How about yourself?" asked Plimpton, eyeing the bloodied shoulder.

"That can wait," said Carter gruffly. "Sort of numb. Doesn't hurt at all."

He started up the slope.

Mary, he saw, was waiting at the top.

... AND THE TRUTH SHALL MAKE YOU FREE

Originally published in 1953, in Future Science Fiction Stories, *this story has been reprinted under the name "The Answers," and it was also the basis of a one-act stage play, not written by Clifford Simak, called "The Ritual Reading." It strongly evokes some of the same responses as the* City *stories—above all, the gut-level feelings of sadness and failure, coming out of the death of dreams and dreaming. (There's an intelligent Dog, too, but not of the sort you'll find in the* City *stories.)*

One can ask oneself whether this story might also be a complete rejection of much of science fiction.

—dww

I

They knew when they stepped out of the ship and saw it. There was, of course, no way that they could have known it, or been sure they knew it, for there was no way to know what one might be looking for. Yet, they did know it for what it was—and three of them stood and looked at it, while the fourth one floated and looked at it. And each of them, in his brain or heart or intuition—whatever you may name it—knew deep inside himself a strange conviction that here finally was the resting place (or one of the resting places) of that legendary fragment of the human race that, millennia before, had broken free of the chains of ordinary humans to make their way into the darkness of the outer galaxy. But whether they fled from mediocrity; or whether they deserted; or whether they left for any one of a dozen other reasons was a thing that no one now might know; for the matter had become an academic question that had split into several cults of erudite belief, and still was fiercely debated in a very learned manner.

In the minds of the four who looked, however, there was no shred of question that here before them lay the place that had been sought—in a more or less haphazard fashion—for a hundred thousand years. It was a place. One hesitated to call it a city, although it probably was a city. It was a place of living, and of learning, and of working, and it had many buildings; but the buildings had been made a part of the landscape and did not outrage the eye with their grossness nor their disregard for the land they stood upon. There was greatness about the place—not a greatness of gigantic stones heaped on one another, nor the greatness of a bold and overwhelming architecture, nor even the greatness of indestructibility. For there was no massiveness of structure, and the architecture seemed quite ordinary; some of the buildings had fallen into disrepair, and others were weathered into a mellowness that blended with the trees and grass of the hills on which they stood.

Still there was a greatness in them, the greatness of humility and purpose—and the greatness, too, of well-ordered life. Looking at them, one knew that he had been wrong in thinking this a city—that this was no city, but an extensive village, with all the connotations that were in the word.

But most of all there was humanness—the subtle touch that marked the buildings as ones that had been planned by human minds, and raised by human hands. You could not put your finger upon any single thing and say, "This thing is human"; any one of those things you put your finger on might have been built or achieved by another race. But when all those single things you might put your finger on were rolled into the whole concept, there could be no doubt that this was a human village.

Sentient beings had hunted for this place, had sought the clue that might lead them to the vanished segment of the race; when they failed, some of them had doubted there had been such a segment—for the story was one that was based upon little more than myth, with the records that told of it often in dispute. There were those, too, who had said that it mattered little if you found the missing fragment, since little that was of any value would come from a race so insignificant as the human race. What were the humans, they would ask you—and would answer before you had a chance to speak. Gadgeteers, they said, gadgeteers who were singularly unstable. Great on gadgets, they would say, but with very little real intelligence. It was, they would point out, only by the slightest margin of intelligence that ever they were accepted into the galactic brotherhood. And, these detractors would remind you, humans had not improved much since. Still marvelous gadgeteers, of course, but strictly third-rate citizens who now quite rightly had been relegated to the backwash of the empire.

The place had been sought, and there had been many failures. It had been sought, but not consistently; there were matters of much greater import than its finding. It was simply an amusing piece of galactic history—or myth, if you would rather. As a project, its discovery had never rated very high.

But here it was, spread out below the high ridge on which the ship had landed; and if any of them wondered why it had not been found before, the answer was simple—there were just too many stars; you could not search them all.

"This is it," said the Dog, speaking in his mind; and he looked slantwise at the Human, wondering what the Human might be thinking; of all of them, the finding of this place must mean the most to him.

"I am glad we found it," said the Dog, speaking directly to the Human; and the Human caught the nuances of the thought, the closeness of the Dog, his great compassion and his brotherhood.

"Now we shall know," the Spider said; and each of them knew, without his actually saying so, that now they'd know if these humans were any different from the other humans—or if they were just the same old humdrum race.

"They were mutants," said the Globe, "or they were supposed to be."

The Human stood there, saying nothing, just looking at the place.

"If we'd tried to find it," said the Dog, "we never would have done it."

"We can't spend much time," the Spider told them. "Just a quick survey, then there's this other business."

"The point is," said the Globe, "we know now that it exists, and where it is. They will send experts out to investigate."

"We stumbled on it," said the Human, half in wonderment; "we just stumbled on it."

The Spider made a thought that sounded like a chuckle, and the Human said no more.

"It's deserted," said the Globe; "they have run away again."

"They may be decadent," said the Spider. "We may find what's left of them huddled in some corner, wondering what it's all about—loaded down with legends and with crazy superstitions."

"I don't think so," said the Dog.

"We can't spend much time," the Spider stated again.

"We *should* spend no time at all," the Globe told him. "We were not sent out to find this place; we have no business letting it delay us."

"Since we've found it," said the Dog, "it would be a shame to go away and leave it, just like that."

"Then let's get at it," said the Spider. "Let's break out the robots and the ground-car."

"If you don't mind," the Human said, "I think that I will walk. The rest of you go ahead; I'll just walk down and take a look around."

"I'll go with you," said the Dog.

"I thank you," said the Human, "but there really is no need."

So they let him go alone. The three of them stayed on the ridge-top, and watched him walk down the hill toward the silent buildings; then they went to activate the robots.

The sun was setting when they returned; the Human was waiting for them, squatting on the ridge, staring at the village.

He did not ask them what they found. It was almost as if he knew, although he could not have found the answer by himself, just walking around.

They told him.

The Dog was kind about it. "It's strange," he said. "There is no evidence of any great development; no hint of anything unusual. In fact, you might guess that they had retrogressed. There are no great engines, no hint of any mechanical ability."

"There are gadgets," said the Human. "Gadgets of comfort and convenience. That is all I saw."

"That is all there is," the Spider said.

"There are no humans," said the Globe. "No life of any kind; no intelligence."

"The experts," said the Dog, "may find something when they come."

"I doubt it," said the Spider.

The Human turned his head away from the village and looked at his three companions. The Dog was sorry, of course, that they had found so little—sorry that the little they had found had been so negative. The Dog was sorry because he still held within himself some measure of racial memory, and of loyalty. The old associations with the human race had been wiped away millennia ago; but the heritage still held—the old heritage of sympathy with, and for, the being that had walked with his ancestors so understandingly.

The Spider was almost pleased about it—pleased that he had found no evidence of greatness, that this last vestige of vanity that might be held by humans now would be dashed forever. The race must now slink back into its corner and stay there, watching the greatness of the Spiders, and the other races, with furtive eyes.

The Globe didn't care. He floated there, at head-level with the Spider and the Dog; it meant little to him whether humans might be proud or humble. Nothing mattered to the Globe except that certain plans went forward; that certain goals were reached; that progress could be measured. Already the Globe had written off this village; already he had erased the story of the mutant humans as a factor that might affect progress, one way or another.

"I think," the Human said, "that I will stay out here for a while. That is, if you don't mind."

"We don't mind," the Globe told him.

"It will be getting dark," the Spider said.

"There'll be stars," the Human said. "There may even be a moon. Did you notice if there was a moon?"

"No," the Spider said.

"We'll be leaving soon," the Dog said to the Human. "I will come out and tell you when we have to leave."

There were stars, of course. They came out when the last flush of the sun still flamed along the west. First there were but a few of the brighter ones; then there were more, and finally the entire heavens was a network of unfamiliar stars. But there was no moon. Or, if there was one, it did not show itself.

Chill crept across the ridge-top and the Human found some sticks of wood lying about—dead branches, and shriveled bushes, and other wood that looked as if it might at one time have been milled and worked—and built himself a fire. It was a small fire, but it flamed brightly in the darkness; he huddled close against it, more for its companionship than for any heat it gave.

He sat beside it, looked down upon the village, and told himself there was something wrong. The greatness of the human race, he told himself, could not have gone so utterly to seed. He was lonely—lonely with a throat-aching loneliness that was more than the loneliness of an alien planet, a chilly ridge-top, and unfamiliar stars. He was lonely for the hope that once had glowed so brightly; for the promise that had gone like dust into nothingness before a morning wind; for a race that huddled in its gadgetry in the backwash of the empire.

Not an empire of humanity, but an empire of Globes and Spiders; of Dogs; and other things for which there was scarcely a description.

There was more to the human race than gadgetry. There was destiny somewhere, and the gadgetry was simply the means to bridge the time until that destiny should become apparent. In a fight for survival, the Human told himself, gadgetry might be the expedient, but it could not be the answer; it could not be the sum total, the final jotting down of any group of beings.

The Dog came and stood beside him, without saying anything. He simply stood there and looked with the Human down at the quiet village that had been quiet so long; the firelight flamed along his coat and he was a thing of beauty, with a certain inherent wildness still existing in him.

Finally the Dog broke the silence that hung above the world and seemed a part of it. "The fire is nice," he said. "I seldom have a fire."

"The fire was first," the Human said. "The first step up. Fire is a symbol to me."

"I have symbols, too," the Dog said, gravely. "Even the Spider has some symbols. But the Globe has none."

"I feel sorry for the Globe," the Human said.

"Don't let your pity wear you down," the Dog told him. "The Globe feels sorry for you. He is sorry for all of us—for everything that is not a Globe."

"Once my people were sorry like that, too," the Human said; "but not any more."

"It's time to go," the Dog said. "I know you would like to stay, but . . ."

"I am staying," said the Human.

"You can't stay," the Dog told him.

"I am staying," the Human said. "I am just a Human, and you can get along without me."

"I thought you would be staying," said the Dog. "Do you want me to go back and get your stuff?"

"If you would be so kind," the Human said. "I'd not like to go myself."

"The Globe will be angry," said the Dog.

"I know it."

"You will be demoted," said the Dog; "it will be a long time before you're allowed to go on a first-class run again."

"I know all that."

"The Spider will say that all humans are crazy. He will say it in a very nasty way."

"I don't care," the Human said; "somehow, I don't care."

"All right, then," said the Dog. "I will go and get your stuff. There are some books, and your clothes, and that little trunk of yours."

"And food," the Human said.

"Yes," declared the Dog; "I would not have forgotten food."

After the ship was gone, the Human picked up the bundles the Dog had brought; in addition to all the Human's food, the Human saw that the Dog had left him some of his own as well.

2

The people of the village had lived a simple and a comfortable life. Much of the comfort paraphernalia had broken down, and all of it had long since ceased to operate; but it was not hard for one to figure out what each of the gadgets did, or once had been designed to do.

They had held a love of beauty, for there still were ruins of their gardens left; and here and there one found a flower, or a flowering shrub that once had been tended carefully for its color and its grace. But these things now had been long forgotten, and had lost the grandeur of their purpose—the beauty they now held was bitter-sweet and faded.

The people had been literate, for there were rows of books upon the shelves; but the books went to dust when they were touched, and one could do no more than wonder at the magic words they held.

There were buildings which, at one time, might have been theatres; there were great forums where the populace may have gathered to hear the wisdom, or the argument, that was the topic of the day.

And even yet one could sense the peace and leisure, the order and the happiness that once had held the place.

There was no greatness. There were no mighty engines, nor the shops to make them. There were no launching platforms, and no other hint that the dwellers in the village had ever dreamed of going to the stars—although they must have known about the stars since their ancestors once had come from space. There were no defenses, and there were no great roads leading from the village into the outer planet.

One felt peace when he walked along the street, but it was a haunted peace—a peace that balanced on a knife's edge; while one wished with all his heart that he could give way to it, and live with it, one was afraid to do so for fear of what might happen.

The Human slept in the homes, clearing away the dust and the fallen debris, building tiny fires to keep him company. He sat outside, on the broken flagstones or the shattered bench, before he went to sleep, and stared up at the stars, and thought how once those stars had made familiar patterns for a happy people. He wandered in the winding paths that were narrower now than they once had been, and hunted for a clue; he did not hunt too strenuously, for there was something here which said you should not hurry, and you should not fret, for there was no purpose in it.

Here once had lain the hope of the human race, a mutant branch of that race that had been greater than the basic race. Here had been the hope of greatness—and there was no greatness. Here was peace and comfort; intelligence and leisure, but nothing else that made itself apparent to the eye.

Although there must be something else, some lesson, some message, some purpose—the Human told himself again and again that this could not be a dead end, that it was more than some blind alley.

On the fifth day, in the center of the village, he found a building that was a little more ornate and somewhat more solidly built—although all the rest were solid enough, for all conscience's sake. There were no windows and the single door was locked and he knew at last that he had found the clue he had been hunting for.

He worked for three days to break into the building, and there was no way that he could. On the fourth day he gave up and walked away—out of the village and across the hills—looking for some thought, or some idea, that might gain him entry to the building. He walked across the hills—as one will pace his study when he is at loss for words, or take a turn in the garden to clear his head for thinking.

And that is how he found the people.

First of all, he saw the smoke coming from one of the hollows that branched down toward the valley where a river ran, a streak of gleaming silver against the green of pasture grass.

He walked cautiously, so that he would not be surprised—but, strangely, without the slightest fear—for there was something in this planet—something in the arching sky, and the song of bird, and the way the wind blew out of the west—that told a man he had not a thing to fear.

Then he saw the house beneath the mighty trees. He saw the orchard and the trees bending with their fruit, and heard the thoughts of people talking back and forth.

He walked down the hill toward the house—not hurrying, for suddenly it had come upon him that there was no need to hurry. And just as suddenly, it seemed that he was coming home; that was the strangest of all, for he had never known a home that resembled this.

They saw him coming when he strode down across the orchard, but they did not rise and come to meet him. They sat where they were and waited—as if he already were a friend of theirs, and his coming was expected.

There was an old lady—with snow-white hair and a prim, neat dress, the collar coming up high at her throat to hide the ravages of age upon the human body. But her face was beautiful— the restful beauty of the very old who sit and rock, and know their day is done, and that their life is full, and that it has been good.

There was a man of middle age or more, who sat beside the woman. The sun had burned his face and neck until they were almost black; and his hands were calloused and pockmarked with old scars, and half-crippled with heavy work. But upon his face, too, was a calmness which was an incomplete reflection of the face beside him—incomplete because it was not as deep and settled, because it could not as yet know the full comfort of old age.

The third one was a young woman and the Human saw the calmness in her, too. She looked back at him out of cool grey eyes; he saw her face was curved and soft, and that she was much younger than he first had thought.

He stopped at the gate, and the man rose and came to where he waited. "You're welcome, stranger," said the man. "We heard you coming since you stepped into the orchard."

"I have been at the village," the Human said. "I am just out for a walk."

"You are from outside?"

"Yes," the Human told him, "I am from outside. My name is David Grahame."

"Come in, David," said the man, opening the gate. "Come and rest with us; there will be food, and we have an extra bed."

He walked along the garden path with the man and came to the bench where the old lady sat.

"My name is Jed," the man said, "and this is my mother, Mary; the other of us is my daughter, Alice."

"So you finally came to us, young man," the old lady said to David.

She patted the bench with a fragile hand. "Here, sit down beside me and let us talk awhile. Jed has chores to do, and Alice will have to cook the supper. But I am old and lazy, and I only sit and talk."

Now that she talked, her eyes were brighter, but the calmness still was in them. "We knew you would come, someday," she said. "We knew someone would come; for surely those who are outside would hunt their mutant kin."

"We found you," David said, "quite by accident."

"We? There are others of you?"

"The others went away; they were not human and they were not interested."

"But you stayed," she said. "You thought there would be things to find. Great secrets to be learned."

"I stayed," said David, "because I had to stay."

"But the secrets? The glory and the power?"

David shook his head. "I don't think I thought of that—not of power and glory. But there must be something else. You sense it walking in the village, and looking in the homes; you sense a certain truth."

"Truth," the old lady said. "Yes, we found Truth."

And the way she said it, "Truth" was capitalized.

He looked quickly at her and she sensed the unspoken, unguarded question that flicked across his mind. "No," she told him, "not religion. Just Truth. The plain and simple Truth."

He almost believed her, for there was a quiet conviction in the way she said it, a deep and solid surety. "The truth of what?" he asked.

"Why, Truth," the old lady said. "Just Truth."

3

It would be something more than a simple truth, of course, it would have nothing to do with machines, and it would concern neither power nor glory. It would be an inner truth—a mental, or a spiritual or a psychological truth—that would have a deep and abiding meaning, the sort of truth that men had followed for years and even followed yet in the wish-worlds of their own creation.

The Human lay in the bed close beneath the roof and listened to the night-wind that blew itself a lullaby along the eaves and shingles. The house was quiet, and the world was quiet, except for the singing wind. The world was quiet, and David Grahame could imagine, lying there, how the galaxy would gradually grow quiet under the magic and the spell of what these human-folk had found.

It must be great, he thought, this truth of theirs. It must be powerful, and imagination-snaring, and all-answering to send them back like this—to separate them from the striving of the galaxy, and send them back to this pastoral life of achieved tranquility in this alien valley; to make them grub the soil for food and cut the trees for warmth; to make them content with the little that they had.

To get along with that little, they must have much of something else, some deep conviction, some inner knowledge that had spelled out to them a meaning to their lives, to the mere fact and living of their lives, that no one else could have.

He lay on the bed, pulled the covers up more comfortably about him, and hugged himself with inner satisfaction.

Man cowered in one corner of the galactic empire, a maker of gadgets—tolerated only because he was a maker of gadgets, and because the other races never could be sure what he might come up with next. They tolerated him, and threw him crumbs enough to keep him friendly, but wasted scant courtesy upon him.

Now, finally, Man had something that would win him a place in the respect and the dignity of the galaxy. For a truth is a thing to be respected.

Peace came to the Human, but he would not let it in; he fought against it so that he could think, so that he could speculate. First he imagined that this must be the truth that the mutant race had found, then he abandoned that idea . . .

Finally the lullabying wind and the sense of peace and the tiredness of his body prevailed against him and he slept. The last thought that he had was: *I must ask them. I must find out.*

But it was days before he asked them, for he sensed that they were watching; he knew that they wondered if he could be trusted with the truth and if he was worthy of it.

He wished to stay; but for politeness sake he said that he must go, and raised no great objection when they said that he must stay. It was as if each one of them knew this was a racial ritual which must be observed, and all were glad when it once was done and was over with.

He worked in the fields with Jed, and got to know the neighbors up and down the valley; he sat long evenings talking with Jed, and his mother and the daughter, and with the other valley folk who dropped in to pass a word or two.

He had expected that they would ask him questions, but they did not ask; it was almost as if they didn't care, as if they so loved this valley where they lived that they did not even think upon the teeming galaxy their far ancestors had left behind to seek, here on this world, a destiny that was better than common human destiny.

The Human did not ask them questions, either; he felt them watching him, and he was afraid that questions would send them fleeing from the strangeness of him.

But he was not a stranger. It took only a day or two for him to know that he could be one of them, so he made himself become one of them; he sat for long hours and talked of common gossip that ran up and down the valley, and it all was kindly gossip. He learned many things—that there were other valleys where other people lived; that the silent, deserted village was something they did not fret about, although each of them seemed to know exactly what it was; that they had no ambition and no hope beyond this life of theirs, and all were well content.

The Human grew content himself, content with the rose-grey mornings; with the dignity of labor; with the pride of growing things. But even as he grew content, he knew he could not be content—that he must find the answer to the truth they had found and must carry that truth back to the waiting galaxy. Before long, a ship would be coming out to explore the village and to study it; and before the ship arrived, he must know the answer. When the ship arrived, he must be standing on the ridge above the village to tell them what he'd found.

One day Jed said to him, "You will be staying with us?"

David shook his head. "I have to go back, Jed; I would like to stay, but I must go back."

Jed spoke slowly, calmly. "You want the Truth? That's it?"

"If you will give it to me," David said.

"It is yours to have," said Jed; "you will not take it back."

That night Jed said to his daughter, "Alice, teach David how to read our writing. It is time he knew."

In the corner by the fireplace, the old lady sat rocking in her chair. "Aye," she said, "it is time he read the Truth."

4

The key had come by special messenger from its custodian, five valleys distant; Jed held it in his hand now, and slid it in the lock of the door, in the building that stood in the center of the old, quiet, long-deserted village.

"This is the first time," Jed said, "that the door has been opened, except for the Ritualistic reading. Each hundred years the door is opened and the Truth is read so that those who then are living may know that it is so."

He turned the key and David heard the click of the tumblers turning in the lock.

"That way," said Jed, "we keep it actual fact; we do not allow it to become a myth.

"It is," he said, "too important a thing to become a myth."

Jed turned the latch and the door swung open just an inch or two. "I said Ritualistic reading," he added, "but perhaps that is not quite right. There is no ritual to it. Three persons are chosen; they come here on the appointed day, and each of them reads the Truth and then goes back as a living witness. There is no more ceremony than there is with you and I."

"It is good of you to do this for me," David said.

"We would do the same for any of our own who should doubt

the Truth," said Jed. "We are a very simple people and we do not believe in red tape or rules; all we do is live.

"In just a little while," he said, "you will understand why we are simple people."

He swung the door wide open and stepped to one side so that David might walk in ahead of him. The place was one large room and it was neat and orderly. There was some dust, but not very much.

Half the room was filled to three quarters of its height with a machine that gleamed in the dull light that came from some source high in the roof.

"This is our machine," said Jed.

And so it was gadgetry, after all. It was another machine, perhaps a cleverer and sleeker machine, but it was still a gadget and the human race still were gadgeteers.

"Doubtless you wondered why you found no machines," said Jed. "The answer is that there is only one and this is it."

"Just one machine!"

"It is an answerer," said Jed. "A logic. With this machine, there is no need of any others."

"You mean it answers questions?"

"It did at one time," said Jed. "I presume it still would if there were any of us who knew how to operate it. But there is no need of asking further questions."

"You can depend on it?" asked David. "That is, you can be sure that it tells the truth?"

Jed said soberly, "My son, our ancestors spent thousands of years making sure that it would tell the truth. They did nothing else. It was not only the lifework of each trained technician, but the lifework of the race. And when they were sure that it would know and tell the truth—when they were certain that there could be no slightest error in the logic of its calculations—they asked two questions of it."

"Two questions?"

"Two questions," Jed said. "And they found the Truth."

"And the Truth?"

"The Truth," Jed said, "is here for you to read. Just as it came out those centuries ago."

He led the way to a table that stood in front of one panel of the great machine. There were two tapes upon the table, lying side by side. The tapes were covered by some sort of transparent preservative.

"The first question," said Jed, "was this: What is the purpose of the universe? Now read the top tape, for that is the answer."

David bent above the table and the answer was upon the tape: *The universe has no purpose. The universe just happened.*

"And the second question . . ." said Jed, but there was no need for him to finish, for what the question had been was implicit in the wording of the second tape: *Life has no significance. Life is an accident.*

"And that," said Jed, "is the Truth we found. That is why we are a simple people."

David lifted stricken eyes and looked at Jed, the descendant of that mutant race that was to have brought power and glory, respect and dignity to the gadgeteering humans.

"I am sorry, son," said Jed; "that is all there is."

They walked out of the room and Jed locked the door and put the key into his pocket.

"They'll be coming soon," said Jed, "the ones who will be sent out to explore the village. I suppose you will be waiting for them?"

David shook his head. "Let's go back home," he said.

CLERICAL ERROR

"Clerical Error" was sent to John W. Campbell, Jr., the editor of Astounding Science Fiction, *in December 1939, under the title of "Man on Jupiter." That date places it within a period during which the author was reputedly in the process of writing a series of stories to be set on each of the planets of our Solar System—a series that probably included "Hunger Death" (Venus) and "Masquerade" (Mercury). (It is also said that the author subsequently abandoned that project.)*

The story, which appeared in the August 1940 issue of Campbell's magazine, happens to be one of several by Simak which feature a theme of humans trying to find medicinal substances on alien planets; but the most important thing about this story, to Cliff's fans, is the fact that this seems to be the Jupiter of his great later story, "Desertion," and I do wonder if Cliff intended to make something of that relationship.

—dww

Fred Franklin knew, better than any of the rest, that death was closing in on them. But he wasn't scared. He was just hopping mad—sore clean through because those beautiful engines of his down in the Hive's sub-floor wouldn't run much longer.

Fred lived for his engines. He liked the swift, smooth hum of power, the blurring whirl of alternators, the exact meshing of whirring gears.

His great, grease-stained hands twitched—as if they were groping for someone's throat.

"If I could just get my hands on that guy back on Earth," he bellowed.

"Whoever he was, he'll probably get canned," said Bill Vickers. "Some shipping clerk, perhaps. A mistake the inspectors should have caught."

"Sure," growled Fred, "the shipping clerk'll get canned. We'll die."

Vickers looked at the atomic engineer soberly. "Just how much longer can you keep them going, Fred?"

The engineer exploded. "You ask me that? I'll tell you this— I'll keep them going until the combustion chamber goes up in smoke, and when that happens we don't need to worry any more."

Vickers shivered, envisioning what would happen when that occurred—if it did occur. He could see the force of uncontrolled atomic power lashing though the engine rooms, ripping through the entire dome.

"The *mercotite* is wearing thin," said Fred. "Too damn thin for safety. If we keep that blast chamber going, we have to have *mercotite*—the *mercotite* that should have been in those boxes and wasn't."

He spat bitterly.

"Copper! What the hell would we want of copper?"

"I've called in all the tractors," said Vickers. "All of them have reported except old Cal Osborn, and he was drunk the last time I talked to him. Maybe he'll show up after a while. As fast as those tractors come in you rip out the *mercotite* in their combustion chambers, use it to patch up and strengthen the big chamber. I know it won't go far, but it will help. Every minute we keep those engines going, every minute we keep juice pouring into these walls is just that much longer for us to live. When those engines stop, we stop, too. We all know that."

"You've called in the men?" asked Dr. Norman Lester. "Does that mean you've given up finding the ship?"

Vickers swung around to face the gray-haired man.

"No," he snapped. "We have to call those tractors in to get *mercotite*. But we aren't giving up the search. I'm going out myself, and I'm coming back with the *mercotite* the *Jovian Ark* was carrying or I don't come back at all. Benny here claims the ship was coming in over Mount Bellow when the signals cut off. It must have struck somewhere over on the other side."

"That's right," said Benny Kern, the radio man. "She was coming in just north of us, still pretty high up, and having a bad time in the storm. Reception wasn't so good, but I was dragging her in. She was riding the directional beam, although it must have been pretty spotty. The sky was full of lightning."

"All very pretty," said Dr. Lester, "but not very convincing. The men who were out searching combed that mountain. How do you figure you'll find anything when they didn't?"

"Look here," snarled Fred, "you keep out of this. A hell of a lot you've done. We tried to get you to help develop a substitute for *mercotite*. All the scientific equipment in the world, all the metal on Jupiter, and what did you do? Not one damn thing."

"I'm a biologist," said Lester, "and I don't know a thing about metals. Neither do my men."

"If it hadn't been for the storm," said Vickers, "we would be all set. The rotors were ready to operate, but the wind twisted them into scrap metal—"

One expects a two-hundred-mile-an-hour wind on Jupiter. It is just an everyday affair—a gentle breeze that eddies and whirls about the giant planet. It doesn't really get gusty until the wind starts blowing at five hundred miles an hour. When it gets up over the thousand-mile-an-hour mark, it might be called a gale. Beyond that it would be a storm.

Jupiter's atmosphere is thick and heavy, composed of nitrogen and hydrogen—mostly hydrogen—and of a souplike consistency. At two hundred miles an hour such an atmosphere would turn mighty rotors, be the source of tremendous power, power such as was needed to maintain the Hive under the ghastly pressures on Jupiter's surface. But at a thousand miles an hour, it would simply smash rotors into junk heaps. That was what had happened.

The Hive had been built five years before by the first spaceships ever to reach the surface of the Solar System's largest member.

It had been built by robots, operated from the ships by remote control. For while man might build on Jupiter and live on Jupiter, and even, in time to come, conquer Jupiter, man never would be able to walk on Jupiter, never would dare to venture out on solid ground.

The gravity wasn't so bad. Only two and one half times Earth gravity. Bad enough, but possible to fit men for it in Earth's conditioning chambers.

But the pressure was something else. Pressure that would make earthly sea-bottom pressure seem almost like a vacuum. Pressure that would turn even steel brittle and shatter it into a million flaky shards.

Men had lived on Jupiter for five years now, but in all that time no man had ever set foot upon the planet, had ever viewed its surface with the naked eye.

The Hive was constructed of an inner shell of durasteel, the toughest, most stubborn alloy man had ever devised, and yet, in itself, not capable of standing up under the weight of Jupiter's vast atmosphere.

Stepping up of the durasteel's electronic tension had made it possible to construct the dome. But to maintain that electronic tension tremendous power was needed—power such as only could be supplied by bursting atoms, or the winds of Jupiter's own atmosphere.

Over the shell of durasteel was fused another shell of quartz, this to protect the alloy against the alkaline rains that poured almost continuously from the heavy clouds.

The same construction applied to the spaceships which ventured down to Jupiter's surface, to the tractors that carried men over its surface, to the scurrying mechanisms, the robots that serve as men's hands on the Solar System's weirdest planet.

No mere haphazard adventure had led men to brave the dangers of Jupiter, but stark necessity. The establishment of the Hive had been almost in the nature of a last desperate effort—a final fling of the dice that might spell life or death for every living thing upon the planets.

For out beyond Jupiter's dense atmosphere stalked a plague, a deadly plague that defied all medicines. It had originated on Mars, which probably explained the fact the first men to reach that planet had found no trace of life but ample evidence life had existed in the past.

For years that deadly germ had lain in wait, and with the coming of man had sprung to life again. From Mars it had gone to Earth, carried there in spaceships, in the bodies of its victims. From Earth to Venus and Mercury, to the few inhabited asteroids. A plague that swept the worlds, that fastened not alone on man, but on every living thing, threatening the extinction of all life.

Frantic research netted exactly nothing. The germ was isolated and recognized, but defied every attempt at control.

In desperation, overlooking no possibility of checking the plague's advance, a Jupiter expedition had been fitted out. For on Jupiter, it was said, one would find a completely alien chemistry—a chemistry that might give some clue, might lead to some method that would stop the plague.

The first expedition failed, one lone ship winning its way back to the Earth. The second expedition failed. But the third, profiting from the tragedies of the other two, won its way through, built the Hive, installed in it the machinery necessary for life.

A fourth expedition brought the chemists and biologists.

Three years of fruitless effort followed.

Jupiter's chemistry *was* alien, there was no doubt of that. So alien, in fact, the research staff took months to orient itself.

There was life on Jupiter—weird plant life, weirder animal life. Life based on ammonia and hydrogen, life that simply evaporated at pressures and temperatures normal to Earth.

Animal life was small and vicious, its metabolism the reverse of Earth-animal life, based on oxidizing foods and reducing air.

Examined microscopically, chemically, bacteriologically, spectrographically, Jupiter's life yielded many secrets—yet not the one the scientists were seeking.

But success finally came. In the gland of one small animal—dubbed the rooter because of its manner of getting food—was found the cure for the deadly plague, and suddenly the Hive on Jupiter became the center of the Solar System's hope.

Now, two years after the discovery of the gland's properties, the fight against the plague was still going on, and the tide was turning, slowly turning, in mankind's favor. But, as was to be expected, man could extract that product of an alien metabolism—but couldn't make it.

Bill Vickers stared at the television screen and groaned.

It was raining again, driving sheets of liquid ammonia, deathly cold, lashing against the eastern cliffs that were the lower slopes of Mount Bellow. Rain driven by the ordinary everyday wind howling along at two hundred miles an hour.

He shifted the screen's vision angle, saw the pens in which hundreds of rooters were kept. The rooters that were the hope of the Solar System, tenderly cared for, bred, raised, killed for their miraculous glands.

A half dozen robots were coming across the valley, carrying loads of the tubers which served as the rooters' food. Not the manlike kind of robots many families on Earth kept as servants, but complicated, complex machines, adapted to do the work man himself could not do—the machines that must serve as proxies for men on this outlandish planet.

"Fred," said Bill, "when the Hive goes it means the lives of millions of people out on those other planets. It will set back the fight against the plague a good five years. They'll have to build another Hive. They'll have to round up a new rooter stock."

"And all," said the engineer bitterly, "because some muddle-headed clerk sent out copper instead of *mercotite*."

Bill nodded.

He could remember that day, weeks before, when they had ripped open the boxes to get a new supply of *mercotite* to reline the atomic combustion chamber. Box after box—all copper, no *mercotite*.

Mercotite—a wondrous metal, found only on the sunward side of the planet Mercury. The only metal known that would stand up under the blast of disintegrating atoms. Without *mercotite*, one could not control atomic power—and without controlled atomic power, the Hive was doomed. Once stop the flow of energy into the durasteel walls and the dome would be shattered by the pressure.

Somewhere out there on the other side of Mount Bellow lay the *Jovian Ark*, carrying a new supply of *mercotite*. Out there on the rim of the valley, also wrecked by the same storm which had wrecked the spaceship, lay the twisted rotors, set up after long weeks of work in the hope they would supply sufficient power to maintain the dome in case the ship failed to arrive on time.

"I got enough metal out of the tractors to patch the chamber up some," said Fred, "but at the best it won't hold out long. It's getting thin in places again. Let that atomic blast once hit steel and it's all up with us."

He stared at the televisor.

"Maybe we ought to pull in all the robots," he said. "Their combustion chambers are pretty small, but we could get some metal out of them."

"Pull in all you want," said Vickers. "I'm going out and have a shot at finding the *Ark*, but I guess Doc Lester is right. There isn't much chance of my finding it when all the others failed."

"Any word from Old Cal?" asked Fred.

Vickers shook his head. "He was blind drunk when he called in last time. He has a stock of liquor cached somewhere and slips out with a bottle every once in a while. It's a wonder he hasn't killed himself a dozen times. Out wandering around with a tractor, carrying a bellyful of rotgut."

Benny Kern stuck his head out of the radio room.

"Call for you," he shouted. "Old Cal."

Vickers' thumb tripped a tumbler on the panel set in his desk. The vision screen flickered for a moment, synchronizing. Then the face of Old Cal Osborn stared out at him.

"Hi, kid," yelped Cal. "How are you? Have a drink on me."

He waved a bottle aloft, took a gusty drink and wiped his mouth.

"Where are you?" Vickers raged. "Didn't you get my call? Why didn't you come in?"

Old Cal stared owlishly out of the screen.

"What the hell?" he said. "We're going to die, anyhow, ain't we? No *mercotite,* no power—no power, no Hive—"

He hiccuped and looked embarrassed.

"You're drunk," snapped Vickers.

"Look, sonny," Old Cal mumbled, "don't be too hard on an old man. An old bird that knows he's going to die has got to have a fling. Just one more drunk, I tells myself—just one more, so I sneaked aboard a couple gallons of the stuff. I says to myself: 'Billy Vickers won't mind, because he'll understand.' Besides—"

"Besides what?" yelled Vickers.

"Well, I found the ship."

"The ship?"

"Sure, sonny, you know the ship I mean. The *Jovian Ark.*"

"You found the *Jovian Ark!*"

"That's right, but it won't do us any good. Not one damned bit of good, sonny. Because, you see, it's at the bottom of a canyon. All smashed to hell and you can't get to it."

Vickers smashed the top of his desk a blow with his fist.

"I don't care where it is," he shouted. "Just so we've found it. We'll reach it somehow!"

Vickers drove savagely. In the television screen set in front of the controls he saw his fog lamps cutting deep swaths of light into the fury of the slashing, howling elements.

The liquid ammonia rain, whipped by the shrieking wind, was a blinding maelstrom. Jagged lightning streaked across the clouds and ripped around the top of Mount Bellow. Weird vegetative formations seemed like gray ghosts in the driving rain, while ahead of the tractor rolled four metal machines, four robots to help get at the shattered *Jovian Ark.*

Scurrying gray and red things scuttled out of the path of the light. Once one of them hurled itself in a streaking charge at one of the robots, slammed hard against the metal of the machine, rolled to the ground and charged again, retreating into the dimness of the rain only after its fury had worn out.

Vicious little things. Poison mean. Intelligent, too, many of them—but just how intelligent it was almost impossible to know.

No big life on Jupiter, for big life simply couldn't live under the awful pressure. Here life had to be small and quick, life built to hug the ground.

The tractor skidded dangerously as the treads slid on smooth rock. Vickers spun the wheel, cursing. An upset now, damaging the machine, would spell the end. For this was the only tractor available. All the others had been dismantled to supply metal for patching the disintegration chamber.

But speed was necessary. The *mercotite* would hold out a few more hours, and that was all.

He cursed as he thought of it—but his curses were more like a chanted prayer.

Damn this planet! Damn Jupiter! A place where a man couldn't walk on the surface, couldn't see with the naked eye. Had to crawl around in tractors. Had to use television because it was simply impossible to build vision ports that would stand up. A place where radio would operate only a few miles, and at that was erratic. No chance of talking to Earth—for no signals could reach higher than fifty miles into that seething atmosphere.

He checked his directional charts, holding his breath, hoping they were right. A man couldn't always be sure on a world like this. A world of terrible cold—120 below Centigrade—of vast pressure, of alien chemistry and metallurgy.

He could hear the roaring of the wind in the high notches and passes of Mount Bellow, the thunderous roaring that had won the peak its two names—Mount Bellow on one side of the valley, Mount Shriek on the other side.

He flipped over the radio control, yelled into the mike.

"Cal. Cal Osborn!"

The radio crackled and chortled, then Cal's ghostly voice came through.

"That you, sonny?"

"Yes, Cal. Have you found anything?"

"Not a thing," Cal replied. "I've looked her over from stem to stern, and there ain't no way of getting down. Its source is right under a cliff, and its mouth is blocked by a landslide. If we had the time we might turn heaters on her, wear it down."

"We haven't got the time," snapped Vickers. "And if we tried heaters we'd probably bring the whole mountain down on top of us."

"Boy," said Cal, "them fellows must have hit that canyon like a ton of bricks. They ironed out like a pancake."

"Listen," said Vickers. "Send your robot down on a line. See what he can do."

"O.K.," agreed Cal, "but I sure ain't fostering no hopes."

Vickers switched the radio off and gave his attention to driving.

Suddenly he felt lonely—lonely and hopeless. Fred would have been a good man to have along in a time like this, but Fred was needed back at the Hive, and anyway, the tractors were built for only one man. Once again the old rule that anything, to survive on Jupiter, must shun size and be shaped like a turtle.

He skirted a mighty cliff, a white, chalky cliff, composed of stuff that on Earth would have been water, but on Jupiter, because of the terrible cold, the crushing atmosphere, was a solid instead. A blue waterfall of liquid ammonia spewed over the cliff, rushing down the mountainside in a swirling torrent. The waterfall was shrouded in a steamy vapor.

The rain still slashed down. From far above came the steady howling of the boisterous wind in the passes.

Vickers flipped on the radio, tried to contact Cal, but there was no answer. Perhaps just another vagary of this giant planet. Radios at any time were poor.

Or it might be Cal had simply passed out.

Vickers spat in disgust. If only there were a real *man* over there at that canyon where the *Jovian Ark* lay shattered! A man like Fred or Eric, or any of a dozen others. But instead the man out there was Old Cal Osborn!

The tractor nosed its way around the cliff, climbed the mountain shoulder, slipping and skidding on the slippery surfaces. Had it not been for the greater gravity, that shoulder would have been impossible to negotiate, but the tractor made it, angled downward to head up a second spur.

The radio suddenly gurgled to life, and Cal's faint voice, distorted and ghostlike, whispered at Vickers.

"Listen, lad, my robot can't do anything. He needs someone down there to work with him. He's pawing around in the wreckage, but he don't know what he's looking for."

"Can't you direct him?" snapped Vickers. "What's the matter?"

"The canyon's deep," said the ghostly voice. "Even with my spot turned on full power I can just make out the wreckage. I can't make out much. If I could just see what that doggoned robot was doing I might be able to help him get somewhere."

Vickers considered. Old Cal was right. It would be hard to see the bottom of a deep canyon. The thick atmosphere played tricks with vision, distorted it, broke up and dissipated light.

"Look, Cal," he said. "We have to get down some way. One of us has to be down there to direct that robot."

An alcoholic hiccup, a ghostly hiccup, blurted out of the radio. Then Old Cal's voice: "O.K., lad. I'll find a way."

The radio went dead. Frantically Vickers tried to raise the old man, but only silence met his efforts.

Vickers bent to his chart, figured swiftly. Only a few miles now. Just a few minutes more to get there. He barreled the tractor savagely up over the spur, turned and flung it at an incline on which the treads spun crazily. But the machine, as if driven by the fierce will of the man at its wheel, moved ahead, protesting, groaning in every beam and plate. It reached the crest of the incline, charged, weaving and bobbing, over upended terrain.

The radio blatted hoarsely.

"I found a way," said Old Cal's voice. "Not much of a way, but maybe I can make it. A sort of trail leading down into the canyon. Looks like some bad turns and pretty narrow—"

"Wait," yelled Vickers. "Wait for me. You're drunk, you fool. You'll never make it. You'll crash."

"Who says I'm drunk?" demanded Cal. "I'm just stimulated. I'll do it better'n you could, sonny. I got—*blurp*—experience."

"Listen to me, Cal," snapped Vickers. "This is an order. You wait for me. I'm going down that trail. I have a chance to make it. You haven't."

"Your orders, mister, don't mean a tarnal damn to me," roared Cal. "Keep your radio open and keep a-coming. I'm going down into that canyon."

Vickers shouted at him, but there was no reply.

The ornery old fool! Vickers knew to a fraction how drunk he was. If he'd been walking, Cal's tracks would have been a sine wave. He'd never reach the bottom of that canyon alive.

Cal had reported before there was no way into the canyon. And now suddenly he had found a way. How did that happen? Was he sure it was a trail—not just a ledge that ran down part way and then snapped off—

He shrieked at the radio again, but only silence greeted him. He heard the hiss of rain against the tractor's hide, the grating of the skidding treads, the screaming of the wind in the passes just above, but that was all.

In the fan of light ahead, the four robots looked like weird goblins, their quartz-covered bodies shining, the deep-blue rain sluicing over them. A monstrous bolt of lightning split the sky and the surrounding landscape, and their bodies were painted a bloody red. Thunder bellowed with mountain-shaking violence.

Then suddenly the tractor was dipping down into a region of upflung topographic nightmare. Fantastic formations loomed in the gray dusk of the rain.

Vickers slowed his speed, wormed his way downward cautiously. He was nearing the canyon's rim, and he couldn't take a chance of overrunning it, flinging the tractor into the depths below.

Ahead of him the robots wheeled to right and left and waited. They had reached the rim.

Vickers stopped the tractor, took readings, found he had struck the canyon too high up the mountainside. Cautiously he edged his way along its edge.

The radio howled at him, loud and clear now: "I'm down, Vickers. Who said I was drunk? And what if I am, but I ain't. The robot is going after the *mercotite.*"

"Are you all right yourself, Cal?" Vickers yelled.

"Sure, kid. But hurry. Throw a line over the side and I'll send it up."

The tractor edged along, its beam flinging a spear of blinding light into the yawning depths.

That beam picked out another light far below, a crumpled mass of wreckage, a tiny form that scurried and ripped and tore at the wreckage.

Swiftly Vickers squared his tractor around. One of the robots grasped the end of the heavy cable wrapped around the drum in front of the tractor. Inside the tractor, Vickers depressed a stud that set the drum in motion.

The robot scurried forward, dropped over the edge of the rim, hanging to the cable. Another robot lowered itself over the edge, grasped the cable, rode down above the first.

"Got the first box out," reported Old Cal's voice. "Those robots just got down there. They'll help a lot."

Minutes passed, breathless minutes, that seemed to drag like eternity.

Then Old Cal's voice again. "Heave away, lad. First three boxes."

Vickers started the drum, used reverse power as an anchorage for the straining tractor. Swiftly the cable rolled in, and over the rim came three lashed metal boxes, ridden by a robot.

Down again and up again with three more boxes. And then three more. And then the final three. Twelve boxes of *mercotite!* Twelve boxes of life for the Hive and the men who lived within it! Twelve boxes of hope for the Solar System!

Old Cal's voice came again, fainter, as if from a long distance away.

"O.K., kid. Load up that stuff and hit for home. I'll be coming up in a little while, but don't wait for me."

Apprehension swept over Vickers.

"Look, Cal, are you sure you're all right?"

"Sure, everything's fine, kid." A long pause and then: "Listen, lad, something I want to tell you—something important. Still got a bottle of good Scotch hid out at the Hive."

There was a longer pause, and when the voice came it was scarcely more than a whisper.

"Up in the room next to the radio shack. No one goes there. Good place to hide it!"

"Cal!" shouted Vickers. "Cal, I can hardly hear you. What's the matter, old man? What's the trouble?"

The whisper, even fainter, was jerky, tremulous: "Maybe you'll want to drink a toast or something."

"Cal!" Vickers yelled. "Cal, answer me!"

But there was no answer. Just the wind screeching in the passes, the growl of thunder in the distant ranges, the hammer of the rain against the tractor's sides.

Savagely, fearfully, Vickers leaped at the controls, swung the machine around, hugging the rim, sweeping the walls with his beam.

Then he saw what he was looking for. A broad ledge, angling sharply downward, starting at the lip of the canyon and reaching far into the depths. But a ledge that broke off before reaching the bottom, a ledge that opened off on empty space. And directly below that blind, blank end lay the pile of wreckage that had been the *Jovian Ark.*

Down there, too, was another pile of wreckage—a pile of wreckage in which a man had lived long enough to accomplish a certain purpose. A man who had taken a chance. A chance his tractor would hold together for a few minutes after that plunge into the canyon. A chance that he himself would not be killed outright.

Vickers cursed softly to himself. He knew to a fraction how drunk Old Cal had been. He was just drunk enough to wabble like a cyclone when he walked, and, being of the breed that started exploring planets when planetary exploration started, he'd been driving explorer tractors the major portion of his lifetime, drunk and sober. He might wabble when he walked, but he'd still drive straighter than most sober men.

And he was just drunk enough to be highly incensed at the suggestion he was drunk, and absolutely determined to prove he wasn't drunk. And, of course, to have lost his sense of judgment. Only a nitwit would-be hero or a thorough and consistent souse like Cal would have thought for an instant that a tractor driven off that ledge, under Jupiter's gravity, would hold together long enough. The blasted machine should, by rights, have opened out like a dropped melon. Instead, the quartz protective layer had simply shattered off, leaving the metal to go a little later as the hydrogen of the atmosphere turned it into sugary-brittle iron hydride.

"Cal, you damned, drunken fool to do—"

The wind swooped down into the canyon, across its lip, and heaved a few hundred tons of ammonia rain on the wreckage with a howl of rage. The wreckage of the *Jovian Ark* didn't change; that was already completely flattened. The shape of the tractor over there, however, suddenly slumped a bit more, and abruptly turned a very deep and lovely blue in the glare of Vickers' lights. The ammonia had gotten into the copper wiring and was washing it out.

Vickers started back for the Hive. "We'll drink a toast," he growled, "but it will *not* be a toast to the *mercotite*. It'll be a toast to a shipping clerk, a little grounded shipping clerk back on Earth—and his speedy and very complete damnation."

SHADOW OF LIFE

———————

"Shadow of Life" is the earliest of three completely unrelated stories by Clifford D. Simak that carried the word "Shadow" in their titles; I think that means something, but I haven't figured out what. It was likely written in mid-1942, not long after the United States was attacked and dragged into World War II, and would be published in Astounding Science Fiction *in March 1943.*

Perhaps as a result of that timing, this story carries a terrible freight of despair, no doubt showing some of Cliff's reaction to the visions (perhaps more obvious to newspapermen of that time than to other civilians) of a world in which war, killing, and evil seemed to be everywhere. As if in a horrible dream sent by Cthulhu, Cliff saw in that moment a universe in which humanity alone seemed not to be bent on the road of war and evil, a cosmos in which an "elder evil" existed on the outer worlds; and the wonder is that he did not, at least in this story, consign humankind to that road, too.

—dww

The thing at the control board tittered in sardonic mockery.

"Your creeds are all in error," it said. "There is nothing but evil."

Stephen Lathrop said wearily: "I've seen enough."

"I've tried to show you the human race is something that never should have been," declared the thing. "Maybe an experiment that went sour. By some queer quirk it took the wrong step, followed the wrong path. It became benevolent. There is no room for benevolence in the Universe. It's not the accepted way of life. I think I've proven that."

"Why did you bother?" Lathrop demanded.

The thing regarded him with fishy eyes. "There was another race. A race that found the answer—"

"We'll find ours, too," growled the human being. "By the time they reach us we'll have the answer. We'll fight them in our own way."

"You can't fight them," said the thing. "There is no way to fight universal evil. The best you can do is hide from it."

The Earthman shrugged. "None of them will reach us for a long time. Now that we know about them, we'll be ready."

The thing at the controls concentrated on the setting of more studs, then said: "You'll never be ready. You're like a candle in the wind, waiting for a gust that will puff you out."

Through the vision plates Lathrop could see the harsh blackness of space, dotted here and there with unfamiliar stars, dusted with faint mists that were distant galaxies.

Somewhere, far back toward the center of the Universe, millions of light-years from where they cruised, lay the Milky Way, home galaxy of the planets that circled Helios.

Lathrop tried to think back the way they'd come, tried to think back to green Earth and red Mars, but time blurred the road of thought and other memories encroached, cold, fear-etched memories that reached for him like taloned, withered claws.

Memories of alien lands acrawl with loathsomeness and venom. Strange planets that were strange not because they were alien, but because of the abysmal terror in the very souls of them. Memories of shambling things that triumphed over pitiful peoples whose only crime was they could not fight back.

He shook his head, as if to shake the memories away, but they wouldn't go. He knew they would never go. They would always walk with him, would wake him screaming from his sleep.

They stayed now, those memories, and shrieked at him—rolling, clanging phrases that bit into his brain. Thundering the soul-searing saga of the elder evil that squatted on the outer worlds. Evil on the move, gobbling up the galaxies, marching down the star streams. Unnatural hungers driving sickening hordes across the gulfs of space to raven and to plunder.

Everything the human race held close, he knew, were alien traits to these races he had seen—not alien in the sense they were not recognized, but more terribly alien in that they could not be recognized. There was simply no place in the make-up of those hordes for the decency and love and loyalty that lay inherent in the people of the Earth. The creeds of Earth could never be their creeds—they could no more understand the attitude of the Earthman than the Earthman could understand their sense of rightness in total evil.

"I don't thank you for what you've done," Stephen Lathrop told the thing.

"I don't expect your thanks," the creature replied. "I've shown you the Universe, a cross section of it, enough so you can see what is in store for the human race."

"I didn't ask to see it," Lathrop said. "I didn't want to see it."

"Of course you didn't," said the thing.

"Why did you take me then?"

"The Earth must know," the thing declared. "The Earth must prepare for the day when this tide of evil moves into its planets."

"And I'm to tell them about it," Lathrop said bitterly. "I'm to become one of the Preachers. One of the Preachers of Evil. I'm to stand on soap boxes of the street corners of Earth. I'm to tramp the sands of Mars to bring the message. I'll be damned if I will do it."

"It would be a service to your race."

"A service to tell them they have to run and hide?" asked Lathrop. "You don't understand the human race. It doesn't hide. It just gets sore and wants to fight. And even if it did want to hide, where would it go?"

"There is a way," the thing persisted.

"Another one of your riddles," Lathrop said. "Trying to drive me mad with the things you hint at. I've gotten along with you. I've even tried to be friendly with you. But I've never reached you, never felt that as two living things we had anything in common. And that isn't right. Just the bare fact we are alive and alone should give us some sense of fellowship."

"You talk of things for which I have no word," the thing declared. "You have so many thoughts that are alien to me."

"Perhaps you understand hatred then?"

"Hatred," it said, "is a thing I know about."

Lathrop watched the creature narrowly as it labored over the control board, adjusting dials, thumbing over trips, pushing studs. His hands opened and closed—hands that were withered with approaching age, but hands that still had brutal strength left in them.

Finally the thing swung away from the board, chuckled faintly at him.

"We're going home," it said.

"Home to Mars?"

"That's right."

Lathrop laughed, a laugh that came between his teeth without curling his lips.

"The trip has been too long," he said. "You'll never get me back in time to do any preaching for you. We're millions of light-years from Mars. I'll die before we get there."

The thing flipped slithery tentacles. "We're close to Mars," it said. "Millions of light-years the long way around, of course, but close by the way I set the co-ordinates."

"The fourth dimension?" asked Lathrop, guessing at something he had long suspected.

"I cannot tell you that," the creature said.

Lathrop nodded at the board. "Automatic, I presume. All we have to do is sit and wait. It'll take us straight to Mars."

"Quite correct," the thing agreed.

"That," said Stephen Lathrop, "is all I want to know."

He rose casually, took a slow step forward, then moved swiftly. The thing grabbed frantically for the weapon in its belt, but was too slow. A single blow sent the weapon flying out of a squirming tentacle. The thing squealed pitifully, but there was no pity in Lathrop's hands. They squeezed the life, surely and methodically, out of the writhing, lashing, squealing body.

The Earthman stood on wide-spread legs and stared down at the sprawling mass.

"That," he said, "is for the years you took away from me. That is for making me grow old seeing things I wished I'd never seen. For never a moment of companionship when the sight of space alone nearly drove me mad."

He dusted his hands together, slowly, thoughtfully, as if he tried to scrub something from them. Then he turned on his heel and walked away.

Suddenly he put out one hand to touch the wall. His fingers pressed hard against it. It was really there. A solid, substantial, metal thing.

That settled it, he thought. Stephen Lathrop, archaeologist, really was inside this ship, had really seen the things that lay in outer space. Stephen Lathrop finally was going home to Mars.

Would Charlie still be there? His lips twisted a bit at the memory. Charlie must have hunted for him for a long time—and when he didn't find him, did he go back to the green Earth he always talked about, or did he return to the city site to carry on the work they had done together? Or might Charlie have died? It would be funny—and hard—to go back to Mars and not have Charlie there.

He pressed his hand hard against the metal once again, just to be sure. It still was there, solid and substantial.

He turned back to look at the dead thing on the floor.

"I wish," he said wistfully, "I'd found out what it was."

* * *

Dr. Charles H. Carter knew he had done a good job. The book was a little dogmatic here and there, perhaps, a little anxious to prove his hypothesis—but after a man had dug and burrowed in the midden heaps of Mars for over twenty years he had a right to be a bit dogmatic.

He picked up the last page of the manuscript and read it over again:

There is, I am convinced, good reason to believe the Martian race may not be extinct, although where it is or why it went there is a question we cannot answer on the basis of our present knowledge.

Perhaps the strongest argument to be advanced in support of the contention the Martians still may be extant is that same situation which has held our knowledge of them to a minimum—the absolute lack of literature and records. Despite extensive search, nothing approaching a Martian library has been found.

That a people, regardless of the manner in which their extinction came about, either slowly and only through final defeat by a long-fought danger, or swiftly by some quickly-striking force, should be able or should wish to destroy or conceal all records seems unlikely. Even if the wish had been present, the exigencies of fighting for survival would have made it difficult of accomplishment. In any event, it would seem far more logical that a people, faced with extinction, would have made every effort to leave behind them some enduring record which might at least save their name from the annihilation which they themselves knew they were about to suffer. The better supposition, it would seem, is that the Martians went somewhere and took their records with them.

Nor do we find in the architecture or the art of Mars any hint of a situation which may have ended in the extinction of the race. That the Martians must have realized their planet was not equipped for the continued support of large populations is shown by many trends in art, particularly the symbolism of the water jug. But nowhere is there evidence of any violent, overshadowing danger. Martian art and architecture pursue, throughout their many periods, a natural development that reflects nothing more than the steady growth of a mature civilization.

It is regrettable more cannot be learned from that unique residuary personality, popularly called the Martian Ghost, still residing within the one Martian city which appears to be of comparatively recent date. In my contacts with the Ghost I have received the definite impression that he, if he wished, might provide the key we seek, that he might furnish definite information concerning the present whereabouts and condition of the Martian race. But in dealing with the Ghost one deals with a form of life which has no parallel in modern knowledge, with understanding further complicated by the fact that it is in substance the image of an alien mind.

Carter laid the page down on his desk, reached for his pipe.

The metallic thing that squatted in one corner of the study moved slightly.

"I take it, doctor, that your work is done," it said.

Carter started, then settled back, tamped tobacco in his pipe.

"I'd almost forgotten about you, Buster," he told the robot. "You sit so still."

The man stared out of the window-port that framed the wild, red emptiness of Mars. Fine, weatherworn sand that whispered when one walked. Off to the left the fantastic towers of harder rock which had resisted the forces that had leveled down the planet. To the right the faintest hint of spires and turreted battlements—the Martian city where dwelt Elmer, the Martian Ghost. Nearer at hand the excavations where twenty years of digging and sifting and studying had netted a pitiful handful of facts about the Martian race—facts that lay within the pages of the manuscript piled on his desk.

"No, Buster," he said, "my work isn't done here. I'm only quitting it. Someone will come along some day and take up where I left off. Perhaps I should stay—but these have been lonely years. I'm running away from loneliness and I am afraid I won't succeed. I've been on the verge of it many times before. But something kept me here—the knowledge it was not only my work I was doing, but someone else's work as well."

"Dr. Lathrop's work," rasped Buster's thoughts.

Carter nodded.

Twenty years ago Steve Lathrop had dropped out of sight. Carter could remember perfectly the morning Steve had left for the little outpost of Red Rocks to get supplies. Each detail of that morning seemed etched into his consciousness. During those intervening years he had lived it over and over again, almost minute by minute, trying to unearth even the tiniest incident that might be a clue. But there had never been a clue. Stephen Lathrop, to all intent and purpose, simply had walked off the face of Mars, vanished without a trace. He had left to get supplies; he had never returned. That, in itself, was the beginning and the end. That was all there was.

Soon he would have to start packing, Carter knew. The manuscript was finished. His notes were all in order. All but a few of the specimens were labeled, ready for packing. The laborers had been discharged. As soon as Alf came back, they would have to get to work. Alf had gone to town three days before and hadn't returned—but that was nothing unusual. Somehow, Carter could feel no irritation toward Alf. After all, an occasion such as this, the end of twenty years of labor, called for a spree of some sort.

The last rays of the setting sun streamed into the window and splashed across the room, lighting up and bringing out the color of the collection of Martian water jugs ranged along the wall. Not a very extensive collection when measured against some of those gathered by professional collectors, but a collection that brought warmth into Carter's soul. Those jugs, in a way, represented the advance of Martian culture, starting with the little lopsided jug over on the left up to the massive symbolic piece of art that marked the peak of the jug cult's development. Jugs from every part of Mars, brought to him by the scrawny, bewhiskered old jug hunters who ranged the deserts in their everlasting search, always hopeful, always confident, always dreaming of the day when they would find the jug that would make them rich.

"Elmer has a guest," said Buster. "Maybe I should be getting back home. Elmer might need me."

"A guest, eh," said Carter, mildly surprised. Elmer had few visitors. At one time the city of the Martian Ghost had been on the itinerary of every tourist, but of late the government had been clamping down. Visitors upset Elmer and inasmuch as Elmer held what amounted to diplomatic status, there was little else the government could do. Occasionally scientists dropped in on Elmer or art students were allowed to spend a short time studying the paintings in the city—the only extensive list of Martian canvases in existence.

"A painter," said Buster. "A painter with pink whiskers. He has a scholarship from one of the academies out on Earth. His name is Harper. He's especially interested in 'The Watchers.'"

Carter knew about "The Watchers," a disturbing, macabre canvas. There was something about its technique that almost turned it alive—as if the artist had mixed his pigments with living fear and horror.

The radiophone on the desk burred softly, almost apologetically. Carter thumbed a tumbler and the ground glass lighted up, revealing a leathery face decorated by a yellow, walruslike mustache, outsize ears and pair of faded blue eyes.

"Hello, Alf," said Carter genially. "Where are you? Expected you back several days ago."

"So help me, doc," said Alf, "they got me in the clink."

"What for this time?" asked Carter, figuring that he knew. Tales of the doings of an alcoholic Alf were among Red Rocks' many legends.

"A bit of jug hunting," Alf confessed, whuffling his mustache.

Carter could see that Alf was fairly sober. His faded eyes were a bit watery, but that was all.

"The Purple Jug again, I suppose," said Carter.

"That's just exactly what it was," said Alf, trying to sound cheerful. "You wouldn't want a fellow to pass up a fortune, would you?"

"The Purple Jug's a myth," said Carter, with a touch of bitterness. "Something someone thought up to get guys like you in trouble. There never was a Purple Jug."

"But Elmer's robot gave me the tip," wailed Alf. "Told me just where to go."

"Sure, I know," said Carter. "Sent you out into the badlands. Worst country on all of Mars. Straight up and down and full of acid bugs. No one's ever found a jug there. No one ever will. Even when the Martians were here, the badlands probably were a wilderness. No one in his right mind, not even a Martian, would live there and you only find jugs where someone has lived."

"Look," yelped Alf, "you don't mean to tell me Buster was playing a joke on me? Those badlands ain't no joke. The acid bugs darn near got my sand buggy and I almost broke my neck three or four times. Then along came the cops and nailed me. Said I was trespassing on Elmer's reservation."

"Certainly Buster was playing a joke on you," said Carter. "He gets bored sitting around and not having much to do. Fellows like you are made to order for him."

"That little whippersnapper can't do this to me," howled Alf. "You wait until I get my hands on him. I'll break him down into a tinker toy."

"You won't be getting your hands on anyone for thirty days or so unless I can talk you out of this," Carter reminded him. "Is the sheriff around?"

"Right here," said Alf. "Told him you'd probably want a word with him. Do the best you can for me."

* * *

Alf's face faded out of the ground glass and the sheriff's came in, a heavy, florid face, but the face of a harassed man.

"Sorry about Alf, doc," he said, "but I'm getting sick and tired of running the boys off the reservation. Thought maybe clapping some of them in jail might help. This reservation business is all damn foolishness, of course, but a law's a law."

"I don't blame you," Carter said. "The Preachers alone are enough to run you ragged."

The sheriff's florid face became almost apoplectic. "Them Preachers," he confided, "are the devil's own breed. Keeping the people stirred up all the time with their talk of evil from the stars and all such crazy notions. Earth's getting tough about it, too. All of them seem to come from Mars and they're riding us to find out how they get that way."

"Just jug hunters gone wacky," declared Carter. "Wandering around in the dessert they get so they talk to themselves and after that anything can happen."

The sheriff wagged his head. "Not so sure about that, doc. They talk pretty convincing—almost make me believe them sometimes. If they're crazy, it's a queer way to go crazy—all of them alike. All of them tell the same story—all of them got a funny look in their eyes."

"How about Alf, sheriff?" asked Carter. "He's my right-hand man and I need him now. Lots of work to do, getting ready to leave."

"Maybe I can stretch a point," said the sheriff, "long as you put it that way. I'll see the district attorney."

"Thanks, sheriff," said Carter. The ground glass clouded and went dead as the connection was snapped at the other end.

The archaeologist swung around slowly from his desk.

"Buster," he challenged, "why did you do that to Alf? You know there is no Purple Jug."

"You accuse me falsely," said Buster. "There is a Purple Jug."

Carter laughed shortly. "It's no use, Buster. You can't get me all steamed up to look for it."

He rose and stretched. "It's time for me to eat," he said. "Would you like to come along and talk with me?"

"No," said the robot. "I'll just sit here and think. I thought of something that will amuse me for a while. I'll see you later."

But when Carter came back, Buster was gone. So was the manuscript that had been lying on the desk. Drawers of filing cases that lined one side of the room had been pried open. The floor was littered with papers, as if someone had pawed through them hurriedly, selecting the ones he wanted, leaving the rest.

Carter stood thunderstruck, hardly believing what he saw. Then he sprang across the room, searched hastily, a sickening realization growing on him.

All the copies of his manuscript, all his notes, all his key research data were gone.

There was no doubt Buster had robbed him. And that meant Elmer had robbed him, for Buster was basically no more than an extension of Elmer, a physical agent for Elmer. Buster was the arms and legs and metallic muscles of a thing that had no arms or legs or muscles.

And Elmer, having robbed him, wanted him to know he had. Buster deliberately had set the stage for suspicion to point him out.

Charles Carter sat down heavily in the chair before his desk, staring at the papers on the floor. And through his brain rang one strident, mocking phrase:

"Twenty years of work. Twenty years of work."

The mistiness that hung among the ornamental girders swirled uneasily with fear. Not the old, ancestral fear that always moved within its being, but a newer, sharper fear. Fear born of the knowledge it had made mistakes—not one alone, but two. And might make a third.

The Earth people, it knew, were clever, far too clever. They guessed too closely. They followed up their guesses with investigation. And they were skeptical. That was the worst of all, their skepticism.

It had taken them many years to recognize and accept him for what he really was—the residual personality of the ancient Martian race. Even now there were those who did not quite believe.

Fear was another thing. The Earthlings knew no fear. Quick, personal glimpses of it undoubtedly they knew. Perhaps even at times a widespread fear might seize them, although only temporarily. As a race they were incapable of the all-obliterating terror that lay forever on the consciousness of Elmer, the Martian Ghost.

But there were some, apparently, who could not comprehend even personal fear, whose thirst for knowledge superseded the acknowledgment of danger, who saw in danger a scientific enigma to be studied rather than a thing to flee.

Stephen Lathrop, Elmer knew, was one of these.

Elmer floated, a cloudy thing that sometimes looked like smoke and then like wispy fog and then again like something one couldn't quite be sure was even there.

He had known he was making a mistake with Lathrop, but at the time it had seemed the thing to do. Such a man, reacting favorably, would have been valuable.

But the result had not been favorable. Elmer knew that much now, knew it in a sudden surge of fear, knew he should have known it twenty years before. But one, he told himself, cannot always be sure when dealing with an alien mind. Earthmen, after all, were newcomers to the planet. A few centuries counted for nothing in the chronology of Mars.

It was unfair that a Ghost be left to make decisions. Those others could not expect him to be infallible. He was nothing more than a blob of ancestral memories, the residue of a race, the pooling of millions of personalities. He was nothing one could prove. He was hardly life at all—just the shadow of a life that had been, the echo of voices stilled forever in the silence of millennia.

Elmer floated gently toward the room below, his mind reaching out toward the brain of the man sitting there. Softly, almost furtively, he sought to probe into the mental processes of the pink-whiskered artist. A froth of ideas, irrelevant thoughts, detached imagining, and then—a blank wall.

Elmer recoiled, terror seizing him again, a wild wave of unreasoning apprehension. It was the same as it had been the many previous times he had tried to reach this mind. Something must be hidden behind that unyielding barrier, something he must know. Never before had there been an Earthman's mind he could not read. Never before had his groping thoughts been blocked. It was baffling—and terrifying.

Mistakes! The idea hammered at him remorselessly. First the mistake with Lathrop. Now this—another mistake. He never should have allowed Peter Harper to come, despite the recommendations of the Earthian embassy, the unquestioned references of the college out on Earth. He would have had right and precedent in such refusal. But he had allowed hundreds of art students and art lovers to view his canvases—to have refused Harper might have aroused suspicion.

The awful idea he was being made the victim of an Earthian plot surged up within him, but he rejected it fiercely. Earthmen never had plotted against him, always made it a meticulous point of honor to accede to all his wishes, to grant him, as the last representative of a great race, considerations over and above those to which his diplomatic status entitled him.

Peter Harper said: "Elmer, your people may have been greater than we know. That painting"—he gestured toward "The Watchers"—"is something no Earthman has the technique to produce."

Elmer's thoughts milled muddily, panic edging in on him. Other Earthmen had said the same thing, but there was a difference. He could read their minds and know they meant what they said.

"You could help us, Elmer," Harper said. "I've often wondered why you haven't."

"Why should I?" Elmer asked.

"Brother races," the man explained. "The Martians and the Earthmen. Your race, whatever happened to them, wouldn't want to keep their knowledge from us."

"I do not have the knowledge of the Martian race." Elmer's thoughts were curt.

"You have some of it. The fourth dimension, for example. Think of what we could do with that. A surgeon could go inside his patient and fix him up without a single knife stroke. We could press a button and go a million miles."

"Then what?" asked Elmer.

"Progress," said Harper. "Certainly you must understand that. Man was Earth-bound. Now he has reached the planets. He's already reaching toward the stars."

"Maybe when you reach the stars you won't like what you find," Elmer declared. "Maybe you'll find things you'd wish you left alone."

Harper grinned and pawed at his pink chin whiskers.

"You're an odd one," he said.

"To you," Elmer said, "the word is 'alien.'"

"Not exactly," declared Harper. "We had things like you back on Earth, only no one except old women believed in them. They were just something to talk about on stormy nights when the wind whistled down the chimney. We called them ghosts, but we never would admit that they were real. Probably ours weren't really real, sort of feeble ghosts, just the beginning of ghosts."

"They never had a chance," said Elmer.

"That's right," Harper agreed. "As a race, we haven't lived long enough. We seldom stay in one place long enough to allow it to soak up the necessary personality. There are a few rather shadowy ghosts in some of the old castles and manor houses in Europe, maybe a few in Asia, but that's about all. The Americans were apartment dwellers, moved every little while or so. A ghost would get started in one pattern and then would have to change over again. I suspect that was at least discouraging, if not fatal."

"I wouldn't know," said Elmer.

"With the Martians, of course, it was different," went on Harper. "Your people lived in their cities for thousands of years, perhaps millions of years. The very stones of the place fairly dripped with personality—the accumulated personality of billions of people—that whatever-you-call-it that stays behind. No wonder the Martian Ghosts got big and tough—"

Metallic feet clicked along the corridor outside. A door opened and Buster rolled in.

"Dr. Carter is here," he said.

"Oh, yes," said Elmer, "he wants to see me about a manuscript."

There was no way to get out. Stephen Lathrop now was convinced of that. Elmer's city, so far as he was concerned, might just as well have been in the depths of space.

In the three days which had passed since he had stumbled in off the desert, he had searched the place methodically. The central spire had been his last chance. But even before he climbed the stairs he knew it was no chance at all. When Elmer decided to make the place a rattrap, he really made it one.

A web of force surrounded the entire city, extending three feet or so from the outer surfaces. Doors would open, so would windows. But that meant nothing, for one could go no farther.

Buster apparently had given up trying to stalk him. Now, it appeared, the game had settled to a deadlock. Buster didn't dare to tackle him so long as he had the weapon and he, on the other hand, couldn't leave the city. Elmer probably had decided on starving him out.

Lathrop knew, deep within him, that he was licked, but that knowledge still was something he would not admit. In the end, logic told him, he would give up, let Elmer wipe out the memory of those twenty years in space, replace them with synthetic memories. Under different circumstances, he might have welcomed such a course, for the things he had seen were not pleasant to remember—certainly Elmer could supply him with a more pleasant past. But the proposition was too highhanded to be accepted without a fight, without at least a struggle to maintain his right to order his own life. Then, too, there was the feeling that if he lost the knowledge of the outer worlds he would be losing something the Earth might need, the opportunity to approach the problem scientifically rather than hysterically, as the Preachers approached it.

He sat down heavily on a step, pulled the weapon from his belt and held it, dangling from a hand that rested on his knee. Although there had been no sign of Buster for a long time, there was no telling when the robot might pop up and once Buster laid a tentacle on him, the game was over.

The weapon as not easy to grip. It was not made for human hands, although its operation was apparent—simply press the button on the side. He shifted it in his hand and studied it. Had it not been for the weapon, he knew, there were times when he would have been tempted to write off that trip through space as the product of an irrational mind.

But there the weapon was, a familiar, tangible thing. For years he had seen it dangling from the belt of the thing that piloted the ship. Even now he remembered how it had flashed in the light from the instrument panel as he knocked it from the grasp of the being, then closed in to make his kill.

He didn't know what the weapon was, but Buster knew and Buster wasn't coming near it.

It was increasingly hard, he found, to continue thinking of the creature of the spaceship as merely a "thing," as something that had no identity, but he knew that despite mounting suspicion, he must continue to think of it as such or give way to illogic.

There was, he knew, good reason to suspect it might have been a member of the old Martian race, although that, he told himself, would be sheer madness. The Martian race was dead.

And yet, Elmer without a doubt had played some part in placing him aboard the ship—and who else but the Martian race would Elmer be in league with? That Elmer had believed, as did the thing, that he would become one of the Preachers of Evil, was evident. That his refusal to so become had enraged Elmer was equally apparent.

Elmer, of course, had taken steps which ordinarily would have protected him against being linked with the junket in space. The Preachers probably did not even dream Elmer had anything to do with their experiences.

For the hundredth time, Lathrop forced his thoughts back along the trail to that interval between the moment he had left the excavation site until the moment he had found himself aboard the spaceship. But the blank still existed—a black, tantalizing lack of memory. Whatever had transpired in that interval had been wiped clean from his brain. He knew now Elmer had done that, hadn't bothered to supply him with fictitious memories to fill in the gap.

Granting, however, that Elmer was engineering the indoctrination of the Preachers, what could be his purpose? Why did he bother about it? What possible interest could he have in whether the human race knew of the evil that existed in the outer worlds—why be so insistent that the race hide from the danger rather than fight it? There was illogic somewhere—perhaps a racial illogic, a wrong way of thinking.

Another funny thing. What had happened to the ship? Of all the incredible happenings, that had been the most insane.

The creature had been right about the ship being automatic.

Snicking, whispering controls had driven it back to Mars in a few weeks' time, had brought it down to a bumpy landing not more than a mile from Elmer's city. That, Lathrop knew, could be explained by engineering—but there was no explanation, no logic in what had happened when he left the ship and walked away.

The craft had shrunk, dwindling until it was almost lost in the sand, until it was no more than an inch or so in length. Lying there, it glistened like a crystal on the desert floor. Then it had shot upward, like a homing bee. Lathrop remembered ducking as it whizzed past his head, remembered watching it, a tiny speck that streaked straight toward the Martian city until he lost it in the glare of the setting sun.

That shrinking must have been automatic, too. There was no hand inside the ship to activate controls. Perhaps the action had become automatic when he opened the port to leave.

Starlight spattered through the narrow portholes in the spire and Lathrop shivered inside his space gear. It was cold there in the tower, for this part of the city was not conditioned against the Martian atmosphere as were some other portions, a concession for Earthly visitors.

From far below came a distant thud of metal striking metal, a rhythmic, marching sound that seemed to climb toward him. Lathrop sat, gun dangling from his knee, starlight sparkling on his helmet, brain buzzing with mystery. Suddenly, he sat erect, tense—that thudding sound was something climbing up the frosty stairs. He waited, wondering what new move might be afoot, realized with a twinge of terror that he was trapped here on the upper step.

Thought calls reached his brain. "Dr. Lathrop, are you up there? Dr. Lathrop!"

"I'm up here, Buster," he called back. "What's eating you?"

"Elmer wants to see you."

Lathrop laughed, said nothing.

"But he really does," insisted the robot. "There's an old friend of yours with him. Dr. Carter."

"It's a trap," said Lathrop. "You ought to think up a better one than that."

"Aw, doc, forget it," pleaded Buster. "It isn't any trap. Carter's really down there."

"What's he there for?" snapped Lathrop. "What's Elmer got against him?"

"He wrote a book—"

Buster's thoughts broke off in wild confusion.

"So he wrote a book."

"Look, doc, I shouldn't have said that," whined Buster. "I wasn't supposed to say it. You caught me unawares."

"You should have made me believe Charlie was down there, all chummy with Elmer, waiting to talk me out of my foolishness. Elmer will chalk one up on you for this."

"Elmer doesn't need to know," suggested Buster. The footsteps stopped. The tower swam in silence.

"I'll think about it," Lathrop finally said. "But I'm not promising anything. If I had a robot that tried to hide things from me, I'd junk him in a hurry."

"Aren't you going to come down, doc?"

"Nope," said Lathrop. "You come up. I'm waiting for you. I have the gun ready. I won't stand for any monkey business."

The footsteps started again, slowly, reluctantly. They climbed for a long minute, then stopped again.

"Doc," said Buster.

"Yes, what is it?"

"You won't hurt me, doc. I got to bring you in this time. Elmer isn't fooling."

"Neither am I," said Lathrop.

The thudding began again, came closer and closer, the frosty steps ringing to the heavy tread of the climbing robot. Buster's bulk heaved itself up the last flight, moved out onto the landing. Facing the stairs, Buster stood waiting, his crystal lenses staring at the man.

"So you came to get me," Lathrop said. He flipped the gun's muzzle at Buster and chuckled.

"You have to come, doc," said Buster. "You just have to come."

"I'll come," said Lathrop, "but first you're going to talk. You're going to tell me a lot of things I need to know."

A flood of protest washed out from Buster's electronic brain. "I can't," he wailed. "I can't!"

Lathrop leveled the gun, his gloved finger covering the button. His eyes grew steellike in the light from the stars.

"Why has Elmer got Charlie?" he demanded. "What did he say in that book?"

Buster hesitated. From where he sat, the Earthman could sense the confusion that tore him.

"O.K.," said Lathrop calmly, "I'll have to let you have it."

"Wait!" shrieked Buster. "I'll tell you!"

His thought-words were tumbling over one another. "Dr. Carter said the Martians might be still alive. Elmer doesn't like that. He doesn't want anyone to even think they're still alive."

"Are they?" snapped Lathrop.

"Yes. Yes, they're still alive. But they aren't here. They're someplace else. They went into another world. They were afraid of the things from outer space. So they made themselves small. Too small to be of any consequence. They reasoned that when the Evil Beings came they would pass right by them, never even guess that they were there."

"The thing that took me out in space was a Martian, then?"

"Yes, they come out of their world, get big again, to take Earthmen out in space. To show them the evil out there, convince them they cannot fight it, hoping they, too, will do what the Martians did."

Lathrop was silent, reflecting, trying to straighten out his mind. At the bottom of the stairs, Buster fidgeted.

"But, Buster, why do they do this? Why don't they let us find out about these things in our own good time? Why don't they let us work out our own salvation? Why do they insist on us following in their footsteps?"

"Because," said Buster, "they know that they are right."

So that was it. A strait-laced dogmatism that in itself portrayed the character and the nature of the Martian race. His guess concerning Elmer's motives then were right, Lathrop knew. The wrong way of thought. A racial illogic that denied there might be many paths to truth. Coupled, perhaps, with an overdeveloped sense of rigid duty to fellow races. There were Earthly parallels.

"Busybodies," Lathrop summed it up.

"What was that?" asked Buster.

"Skip it," Lathrop told him. "It doesn't matter. You wouldn't understand."

"There are many things," said Buster, sadly, "that I don't understand. Maybe Elmer does, but I don't think he does. It doesn't bother him. That's because he's a Ghost and I'm only a robot. You see, he's sure he's right. I can't be sure. I wish I could be. It would make things easier."

The Earthman grinned at the robot, flipped the gun.

"You Earthmen think differently," Buster went on. "Your minds are limber. You never say a thing is right until you've proven it. You never say a thing's impossible until you've proven that. And one right, so far as you are concerned, isn't the only right. To you it doesn't matter how you do a thing just so you get it done."

"That, Buster," said Lathrop gently, "is because we're a young race. We haven't gotten hidebound yet. Age may give a race a different viewpoint, an arrogant, unswerving viewpoint that makes it hard to get at truth. The Martians should come to us straightforward, explain the situation. They shouldn't try to propagandize us. The human race, from bitter experience, hates propaganda, can spot it a mile away. That's why we're suspicious of the Preachers, make things so tough for them."

"The Martians don't trust you," Buster said. "You take over things."

Lathrop nodded. It was, he realized, a legitimate criticism.

"They're a cautious people," Buster went on. "Caution played a part in the course they took. They wanted to be sure, you see. When the future of the race was at stake, they couldn't take a chance. Now they're afraid of the human race—not because of what it can do now, but what it might do later. And still they know you are the closest to them, in thought and temperament, of any peoples in the Universe. They feel that for that reason they should help you."

"Look, Buster," said Lathrop, "you told me they became small. You mean they went into a subatomic universe?"

"Yes," said Buster. "They found a principle. It was based on the fourth dimension."

"What has the fourth dimension got to do with being small?"

"I don't know," said Buster.

Lathrop got to his feet. "All right," he said. "We'll see Elmer now."

He moved slowly down the stairs, the weapon dangling from a hand that swung by his side. Below, Buster waited, meekly.

Suddenly Buster moved, straight up the stairs, charging with tentacles flailing. Lathrop jerked back, retreating before the rush. For a fumbling moment he held his breath as he brought up the clumsy gun and pressed the button.

A tentacle slammed against his shoulder and knocked him sidewise even as he fired. He brought up against the stone wall of the staircase with a jolt, the gun still hissing in his hand.

For an instant Buster halted as the faint blue radiance from the weapon spattered on his armor, then tottered, half fell, regained erectness with an effort. Slowly at first, then with a rush, he began to shrink—as if he were falling in upon himself.

Lathrop lifted his finger from the button, lowered the gun. Buster was trying to scramble up the steps, still trying to get at him, but the stairs now were too high for him to negotiate.

In stricken silence, Lathrop watched him grow smaller and smaller, just as the spaceship had grown smaller out there on the desert.

Thrusting the gun back into his belt, Lathrop knelt on the stairs and watched the frantic running of the tiny robot, running as if he were trying to escape from something, trapped by his very smallness on a single tread.

Buster was no more than two inches tall, seemed to be growing no smaller. Gently, Lathrop reached down and picked him up. He shuddered as he held the robot in his hand.

Buster, he knew, had almost succeeded in his purpose, had almost captured him. Had lulled him to sleep by his almost human attributes, by his seeming friendliness. Perhaps Buster had figured out it was the only way to get him.

He lifted his hand until it was level with his face. Buster waved stubby tentacles at him.

"You almost did it, chum," said Lathrop.

A feeble thought piped back at him: "You wait until Elmer gets at you!"

Lathrop said grimly: "I have Elmer where I want him now."

He tucked the squirming Buster carefully in a pocket and started down the stairs.

Outside the door that had been locked to keep him in, Peter Harper carefully checked himself. His beard, he decided, was just a shade too red. He concentrated on it and the beard grew pink.

"The fools!" he hissed in contempt at the still-locked door.

His body, he knew, was all right—just as it had been before. But his mind was in a mess. Standing rigidly, he sought to smooth it into pattern, forcing it into human channels, superimposing upon it the philosophy he hated.

All this, he told himself, world be over soon. The end of his mission finally was in sight—the mission he had worked so hard to carry out.

Footsteps were coming down the corridor and Harper forced himself to relax. He fumbled in his jacket packet for a cigarette, was calmly lighting it as Stephen Lathrop, still clad in space gear, came around the corner.

"You must be Harper," Lathrop said. "I heard that you were here."

"Just for a time," said Harper. "Studying the canvases."

"You are lucky. Not many people have that chance."

"Lucky. Oh, yes. Very lucky." Harper rolled the phrases on his tongue.

Lathrop crinkled his nose. "Do you smell anything?" he asked.

Harper took the cigarette from between his lips. "It might be this. It's not a usual brand."

Lathrop shook his head. "Couldn't be. Just caught a whiff. Like something dead."

Lathrop's eyes swept the man from head to foot, widened a bit at the alarming whiskers.

"The beard is quite natural, I assure you," Harper declared.

"I do not doubt it," Lathrop said. "You should wear a purple tie."

Without another word, he wheeled and tramped away. Harper watched him go.

"Purple tie!" spat Harper. Hate twisted his face.

Buster scurried back and forth across the table top, tiny feet beating out a frenzied minor patter.

"There is no use in arguing," Elmer said. "This talk of Earthmen co-operating with the Martians is impossible. It would never work. They'd be at one another's throats before they were acquainted. You, Lathrop, killed the Martian out in space. There was no provocation. You simply murdered him."

"He got in my hair," said Lathrop. "He'd been in it for almost twenty years."

"That's what I mean," said Elmer. "If the two races could get along, they'd be unbeatable. But they couldn't get along. They'd grate on one another's nerves. You have no idea the gulf that separates them—not so much the gulf of knowledge, for that could be bridged, nor a lack of co-operation, for the Martians know that as well as the race of Earth, but temperamentally they would be poles apart."

Carter nodded, understandingly: "They'd be old fossils and we'd be young squirts."

"But we could work at long range," insisted Lathrop. "They could stay in their subatomic world, we could stay where we are. Elmer could act as the go-between."

"Impossible," Carter argued. "There is the time angle to consider. A few days for us must be a generation for them. Everything would be speeded up in their world—even the rate of living. The time factor would be basically different. We could not co-ordinate our effort."

"I see," said Lathrop. He tapped his fingers on the table top. Buster scurried to the other side, as far as he could get from the tapping fingers.

Lathrop shot a quick glance at Elmer. "Where does that leave us?"

"Just where we started," Elmer said. "You've made Buster useless to me, but that is of little matter. Another robot can be sent me."

"Maybe Buster will grow up again," Lathrop suggested.

Elmer was in no mood for jokes. "You have the weapon," he went on, "But that is worthless against me. With Buster gone, you have cheated yourself out of a quick death in case you refuse to have your memories replaced. But that is inconsequential, too. I can let you starve."

"What a happy soul you are!" said Carter, dryly.

"I suppose I should say I regret the situation," Elmer said. "But I don't. You must understand I can't let you go. In order that the Martian plan may go on, the knowledge you hold must never reach your race. For once your race knew the Martians were alive, they would find a way to ferret them out."

"And," suggested Lathrop, "the Evil Beings must continue to be something mystic, something not quite real, something for fools to believe in."

Elmer was frank. "That is right. For if your people knew the truth they would take direct action. And that would be wrong. One cannot fight the Evil Ones, one can only hide."

"How are you so sure?" snapped Carter.

"The Martians," said Elmer, solemnly, "exhausted every other possibility. They proved there could be no other way."

Lathrop chuckled in his corner. "There is one thing you have forgotten, Elmer."

"What is that?"

"Harper," said Lathrop. "What are you going to do about Harper?"

"Harper," declared Elmer, "will leave here in a few days. He will never know what happened. Not even that you were here."

"Oh, yes, he will," said Lathrop. "I just talked to him. On my way to see you."

Elmer writhed uneasily. "That's impossible. Buster locked him in his room."

"Locks," declared Lathrop, "don't mean a thing to Harper."

Carter started at the tone of Lathrop's voice. "What do you mean?" he asked.

"Harper," Lathrop started to say, "is a—" but a scream from the next room cut him short. A scream followed by the snickering of a blaster.

The two men sprang to their feet, stood in breathless silence. Elmer was a streak of fog flashing through the air.

"Come on!" yelled Lathrop. Together the two humans followed Elmer, who had faded through the door.

Starlight from the tall windows lit the other room with spangled light and shade. In it figures moved, unreal figures, like trick photography on a stereovision screen.

Beside one of the windows stood a man, blaster at his hip. Advancing upon him, crouching like a beast of prey stalking food, was another man. The smell of burned flesh tainted the room as the blaster whispered.

Something had happened to the painting of "The Watchers." It had swung on a pivot in its center, revealing behind it a cavern of blackness. Starlight was shattered by a glinting object that stood within the darkness.

The man who held the blaster was talking, talking in a baffled, ferocious, savage undertone, talking to the thing that advanced upon him, a rattle of words that had no meaning, half profanity, half pure terror, all bordering on madness.

"Alf!" shrieked Carter. But Alf didn't seem to hear him, went on talking. The thing that stalked him, however, swung about, huddled for an indecisive instant.

"Light!" yelled Lathrop. "Turn on those lights!"

He heard Carter fumbling in the darkness, hunting for the switch. Scarcely breathing, he stood and waited, the Martian weapon in his hand.

The man in the center of the room was shambling toward him now, but he knew he didn't dare to shoot until the lights were on. He had to be sure what happened.

The switch clicked and Lathrop blinked in the sudden flood of light. Before him crouched Peter Harper, clothes ripped to smoldering ribbons, face half eaten away by the blaster, one arm gone—crouching as if to spring.

Lathrop snapped the weapon up, pressed the button. The blue radiance flamed out, bored into Peter Harper.

There was no shrinking this time. The spear of blue seemed to slam the man back on the floor and pin him there. He writhed and blurred and ran together. The clothes were gone, the eaten face, with the scraggly, pink whiskers disappeared. Instead came taloned claws and a face that had terrible eyes and a parrot beak. A thing that mewed and howled and yammered. A thing that struggled in vicious convulsions and melted—melted and stank.

Carter stared in horror, hand covering his nose. Lathrop released the pressure on the trip, held the gun alertly.

"One of those things from space," he said, his voice tense and hard. "One of the Evil Beings."

Alf staggered down the room, like a drunken man.

"I just climbed through the window," he mumbled. "I just climbed through the window—"

"How did you get in here?" Carter yelled at him. "Elmer has the city screened."

"The screen," said Elmer's thoughts, "works only one way. It keeps you in, it doesn't keep you out."

Carter turned his attention to the mess upon the floor, trying not to gag. "He wanted something," he said. "He came for something."

"He came because he was afraid," Lathrop declared. "There is something here those races are afraid of. Something they had to get at and destroy."

Alf grabbed at Carter's arm. "Charlie," he whimpered, "tell me if it's true. Maybe I'm drunk. Maybe I got them D.T.'s again."

Carter jerked away. "What's the matter with you, Alf?" he snapped.

"The Purple Jug," gasped Alf. "So help me, it's the Purple Jug."

They saw it then.

The Purple Jug was the thing that had stood in the cavern back of "The Watchers." It was the thing that had shattered the starlight.

It was a thing of beauty, of elegance and grace. A piece of art that snatched one's breath away, that made a hurt rise in the throat and strangle one.

"It wasn't like you said," Alf accused Carter. "It wasn't just a myth."

Something flashed above the jug's narrow lip, a silvery streak that struck fire with the light and soared like a burnished will-o'-

the-wisp out into the room. Something that swelled and grew—grew until it was fist size and one could see it was a tiny space craft.

"One of the Martian ships!" yelled Lathrop. "One of them coming out of the subatomic!"

And as the last words fell from his lips, he stiffened, grew rigid with the knowledge that snapped into his brain.

"You're quite right," said Elmer. "The Purple Jug is the home of the Martian race. It contains the subatomic universe to which they fled."

Lathrop glanced up, saw the shimmery blot that was Elmer up against the roof.

"Then the jug was what Harper wanted," Carter said, his voice just a bit too calm, calm to keep the terror out.

The spaceship had settled on the floor, was rapidly expanding.

"Quick, Elmer," urged Lathrop, "tell me how the Martians grew small."

Elmer was silent.

"Buster said it was tied up with the fourth dimension," Lathrop said. "I can't figure what the fourth dimension has to do with it."

Elmer still was silent, silent so long Lathrop thought he wasn't going to speak. But finally his thoughts came, spaced and measured with care, precise:

"To understand it you must think of all things as having a fourth dimension or fourth-dimensional possibilities, although all things do not have a fourth-dimensional sense. The Martians haven't. Neither have the Earthmen. We can't recognize the fourth dimension in actuality, although we can in theory.

"To become small, the Martians simply extended themselves in the direction of the fourth dimension. They lost mass in the fourth-dimensional direction, which reduced their size in the other three dimensions. To put it graphically, they took the greater part of themselves and shoved that greater part away where it wouldn't bother them. They became subatomically small in the first three dimensions, extended their fourth dimension billions of times its original mass."

Lathrop nodded slowly, thoughtfully. It was a novel idea— all things had a fourth dimension even if they didn't know it, couldn't know it, since they had no sense which would recognize the fourth dimension.

"Like stretching a rubber band," said Carter. "It becomes longer but thinner. Its mass is increased in length, reduced in breadth and thickness."

"Exactly," said Elmer. "They reverse the process to become larger again, drawing mass from the fourth-dimensional direction."

Silence fell, was broken by the soft whine of whirling metal. The entrance port of the spaceship, now grown to normal size, was opening.

The port fell smoothly back and a Martian waddled out. Lathrop stood rooted to the floor, felt the short hairs on the back of his neck stirring, struggling to arise as hackles.

The Martian waddled forward and stopped in front of them, his tentacles writhing gently. But when he spoke, he did not address the humans. He spoke to Elmer.

"You have shown them the jug?"

"I did not show it to them," Elmer said. "They saved it for us. They killed an Evil One who masqueraded as a human. He would have stolen it, perhaps destroyed it. Lathrop recognized him."

"I smelled him," Lathrop said.

The Martian did not notice Lathrop or the others. It was as if they weren't there, as if Lathrop hadn't spoken.

"You have failed your duty," the Martian said to Elmer.

"I am beyond duty," Elmer replied. "I owe you nothing. I'm not even one of you. I'm just a shadow of those of you who have been. There are many times I do not think as you do. That's because your thinking has outstripped me and because I'm still living in the past and can't understand some of the philosophy you hold today. A part of me must be always in the past, because the past accounts for all of me. For countless centuries I lived here with never a sign of recognition from you. It wasn't until you needed me that you came out of your Universe to find me. You asked my help and I agreed. Agreed because the memories that make me up gave me racial pride, because I couldn't let my own race down. And yet, in face of all that, you talk to me of duty."

"The Earthmen," said the Martian deliberately, "must die."

"The Earthmen," Lathrop declared, "don't intend to die."

Then, for the first time, the Martian faced him, stared at him with fish-bleak eyes. And Lathrop, staring back, felt slow, cold anger creep upon him. Anger at the arrogance, the insolence, the scarcely veiled belief that the Earth race was inferior, that some of its members must die because a Martian said they must. Arrogance that made the Martians believe they could conduct a crusade to bend the human race to the Martian way of thinking, use human beings to sell the race the dogma that had sent the Martians fleeing before a threat from the outer stars.

"I killed one of you before," snapped Lathrop, "with my bare hands."

It wasn't what he would have liked to have said. It was even a childish thing to say.

Through his mind ran bits of history, snatched from the Earthian past—before space travel. Bits that told of the way inferior races had been propagandized and browbeaten into trends of thought by men who wouldn't wipe their feet on them even while they sought to dictate their ways of life. And here it was again!

He would have liked to have told the Martian that, but it would have taken too long, maybe the Martian wouldn't even understand.

"Where's the robot?" asked the Martian.

"Yeah, where's Buster?" yelped Alf. "I got a score to settle with that rattletrap. That's why I came here. I swore I'd bust him down into a tinker toy and so help me—"

"Keep quiet, Alf," said Carter. "Buster is a toy now. One that scoots along the floor."

"Get going," Lathrop told the Martian. "Buster isn't here to help you."

The Martian backed away. Lathrop sneered at him.

"Run, damn you, run! You're good at that. You ran away from the things out on the stars. You ran away and hid."

"It was the only thing to do," the Martian's thoughts were blubbery.

Lathrop whooped in sudden laughter. "You only think you hid. You're like an ostrich sticking its head into the sand. You hid in three dimensions, yes, but you ran up a fourth-dimensional flag for all the Universe to see. Didn't you realize, you fool, that the Evil Beings might have fourth-dimensional senses, that when you strung your fourth-dimensional selves all to hell and gone you were practically inviting them to come and get you?"

"It's not true," said the Martian smugly. "It couldn't be true. We figured it all out. There is no chance for error. We are right."

Lathrop spat in disgust. Disgust at something that was old and doddering and didn't even know it.

The Martian sidled slowly away, then made a sudden dash, scooped up the Purple Jug, hugging it close against him.

"Stop him!" shrieked Elmer, and fear and terror rode up and down the shriek.

The Martian lunged for the open door of the spaceship, still hugging the jug. Lathrop hurled himself forward, flattening in a flying tackle. His hands fell short, scraped a leathery body, clawing fiercely, closed upon an elephantine leg. A tentacle spatted at his face, broke his grip upon the leg, sent him rolling on the floor.

Alf's blaster crackled and the Martian moaned in high-pitched pain.

"Stop him! Stop him!" Elmer's thoughts were sobbing now.

But there was no stopping him. The Martian already was in the ship, the port was swinging home.

Lathrop pulled himself to one knee, watched the port whirling, the ship already starting to grow small.

"There's no use," he said to Elmer.

"In a way," said Carter, "that fellow is a hero. He's throwing away his own life to save his race."

"To save his race," Lathrop echoed bitterly. "He can't save his race. They're lost already. They were lost the first time they did a thing and said that it was right, irrevocably right—that it couldn't be wrong."

"He can take his ship down into the subatomic," argued Carter, "and then the jug will be subatomic, too. We'll never find it. No one will ever find it. But he, himself, can't get back into it. He's barring himself from his own Universe."

"It can be found," said Lathrop. "It can be found no matter how small he makes it. Maybe it wouldn't even survive being pushed down into a state smaller than the subatomic, but if it does that only means the mass pushed into the fourth-dimensional direction will become longer or greater or whatever happens to mass in the fourth dimension. And that will make it all the easier for those chaps out on the stars to spot it."

The ship was no bigger than the end of one's finger when it rose into the air. In a moment it was a mote dancing in the light and then was gone entirely.

Carter stared at the space where it had been. "That's that," he said. "Now we fight alone."

"We fight better alone," growled Lathrop. He patted the weapon at his side. "Harper died when I turned this on him. He didn't shrink, like Buster. It acted differently on the two of them. There's something in this gun those babies are afraid of.

The Martians should have known it, but they didn't. They were too sure that they were right. They said the record was closed, but that didn't make it closed."

He patted the gun again. "That's why Harper, or whatever Harper was, wanted to get the jug. He and his race didn't feel safe so long as there was any race in the Universe holding a working knowledge of the fourth dimension."

"Harper," said Elmer, "had a fourth-dimensional sense."

Lathrop nodded. "The Martians didn't have such a sense, couldn't *feel* in the fourth dimension. So they never knew it when they poured themselves into the fourth dimension. But when Harper started being shoved into the fourth dimension, it hurt. It hurt like hell. It killed him."

Carter shrugged. "It's not much to go on."

"The human race," Lathrop reminded him, "has gone a long way on less. The gun is the starting point. From it we learn the basic principle. Pretty soon we'll be able to make Buster his regular size again. And after that we'll be able to do something else. And then we'll find another fact. We'll edge up on it. In the end we'll know more about the fourth dimension than the Martians did. And we'll have a weapon none of the Evil Beings dare to face."

"We'll do all that," said Carter, "if Elmer lets us go. He still can insist that we stay right here and starve."

"You may go," said Elmer.

They stood, the three of them, staring at the ceiling, where Elmer fluttered wispily.

"You may go," Elmer said again, and there was a bit of insistence in his voice as if he wished they would. "You will find a switch in the hiding place back of where the jug stood. It controls the screen."

They waited in silence while Carter snapped the switch.

"Good night," said Elmer and in his thoughts was a weight of sorrow, a sorrow that seemed to be wrenched out of a millennia of life.

They turned to go, but before they reached the door he called them back.

"Perhaps you would take Buster. Take care of him until you can restore him to normal size again."

"Certainly," said Lathrop.

"And, gentlemen," said Elmer, "just one other thing."

"Yes, what is it, Elmer?"

"There'll be times," said Elmer, "when you won't understand. Times when you get stuck."

"I don't doubt it," Carter admitted.

"When those times come," said Elmer, "come around and see me. Maybe I can help."

"Thank you, Elmer," said Lathrop.

Then he went into the other room for Buster.

INFILTRATION

A January entry in Clifford Simak's journal for 1941 mentions that he was finishing a story that he called "Earth Can't Take Chances," and early in February he had it typed and ready to be sent to Astounding—but editor John W. Campbell. Jr., rejected it. During the rest of the year the story would be rejected in turn by Amazing, Wonder Stories, *and* Comet. *I believe the story then underwent a change of name, and was again submitted to* Astounding, *as "Infiltration"— but was again rejected. Finally, in the autumn of 1942, it would be bought by a publication called* Future Fantasy—*but would, for reasons unknown to me, be published in the July 1943 issue of* Science Fiction Stories. *Cliff was paid only $30 for it, which perhaps reflected both its brevity and the magazine's status in the marketplace. (It's possible that we're dealing with two different stories here; although there's just no information to clarify that situation any further, the phrase "Earth can't take chances" does occur in this story.)*

"Infiltration" may be considered a kind of homage to H.G. Wells's War of the Worlds, *but to me the story is most interesting because it comes close to being a parody of Cliff Simak's preference for telling stories through the eyes of common folk. It contains suggestions (including his mentions of the Eaters) of a relationship to other, more famous, Simak stories—and it's another of those early Simak stories in which he described a telephone as "snarling," or something else more evocative than "ringing."*

—*dww*

Constable Chet Newton polished his star with his coat sleeve, shucked up his trousers and started once again to saunter the length of the midway at the Brown county fair, keeping an eagle eye cocked for disorder.

The barker in front of the "Monsters From Mars" tent was striking up a new spiel.

"Right this way, ladies and gentlemen," he yodeled. "Right this way for the greatest wonder of the world. Animals actually brought back from Mars. Living, breathing animals . . ."

"There ain't never been nobody on Mars," yelled a heckler in the assembling crowd. "Nobody . . ."

The barker silenced him with imperious gestures while the crowd snickered and chortled in enjoyment.

"So you think no one has ever been to Mars," said the barker. "Mister, your memory is awfully short. You remember Steven H. Allen, don't you? The man who landed in Arizona in a rocket and said he had been to Mars?"

"Sure," yelped the heckler, "but he was a fake. He was . . ."

The barker drew his face into mournful lines, leaned over, assumed a confidential tone.

"Yes, ladies and gentlemen, that is what the world called Steve Allen. A fake! Learned professors examined his rocket ship and labeled him a fake. And the world took up the cry. Fake, they yelled. Fake, fake, fake."

The barker's voice rose and soared . . . then again the confidential tone . . .

"But Steve Allen was no fake. He really went to Mars, despite what the professors said. That is a fact the world cannot shout down. And inside this tent are the things that he brought back . . . animals that he captured on the red deserts of the ancient planet Mars. Animals that are alien to this world . . ."

Constable Chet Newton yawned. All of this was old stuff to him. He had been hearing it for hours. As soon as the barker started his spiel the planted heckler would show up and shoot off his face. It went big with the crowd. They ate it up. There was nothing like an argument to get a crowd together.

Chet gazed up at the canvas banners that flapped before the tent. Occupying the central position of honor was a larger banner portraying a dragon-like beast with horns and fire-breathing nostrils, with a back that looked like a picket fence and claws that looked like scythes.

The barker was pointing at that banner now and shouting:

"The Eater. So ferocious that mere bars of steel will not hold him. But you need not fear him, for we have caged him in electricity . . . in a cage of heavy netting through which flows an electrical current. It is the only thing he fears. Nothing else short of armor plate would hold him. To supply the heavy load of power which we need, and so we do not have to rely on regular power lines, we carry generating equipment with stand-by units ready at all times. We cannot afford to take a chance. Listen to that sound . . ."

He held up his hand and from the tent came "put put put."

"That is the engine running the generating plant," the barker explained.

"Horse feathers," blared a throaty voice.

The barker jumped. Here was something that wasn't on the schedule.

"Who said that?" he demanded.

"I did," yelled the voice. "I been to your danged show six times and I'm here to say it ain't so wonderful. Just a bunch of mangy animals . . ."

Chet Newton saw that it was old Pop Hansen, drunk again. Pop lived in a tar-paper shack on the edge of the fair grounds and every year he made himself a nuisance. Chet started edging through the crowd.

". . . I got better animals than that in my little old shack," clarioned Pop in his whiskey tenor. "An' I won't charge you nothin' to see 'em. I got a purple crocodile all staked out and there are green rabbits runnin' all over."

"The man is drunk," yelled the barker.

"You're dang right I'm drunk," agreed Pop, "but I'm a better man than you are, drunk or sober. I'll come up and fight you if you want me to . . ."

"You pipe down," Pop," warned Chet, who had wormed his way to the old man's elbow. "You pipe down or I'll heave you in the can."

"I'll fight both of you," screeched Pop. "I'll lick the 'tarnal . . ."

On the outside of the crowd someone was yelling:

"Chet! Chet!"

"What is it?" roared Chet.

"There's a fight up at the cattle barns," yelled the man. "You gotta get there and stop them before somebody's killed."

Chet charged through the crowd.

"Who is it?" he demanded.

"Abner Hill and Louie Smith," gasped the informant. "They're going after one another with pitch forks."

"I knew it," said Chet. "I knew there'd be trouble there. Just as soon as I saw Abner took the blue ribbon on that bull of his'n, I knew there'd be hell to pay. Louie had been braggin' all over how he was going to get it this year."

But by the time Chet arrived, puffing from his run, the two contestants had been separated. Jake Carter, elderly and peppery publisher of the *Weekly Clarion*, had stopped the fight and was giving them a talking to.

"You boys ought to be plumb ashamed of yourselves," he was telling them, brandishing a pitch fork at the two. "I have a good mind to light into the both of you and whale the living tar right out of you. Fighting over a blue ribbon."

"Dagnab it," said Abner, "Louie started it."

"You should have reasoned with him," said Carter.

"You can't reason with a pitch fork, Jake," said Abner. "You know that as well as I do."

"Listen, you two," said Chet, still panting, "you got to cut this out. Any more of it and I'll run you in."

"He cheated me out of that ribbon," declared Louie. "The low-down skunk got next to the judges. I saw him downtown the other night, setting up the drinks for them."

"I don't give a dang what he done," said Chet. "I'm here to uphold law and order and, by cracky, I'm upholding it."

He shucked up his pants.

Carter stabbed the pitch fork in a bale of hay.

"Long as you're here," he said to Chet, "I'll be getting along. You'd ought to lock those two fellows up in a cage and let them fight it out. Maybe they'd get it out of their systems."

Chet spat disgustedly. "They wouldn't fight with bare hands," he said. "Only time they come to blows is when one of them has a club or something."

Carter found Paul Lawrence, the county agricultural agent, in the 4-H building.

"Pretty nice fair, Paul," he said. "Seems to me I can't remember a nicer one and I been writing up Brown county fairs for almost 40 years."

The county agent agreed. "Entry list biggest on record. And the quality of the stuff is finer than ever. I only hope we don't pick up any of those diseases that are breaking out down in Iowa and Nebraska."

"Is there anything new on them?" asked the editor.

The county agent shook his head. "Thought at first it might be hoof and mouth. Then thought it might be blackleg. But it isn't either one. They have corps of government men down there, but they don't seem to be making much headway. Seems to be spreading, too."

"They'll stop it," declared Carter confidently. "Other new diseases have broken out from time to time and they've always got them under control before they spread too far. Tough on the folks down in those sections, though."

"Yeah, it is," said Lawrence. "By the way, how are your roses?"

Carter's chest stuck out. "Better than ever. Grew some new varieties this year. Walked away with all the prizes at the show."

"I noticed that."

"Yes, sir," said the editor, "soon as I can get away from this danged paper of mine I'm going to settle down to growing roses. Nothing more interesting than a rose . . . no sir, nothing more interesting . . ."

Benny Short leaned his elbows on the counter of his shooting gallery concession and glowered at the "Monsters From Mars" tent.

"How's business, Benny?" asked the dwarf from the freak show two doors up.

"Ain't bad," said Benny. "All these yokels think they can shoot. Some of them can, too, but not with the sights I have on these rifles. Can't nobody hit anything the way I got those sights fixed."

"You look kinda frazzled," commented the dwarf.

"I am frazzled," agreed Benny. "All wore down to the quick. I ain't had a night's sleep in God knows how long."

"Conscience bothering you?"

"Not my conscience. It's that damn engine the Martian people have. Claim they use it to run their generator. Just props, that's all. Props. Something to get the yokels' interest. But why do they have to run it all night long, I ask you? Night and day it goes. Put, put, put. I haven't closed an eye."

He speared a finger at the dwarf.

"You know what I got a damn good notion to do. I got a notion I'm going in there some night and smash that engine all to hell."

"Now you're talking," said the dwarf. "Folks probably would hand you a medal for it. Them Martians have the rest of them all burned up. Taking all the business. And just a fake, too. Who'd think anyone would fall for a thing like that. And while they're packing 'em in, look at us. A good honest freak show and we haven't had a full house for weeks."

Inside the Monsters From Mars tent the barker was closing one of his lectures.

He had gotten to Dopey.

"And this is Dopey. You can see why we call him that. He sleeps all the time . . . or seems to sleep. He doesn't eat much . . . just takes it easy all day long. . . ."

Dopey, a small round ball of fur, uncurled slightly inside his glass cage and opened one eye. The eye was a surprise. It was red and vicious and sparkled with rage.

"He's always sore when someone wakes him up," the barker said.

He led the way to another glass cage where rested a thing that resembled nothing quite so much as a prairie tumbleweed. Even in the cage, which had little, if any air motion, it was on the go . . . floating and bumping about, never quiet, never still.

"This is the Tumbler," said the barker. "A bundle of nerves. An ideal form of life for open deserts. Even the slight winds of Mars will blow it many hundred miles a day. We had three of them to start with but this is the only one left. Even our utmost care has failed to keep them alive.

"Despite the fact that these cages simulate Martian conditions, the Tumbler does not seem to thrive in close confinement. To live he needs the wide expanses of his Martian home. We have drained the cages of air until they are almost a vacuum, we have introduced ozone, we have lowered the temperature. We have tried to create for the Tumbler the exact conditions of his natural habitat, but still he isn't satisfied. He wants to roam . . ."

And now the crowd stood before the cage of the Eater, a mighty beast of dirty yellow, with razor claws and terrible fangs and sharp, wicked horns. His back was saw-toothed, like the backs of some of the old dinosaurs of Earth, and there was a metallic sheen to his hide.

"A siliceous form of life," said the barker. "Formed of silica instead of carbon. Possibly he is the sole survivor of some Martian type of long ago. He alone of all Martian animals needs no conditioning to live on Earth. He could live anywhere."

The Eater coughed boomingly and stuck out a mighty taloned claw toward the glowing net that fenced him in, then cautiously withdrew it. He'd touched that net before.

Benny Short cautiously raised the edge of the tent at the rear of the Martian show. The interior was dark . . . dark except for a strange flicker of radiance from the operating engine.

No one seemed to be there in the dark. Except for the engine, everything was quiet.

The last of the lights had gone out on the midway fronts. The crowd had gone home. From far away came the droning of a car.

Benny hitched forward easily, drew himself inside. Crouching, he reached a hand under the canvas, hauled in a heavy sledge. Still crouching, he weighed it in his hand.

"I'll get some sleep tonight," he said softly, grinning in the darkness.

Foot by foot he made his way forward, took a stance before the dimly seen machine. Easily he slung up the sledge, heaved it high above his head, smashed it down.

There was a brittle crash as if the engine had been shattered into shards. The strange flicker of radiance flared and mounted, seeming to come from nowhere . . . and suddenly was a sheet of brilliance that for an instant silhouetted the concessionaire and his sledge against the canvas background and then, as he turned to flee, reached out and smothered him.

In the front part of the tent the Eater jerked to stark attention, saw the flame flicker and die in the net around him.

With a cough of triumph he lunged at the netting. It parted and he plowed onward, snapped off a tent pole, ripped through the canvas wall, trotted cockily down the center of the midway.

Chet Newton, making his final rounds before he went home, saw the thing coming toward him, hauled frantically at the old six-shooter in his belt.

The first shot missed. The second struck the beast. Chet knew it struck him. He heard it strike and richochet wickedly off into the night. He fired again and again, the bullets sliding off the gleaming coat and screaming out over the fairgrounds.

With a yelp of panic, Chet fled. He tore his way up the embankment to the race course, spurted swiftly for the grand-stand. Halfway there, he stopped and looked back.

There was no sign of the Eater.

Sitting on the steps of his tar-paper shack, Pop Hansen had just finished one bottle of moonshine, was reaching under the steps to get another.

Then came the sound of shots down on the fairgrounds. He pricked up his ears.

"Some sort of ruckus down there," he hiccoughed. He essayed to raise from the steps, lost his balance and fell back.

"Oh, well," he pronounced judiciously. "I've had enough fun for one day."

He groped anxiously for the bottle, finally found it and hauled it out.

With a crash the fairgrounds' fence came down and the Eater came through. He just grazed the tar-paper shack and went on into the woods, taking down a couple of trees that stood in his way.

Eyes staring glassily, Pop solemnly replaced the bottle, still unopened.

"When they get that big," he told himself regretfully, "it's time to quit the hooch."

Constable Newton was in Sheriff Alf Tanner's office, telling him what had happened, when the man burst into the office.

"I'm the owner of the Monsters from Mars show out at the fair," he gasped. "The Eater is loose!"

"So Chet's been telling me," said Sheriff Alf.

"My name," said the man, "is William F. Howard. I got here as quick as I could. The animal is dangerous. We have to round it up . . ."

The sheriff eyed him suspiciously.

"Just what kind of an animal is this?"

"'Tain't no animal from Mars," declared Chet. "That's just a lot of hokum. No one's ever been to Mars."

"No, of course," said Howard. "It's not an animal from Mars. But it really is a most extraordinary animal. From Patagonia. A friend of mine secured it for me. Probably it's a survival from the age of dinosaurs. There's some wild country down there . . ."

"That sounds fishy to me," said Chet. "Seems if it was a sur . . . a surv . . . well, whatever you said it was, that some museum or zoo would have got it instead of you."

"What difference does it make?" raged Howard. "Here we stand arguing when we should be trying to catch it."

The telephone rang, sharply, persistently.

The sheriff picked it up.

"Sheriff speaking," he said, in his best dignity-of-office voice.

A high-pitched woman's voice cut into the room.

"This is Mrs. Jones. Over on the old Blackburn place. You gotta get right over here, Sheriff. Something's out in the barn-yard trying to tear down the barn. It's already gone through the chicken house. Something big and awful. Tommy's gone out with a gun, though I tried to keep him in . . ."

"I'll be right out," the sheriff yelled.

He wheeled from the phone.

"It's over at Tommy Jones' place," he said. "We got to get a hustle on. Chet, you get the machine gun and let's get going . . ."

* * *

But when they got there the thing was gone. It had left the place a shambles. One side was ripped out of the barn and inside a dozen milch cows and three horses were slumped in their stanchions and stalls. The animals were dead. They looked like punctured balloons. Each bore a single wound.

The pigs, in their pasture, were the same and all about the barnyard lay the fluffy rags of feathers that once had been chickens.

Mrs. Jones was wailing and wringing her hands.

"All my best pullets," she screamed. "And I worked so hard to raise them. Chasing them in and out of the rain so they wouldn't drown and fixing up the coops so the skunks couldn't get at them."

"I'm going to have the law on somebody for this," stormed Jones. "I'm going to find out where that thing came from and I'm going to make somebody pay . . ."

"The animal is mine," said Howard. "It escaped from my show up at the fairgrounds. I'm sure we can reach some settlement."

"You bet we'll reach some settlement," Jones ranted. "How would you like a bunch of knuckles right smack in the puss?"

"Cut it out, Tommy," commanded Sheriff Alf. "Mr. Howard has told you he would pay. What more do you want?"

"I'm going into town with you," said Jones. "I'm going to slap an injunction on his show. I'm going to fix it so he can't move a foot until he's paid me every dime he owes me. Look at that barn. Cost a couple, three hundred bucks to fix that up and . . ."

"And don't forget my pullets, Tommy," wailed Mrs. Jones.

The sheriff was nodding with weariness when morning came.

It had been a strenuous night. They had tracked the Eater across three stubble fields, through a field of corn in which he had left a broad, unmistakable path. Then the trail had led into Kinney swamp. After floundering through the muck and mud for two hours, they finally had lost the tracks and given up.

Now the wires were humming, calling for help from the state capital. The newspapers at Minneapolis had besieged the sheriff with calls. The Associated Press and United Press wanted statements.

The sheriff mopped his brow and glared at the telephone, daring it to ring again.

Feet pounded in the hall outside and Abner Hill stalked into the office.

"Howdy," said Sheriff Alf. "What gets you up so early, Abner?"

Abner was fit to be tied. The sheriff could see that.

"I want you to go out and haul in Louie Smith," he snapped.

"Now, wait," said the sheriff. "I can't do that without no warrant. I know you fellows had a set-to up at the fair the other day, but you can't . . ."

"He poisoned my bull," stormed Abner. "The bull is dead . . . dead of poisoning and there ain't nobody but Louie could have done it. He's sore because I got that blue ribbon after he'd bragged all over the county he was going to get it."

"How do you know Louie did it?"

"Stands to reason he did. Nobody else is sore at me. And someone poisoned that bull."

The telephone snarled at the sheriff.

"Hello. What now?"

"This is Paul Lawrence, Sheriff," came the voice of the county agent. "Something's funny out at the cattle barns. Somebody has poisoned a lot of stock."

"Abner Hill is here now," said the sheriff. "Says his prize bull was poisoned. Seems to think Louie Smith might have done it."

"Couldn't have been Louie," argued the county agent. "Because his bull is dead, too."

"All right," said the sheriff. "I'll come up."

The phone rang again. "Well, what do you want?" Sheriff Alf bawled.

"This is Chet. Seems we been missing something. We got a murder on our hands."

"A murder!"

"Yep. Dead feller in the Martian tent. Burned black as a boot. Pretty nigh scorched to a cinder. He's laying alongside some busted machinery. Looks like he might have busted it himself. Sledge hammer right beside him."

"Who is he?"

"Don't know. But the jasper next door to the tent, the feller that ran the shooting gallery, is missing. Might be him. And that's not all . . ."

"NO?"

"No, it ain't. There aren't any animals in them cages. Just little heaps of ashes. And I found some trunks . . ."

"Of course," said the sheriff. "Show people live out of trunks."

"But just you wait till you hear what I found in them. One of them was filled with a whole hell's slew of little bottles . . . the kind doctors carry around with them . . ."

"Phials?"

"That's it . . . that's what they are. And all of them are filled with messy-looking stuff. Another trunk was just oozing with bugs. All kinds of bugs. Packed away, neat and snug, in little compartments."

"Well, I'll be damned," said the sheriff. "What would anyone be wanting with that many bugs?"

"Search me," said Chet. "Maybe you better come up and have a look for yourself. Maybe you could get Joe Saunders, over at the garage, to come up with you. Joe might know what kind of a machine the dead feller smashed. Sort of funny-looking contraption."

"O.K.," said the sheriff, hanging up.

"And this was the day," he said to himself, "that I was going fishing."

* * *

Night had fallen. The sheriff sat with his feet up on his desk, hat pulled over his eyes, snores issuing from under it.

Chet was playing solitaire.

Feet clumped swiftly up the stairs and into the corridor. Paul Lawrence rushed into the office, a map clutched in his hand.

"Hey, Alf!" he yelled. "Wake up. I got an idea!"

The sheriff's feet clopped off the desk and onto the floor. He snatched his hat off his face and blinked.

"Dang it," he complained, "can't you leave me alone? Seems like I ain't had a minute's peace for days. Newspapermen and crime bureau men swarming all over the place, pestering a fellow."

"But look here," said the county agent. "Just take a look at this map."

He spread it on top of the desk. It showed the middle western states. Across it a red line snaked across Kansas, Nebraska, Iowa and Minnesota. Several towns were ringed with red.

"Can't make head nor tail of it," said the sheriff, squinting with sleep-rimmed eyes. "Are you sure you're feeling all right, Paul?"

"Certainly I am," said the county agent. "That red line is the route travelled by the carnival, the outfit up at the fairgrounds. Those towns circled in red are where the diseases have started. Look, Junction City, in Kansas. Disease has wiped out almost all of the livestock there. The wheat is ruined by strange fungi. Insects are playing hell with the fruit and corn."

His finger ran along the red trail.

"See, we jump all these towns where the carnival played until we reach Sabetha, then up into Nebraska, skipping towns until we come to Nebraska City. At both of these places the same thing happened as at Junction City. Then over into Iowa . . ."

"Wait a minute," yelped the sheriff. "Maybe you got something there. You think the same thing is happening here."

The county agent's face was grim. "I know it is. Almost all the livestock at the fair is dead. One man took his cattle home in a hurry this morning, figuring he might save them. His whole herd is sick now. He was just in to see me. He's afraid he's going to lose everything he has.

"And this morning Jake Carter came in, madder than a wet hen. He'd found some funny kind of bugs on his roses. I sent him to St. Paul with some of them. Thought maybe the University Farm boys up there might be able to identify them."

"And you think the carnival has something to do with it?"

Lawrence slapped the map with the back of his hand.

"It's all there, Alf. It hasn't happened every place the carnival has been, but every place it has happened the carnival has played. There could be a connection . . . I think there is."

Chet dropped his cards and came over to the table.

"Might be something to it, Sheriff," he said. "Remember them bugs I found in the trunk. And those phials might have been cultures. Disease cultures."

"Grab that chap who was running the Mars show," suggested the county agent, "and you might find out something."

"Grab him!" yelled the sheriff. "What do you think I been trying to do all day? We ain't seen hide nor hair of him since this morning. After we got back from chasing that critter of his'n he stepped out. Said he was going to get a cup of coffee. We ain't seen him since."

"It sure looks screwy to me," said Chet. "Why, even that machinery in the tent. Supposed to be an engine and a generator, least ways that's what he told the customers. A generator to supply juice to keep the Eater caged. But Joe Saunders looked it over, what was left of it, and he says it ain't like no generator he ever saw before. In fact, Joe says it ain't like anything he ever saw before."

The phone rang. The sheriff reached for it.

"It's for you, Paul. Long distance. Jake calling. Girls over at Central must have figured you would be here."

The county agent picked up the instrument.

"Hello," he said. "That you, Jake? What did you find out?"

"I got them running around in circles," said the editor. "They can't believe their eyes. Say they never saw nothing like them bugs. They say . . ." he lowered his voice . . . "they say that if they didn't know it was impossible they'd believe those bugs came from another planet. They don't fit in with nothing ever found on earth. They been trying . . ."

Central's voice cut in. "Sorry. Would you mind? An urgent call for the sheriff."

"Certainly not," said Paul. "It's for you, Alf."

The sheriff took it.

"Sheriff," yelled the voice. "This is Louie Smith. Hell's broke loose out here. That Martian animal just went through my barnyard like a whirlwind through a strawstack. Didn't miss a single thing. And now there's something going on down in the south forty. Funny calls. Like nothing no one's ever heard before. Makes a man's blood run cold to listen."

"You stay inside, Louie," shouted the sheriff. "Just stick tight. We'll be there soon as four wheels can get us there."

The calls in the south forty were enough to chill one's blood. Utterly weird, they ululated into the star-sprinkled sky, seemed filled with all the rage and terror that the world had ever known. And there was about them an unearthliness that made a man's teeth chatter and chilled the marrow in his bones.

Chet cuddled the sub-machine gun against his chest as they advanced across the field.

"Just let me get one crack at whatever's making all that hullabaloo," he said, "and I'll guarantee I'll pipe it down. Did you ever hear such God-awful goings-on in all your life?"

"You shut your trap, Chet," warned the sheriff. "Don't want to scare it off."

The dreadful wailing rose again, this time with a sinister and insistent note.

The sheriff hissed a warning. A tree-studded knoll stood at the lower end of the field and the sheriff pointed at it.

A man stood on the knoll, outlined against the rising moon.

The men in the field crouched and watched. The man stood motionless and from the direction of the knoll came the alien caterwauling.

"Do you suppose he could be doing that?" whispered the county agent. From the lower edge of the field something was advancing toward the knoll. Serrated back and twin horns bobbed and weaved as the creature trotted forward. White teeth shone viciously in the moonlight and the hide of the thing seemed to strike sparks where the moon beams hit it.

Chet raised the gun to his shoulder. "Shall I let him have it, sheriff?"

"Wait," said the sheriff. "It's the Eater. We want to make sure of him."

The Eater was climbing the knoll now and the man still stood there, although the calls had ceased.

"Why doesn't the damn fool run?" cried the county agent.

But instead of running the man was walking down the knoll toward the Eater and to the ears of the waiting men came soft, cooing calls, the kind of talk a kind man reserves for his animals. As if the Eater might have been a pet the man was trying to coax home.

Both the man and the Eater stopped, only a few yards separating them, the man still making the coaxing, affectionate sounds. The Eater pawed the ground, arched his back. The man moved forward slowly, hands outstretched, still talking to the animal.

And then the Eater charged. The man turned, started to run, tripped and fell.

Chet was running forward, yelling, the gun pressed against his hip. The sheriff and county agent followed.

They saw the man flip over, roll away from the charge and struggle to his knees. The Eater skidded to turn, was charging back. But the man had something in his hand, was aiming it at the Eater. A cone of blue radiance lashed out and caught the animal. Great portions of the Eater turned red and puffed into acrid smoke. The blue cone still bore at the beast but it still came on.

The night echoed to the thud as the battering ram of a head caught the man and tossed him. Strange rasping, tearing sounds ensued at the Eater reared and trampled the fallen, broken thing.

There was no outcry from the battered figure on the ground, no sound of rage from the attacking Eater . . . just those terrible rending sounds as gleaming hoofs raced and smashed.

But the dull red glow set by the blue cone spread upon the Eater's body, spread like swiftly creeping fire . . . although there was no smell of burning flesh . . . merely acrid smoke that steamed and eddied above the knoll, rising into the clear blue of the night.

Charging up the slope, the three men saw the Eater stagger away from the mangled body, slump into a heap of something that looked for all the world like a heap of molten metal.

The man was stretched on the ground, body ripped apart, skull cracked open. One arm, torn from its socket, lay yards away. One leg was twisted off at the knee.

And out of the broken skull came something . . . something that was black and loathesome and many armed. Something that stared at the three with terrible eyes of angry red.

For one long moment it watched them, then slowly crawled back into the skull again. The man's body writhed and twisted, finally gained a sitting position. The jaw moved slowly, awkwardly. Distorted sounds came out of the wagging jaws, sounds that tried to be words and failed.

Then the body flopped down again and the loathesome thing scuttled from the smashed brain case. It darted rapidly away, moving like a furtive crawfish, a terrible, repulsive alien thing that made one's gorge rise by the very sight of it.

Chet's gun snapped to his shoulder and the field and woods reverberated with its yammering. The black thing thrashed and bounced to the impact of the bullets and then lay still.

The sheriff turned angrily on the constable. "Damn you, Chet, what did you do that for?"

Chet lowered the gun and stared at the thing with revulsion on his face.

"It gave me the creeps," he said.

The county agent said: "Perhaps it's better that he did."

"What do you mean by that?" demanded the sheriff.

"Take a look at that body . . . the man's body, I mean. Do you recognize it?"

The sheriff looked. The moon shone full upon the broken features.

"Howard!" exclaimed the sheriff. "William F. Howard. The owner of the Martian show!"

The sheriff's jaw hung slack. "Paul, it can't be that! It was all just a fake. Nobody's ever been to Mars!"

"Perhaps not," said the county agent. "But that doesn't mean the Martians haven't come to Earth."

The thing seemed less plausible, more fantastic, back in the sheriff's lights . . . but the proof was there.

"Examine that body," said the county agent. "A clever thing of steel and plastics. Intricate machinery in it, too. Until a few hours ago it passed for a man who called himself William F. Howard. You talked to him, Sheriff. And so did Chet. He fooled you both. He fooled everyone he talked to. Everyone thought he was a man. And yet he wasn't . . . he was just a machine to house that filthy thing Chet killed."

The sheriff wiped his brow. "Do you really think that thing was a Martian, Paul? That the show really was a Martian show?"

"Perhaps," said the county agent. "If it was it was a clever way to masquerade. Announce yourself as something grotesque enough, impossible enough and you can be that thing and no one will believe you."

"But look here," Chet broke in, "what would them Martians be doing traipsing all over with a show? If they wanted us to believe they were Martians they could have gone to some of these here professors and proved it and if they didn't want us to believe it . . ."

The county agent shook his head wearily. "Who can tell how an alien brain would work? Or what purposes an alien brain might hold? Looking at it the way a human being would look at it, a fifth column might be the answer. A fifth column from Mars . . . trying to soften Earth up before they took us over. That would fit. Enough diseases, enough strange insects removed from their natural enemies, enough fungi would do the trick. They could starve us out . . . have us beaten before the first war-rocket blasted off from Mars.

"Perhaps they would wipe out some Earth species with their diseases and their insects, establish some of their own on Earth. Most of them probably couldn't adapt themselves to Earth conditions, but some of them could. Given time, the Martians could transform parts of Earth into a little Mars . . . weeding out Earth life, replacing it with Martian life. Even now we can't be sure. Maybe the work is further progressed than we can guess. Maybe some of our unwanted, noxious plants really may be Martian plants . . ."

Chet shucked up his pants and spat contemptuously.

"You're plumb batty," he declared.

"I didn't say that is what happened," explained the county agent. "I said that was what might have happened. That would form a logical *human* explanation. But possibly it isn't the human explanation that we want. From the Martian viewpoint . . . if Howard was a Martian . . . the explanation might be something entirely different. Probably would be. We are dealing with a thing beyond our depth."

"There's something wrong, you can bet your eye teeth on that," announced the sheriff. "Something that needs a whale of a lot of explaining. Take that there Eater . . ."

"An animal formed of silicon instead of carbon," said the county agent. "Probable, not very possible . . . but there it was. All three of us saw what happened to it. We know it wasn't flesh and blood. We know it wasn't something that belonged to Earth. It, alone, if nothing else, should convince us that we're dealing with something alien, something from out in space.

"That blue cone that set the Eater on fire is another thing. Looks a lot like a flashlight. Something like a gun, too. But it isn't either one. The scientists will have a holiday with it, if they don't kill themselves taking it apart.

"Then there were the other animals. Too bad we haven't got them. They might give us some more data to go on. But Howard apparently destroyed them when he knew the jig was up. He was afraid that, examined closely enough, they might give him away. And the machine in the tent. Joe was right. It couldn't have been a generator . . . at least not the kind of generator we know. Probably was used to keep the Eater caged, but just how it worked, we can't know."

"What I can't figure out," said the sheriff, "is why Howard or the thing that was Howard . . . tried to make up to the Eater. He must have known it was dangerous. But he took the chance . . . there must have been a reason."

The county agent shook his head. "Undoubtedly there was. Maybe the Eater was his pet. A man will risk his life to help a dog he loves. But, again, we don't know. We're trying to apply human logic to alien motives."

"Look here," challenged Chet, "if all this stuff you been dreaming up is true, what are we going to do about it?"

"Notify the proper authorities," snapped the sheriff. "The state crime bureau. Maybe even the FBI, by cracky."

"That's right," agreed the county agent. "We'll have to watch. From now on, Earth can't take chances. There may be others.

Perhaps not masquerading as road shows, but in other ways. For what purpose we cannot be sure except that it bodes no good for Earth. Fifth column. Infiltration. Illegal immigration. Call it what you will. It has to be checked. We have to watch . . . we can't take anything for granted anymore. Lord knows how long this has been going on . . . how many calamities really have been due to the work of things like these."

Chet shuddered. "So help me, you got me goose pimples all over. I'll never feel safe again."

Slow feet shuffled toward the door. The three men tensed. Pop Hansen stumbled into the room. His liquor-muddled face stared at them.

"Say," he blurted, "any of you guys seen this feller that has the Martian show?"

The sheriff bristled.

"What do you want of him?"

"Thought maybe I'd make a little deal."

"A little deal?"

The old drunkard blinked.

"Yeah, a deal. I got a candy-striped elephant . . ."

THE MARATHON PHOTOGRAPH

It was not often that Cliff Simak wrote in the voice of a university professor; but in this case, it was appropriate to contrast the narrator with the ancient story that lay at the heart of its events.

You readers can of course read that old story, as told in the text, for yourselves. But I thought you might be interested to know that the old story was not made up by Cliff, but was an adaptation of a story that was hundred-year-old folklore when he heard it as a boy in southwestern Wisconsin. As Cliff told it to me, two soldiers who were stationed at a U.S. Army fort in that area had deserted, taking with them a payroll that had just arrived. The payroll consisted of a heavy load of silver dollars—there were no banks in the area, so that was how federal payrolls were met. One could see the temptation. . . .

Alas, the story went on to say that the deserters, loaded down with the heavy coins, lost it all when they tried to canoe down the Mississippi, only to get caught in a whirlpool that sometimes formed where the Wisconsin River rushed into the Mississippi.

This story was written for inclusion in the original anthology Threads of Time: Three Original Novellas of Science Fiction, *which was edited by Robert Silverberg and published by Thomas Nelson & Son in 1974.*

—dww

There is no point in putting this account on paper. For me, a stolid professor of geology, it is an exercise in futility, eating up time that would be better spent in working on my long-projected, oft-delayed text on the Precambrian, for the purpose of which I still am on a two-quarter leave of absence, which my bank account can ill afford. If I were a writer of fiction I could make a story out of it, representing it as no more than a tale of the imagination, but at least with some chance of placing it before the public. If I were anything other than a dry-as-dust college professor. I could write it as a factual account (which, of course, it would be) and submit it to one of the so-called fact magazines that deal in raw sensationalism, with content on such things as treasure hunts, flying saucers, and the underground—and again with the good chance that it might see the light of print, with at least some of the more moronic readers according it some credence. But a college professor is not supposed to write for such media and most assuredly would feel the full weight of academic censure should he do so. There always is, of course, the subterfuge of writing under an assumed name and changing the names of those who appear in the text, but even should I not shrink from this (which I do) it would offer only poor protection, since at least part of the story is known to many others and, accordingly, I could be identified quite easily.

Yet, in spite of all these arguments, I find that I must write down what happened. White paper covered with the squiggles of my penmanship may, after a fashion, serve the function of the confessional, lifting from my soul and mind the burden of a lonely knowledge. Or it may be that subconsciously I hope, by putting it down in a somewhat orderly fashion, to uncover some new understanding or some justification for my action which had escaped me heretofore. Anyone reading this—although I am rather certain no one ever will—must at once perceive that I have little understanding of those psychological factors that drive me to what must seem a rather silly task. Yet, if the book on the

Precambrian is ever to be finished, it seems, this account must be finished first. The ghost of the future must be laid to rest before I venture into the past.

I find some trouble in determining where to start. My writing for academic journals, I realize, cannot serve as a model for this effort. But it does seem to me that the approach in any writing chore must be logical to some degree at least, and that the content must be organized in some orderly fashion. So it appears that a good place to start might be with the bears.

It had been a bad summer for the bears. The berry crop had failed and the acorns would not ripen until fall. The bears dug for roots, ripped open rotten logs to get at grubs and ants and other insects that might be hidden there, labored long and furiously to dig out mice and gophers, or tried, with minimal success, to scoop trout from the steams. Some of them, driven by their hunger, drifted out of the hills to nearby tiny towns or lurked in the vicinity of resorts, coming out at night from their hiding places to carry out raids upon garbage cans. These activities created a great furor, with the nightly locking and barring of doors and windows and an industrious oiling of guns. There was some shooting, with one scrawny bruin, a wandering dog, and a cow falling victims to the hunters. The Division of Wildlife of the State Conservation Department issued the kind of weighty, rather pompous warning that is characteristic of entrenched bureaucracy, recommending that bears be left alone; they were a hungry tribe, consequently out of temper, and could be dangerous.

The accuracy of the warning was borne out in a day or two by the death of Stefan, the caretaker at the Lodge back in the hills, only a half mile or less from the cabin that Neville Piper and I had built a dozen years or more ago, driving up from the university and working on it of weekends. It had taken, for all its modest proportions, a couple of years to build.

I realize that if I were a really skillful writer I'd go on with the story and in the course of telling it weave in all the background information. But I know that if I try it, I will be awkward at it; the writing of geological papers intended for scientific journals is not the kind of thing that trains one for that kind of writing craftmanship. So, rather than attempt it and get all tangled up, it might be a good idea to stop right here and write what I knew at that time about the Lodge.

Actually, I didn't know too much about it, nor did anyone. Dora, who ran the Trading Post, a fanciful name for an old-fashioned general store that stood all by itself where the road into the hills branched off from the valley road, for years had carried deep resentment against the people who occasionally came to the Lodge because she had been able to learn almost nothing of them. About all that she knew was that they came from Chicago, although, when pressed upon the point, she wasn't even sure of that. Dora knew almost all the summer visitors in the hills. I think that over the years she had come to think of them as family. She knew them by their first names and where they lived and how they made a living, plus any other information of interest that might be attached to them. She knew, for example, how for years I had been trying to write my book, and she was quite aware that not only was Neville a famous Greek historian, but that he also was widely known as a photographer of wildlife and nature. She had managed to get hold of three or four of those coffee-table books that had used some of Neville's work and showed them to all comers. She knew all about the honors that had been conferred upon him for his photographic study of asters. She knew about his divorce and his remarriage and how that hadn't worked out, either. And while her accounts of the subject may have been somewhat short of accuracy, they did not lack in detail. She knew I'd never married, and alternately she was enraged at me for my attitude, then sympathetic toward my plight. I never could decide whether it was her rage or her pity that incensed me most. After all, it was none of her damn business, but she made everything her business.

So far as technology is concerned, the hills are a backward place. There is no electricity, no gas, no mail service, no telephones. The Trading Post has a sub-postoffice and a telephone, and for this reason, as well as for the groceries and the other items carried on its shelves, it is a sort of central hub for the summer visitors. If you were going to stay for any length of time, you had your mail forwarded, and if you needed a telephone, the Trading Post had the nearest one. It was inconvenient, of course, but few of the visitors minded, for the greater part of them came into the hills to hide away momentarily from the outside world. Most of them came from only a few hundred miles away, but there were some who lived as far away as the East Coast. These visitors flew into Chicago, as a rule, and boarded the Galloping Goose to fly to Pine Bend, about thirty miles from the hills, renting cars to travel the rest of the way. The Galloping Goose was the Northlands Airline, a regional company that served the smaller cities in a four-state area. Despite its ancient equipment, it did a creditable job, usually getting in on time, and with one of the finest safety records of any airline in existence. There was one hazard; if the weather was bad at a certain landing field, the pilot didn't even try to land, but skipped that particular stop. The fields had no lights and there were no towers, and when there was a storm or a field socked in by fog, the pilots took no chances—which may help to explain the excellent safety record. There were many friendly jokes attached to the Galloping Goose, most of them with no basis of truth whatever. For example, it was untrue that at Pine Bend someone had to go out and drive the deer off the runway before a plane could land. Personally, over the years, I developed a very friendly, almost possessive feeling toward the Galloping Goose—not because I used it, for I never did, but because its planes flew on their regular schedules over our cabin. Out fishing, I'd hear one of them approaching and I would stand and watch it pass over, and after a time I found myself sort of anticipating a flight—the way one would watch a clock.

I see that I am wandering. I really started out to tell about the Lodge.

The Lodge was called the Lodge because of all the summer places in the hills it was the largest and the only one that was pretentious in the least. Also, as it turned out, it had been the first. Humphrey Highmore, not Dora, had been the one who told me the most about the Lodge. Humphrey was a ponderous old man who prided himself on being the unofficial historian of Woodman County. He scrabbled out a living of sorts by painting and hanging wallpaper, but he was first and foremost a historian. He pestered Neville every chance he got and was considerably put out because Neville never was able to generate much interest in purely local history.

The Lodge had been built, Humphrey told me, somewhat more than forty years before, long before anyone else had evinced an interest in the hills as a vacation area. All the old-time residents, at the time, thought that whoever was building it was out of his right mind. There was nothing back in those hills but a few trout streams and, in good years, some grouse shooting, although there were years when there weren't many grouse. It was a long way from any proper place, and the land, of course, was worthless. It was too rough to farm, and the timber was so heavy it was no good for pasture, and the land was too rough to harvest timber. Most of it was tax-forfeited land.

And here came this madman, whoever he might be, and spent a lot of money not only to erect the Lodge, but to build five miles of road through the nightmare hills to reach it. Humphrey, who had told me the story on several occasions, always indicated at this point a further source of irritation that perhaps would have been felt most keenly by a devoted historian—no one had ever really learned who this madman was. So far as anyone knew, he had never appeared upon the scene during the time the Lodge and road were being built. All the work had been done by contractors, with the contracts let by letter through a legal firm. Humphrey thought the firm was based in Chicago, but he wasn't sure. Whether the builder ever actually visited the Lodge after it was built was not known, either. People did come to stay in it occasionally, but no one ever saw them come or leave. They never came down to the Trading Post to make any purchases or to pick up mail or make a phone call. The buying that was done or other chores that needed to be performed were done by Stefan, who seemed to be the caretaker, although not even that was certain. Stefan, no last name. Stefan, period. "Like he was trying to hide something," Humphrey told me. "He never talked, and if you asked him anything, he managed not to answer. You'd think a man would tell you his last name if you should ask him. But not Stefan." On his infrequent trips out from the Lodge, Stefan always drove a Cadillac. Most men usually are willing to talk about their cars, said Humphrey, and a Cadillac was seen seldom enough in these parts that there were a lot of people who would have liked to talk about it, to ask questions about it. But Stefan wouldn't talk about the Cadillac. To Dora and Humphrey he was an irritating man.

It had taken several months, Humphrey said, to get the road into the Lodge built. He explained that at the time he had been off in another part of the county and had not paid much attention to the Lodge, but in later years he had talked with the son of the man who had the contract to build the road. The road as it first was built was good enough for trucks to haul in the material to build the Lodge, but once it had been built the track was fairly well torn up by truck traffic, so there had been a second contract let to bring the road back to first-class condition. "I suppose a good road was needed for the Cadillac," Humphrey said. "Even from the first it was a Cadillac. Not the same Cadillac, of course, although I'm not sure how many."

Humphrey always had plenty of stories to tell; he bubbled with them. He had a pathological need to communicate, and he was not bothered too much by repetition. He had two favorite topics. One, of course, was the mystery of the Lodge—if it really was a mystery. Humphrey thought it was. His other favorite was the lost mine. If there was a lost mine, it would have had to have been a lead mine. There were lead deposits all through the area. Humphrey never admitted it was a lead mine; he made it sound as if it might be gold.

As I gathered it, the lost-mine story had been floating around for a long time before Humphrey fastened hold of it. That there was such a story was no great surprise—there are few areas that do not possess at least one legendary lost mine or buried treasure. Such stories are harmless local myths and at times even pleasant ones, but at least subconsciously they are recognized for what they are, and it is seldom that anyone pays much attention to them. Humphrey did, however, pay attention to the story; he ran it down relentlessly, chasing after clues, reporting breathlessly to anyone who would listen to him his latest scrap of information or imagined information.

On that July morning when it all began I drove down to the Trading Post to buy some bacon and pick up our mail. Neville had planned to make the trip so that I could get started on the textbook project, but after several rainy days the sun had come out and during all the rainy spell he'd been praying for a few hours of sunlight to photograph a stand of pink lady's slippers that were in bloom a short distance below the bridge just beyond the Lodge. He had been down there for several days in the rain, floundering around, getting soaked to the skin and taking pictures. The pictures had been fine, as his pictures always are. Still, he needed sunlight for the best result.

When I left, he'd had all his equipment spread out on the kitchen table, selecting what he'd need to take along. Neville is a fussy photographer—I guess most photographers are, the ones who are interested in their work. He had more gadgets than you can imagine, and each of those gadgets, as I understand it, is built for a specific task. It's his fussiness, I suppose, and all those gadgets he has collected, that make him the outstanding photographer he is.

When I arrived at the Trading Post, Humphrey was there, sitting all by himself in one of the several chairs pulled up around the cold heating stove that stood in the center of the store. He had the look of someone who was waiting for a victim, and I didn't have it in my heart to disappoint him. So after buying the bacon and picking up the mail, I went back to the stove and sat down in the chair next to him.

He didn't waste any time in idle chatter; he got right down to business.

"I've told you, I think," he said, "about the lost mine."

"Yes," I said. "We have discussed it several times."

"You recall the main thrust of the story," he said. "How it was supposed to have been discovered by two deserters from Fort Crawford who were hiding in the hills. That would have been back in the 1830s or so. As the story went, the mine was discovered in a cave—that is, there was a cave, and cropping out in the cave was a drift of mineral, very rich, I understand."

"What I've never been able to figure out about it," I said, "is even if they found the mine, why they should have bothered to try to work it. It would have been lead, wouldn't it?"

"Yes," said Humphrey, somewhat reluctantly, "I suppose it would have been."

"Think of the problem of getting it out," I said. "I suppose they would have had to smelt the ore and cast it into pigs and then bring in pack animals to get out the pigs. And all the time with the Army with an eye out for them."

"I suppose you're right," said Humphrey, "but there's magic in a mine. The very idea of finding riches in the earth is somehow exciting. Even if there's no way to work it . . ."

"You've made your point," I said. "I think I understand."

"Well, in any case," said Humphrey, "they never really worked it. They started to, but something happened and they pulled out.

Left the country and were never seen again. They are supposed to have told someone that they cut logs to conceal the cave mouth and shoveled dirt over the logs. To hide the mine from anyone else, you understand. Figuring maybe some day they'd come back and work it. I've often wondered, if all this is true, why they never did come back. You know, Andrew, I think that now I have the answer. Not only the answer, but the first really solid evidence that the old story is not a myth. I think as well that I may be able to identify that hitherto unknown person who got the story started."

"Some new evidence?" I asked.

"Yes, quite by chance," he said. "Knowing I am interested in the history of this area, people often bring me things they find— old things, like letters or clippings from old newspapers. You know the kind of stuff."

I said, indeed, I did. He had me interested, but even if I hadn't been I'd let him get started on it and I had to hear him out.

"The other day," he said, "a man from the eastern part of the county brought me a journal he'd found in an old box in the attic. The farmhouse had been built by his grandfather, say a hundred years or more ago, and the farm had stayed in the family ever since. The man who brought me the journal is the present owner of it. The journal apparently had been written by his great-grandfather, the father of the man who originally settled on the farm. This great-grandfather, for several years when he was a young man, had run a trading post up on the Kickapoo, trading with the Sauks and Foxes who still were in the area. Not much of a business, apparently, but he made a living out of it. Did some trapping on his own and that helped. The journal covers a period of about three years, from 1828 well into '31. Entries for almost every day, sometimes only a single sentence, but entries. At other times several pages filled, summarizing events of the past few weeks, previously only mentioned sketchily or not at all . . ."

"There was mention of a mine?" I asked, getting a bit impatient. Left to himself, he could have rambled on for hours.

"Toward the end of it," he said. "August of '31, I think. I can't recall the date. Two men who I take to have been the deserters came to the post late one evening, seeking food and shelter. It had been some time since our journalist had seen another white man, and I would suspect they made a night of it, sitting up and drinking. They would not have told him what they did if they'd not had a few too many. They didn't out and out say they were deserters, but he suspected it. The fort authorities had asked him some time before to be on the lookout for them. But it appears he had been having some trouble with the military and was not about to help the fort. So it would have been safe enough for the two to have told him they were deserters, although apparently they didn't. They told him about the mine, however, and pinpointed it close enough so he could guess that it was somewhere in these hills. They told him the story that has come down to us, little changed. How they cut the logs to cover up the cave mouth before they left.

"But they told him something else that has not come down to us—why they fled the country. Something scared them, something they found in the mine. They didn't know what it was; they never got close enough to it to find out. It ticked at them, they said; it sat there and ticked at them. Not regular, like a clock, but erratically, like it might be trying to talk with them, they said. Warning them, perhaps. Threatening them. When they first encountered it, apparently, they went out into the open, like a shot, scared stiff. It must have been an eerie sort of feeling. Then, getting a little over it and feeling sheepish about being scared so easily, they went back into the cave, and as soon as they stepped inside it, the ticking started up again. That did it. You must remember that more than a century ago, when all this happened, men were somewhat more inclined to superstitions than they are now, more easily frightened by what might appear to be supernatural. I remember a fine old Irish gentleman who lived on a farm near my father's farm. When I was a small boy he was well into his seventies, and I, of course, did not hear his story of the graveyard ghost. But in later years I did hear my father tell it many times. It appears that one night, driving home in a cart that he habitually used in his travels about the countryside, he saw or thought he saw a white-sheeted ghost in the graveyard only a few miles from his home. Ever after that, when he was out at night and coming home, upon approaching the cemetery he would whip up his horse and go past the cemetery as fast as good horseflesh could carry him."

"It was after the second ticking incident that they left," I said.

"Yes, apparently. The journal's not entirely clear. The keeper of the journal was no great writer, you must understand. His syntax leaves much to be desired and his spelling takes a moderate amount of deciphering. But, yes, it seems they did light out after that second incident. The wonder is, frightened as they seemed to be, that they took the time to conceal the cave."

The screen door banged and I turned around to see who it was. It was Neville. He stopped just inside the door and stood there, straight and calm, the way he always is, but a bit stiffer in his straightness, it seemed to me, than was usual.

"Dora," he said to the woman behind the counter, "I wonder if you'd phone the sheriff for me."

I got up from the chair. "The sheriff?" I asked. "What do you want the sheriff for?"

He didn't answer me immediately. He spoke to Dora. "Tell him that Stefan, up at the Lodge, is dead. Killed by a bear, it seems. Just below the bridge this side of the Lodge. The one over Killdeer Creek."

Humphrey was on his feet by this time. "Are you sure he's dead?" he asked.

"Reasonably certain," said Neville. "I didn't touch him, of course. But his throat's ripped out and it would seem his neck is broken. There are bear tracks all about. The slope down to the stream is muddy from the rains and the tracks are clearly seen."

Dora was on the phone. Neville said to her, "I'm going back. I don't think he should be left alone."

"The bear won't come back," said Humphrey. "Granted, they are hungry. But if he didn't eat him at the time . . ."

"Nevertheless," said Neville, "I am going back. It's not decent to leave him there any longer than is necessary. Andy, do you want to follow me?"

"Certainly," I said.

Humphrey dealt himself in. "I'll wait for the sheriff," he said. "When he comes along, I'll flag him down and ride along with him."

Neville and I got back to the bridge half an hour or so before the sheriff and Humphrey showed up. We parked our cars and walked down below the bridge. And there, only a few yards from the creek, was Stefan.

"We better sit down up here," said Neville. "There's nothing we can do but watch. We don't want to go tracking up the place. There's not much doubt what happened, but the sheriff will want the area to be left undisturbed."

We found adjacent boulders and sat down upon them. Neville glanced at the sky. It was clouding up again. "There goes my chance for pictures," he said. "And those blooms only have another day or two to go. Besides . . ."

He said that "besides" and then he stopped. As if there were something he had been about to tell me and then decided not to. I didn't question him. Maybe one of the reasons we've been friends so long is that we do not question one another.

"There are some good trout in that pool just below the bridge," I said. "One of these days I'm going after them. I picked up some new flies before I drove up. Maybe they'll do the job."

"I have to go back to the university," said Neville. "Tonight, if I can. Tomorrow morning at the latest."

I was surprised. "I thought you were staying for another week or two."

"Something came up," he said.

We sat and passed away the time with inconsequential talk until the sheriff arrived. As I looked at Stefan sprawled out on the stream bank, it seemed to me that he looked smaller than I remembered him. I found myself wondering if life added an extra dimension to a man. Take life away, would the man grow smaller? He lay with his face up to the sky, and there were flies and other insects crawling on his face. The position of his head concealed his torn-out throat, but there were bright specks of red still on the leaves and forest loam, blood that as yet had not turned to brown. I tried to make out the bear tracks that Neville had mentioned, but I was too distant from the body to make them out.

The sheriff turned out to be a genial man, soft-spoken, unofficious. He was a big man, rather fleshy. He looked like the TV stereotype of a hick-town sheriff, but he didn't talk or act like one. He came clambering down the bank, with Humphrey following. He spoke to Neville, "You are Mr. Piper. I think we met several years ago. And you must be Mr. Thornton. I don't think we've ever met. You're a geologist, I understand."

We shook hands and the sheriff said to Neville, "You asked Dora to call. She said you were the one who found the body."

"I was on my way to photograph some flowers," said Neville. "He's just the way I found him. I touched nothing. It was apparent he was dead. There were bear tracks."

"The ambulance will be along any minute now," the sheriff said. "Let's have a look."

We went down and had a look. There was nothing much to see. It was rather horrible, of course, but the body, the man reduced by the absence of life, was so small and insignificant that it had little impact. Balanced against the brawling stream, the sweeping extent of birch and pine, the deep silence of the wilderness, the fact of human death canceled out to very little.

"Well," the sheriff said, "I guess I better have a closer look. This is something that I always hate to do, but it goes with the job."

He bent over the body and began going through the pockets. He looked through the pockets of the jacket and the shirt and had to roll the body a little to explore the back pockets of the trousers. He came up with nothing.

He straightened up and looked at us. "That's funny," he said. "Nothing. Not even a billfold. No papers. He had no pocket-knife; most men carry pocketknives. I don't think I've ever run into that before. Even the filthiest old bum, dead in some back alley, always has something on him—an old letter, a photograph, faded and torn, from long ago, a piece of twine, a knife, something. But this one is absolutely clean."

He stepped away, shaking his head. "I can't figure it," he said. "Stands to reason a man would have something on him." He looked at Neville. "You didn't go through his pockets, did you? No, of course you didn't. I don't know why I asked."

"You're right," Neville said. "I didn't."

We went back to the road. The sheriff played a dirty trick on Humphrey, and perhaps there was justice in that because Humphrey really had no right to be there.

"I think," the sheriff said, "we'd better go up to the Lodge."

"I doubt there's anyone around," I said. "For the last couple of days I've seen no one there, not even Stefan."

"I think, anyhow, we should have a look," the sheriff said. "Just in case there should be someone. Somebody should be notified. Perhaps Humphrey won't mind staying here to flag down the ambulance."

Humphrey did mind, naturally, but there was nothing he could do about it. Here was the chance to go up to the Lodge, probably to go inside it, and he was being counted out. But he did what he had to do with fairly good grace and said that he would stay.

Passing by the Lodge, of course, one could see that it was a massive structure, half camouflaged by native trees and planted shrubbery. But it was not until one drove up to it, going up the driveway that led to the detached garage that housed the Cadillac, that an adequate idea could be gained of the size of it. From the driveway it became apparent that its true dimensions, as seen from the road, were masked by the fact that it crouched against the hill that rose back of it. By some strange trick of perspective it seemed from the road to be dwarfed by the hill.

The sheriff got out of his car as we drove our cars back of his and parked. "Funny," said the sheriff. "In all these years I have never been here."

I was thinking the same thing. On a number of occasions, driving past, I had waved to Stefan, if he happened to be out, but I had never stopped. Sometimes Stefan waved back, most of the time he didn't.

The garage door was open and the Cadillac parked inside. It seemed to me, as I looked at it, that there was a strangeness to the garage. Then, quite suddenly, I realized what the strangeness was. Except for the Cadillac, the garage was empty; it had not been used as a storage catch-all, the fate of most garages.

A flight of flagstone steps ran up from the driveway to a terrace and the narrow strip of level ground that lay in front of the house. The lawn was intended to be gay, with garden umbrellas, but the gaiety fell a little short, the canvas torn by the wind and faded by the sun.

No one was about. More than that, the place—the house, the lawn, all of it—had an empty feel to it. It felt like a place that never had been lived in, as if it had been built those forty years ago and then been allowed to stand, to age and weather, with no one ever standing underneath its roof. It was a strange sensation and I wondered what was the matter with me that I should be thinking it. I knew that I was wrong. Stefan had done a lot of living here, and occasionally there had been others.

"Well," the sheriff said, "I suppose we should go up and see if anyone is home." I sensed the sheriff felt uncomfortable. I felt uncomfortable myself, as if, somehow, I were an unwelcome guest, as if I'd come to a party, the kind of party that you simply do not crash, without an invitation. All these years the people of this house (whoever they might be) had made it a point of honor that they wished to be left alone, and here we were, invading their fiercely protected privacy, using a tragedy as a pretext.

The sheriff went heavy-footed up the flagstone stairs, with Neville and me following close behind. We came out on a stone patio that led up to the front door. The sheriff rapped on the door. When there was no answer, he pounded on it. I think that all he was doing was going through the motions; he had sensed as well as I had that there was no one there.

He put his hand on the latch and pressed it with his thumb. The door came open and he stuck his head inside. "Anyone home?" he asked, and then, scarcely waiting for an answer, went on in.

The door opened on a large room; I suppose you would call it the living room, although it was larger than any living room I had ever seen. A lounge would have described it better. The windows facing the road were heavily draped and the place was dark. There were chairs scattered all about, and a monstrous stone fireplace was opposite the windows. But I only glimpsed these things, for standing in the middle of the room, in almost the exact center of it, stood an object that caught my gaze and held it.

The sheriff shuffled slowly forward. "What the hell is that?" he rumbled.

It was some sort of transparent box standing on a platform elevated a foot or so above the floor. A framework of what appeared to be metal held the box in place. Inside the box were unsupported green stripes, like the yardage stripes that mark off a football field. But the stripes didn't run the way they would on a football field. They were canted at all angles and were of no uniform length. Some of them were short, others long, some of them had zigzags in them. Scattered amid the markings, with no particular pattern, were a number of glowing red and blue dots.

The sheriff stopped when he got to the box and stood looking down on it. He asked, gently, "Mr. Piper, have you ever seen anything like this?"

"Never," Neville said.

I squatted down, squinting at the box, looking for any sign of wires on which the colored dots might be strung. There was no sign of wires. I poked a finger at the box and struck something hard. Not glass; I would have known the feel of glass. This was something else. I tried several other places and each time the hardness stopped my probing finger.

"What do you make of it, Mr. Thornton?" asked the sheriff.

I made a stupid answer. "It isn't glass," I said.

Suddenly one of the blue dots changed position. It didn't move from one position to another; it jumped so fast I couldn't see it move. It was at one place and suddenly it was at another place, some three or four inches from where it had been.

"Hey," I said, "the damn thing works!"

"A game of some sort," the sheriff said, uncertainly.

"I wouldn't know," said Neville. "There is no evidence upon which to speculate."

"I suppose not," said the sheriff. "Funny setup, though."

He moved across the room to the windows, started fumbling at the drapes. "Got to get some light in here," he said.

I stayed squatting, watching the box. None of the other dots moved.

"Four feet, I'd say," said Neville.

"Four feet?"

"The box. Four feet square. A cube. Four feet on each side."

I agreed with him. "Close to it," I said.

The sheriff got the drapes open and daylight poured into the room. I got up from my crouch and looked around. The place had a barren look. There was carpeting on the floor. Chairs. Sofas. End tables. Candelabra with wilted candles in them. The fireplace. But no paintings on the walls. No figurines on the fireplace mantel. No small pieces at all. Just the furniture.

"It looks," said Neville, "as if no one ever quite finished moving in."

"Well," said the sheriff, "let's get to work. Let's see if we can find anything that will give us a clue to who should be notified of Stefan's death."

We went through the place. It didn't take us long. All the other rooms were as barren as the lounge. Necessary furniture. That was all. Not a single scrap of paper. Nothing.

Out on the driveway, the sheriff shrugged in resignation. "It seems unbelievable," he said.

"What do you do now?" I asked.

"The county registrar of deeds can tell me who owns the place."

It was almost noon by the time Neville and I got back to the cabin. I started to fry some eggs and bacon. I had the bacon in the pan when Neville stopped me. "Don't bother with it now," he said. "We can eat a little later. There's something I have to show you."

His voice was more tense than I had ever heard it.

"What's the trouble, Neville?"

"This," he said. He reached into his jacket pocket, took something out of it, placed it on the kitchen table. It was a cube, perhaps four inches to the side. It appeared to be translucent.

"Take a look at it," he said. "Tell me what you make of it."

I picked it up. It was heavier than I expected. I weighed it in my hand, puzzled by it.

"Look at it," he said. "Look into it. Bring it up close to your face and look inside it. That's the only way to see it."

At first I saw nothing. Then I brought it closer to my eyes and there, captured inside of it, I could see what appeared to be an ancient battle scene. The figures were small, but lifelike and in full color. There was artistry in the cube; whoever had fabricated it had been a master of his craft.

I saw that not only were there warlike figures, but a background as well—a level plain, and in the distance a body of water and off to the right some hills.

"Beautiful," I said. "Where did you get it?"

"Beautiful? Is that all you can say?"

"Impressive," I said, "if you like that better. But you didn't answer me. Where did you get it?"

"It was lying beside Stefan's body. He'd been carrying it in the pocket of his jacket, more than likely. The bear had ripped the pocket."

I handed the cube back to him. "Strange thing," I said, "for a man to be carrying about."

"Exactly," Neville said. "My thought exactly. It had a strange look to it. Not like plastic, not like glass. You've noticed?"

"Yes," I said. "Come to think of it, a strange feel, too. A hardness, but no texture to the hardness. Like that box in the center of the room back at the Lodge."

"Even facing the fact of death," said Neville, "startled by the fact of human death, I still was fascinated by the cube lying there beside the body. It is strange how one reacts to shock. I suppose that often we may fasten our attention on some trivial matter, not entirely disassociated from the shock, but not entirely a part of it, either, in an unconscious effort to lessen the impact that might be too great if allowed to come in all at once. By accepting the shock gradually, it becomes acceptable. I don't know, I'm not enough of a psychologist to know, no psychologist at all, of course. But there was the cube and there was Stefan, and as I looked at the cube it seemed to me, rather illogically, that the cube was more important than Stefan. Which, I suppose, is understandable, for Stefan, all these years, had been an object rather than a person, someone that we waved to as we drove past but almost never spoke to, a man one never really met face to face.

"This may all seem strange to you, Andy, and I am a bit surprised myself, for until this moment I have not really considered how I felt when I found the body, never sorted out my reactions. So, to get on with it, I picked up the cube, which I am aware I should not have done, and holding it in my hand and turning it to try to determine what it was, I saw a glint of color from inside it, so I lifted it closer to look at it and saw what you saw just now. And having seen it, there was no question in my mind at all of dropping it back where I found it. I've never been more shaken in my life. I stood there, with the cold sweat breaking out on me, shaking like a leaf . . ."

"But, Neville, why?" I asked. "I'll admit it is a clever thing, a beautiful piece of work, but . . ."

"You mean you didn't recognize it?"

"You mean the picture in the cube? Why should I?"

"Because it is a photograph of the Battle of Marathon."

I gasped. "A photograph? Marathon! How can you know? You are going dotty, Neville."

"I know because I know the Plain of Marathon," he said. "I spent three weeks there two years ago—remember? Camping on the field. Tramping up and down the battlefield. Trying to get the feel of it. And I did get the feel of it. I walked the line of battle. I traced the Persians' flight. I lived that goddamn battle, Andy. There were times, standing in the silence, I could hear the shouting."

"But you said a photograph. That thing's not any photograph. There's not a camera made . . ."

"I know, but look at this." He handed back the cube. "Have another look," he said.

I had another look. "There's something wrong," I said. "There isn't any water, and there was before. There was a lake off in the distance."

"Not a lake," said Neville. "The Bay of Marathon. Now you are seeing hills, or perhaps a distant marsh. And there is still a battle."

"A hill," I said. "Not too big a hill. What the hell is going on?"

"Turn it. Look through another face."

I turned it. "A marsh this time. Way off. And a sort of swale. A dry creek bed."

"The Charadra," said Neville. "A stream. Really two streams. In September, when the battle was fought, the streams no longer ran. The beds were dry. You're looking along the route the Persians fled. Look to your right. Some pine trees."

"They look like pines."

"The Schoenia. Pines growing on a sandy beach between the marsh and the sea. The Persian boats are pulled up on that beach, but you can't see them."

I put the cube back on the table. "What kind of gag is this?" I asked, half angrily. "What are you trying to prove?"

He almost pleaded with me. "I told you, Andy. I'm not trying to prove anything at all. That cube is a photograph of Marathon, of the battle that was fought almost twenty-five centuries ago. I don't know who photographed it or how it was photographed, but I am certain that is what it is. It's no snap judgment on my part. I know. I have examined it more closely than you have. After you left for the Trading Post I decided that instead of driving my car, I'd walk down to the bridge. It's only half a mile or so. It was a fine morning and I felt like a walk. So when I found Stefan I had to come back here to get the car, and I must confess I did not drive to the Trading Post immediately. I know I should have, but I was so excited about the cube—I was fairly sure what it was, but not absolutely certain, the way I am now—and a half hour one way or the other meant nothing whatsoever to Stefan any more. So I took the time to have a good look at the cube and I used a glass on it. Here," he said, digging around in his pocket, taking out a reading glass. "Here, use this. The picture doesn't break up with magnification. Those are no toy figures in there, no fabrications, no clever make-believes. They are flesh-and-blood men. Look at the expressions on their faces. Note that details become clearer."

He was right. Under the glass, the details were sharper, the faces became more human. The beards were not pasted-on beards, not painted-on beards; they were really beards. One Greek hoplite, his mouth open in a shout, had a missing front tooth, and little beads of blood had oozed out of a minor bruise across one cheek.

"Somewhere," said Neville, "there is a projector, or whatever it is called. You drop the cube into it and the scene is reproduced. You are standing in the middle of the battle, in a frozen thousandth-second of the battle . . ."

"But there is no such thing," I said.

"Neither is there a camera that would take a photograph of this sort. It's not only a three-dimensional photograph but an all-angles photograph. Look through one face of it and you see the bay, look through another and you see the marsh. Rotate it through three hundred and sixty degrees and you see the battle all around you. You see it all as it was happening in that thousandth of a second."

I put the cube and the reading glass back on the table. "Now, listen," I said. "You say this had fallen out of Stefan's pocket. Tell me this—how did Stefan get it?"

"Andy, I don't know. First we'd have to know who Stefan was. Tell me what you know about Stefan. Tell me what you know about the other people who come to the Lodge."

"I don't know a thing about Stefan or the others," I said. "Nor do you. Nor does anyone else."

"Remember," Neville reminded me, "how when the sheriff looked for identification on Stefan's body, he found nothing. No billfold. No scrap of paper. Nothing. How could a man get by without a social security card? Even if he had no other identification . . ."

"He might not have wanted to be identified," I said. "He carried nothing so that if something happened to him, there'd be no way for anyone to know who he was."

"The same thought crossed my mind," said Neville. "And the Lodge. It was as clean of paper as Stefan's body."

I had been standing all this time, but now I sat down at the table. "Maybe it's time," I said, "that we start saying out loud some of the things we have been thinking. If that cube is what you say it is, it means that someone with greater technical skills than we have has traveled in time to take the photograph. It couldn't be an artifact. Back when Marathon was fought no one had ever dreamed of the possibility of even a simple photograph. No one from the present time could take the kind of photograph there is in the cube. So we've got two factors—time travel and time travel done by someone from the future, where an advanced technology might make that photograph possible."

Neville nodded. "That has to be the answer, Andy. But you'll not find a responsible physicist who'll concede even the faintest hope that time travel is possible. And if it should be, some time in the future, why should the travelers be here? There's nothing here that could possibly attract them."

"A hideout," I said. "When the Lodge was built, forty years ago, these hills were a good hideout."

"One thing puzzles me," said Neville. "The emptiness of the Lodge. If you were traveling in time, wouldn't you bring back some artifacts? Wouldn't you want something to put up on the mantel?"

"It might be only a stopping place. A place to spend the night every now and then."

He reached out and took the cube and glass. "One thing bothers me," he said. "I should have turned this over to the sheriff."

"What in the world for?" I asked. "It would only confuse him more, and he's confused enough already."

"But it's evidence."

"Evidence, hell," I said. "This is no murder. There's no question what did Stefan in. There's no mystery to it; there's nothing to be solved."

"You don't blame me, Andy, for wanting to keep it? It's not mine, I know. I have no right to it."

"If it's what you think it is," I said, "you have more right to it than anyone I know. Four studies in the *Journal of Hellenic Studies,* all on Marathon . . ."

"Only three on Marathon," he said. "One of them concerned the pre-historic Danube Thoroughfare. Some of the bronzes found there seemed to have some connection with Troy. There have been times when I have had some regrets about that paper. Since then I've told myself I wandered somewhat far afield."

He dropped the cube back into his pocket. "I might as well get started," he said. "I want to reach the university before nightfall. There are hundreds of color slides in my files, taken on the plain of Marathon, and I want to make some comparison checks. Also I want to get some greater magnification than this reading glass affords."

He stood up, hesitating for a moment. "You want to come with me, Andy? We could be back in a few days."

I shook my head. "I have to get down to work," I said. "If I don't get that damn book written this time around, I'll never write it."

He went into his bedroom and came out with his briefcase.

I stood in the cabin door and watched him drive off. He'd get no sleep this night, I knew. Once back in his office, he'd spend the night working with the photograph of Marathon. I was surprised to find how easy it had become to think of it as a photograph of Marathon. I had come to accept, I realized, what Neville said about it. If there was anyone who would know, I told myself, he would be the one. Neville Piper was among the half dozen men in the world who could be regarded as experts on the Persian campaign of 490 BC. If he said it was Marathon, I stood ready to believe him.

I went out on the porch and sat down in a chair, looking out over the tangled wilderness of the hills. I knew I shouldn't be sitting there. I had an attache case and a whisky carton, both filled with notes and half-written chapters, some of them only roughed out and others only needing polishing and checking. I had a brand-new ream of paper and I'd had the typewriter cleaned and oiled—and here I sat out on the porch, staring off into nothing.

But somehow I couldn't make myself get up and go in to work. I couldn't get Stefan or any of the rest of it out of my mind— Stefan, the cube, Stefan's empty pockets, and the empty Lodge, empty of everything except that incredible contraption that the sheriff had thought might be some sort of game. Thinking about it, I was fairly certain it wasn't any game, although, for the life of me, I couldn't imagine what it was.

I sat there stupid, not moving, not wanting to move, sitting there trying to absorb and put together all the strange happenings, listening with half an ear to the sound of wind in the pines that grew just down the hill, the shrill chirring of a startled chipmunk, the squalling of a jay.

Then I became aware of another sound, a distant sound, a droning that steadily grew louder, and I knew it was the noon flight of the Galloping Goose, heading north after stopping at Pine Bend. I got out of my chair and went into the yard, waiting for the plane to come over the treetops. When it showed up it seemed to be flying lower than it usually did, and I wondered if there might be something wrong, although, except for the lower-than-usual altitude, it seemed to be all right. Then, when it was almost directly above me, something apparently did happen. Suddenly the plane, which had been flying level, perhaps actually climbing, although from the ground that would not have been immediately apparent—suddenly the plane went into a bank, dipping one wing and raising the other, and watching it, I had for an instant the distinct impression that it had shuddered. It banked and seemed to wobble, as if it might be staggering. Then, just as it disappeared above the tree-tops, it seemed to right itself and go on as before.

It all had happened so swiftly that I really had seen nothing that I could pin down. Somehow, however, I had the impression that the plane had hit something, although what might be up there to hit I could not imagine. It seemed to me I had read somewhere about planes coming to grief by running into flocks of birds. But that, I remembered, almost always happened on approach or takeoff. Despite the fact that the Galloping Goose had appeared to be flying lower than usual, I realized it probably had been flying too high for birds to be a hazard.

I had glanced down and now, for some reason I don't remember, perhaps for no reason at all, I glanced up at the sky and saw a dark dot hanging almost directly over me. As I watched it got larger, and I could see that it was something falling. It was wobbling about as if it might be tumbling in its fall. From the distance that I viewed it, it looked remarkably like a suitcase, and the thought occurred to me that a piece of luggage may have fallen or been thrown from the plane. Then I realized the improbability of throwing anything from a plane in flight, and realized, as well, that if a cargo hatch had popped open, there'd be more than one piece of luggage falling to the ground.

The whole thing was ridiculous, of course, but it didn't seem ridiculous while I stood there watching the flapping, tumbling whatever-it-was falling toward the ground. Afterward it did seem ridiculous, but not at that time.

For a moment it seemed to be rushing straight down upon me. I even took a couple of steps to one side so it wouldn't hit me, before I saw that it would come to earth a short distance down the slope below the cabin.

It came crashing down, brushing through the branches of a maple tree, and when it hit the ground it made a soggy thud. In the last few seconds before it hit the tree I could see it was not a piece of luggage. It was hard to make out what it was, but it did look something like a saddle, and of all the things a man would expect to come falling from the sky a saddle would have been the last upon the list.

When I heard it hit, I went running down the slope and there, in a dry ravine below the road, I found it—and it was a saddle, although no kind of saddle I had ever seen before. But it did have stirrups and a seat and what I took to be an adaptation of a saddle horn. It was scratched up a bit, but it really wasn't damaged much. It had fallen in a deep drift of leaves, and the leaves had cushioned its fall. There was, I saw, a rather deep dent in the saddle horn, if that was what it was.

It was heavy, but I managed to hoist it on one shoulder and went puffing and panting up the slope. Back at the cabin I dumped it on the porch floor and it lay all humped up, but when I straightened it out there was no doubt that it was a saddle. The seat was wide and ample and the stirrups were cinched up to the right length for an ordinary man. The horn rose somewhat higher than one would find in an ordinary saddle and was considerably larger and flattened on the top, with what seemed to be control buttons set into its face. The entire structure of the horn was shaped like an elongated box. The saddle was constructed of a good grade of heavy leather, and from the feel of it the frame was made of metal. But leather covered all of it and no metal could be seen. Attached to the forward saddle skirts were two closed saddlebags.

I squatted on the floor beside the saddle and my fingers itched to open up the bags, but I didn't do it for a time. I squatted there and tried to fight down the thought that had popped into my head—not that I wanted to do away with it, to banish it, but rather to bring it down to proper perspective, carve it down in size a bit.

Now let's be logical, I told myself. Let's put down the facts we have. First there is a saddle and the saddle is a fact. It is something one can see and touch. It fell out of the sky and that is another fact—for I had seen it fall. It had fallen after the Galloping Goose had gone through a rather strange maneuver—and that probably could be better listed as an observation rather than a fact.

It all seemed clear to me. The saddle had been up there in the sky and the Galloping Goose had come along and collided with it. After the collision the saddle had fallen from the sky. But, I cautioned myself, I could not be sure of that. I could be sure the saddle had fallen from the sky, but I couldn't be positively sure the plane had caused the fall. Fairly sure, of course, but not entirely so.

Questions rattled in my mind, and on the heel of questions, answers. I pushed both the questions and the answers back and stayed looking at the saddlebags. They lay quite flat, and there was no bulge to them. Although, I told myself, there might be something in them. It wouldn't need to be too much. A clue was all I needed. A clue that would give some support to that one big answer roaring in my brain.

I hunkered down and opened up the first bag. There was nothing in it. I opened the second bag and there was nothing in it, either. Empty—as empty as Stefan's pockets, as empty as the Lodge.

I got up and staggered to the chair and sat weakly in it. The saddle sprawled upon the porch floor and I tried not to look at it.

A time machine, I asked myself—a traveling time machine? You got into the saddle and rose up in the air, then you turned it on and went where you wished in time. But, hell, I told myself, it wouldn't work. Even if you could blind yourself to the impossibility of time travel, there still were a dozen easy reasons why it wouldn't work. I must be insane, I told myself, to even think about it. But tell me, said that mocking, illogical portion of my mind that I didn't even know I had—tell me this, what would a saddle be doing up there in the sky?

I got down on the porch floor on all fours and looked the saddle over. I examined it inch by inch. Hoping, I suppose, for an impression somewhere in the leather which would read: TEXAS SADDLE AND LEATHER CORP., HOUSTON, or something of the sort, anything at all to take my imagination off the hook. I found nothing. There was no imprint or tag to tell the saddle's origin. I felt cold feet walking on my spine. I picked up the saddle and took it in the cabin, tossed it on the floor of the closet off my bedroom and shut the door. Then, halfway back to the porch, I turned around and went back again and threw a pair of trousers and an old sweatshirt over the saddle so it would be hidden. I went back to the porch and sat there, thinking I should get at the book but knowing I'd have to wait for a while before I would get to it. I tried to watch the birds and chipmunks and the other creatures that skittered about the woods, but couldn't seem to work up too much interest in them. I thought about going fishing but decided not to. After a while I cooked some eggs and bacon and, after eating, went out on the porch again.

About three o'clock the sheriff drove up, parked his car and came up on the porch to sit with me.

"I'm not getting anywhere," he said. "I checked the records and the Lodge is owned by a legal firm down in Chicago. They hold the deed and pay the taxes and I suppose that's owning it. So I phoned and got an answering service. At one thirty in the afternoon I got an answering service. And it took a while before they told me it was an answering service. Now, just why should a firm of lawyers be using an answering service at that hour of the day? They wouldn't all of them be in court. They wouldn't all of them be off on vacation, and even if they were, there'd be at least one secretary to take their calls."

"Maybe," I said, "it is a one-man operation."

The sheriff grunted. "Doesn't sound like it. Jackson, Smith, Dill, Hoen, and Ecklund. Took the answering service gal half a minute to get it out of her mouth. She sort of sang it. She had to sing it, I figured, or she'd never make it. Say, where is Piper?"

"He had to go back to the university."

"He didn't tell me he was going back."

"He just failed to mention it," I said. "He'd known for several days he had to go back today. Any reason he shouldn't have?"

"No," said the sheriff. "I guess not. No doubt at all what happened to Stefan. You wouldn't remember, would you, what his last name was?"

"I never knew it," I said.

"Well, so much for that," the sheriff said. "A little embarrassing to have a corpse you don't know the name of. Especially a man who had lived here as long as he had. Stopped at the Lodge on my way up and there's still no one there."

The sheriff stayed for an hour or more. He acted like a man who didn't want to go back to town, who hated to get back to his office. We talked about the fishing, and he said that some day he'd come out and fish Killdeer Creek with me. We talked about grouse. I told him I'd seen a fair amount of them. We talked about the old days when people hunted ginseng in the hills and how you almost never found any ginseng now. Finally he got up and left.

I listened to the six o'clock radio news and again at ten and nothing was said about the Galloping Goose running into anything after it left Pine Bend. I went to bed after that, figuring that I wouldn't sleep, for I was still too excited, but I did. It had been a trying day and I was all worn out.

After breakfast I decided to go fishing. When I got to the bridge over Killdeer Creek a woman was standing on the bridge. I had taken a good look at the Lodge when I drove past and it still seemed to be deserted. But the woman was someone I had never seen before, and for no good reason I immediately figured she was someone from the Lodge. She was a blonde, a skinny sort of woman. She wore vivid yellow shorts and a skimpy yellow bra, but the bra seemed quite adequate, for she hadn't much to cover. Her hair was skinned back from her face and hung in a short ponytail down her back. She was leaning on the bridge railing, looking down into the pool. When I pulled the car over on the shoulder of the road just short of the bridge and got out, she turned her face toward me. The face was as skinny as her body. The structure of the jaw and cheekbones stood out beneath the skin, and the face had a sharp, almost pointed look.

"Is this where you found him?" she asked.

"I was not the one who found him," I said, "but, yes, this is where he was found. On the other side of the creek, just below the bridge."

"Stefan was a fool," she said.

"I didn't know the man," I said. I thought it strange that she should speak as she did of him. After all, the man was dead.

"Were you a friend of his?" I asked.

"He had no friends," she said. "He had this silly hobby."

"No hobby," I said, "is really silly if the hobbyist gets something out of it. I know a man who collects matchbook covers." I didn't know anyone who collected matchbook covers. I just thought it was a good example of a rather pointless hobby.

"Did he have anything on him?" she asked. "Anything in his pockets?"

It seemed a rather strange question for her to ask, but I answered her. "Nothing," I said. "No identification. They don't know who he was."

"Why, of course they do," she said. "They know he was Stefan. That's all we ever knew of him. That's all anyone needs to know."

I heard footsteps behind me and swung around. A man was close behind me.

"Angela," he said to the woman, "you know you shouldn't be out here. What's the matter with you? Are you drunk again? You've been warned to leave the stuff alone."

He said to me, "Sorry if she's been bothering you."

"Not at all," I said. "We've been talking. It's been most interesting."

He was a bit shorter than I was, perhaps a little heavier, for he ran to chunkiness. His face ran to fullness and his hair was clipped short. He wore a checkered sports shirt and blue jeans, with heavy work shoes on his feet.

"We were talking about Stefan," said the woman, and her voice carried the impression that she was embarrassing him and was glad of the chance to do so. "About Stefan and his silly hobby."

"But you are not interested in any hobbies he might have had," said checkered shirt to me.

"Certainly I am," I told him. "I find it fascinating."

"Come along," he said to Angela. "Back to the house with you."

She came down off the bridge and stood beside him. She looked at me. "I'll see you again," she said.

"I hope so," I told her. Before she had a chance to say any more he had taken her by the arm and turned her around and the two of them went marching down the road toward the Lodge. He didn't even say good-bye. He was a surly bastard.

There had been a lot going on between the two of them, I knew, that I had not understood. Most of it, I sensed, had to do with Stefan's hobby, and I wondered if the cubic photograph could have been the hobby. Thinking of it, I was fairly sure that my suspicion was correct. Angela had called his hobby silly, though, and it seemed to me that taking a photograph of Marathon was anything but silly.

There were a lot of things, I realized, I would have liked to talk with them about. When and how they'd gotten word of Stefan's death and when they'd gotten to the Lodge and how. Ordinarily when people came to the Lodge they flew into Pine Bend and Stefan took the Cadillac down to get them. Probably, I told myself, they'd hired someone to drive them up; after all, it didn't really matter. Come to think of it, no one really knew that Stefan had driven to Pine Bend to meet arrivals; we had just always assumed he had. I was a little disgusted with myself for wondering all those petty things; I was getting as nosy, I told myself, as Dora.

I lifted the rod out of the car and rigged it up, then got into my waders and went clumping down the embankment to the pool below the bridge.

I knew there were big trout in the pool, but I couldn't really put my heart into fishing. All the time that I was working at it, I was thinking of Stefan's body, stretched out on the bank across the stream. Every now and then I caught myself looking over my shoulder at the spot where he had been found. I got no strikes and no wonder, for I was too preoccupied with Stefan to pay attention to the fishing.

So I left the pool and went down the stream, walking in the shallow stretches, climbing out when I reached pools too deep for my waders. I left the scene of Stefan's death behind me and settled down to business. I hooked and landed one fair brookie in a stretch of rapid water at the head of a small pool, failed to set the hook when a big one, probably a rainbow, made a vicious lunge as the fly floated down the smooth water of a pool, edging in toward a cutbank where the big trout waited. I hauled in the line and made another cast to let the fly float in the self-same pattern, but there was no second strike. The big fellow that had made the strike might have felt the hook and was having none of it. I fished the pool thoroughly, but without a further strike. Several hundred feet beyond the pool I netted another brookie, perhaps a little bigger than the first one.

I climbed out on the bank and sat down on a rotting log, debating whether I should go on or quit. My fishing had not been too successful, but I had two fish, enough for supper, and there was that book on the Precambrian waiting at the cabin. I didn't want to quit. I wanted to keep on down the stream, not so much, perhaps, to keep on fishing as simply to stay out-of-doors, perhaps to stay away from the work that waited at the cabin. And, thinking that, I wondered rather seriously for the first time, I am sure, if I'd ever get the book done, whether I actually wanted to get it done. I had published little else and the department had excused the failure in light of knowing that I had the book, that I was working on it. I had been given the leave of absence to finish it, and I knew that I damn well better finish it. And yet I sat there, miserable, wondering if I'd ever finish it, knowing that through all the summer I'd use every excuse I could find not to work on it.

I thought of Neville's patch of lady's slippers and wondered if I should take the time to go and look for them. There was no reason that I should, of course, but I told myself that if I didn't see them now, in a few more days the blooms would be gone and I'd miss the seeing of them, for this year at least. But I made no move to go; I just stayed sitting there. I wasn't absolutely sure where the lady's slippers were, but from what Neville had said I didn't think I'd have much trouble finding them. Still I kept on sitting.

I've often wondered since what it was that kept me sitting on that rotten log. I could have continued with my fishing, I could have gone back to the car, I could have gone in search of Neville's lady's slippers. But I did none of these. And because I didn't, I now sit here writing this account when I should be working on my book.

Before I go any further, perhaps I should explain that Killdeer Creek lies deep in a wooded ravine between two steeply sloping hills. The bed of the creek lies in St. Peter sandstone, but a slight distance up either hillside there are outcroppings of the Platteville limestone, although in large part these outcroppings may go quite unnoticed because in most instances they are masked by trees.

On the slope across the stream from me something was rustling around in the underlay of last autumn's leaves, and when I looked to see what was going on it took several seconds before I spotted the squirrel that was causing the commotion. He was nosing around, digging here and there, perhaps in hope of finding a nut left over from the autumn. He must somehow have sensed me watching, for suddenly he panicked and went scampering up the hillside. Veering to the right, he whipped into a small rock shelter. These tiny rock shelters are common in the hills, small areas of softer stone having eroded away and been capped by a layer of harder stone projecting out above them.

I sat quietly watching the shelter, and after a few minutes the squirrel came sneaking out. He sat upright and looked around, alert to any danger, then flashed up the hill again. A few yards above the rock shelter he crossed a small area of raw earth where the recent rains apparently had washed away loose ground cover and gouged into the underlying clay.

I followed his flight across the gouge and for a short distance up the hill, then my mind caught up with me and my eyes came back to focus on what they had seen, but which had been delayed in its registration on my brain. Protruding from that area of raw earth were not one but two logs, or rather the ends of two logs. Above the topmost log the ground appeared to have caved in, leaving a small depression, and just above the depression was another limestone outcropping.

I sat frozen, and my startled mind said no, that it was all imagination. But hammering through my skull were the words that Humphrey Highmore had spoken to me only the day before: "They cut logs to conceal the cave mouth and shoveled dirt over the logs to conceal the mine."

You're stark, staring mad, I told myself; you're as bad as Humphrey. But the idea still persisted, although I tried to fight it down. A man simply did not sit down on a rotting forest log and find a legendary mine.

To give myself something to do, I unshipped my rod, dropped the reel into my pocket. Over the ages, I told myself, a couple of trees could have fallen and been covered by the slow accumulations of time. But the more I looked at those two logs, the less it seemed that way.

Although I was too far away to see them, I found myself believing I could discern the bite of ax strokes upon the logs' protruding ends.

I crossed the stream and began clambering up the slope. The going was slow, the hill so steep that I found myself grabbing hold of saplings to help pull myself forward. When I reached the small rock shelter into which the squirrel had popped, I paused to catch my breath. I saw that the shelter was somewhat larger than I had thought; a drift of dried autumn leaves had become lodged against the open face and made it seem smaller than it was. The floor of it was flat and a few feathers lay upon it; the floor was white with the chalkiness of old bird droppings. Perhaps, I thought, it had been used for centuries as a sanctuary for ruffed grouse, or possibly by quail, although there were no longer very many quail. Toward the farther end of the shelter a small rock fall from the roof above seemed rather recent; in a few years, I told myself, other rock falls would occur and there'd no longer be a shelter. I felt sorry for the grouse, it was such a snug retreat for them against the night or weather.

Having gotten back my breath, I went on up the slope to where I'd seen the logs. Kneeling beside them, I knew I had found the mine. The wood was punky and wet from recent rains, but there could be no mistaking the still-existent evidence that they had been cut to a proper length by ax work. I could not quite believe my eyes and ran a hand across their cut ends for confirmation. And as I squatted there, stupidly running my hand back and forth over the wood, something ticked at me.

I went cold inside my guts and crouched hunched over, as if expecting someone or something to clout me on the head. There was nothing in the sound that was sinister; it was, in fact, a very gentle ticking, almost companionable—but this was not the place for it. And now there was no doubt at all that I had found the mine, for it had been a ticking that had driven the miners in terror from the hills.

I came to my feet and for a moment felt an illogical but powerful urge to go plunging down the hill, to put as much distance as possible between myself and this thing that ticked. The feeling didn't go away, but I stood against it and once I had managed to stand against it, it didn't seem quite so bad. I drove myself, literally drove myself, my feet not wanting to move but my brain making them move, the few feet up the slope to where the depression fell away above the logs. I could see that the depression extended deep into the ground, and I went down on my knees beside it. There seemed no bottom to it. I thrust my face down close above it and smelled the darkness and the coldness of another world. The cave, I knew, lay beneath my feet, and out of the opening into it came a wild, excited chittering of ticks.

"OK," I said. "OK, just take it easy. I'll be back to get you."

I don't know why I said it. The words had come out of me without any conscious thought, as if some part of me of which I was not aware had grasped a situation I was unaware of and had answered for me, speaking to the thing that ticked and chittered as if it were a person.

I straightened, and even though the day was warm, I shivered. I would need a shovel, perhaps something that would play the part of a crowbar—the opening was too small and would have to be enlarged. And I would need, as well, a flashlight.

As I started to turn away, the ticking came again, a somewhat frantic and excited sound. "It's all right," I said. "I'll be back. I promise."

I was back in less than an hour. I had a shovel, a flashlight, my geologist's hammer, and a length of rope. I had not been able to find anything that resembled a crowbar, so I had brought along a pick that Neville and I had used when we had dug a trench to put in the footings for the cabin.

The thing inside the cave began ticking at me as I toiled up the slope, but now it sounded like a contented ticking, as if it knew I was coming back to get it. During the time that I had been gone, I'd had it out with myself on that score. You acted like a damn excited fool, I'd told myself. You allowed yourself to be stampeded into the acceptance of a fantasy situation that could not possibly exist. You can be excused for what you did in the unthinking excitement of the moment; you acted under shock impact and were illogical. But you're illogical no longer. You've had time to think it over and now you know it's not a living thing down there in the cave, not a personality. Whatever is in there ticks, but it was ticking more than a century ago and it's unlikely that any living thing that was there more than a hundred years ago, and God knows how much longer ago than that, would still be there, alive and ticking. What you'll find will either be a mechanism of some sort or you'll find a perfectly natural explanation. And once having found it, you'll wonder why in hell you hadn't thought of it before.

I admit that while I had been talking so harshly to myself I hadn't examined that bit about finding a mechanism too closely. I had, I suspect, shied away from it because I didn't want to ask the question that would follow—what kind of mechanism, made by whom and for what purpose and how did it come to be there?

The thing to do, I told myself, was to rip out the logs, enlarge the opening, get down into the cave and find out what was going on. I was scared, of course. I had a right to be scared. I had thought of seeking out Humphrey (because Humphrey was the one man who had the right to be there), the sheriff, even that bastard at the Lodge. But I decided against it. I was surprised to find that I had become somewhat secretive about this business—afraid, perhaps, that it would come to nothing in the end and that I would become the laughingstock of the neighborhood.

So I got down to business. I shoveled away some dirt from around the logs, drove the pick between the logs and heaved. The bottom log came loose with less effort than I had expected, and I grabbed it with my hands and hauled it out. With the bottom log gone, the one on top of it was easily removed. Underneath the second log I could see another, but there was no need to bother with it, for with the two logs out, the way into the cave was open.

I shined the flashlight down into the cavity and saw that the floor was only about three feet down.

All the time that I had been working, the ticking had been going on, but I had paid little attention to it. I suppose I was getting somewhat accustomed to it. Or maybe I was consciously trying not to pay attention to it. Coming out of the dark maw of the cave, it was a spooky sound.

I let the shovel and the pick down into the cave, then, holding the flashlight, slid in myself. Once I hit the floor, I flashed the light into the cave's interior and was surprised to see it was rather small—ten feet wide or so and half again as deep, with the roof some three feet above my head. It was dry—there was very little overlay above it, and the slope was so steep that most of the water ran off without a chance to seep down into the cave.

I directed the light at the back of it and could see where the miners, more than a century ago, had done some digging. There were a couple of heaps of broken rock lying against the back wall of the cave, rocks that had been pried out of the rather thin-layered structure of the Platteville limestone.

The ticking came from the back of the cave. I stalked it step by cautious step. I could feel the short hairs at the back of my neck prickling but I kept on. I found it at the very back of the cave, protruding from one of the strata that had been broken by the miners. And, having found it, I sat flat upon my seat, keeping the light trained directly on it. Sitting there, with all the wind of courage drained out of me, I stared at it.

It really wasn't anything to be afraid of. It was not alive. It was, by rough definition, the mechanism I had told myself I'd find. It was cemented in the rock, only a part of it revealed.

It chittered at me and I said nothing back. If you'd paid me a million, I could have said nothing back.

Its end was a blunted point and seemed to be attached to some sort of cylinder. The cylinder, I estimated, was four inches or so in diameter. Above and all around it I could see the rough edges of the break that must have been made when the miners had worried off the forepart of the stone in which it was embedded.

And that was the hell of it—embedded!

The blunt end of the cylinder ticked at me.

"Oh, shut up," I said. For not only was I frightened, I was exasperated. It was, I told myself, impossible. Someone, I thought, was pulling my leg, but for the life of me I couldn't figure who it might be or how they could have done it.

A rattle of falling rock and earth brought me around to face the entrance of the cave. I saw that someone stood there, but for a moment I couldn't make out who it was.

"What the hell do you mean," I asked, "sneaking up on me?"

"I'm sorry that I startled you," the intruder said. "Please believe me, I did not intend to do so. But it seems that you have found what we've been looking for."

I thought I recognized the voice and now I saw who it was—the man who had come from the Lodge to get the woman he called Angela.

"Oh, it's you," I said. I didn't try to conceal my dislike of him.

"Thornton," he said, "we have to make a deal. We must have what you have found."

He came across the cave and stood above me. The cylinder made a few excited clicks, then fell silent.

He squatted down beside me. "Let's have a look," he said.

When I turned I had moved the flashlight. Now I brought it back to shine on the blunted nose of the cylinder.

"Have you got a name?" I asked.

"Sure. My name is Charles."

"OK, Charles," I said. "You say you want this thing. As a start, perhaps, you can tell me what it is. And be damn careful what you tell me. For my part, I can tell you that it's embedded in the stone. See how the stone comes up close against it. No hole was ever bored to insert it. The limestone's wrapped around it. Do you have any idea what that means?"

He gulped, but didn't answer.

"I can tell you," I said, "and you won't believe it. This is Platteville limestone. It was formed at the bottom of an Ordovician sea at least four hundred million years ago, which means this thing is an artifact from at least as long ago. It fell into the sea, and when the limestone formed it was embedded in it. Now speak up and tell me what it is."

He didn't answer me. He took a different tack. "You know what we are," he said.

"I have a good idea."

"And you're not about to talk of it."

"I think it most unlikely," I said. "To begin with, no one would believe me."

"So there's no use in my pretending."

"I rather doubt there is," I said. "You see, I have the saddle and Neville has the Marathon photograph."

"The what kind of photograph?"

"The Marathon photograph. Marathon was a battle fought two and a half millennia ago. It fell from Stefan's pocket. Neville found it when he found the body."

"So that is it," he said.

"That is it," I said, "and if you think you can come in here and demand this thing that I have found—"

"It's not a matter of demanding," he assured me, "nor of taking. We are beyond all demanding and all taking. We are civilized, you see."

"Yeah," I said. "Civilized."

"Look," he said, almost pleading, "there is no reason not to tell you. There were a people—you say four hundred million years ago, so I suppose it could have been that long ago . . ."

"A people?" I asked. "What people? Four hundred million years ago there weren't any people."

"Not here," he said. "Not on Earth. On another planet."

"How would you know?" I asked.

"Because we found the planet."

"We? You talk of we. Just who are 'we'?"

"Myself. Angela. Stefan. Others like us. What is left of the human race. Stefan was different, though. Stefan was a throwback, a mistake."

"You're jabbering," I said. "You don't make any sense. You're from up ahead, in the future, is that it?"

It was all insane, I told myself. Insane to ask that question. Asking as if it were just an ordinary thing, not to be greatly wondered at.

"Yes," he said. "A different world. You would not recognize it. Or the people in it."

"I recognize you," I said. "You seem like anybody else. You're no different than anyone I know."

He sighed, a patronizing sigh. "Think, Thornton," he said. "If you were to go back to a barbarian age, would you wear a jacket and a pair of slacks? Would you talk twentieth-century English? Would you—"

"No, of course not. I would wear a wolfskin and I'd learn—so that is it," I said. "Barbarian."

"The term is relative," he said. "If I've offended you—"

"Not in the least," I said. I had to be fair about it. Depending on how far in time he had traveled, we might be barbarian. "You were telling me about a planet you had found."

"Burned out," he said. "The sun had novaed. All the water gone. The soil burned to powdered ash. You said half a billion years?"

"Almost that long," I said.

"It could have been," he said. "The star is a white dwarf now. That would have been time enough. The planet had been inhabited by an intelligence. We found—"

"You mean you, personally? You saw this planet?"

He shook his head. "Not I. No one of my generation. Others. A thousand years ago."

"In a thousand years," I said, "a lot could happen . . ."

"Yes, I know. Much is forgotten in a thousand years. But not this. We remember well; this is not a myth. You see, in all the time we've been out in space this is the first evidence of intelligence we found. There had been cities on that planet—well, maybe not cities, but structures. Nothing left, of course, but the stone that had been used in building them. It still was there, or most of it, stone on stone, much as it had been when it was laid. Some destruction, of course. Earthquakes, probably. No real weathering. Nothing left to cause weathering. All the water gone and the atmosphere as well. I forgot to say the atmosphere was gone."

"Come to the point," I said, rather brutally. "This is all wonderful, of course. And very entertaining . . ."

"You don't believe me?"

"I can't be sure," I said. "But go on, anyhow."

"You can imagine," he said, "how avidly and thoroughly our people examined the ruins of the structures. The work was, after a time, discouraging, for the ruins could tell us very little. Then, finally, a graven stone was found . . ."

"A graven stone?"

"A message stone. A slab of stone with a message carved upon it."

"Don't tell me that you found this stone and then, right off, you read the message."

"Not words," he said. "Not symbols. Pictures. You have a word. Funny pictures."

"Cartoons," I said.

"Cartoons. That is right. The cartoons told the story. The people of that planet knew their sun was about to nova. They had some space capability, but not enough to move a total population. What was worse, there was no planet they had ever found that could support their kind of life. I suspect it was much like our life, the same basis as our life. Oxygen and carbon. They didn't look like us. They were bugs. Many-legged, many-armed. Perhaps, in many ways, a more efficient organism than ourselves.

They knew they were finished. Perhaps not all of them. They might have hoped they still could find a planet where a few of them could live. That way the germ plasma could be preserved, if they were lucky. The plasma, but not the civilization, not their culture. Locating to another planet, having to come to grips with that planet and perhaps only a few of them to do it, they knew they would lose their culture, that it would be forgotten, that the few survivors could not maintain and preserve what they had achieved over many thousands of years. And it seemed important that at least the basics of their culture should be preserved, that it should not be lost to the rest of the galaxy. They were facing the prospect of cultural death. Do you have any idea of what the impact of cultural death might be like?"

"Like any other death," I said. "Death is death. Someone turns out the light."

"Not quite," he said. "Not quite like any other death. No one likes the prospect of death. It may not be death itself, but the loss of identity we fear. The fear of being blotted out. Many men facing death are able to await it calmly because they feel they've made a good job out of life. They have done certain tasks or have stood for something they feel will cause them to be remembered. They are, you see, not losing identity entirely. They will be remembered, and that in itself is a matter of some identity. This is important for the individual; it is even more important for a race—a race proud of the culture it has built. Racial identity is even more important than individual identity. It is not too difficult for a man to accept the inevitability of his own death; it is almost impossible for him to accept the fact that some day there may be no humans, that the species will have disappeared."

"I think I see," I said. I had never thought of it before.

"So this race on the planet soon to be dead," he said, "took steps to preserve their culture. They broke it down to its basic concepts and essentials and they recorded it and put it into capsules . . ."

I started in surprise. "You mean this?" I asked, gesturing at the cylinder enclosed within the stone.

"It is my hope," he said, far too calmly, far too surely.

"You must be nuts," I said. "First for believing all this . . ."

"There were many capsules," he said. "There was a number indicated, but since we could not decipher their notation . . ."

"But they must have broadcast them. Simply flung them into space."

He shook his head. "They aimed them at suns. Given the kind of technology they had, many would have reached their destinations. They were gambling that one of them would come to earth on some distant planet and be picked up by some intelligence with enough curiosity and enough ingenuity . . ."

"They would have burned up when they entered the atmosphere."

"Not necessarily. The technology . . ."

"Four hundred million years ago," I said. "That long ago this precious planet of yours could have been across the galaxy from us."

"We did not know, of course, how long ago," he said, stubbornly, "but from our calculations our sun and their sun would never have been impossibly far apart. They have matched galactic orbits."

I squatted there and tried to think, and all I had was a roaring in the brain. It was impossible to believe, but there was the cylinder, embedded in the stone, a cylinder that ticked industriously to call attention to itself.

"The ticking," said Charles, as if he knew my thoughts, "is something we had never thought of. Perhaps it's activated when anything fulfilling certain biological requirements comes within a certain distance of it. But, then, of course, we never expected to stumble upon one of the capsules."

"What did you expect, then?" I asked. "From what you've said, you have been hunting for a capsule."

"Not really hunting for one," he told me. "Just hoping we'd find some evidence that some time in the past one had been found.

Either found and destroyed or lost—maybe found and at least a portion of its message extracted from it, extracted perhaps, then lost again because it did not fit in with human thought. Always hoping, of course, that we might find one tucked away in some obscure hiding place, in a small museum, maybe, in an attic or a storeroom of an ancient house, in some old temple ruin."

"But why come back into the past, why come here? Surely in your own time—"

"You do not understand," he said. "In our time there is very little left. Very little of the past. The past does not last forever—either materially or intellectually. The intellectual past is twisted and distorted; the material past, the records and the ruins of it, are destroyed or lost or decay away. And if by 'here' you mean in this particular place and time, we do few operations here. The Lodge—I understand that is what you call it—is what in your time you might term a rest and recreation area."

"But the years you've spent at it," I said. "All these years in a search that had so little chance."

"There is more to it than that," he said. "The finding of an alien capsule, how would you say it in the idiom of today? The finding of a capsule is the big prize on the board. It was something we were always on the lookout for, our investigative sense was always tuned to some hint that one might exist or at one time had existed. But we did not spend all our time—"

"Investigative? You said investigative. Just what the hell are you investigating?"

"History," he said. "Human history. I thought there was no question that you would have guessed it."

"I am stupid," I said. "I didn't guess it. You must have shelves of history. All you have to do is read it."

"As I told you, there's not much of the past left. When there are nuclear wars and a large part of the planet goes back to barbarism, the past goes down the drain. And what little there is left becomes very hard to find."

"So there will be nuclear wars," I said. "We had begun to hope that Earth might never have to face that. Could you tell me—"

"No," said Charles, "I can't."

We hunkered there, the two of us, looking at the capsule.

"You want it?" I asked.

He nodded.

"If we can get it out undamaged," I said.

The capsule clucked quietly at us, companionably.

I pulled the rock hammer out of my belt.

"Here," I said, handing him the flashlight.

He took it and held it with its light trained on the capsule while I leaned close and studied the rock.

"We might be in luck," I said. "There is a bedding plane, a seam, running just below the capsule. Limestone's funny stuff. The layers can be either thick or thin. Sometimes it peels, sometimes it has to be broken."

I tapped the bedding plane with the hammer. The stone flaked under the blows. Turning the hammer around to use the chisel end, I pecked away at the seam.

"Hand me the pick," I said, and he handed it to me.

I had little room to work in, but I managed to drive the sharp end of the pick deep into the seam and a layer of the limestone peeled away and fell. The capsule was exposed along its lower side, and it took only a little more judicious chipping away of the rock to free it. It was some eighteen inches long and heavier than I had imagined it would be.

Charles put the flashlight down on the floor of the cave and reached out his hands for it.

"Not so fast," I said. "We have a deal to make."

"You can keep the saddle."

"I already have it," I said. "I intend to keep it."

"We'll repair it for you. We'll even exchange a new one for it. We'll teach you how to use it."

"I don't think so," I said. "I'm satisfied right here. I know how to get along right here. Seems to me a man could get into a lot of trouble taking off to other times. Now if you had some more photographs like the Marathon photograph . . . Say a couple of hundred of them, of selected subjects."

He put his hands up to his head in anguish.

"But we don't," he said. "We never take such photographs."

"Stefan took them."

He choked in frustration. "How can I make you understand! Stefan was a freak, a throwback. He got kicks out of violence, out of blood. That's why we kept him here. That was why he was never allowed to go out in the field. He sneaked out whenever he could and took what you call the photographs. There is a name for them . . ."

"Holographs," I said.

"I guess that's the word. A mechanism using the laser principle. It was a mistake to put him on our team. It meant we had to cover up for him. We couldn't report or admit what he was doing. We had to consider the honor of the team. We talked with him, we pleaded with him, but he was beyond all shame. He was a psychopath. How he ever succeeded in covering up his condition so he could be appointed to the team—"

"Psychopaths," I said, "are tricky."

He pleaded with me, "Now you understand?"

"Not too well," I said. "You stand aghast at violence. You are turned off by blood. And yet you study history and, more often than not, history turns on violence. It can be a bloody business."

He shuddered. "We find enough of it. We are repelled by it, but it's sometimes necessary to consider it. We do not enjoy it: Stefan did enjoy it. He knew how we felt about it. He hid away his photographs, afraid we would destroy them. We would have if we'd found them."

"You hunted for them," I said.

"Everywhere. We never found their hiding place."

"So there are some around?"

"I suppose there are. But if you think they can be found, forget it. You said psychopaths are tricky."

"Yes, I guess I did," I said. "In such a case, there can't be any deal."

"You mean you'll keep the capsule?"

I nodded and tucked it underneath my arm.

"But why?" he shouted. "Why?"

"If it's valuable to you," I told him, "it should be valuable to us."

And I thought to myself, what in the name of Holy Christ am I doing here, hunkered down in a cave that was an olden mine, arguing with a man out of the human future about a silly cylinder out of the nonhuman past?

"You would have no way to come by the information that the capsule carries," he said.

"How about yourself? How about your people?"

"They'd have a better chance. We can't be entirely sure, of course, but we'd have a better chance."

"I suppose," I said, "that you expect to find some nonhuman knowledge, a cultural concept based on nonhuman values. You expect a lot of new ideas, a windfall of new concepts, some of which could be grafted on your culture, some of which could not."

"That's the whole point, Thornton. Even if you could extract the knowledge, how would your age put it to use? Don't forget that some of it, perhaps much of it, might run counter to your present concepts. What if it said that human rights must take precedence, both in theory and in practice, over property rights? In practice as well as in theory—right now, of course, human rights do in certain aspects take precedence in theory, even in law, but how about in practice? What if you found something that condemned nationalism and gave a formula for its being done away with? What if it proved patriotism were so much utter hogwash? Not that we can expect the contents of this capsule to deal with such things as human rights and nationalism. The information in this capsule, I would suspect, will include a lot of things we've never even thought of. How do you think the present day, your present day, would take to such divergence from what you consider as the norm? I can tell you. It would be disregarded, it would be swept beneath the rug, it would be laughed and sneered to nothing. You might as well smash this capsule into bits as give it to your people."

"How about yourselves?" I asked. "How can you be sure you'll put it to good use?"

"We have to," he said. "If you saw Earth as it is up in my time, you would know we'd have to. Sure, we can travel out in space. We can travel into time. But with all these things, we still are hanging on by our fingernails. We'll use it; we'll use anything at all to keep the human race in business. We are the end product of thousands of years of mismanagement and bungling—your mismanagement and bungling. Why do you think we spend our lives in coming back to study history? For the fun of it? The adventure? No, I tell you, no. We do it to find where and how the human race went wrong, hoping to glean some insight into how it might have gone right, but didn't. To find an old lost knowledge that might be put to better use than you ever put it to. We are the lost race digging through the garbage of men who lived before us."

"You're sniveling," I said. "You are feeling sorry for yourself."

"I suppose so," he said. "I'm sorry. We no longer are the frozen-faced realists of this time, afraid of emotion, any more than you are the rough, tough barbarian you'd meet if you went back a couple of thousand years. The human race has changed. We are the ones who were stripped naked. We decided long ago we could no longer afford the luxury of violence, of cutthroat economic competition, of national pride. We are not the same people you know. I don't say we are better, only different and with different viewpoints. If we want to weep, we weep; if we want to sing, we sing."

I didn't say anything; I just kept looking at him.

"And if you keep the capsule," he asked, "what will you do with it, you personally, not your culture? To whom would you give it, whom would you tell about it? Who would listen to your explanation? Could you survive the scarcely hidden disbelief and laughter? How could you, once you'd told your story, the story I have told you—how could you face your colleagues and your students?"

"I guess I couldn't," I said. "Here, take the goddamn thing."

He reached out and took it. "I thank you very much," he said. "You have earned our gratitude."

I felt all cut up inside. I wasn't sure of anything. To have something in one's hand, I thought, that might change the world, then give it away, be forced to give it away because I knew that in my time it would not be used, that there could be no hope that it would be used—that was tough to take. I might have felt different about it, I knew, if I could have given the cylinder to someone else than this little twerp. I didn't know why I disliked him; I had never even asked myself what there was to dislike about him. Then, suddenly, I knew; it all came to me. I disliked him because there were too many centuries between us. He was still a human, sure, but not the same kind of human as I was. Time had made a difference between us. I had no idea of how many years there might be between us—I hadn't even asked him, and I wondered why I hadn't. Times change and people change, and those cumulative changes had made us different kinds of humans.

"If you'll come up to the house," he said, "I could find a drink."

"Go to hell," I said.

He started to leave, then turned back to me. "I hate to leave like this," he said. "I know how you must feel. You don't like me, I am sure, and I can't with all honesty say I care too much for you. But you have done a great, although unwitting, service for us, and I have a deep sense of gratitude. Aside from all of that, we are two human beings. Please don't shame me, Thornton. Please accord me the luxury of being decent to you."

I grunted boorishly at him, but I got up, picked up the tools and followed after him.

When we came into the Lodge, Angela was slumped in a chair. A whiskey bottle stood on the table beside her. She struggled to her feet and waved a half-filled glass at me, spilling liquor on the rug.

"You must not mind her," Charles said to me. "She is compensating."

"And who the hell wouldn't compensate?" she asked. "After months of tracking down and keeping up with Villon in the stews of fifteenth-century Paris . . ."

"Villon," I said, not quite making it a question.

"Yes, Francois Villon. You have heard of him?"

"Yes," I said. "I have heard of him. But why . . ."

She gestured at Charles. "Ask the mastermind," she said. "He's the one who figures it all out. A man out of his time, he said. Find this Villon, a man out of his time. A genius when there were few geniuses. Pluck wisdom from him. Find out who he really was. And so I found him and he was just a filthy poet, a burglar, a chaser after women, a brawler, a jailbird." She said to me, "The past human race was a bunch of slimy bastards, and the people of your time are no better than the others that have come before you. You're all a bunch of slimy bastards."

"Angela," Charles said, sharply, "Mr. Thornton is our guest."

She swung on him. "And you," she said, "while I'm wading through the stench and depravity and obscenity of medieval Paris, where are you? In a little monastery library somewhere in the Balkans, feeling sanctimonious and holy, and no doubt somewhat supercilious, pawing through parchments, searching on slimmest rumor for evidence of something that you damn well know never did exist."

"But, my dear," he said, "it does exist."

He put the cylinder on the table beside the whiskey bottle.

She stared at it, swaying a little. "So you finally found it, you little son of a bitch," she said. "Now you can go home and lord it over everyone. You can live out your life as the little creep who finally found a capsule. There's one good thing about it—the team will be rid of you."

"Shut up," said Charles. "I didn't find it. Mr. Thornton found it."

She looked at me. "How come you knew about it?" she asked.

"I told him about it," said Charles.

"Oh, great," she said. "So now he knows about us."

"He did, anyhow," said Charles. "So, I suspect, does Mr. Piper. They found one of Stefan's cubes, and when the plane hit Stefan's parked saddle, it fell in Mr. Thornton's yard. These men aren't stupid, dear."

I told him, "It is good of you to say so."

"And the sheriff, too," she said. "The two of them and the sheriff came snooping yesterday."

"I don't think the sheriff knows," I said. "The sheriff doesn't know about the saddle or the cube. All he saw was that contraption over there. He thought it might be a game of some sort."

"But you know it's not a game."

"I don't know what it is," I said.

"It's a map," said Charles. "It shows when and where we are."

"All the others can look at it," said Angela, "or another like it and know where all the others are."

She pointed. "That is us down there," she said.

It made no sense to me. I could see why they'd need a map like that, but not how it could work.

She moved closer to me and took me by the hand. "Look down," she said. "Look down into the center of it. Let's move closer to it and look down into the center of it."

"Angela," warned Charles, "you know that's not allowed."

"For the love of Christ," she said, "he has something coming to him. He found that stinking cylinder and gave it to you."

"Look," I said, "whatever is going on, leave me out of it." I tried to pull my hand away, but she hung on to it, her nails cutting into my flesh.

"You're drunk," said Charles. "You are drunk again. You don't know what you're doing." There was something in his voice that told me he was afraid of her.

"Sure, I'm drunk," she said, "but not all that drunk. Just drunk enough to be a little human. Just drunk enough to be a little decent."

"Down," she said to me. "Look down into the center of it." And I did, God help me, look down into the center of that weird contraption. I guess I must have thought that looking down into it might humor her and end the situation. That's just a guess, however; I don't honestly remember for what reason, if I had a reason, I looked down into it. Later on—but the point is that it was later on and not at that particular moment—I did some wondering if she might have been a witch, then asked myself what a witch might be, and got so tangled up in trying to figure out a definition that it all came to nothing.

But, anyhow, I looked down and there was nothing I could see except a lot of swirling mist—the mist was dark instead of white. There was something about it that I didn't like, a certain frightfulness to it, and I went to step away, but before I could take the step the dark mist inside the cubicle seemed to expand rapidly and engulf me.

The world went away from me and I was a consciousness inside a blackness that seemed to hold neither time nor space, a medium that was suspended in a nothingness in which there was no room for anything or anyone but the consciousness—not the body, but the consciousness—of myself and Angela.

For she still was with me in that black nothingness and I still could feel her hand in mine, although even as I felt the pressure of her hand I told myself it could not be her hand, for in this place neither of us had hands; there was no place or room for hands. Once I had said that to myself, I realized that it was not her hand that I seemed to feel so much as the presence of her, the essence of her being, which seemed to be coalescing with my being as if we had ceased to be two personalities, but had in some strange way become a single personality, although not so much a part of one another as to have lost our identities.

I felt a scream rising in my throat, but I had no throat and I had no mouth and there was no way to scream. I wondered, in something close to terror, what had happened to my body and if I'd ever get it back. As I tried to scream I sensed Angela moving closer, as if she might be extending comfort. And there was comfort, certainly, in knowing she was there. I don't think she spoke to me or actually did anything at all, but I seemed to realize somehow that there were just the two of us in this great nothingness and that there was no room for more than just the two of us; that here there was no place for fear or even for surprise.

Then the dark nothingness drained away, but the draining did not give us back our bodies. We still were disembodied beings, hanging for a moment over a nightmare landscape that was bleak and dark, a barren plain that swept away to jagged mountains notched against the sky. We hung there for a moment only, not really long enough to see where we were—as if a picture had been flashed upon a screen, then suddenly cut off. A glimpse was all I had.

Then we were back in the empty nothingness and Angela had her arms around me—all of her around me—and it was very strange, for she had no arms or body and neither did I, but it seemed to make no difference. The touch of her was comforting, as it had been before, but this time more than comforting, and in that nothingness my soul and mind and the memory of my body cried out to her as another human being and another life. Instinctively, I reached out for her—and reached out within everything I had or had ever had until the semblance of what we once had been intertwined and meshed and we melted into one another. Our beings came together, our minds, our souls, our bodies. In that moment we knew one another in a way that would have been impossible under other circumstances. We crawled into one another until there were not two of us, but one. It was sexual, in part, but far more than sexual. It was the kind of experience that is sought in a sexual embrace but never quite achieved. It was complete fulfillment and it did not subside. It reached a high and stayed there. It was an ecstasy that kept on and on, and it could have gone on forever, I suppose, if it had not been for that one little dirty corner of my busy brain that somehow stood aside and wondered how it might have been with someone other than a bitch like Angela.

That did it. The magic went away. The nothingness went away. We were back in the Lodge, standing beside the strange contraption. We still were holding hands, and she dropped my hand and turned to face me. Her face was white with fury, her voice cold.

"Remember this," she said. "No woman will ever be quite the same again."

Charles, still standing where he had been before, picked up the nearly empty whiskey bottle. He laughed, a knowing and insulting laugh. "I promised you a drink," he said. "You probably need one now."

"Yes, you did," I said. I started across the room toward him, and he picked up the glass that Angela had been using and began to pour the drink. "We are short of glasses," he said. "Under the circumstances, I don't imagine you will mind."

I let him have it, squarely in the face. He was not expecting it, and when he saw the fist coming in it was too late for him to duck. I caught him in the mouth and he went back and down as if he had been sledged. The glass and bottle fell from his hands and rolled across the carpeting, both of them spewing whiskey.

I felt good about belting him. I had wanted to do it ever since I saw him for the first time that morning. Thinking that, I was aghast that so little time had passed.

He didn't try to get up. Maybe he couldn't; maybe he was out. For all I cared he might as well be dead.

I turned and walked toward the door. As I opened it, I looked back. Angela was standing where I'd left her, and she didn't stir when I looked at her. I tried to think of something I should say to her, but nothing came to mind. I suspect it was just as well.

My car was standing in the driveway and the sun was far down the western sky. I took a deep breath—I suppose, unconsciously, I was trying to wipe away any clinging odor of the fog of nothingness, although, to tell the truth, I had never noticed any odor.

When I got into the car and put my hands on the wheel, I noticed that the knuckles of my right hand were bleeding. When I wiped the blood off on my shirt, I could see the toothmarks.

Back at the cabin I parked the car and, climbing to the porch, sat down in a chair. I didn't do a thing, just stayed sitting there. The Galloping Goose came over, heading south. Robins scratched in the leaves underneath the brush beyond our patch of lawn. A sparrow sang as the sun went down.

When it was dark and the lightning bugs came out, I went indoors and made myself some supper. After I had eaten I went out on the porch again, and now I found that I could think a bit, although the thinking made no sense.

The thing that stuck closest to my mind was that brief glimpse I'd gotten of the bleak, dark landscape. It had only been a glimpse, a flashing on and off, but it must have been impressed deeply on my brain. For I found that there were details I had not been aware of, that I would have sworn I had never seen. The plain had seemed level in its blackness, but now I could recall that it was not entirely level, that there were mounds upon it and here and there jagged spears extending upward that could be nothing else than the stumps of shattered masonry. And I knew as well, or seemed to know, that the blackness of the plain was the blackness of molten rock, frozen forever as a monument of that time when the soil and rock beneath had bubbled in a sudden fire.

It was the future, I was certain, that Angela had shown me, the future from which she and the other scavengers had come, probing back across unknown centuries to find out not only what their far forebears had known, but as well those things they might have uncovered or discovered, but had not really known. Although I wondered, as I thought of it, what could possibly have been the so-far-unrecognized significance of a man like Villon? A poet, sure, an accomplished medieval poet who had a modern flair and flavor, but as well a thief and a vagabond who must at many times have felt the shadow of the hangman's noose brush against his neck.

What had we missed in Villon, I wondered, what might we have missed in many other events and men? What could be the significance that we had missed and which had been recognized and now was sought by our far descendants in that black and frozen world up ahead of us? Sought by those who now came back among us to sift through the dustbins of our history, seeking what we unknowingly might have thrown away.

If we could only talk with them, I thought, if only they would talk with us—and even as I thought it, I knew how impossible it was. There was about them a supercilious quality that would not allow them to, that we would never stand for in that it scarcely masked the contempt that they felt for us. It would be akin to a radio astronomer going back to ancient Babylon to talk with a priest-astronomer. In both cases, I knew, the gulf would not be only one of knowledge but of attitude.

A faithful whippoorwill that clocked in every evening shortly after dusk began his haunted chugging. Listening to it, I sat and let the woodland peace creep in. I'd forget it all, I told myself, I'd wipe it from my mind—I had a book to write. There was no purpose and no need to fret about something that would not happen for God knows how many millennia from now.

I knew, of course, that I was wrong. This was not something that could be forgotten. Too much had happened, too much remained unsaid for the incident to be ignored. There probably was, as well, too much at stake, although when I tried to sort out what specifically might be at stake, I had no luck at all. There were questions that needed answering, explanations to be given, a fuller story to be told. And there was just one place to get those questions answered.

I went down off the porch and got into the car. The Lodge was dark when I pulled into the driveway. There was no answer to my knock; when I tried the latch the door came open. I stepped inside and stood in the dark, not calling out. I think I knew there was no one there. My eyes became somewhat accustomed to the dark. Moving cautiously, alert to chairs that might trip me up, I went into the room. My foot crunched on something and I stopped in midstride. Then I saw it—the shattered wreckage of the time-map. I found a pack of matches in my pocket and struck one of them. In the brief flaring of its light I saw that the cubicle had been smashed. Someone, I guessed, had taken a maul, or perhaps a rock to it.

The match burned down and I shook it out. I turned about and left, shutting the door behind me. And now, I thought, the people of the hills would have another mystery about which to speculate. There was the shattered time-map, of course, which when it was found would be a topic of conversation for a year or more at most. The real mystery, however, would be the question of what had happened to the people of the Lodge—the story of how one summer they had disappeared, leaving the Cadillac standing in the garage, and had not come back again. The unpaid taxes would pile up, and at some time in the future someone might pay up the taxes and get title to the place, but that would make no difference to the legend. Through many years to come the story would be told at the Trading Post, and given time the Lodge might become a haunted house and thus the story would be ensured a special kind of immortality.

Back at the cabin, with the fireflies winking in the woods

and the faithful whippoorwill chunking from across the hollow, I tried to console myself by thinking I had done everything that a man could do, although I had the horrid feeling I had failed. And I realized, as well, that now I had lost any chance I might have to do anything at all. This, then, had to be the end of it. The best thing for me, I told myself, was to get back to the book in the hope that as I worked I might forget—or, if not forget, ease the sharpness of the memory.

I tried. For three whole days I tried. I drove myself and got some writing done. When I read it over, I tore it up and wrote it once again. The second draft was no better than the first.

While I sat working at the kitchen table I could feel the saddle in the closet sneaking up on me. I took it out of the closet and, dragging it down the hill, chucked it in a deep ravine. It didn't help; it still sneaked up on me. So I went down into the ravine and retrieved it, throwing it back into the closet.

Running out of groceries, I went to the Trading Post. Humphrey was sitting outside the door, his chair tipped back against the building. I picked up the groceries and a letter from Neville. I sat an hour or two with Humphrey while he talked about the mine. I let him do the talking; I was afraid to say anything for fear I'd make a conversational slip and tip him off to what I knew about it.

The letter from Neville was short, written by a man who was in a hurry. He was off for Greece, he wrote—"I need to see Marathon again."

Returning home with the groceries, I bundled up the notes and drafts I had been working on and jammed them in the briefcase, then went fishing. Fishing helped, I think. If I could have gone on fishing, it would have been all right. If I could have spent the summer fishing, I might have worked it out. But the fishing didn't last long.

I had picked up three fairly good trout by the time I reached the place from which, sitting on a log, I had spotted the protruding log ends that had led me to the mine.

Standing in the stream and looking up the hill, I could see the entrance to the mine, and a short distance below it the rock shelter into which the squirrel had dived.

Then my mind played a sneaky trick on me. Looking at the rock shelter, the thought struck me—that hidden, obscure bit of evidence that had been lying in the back part of my mind, unnoticed until now. I have often wondered since why it could not have passed me by, why it would not have remained hidden, why the computer in my brain felt compelled to haul it forth.

When I had glanced into the shelter, I recalled, I had seen the drifting feathers and the chalky droppings of the birds that had used it for a shelter, while toward the farther end there had been a small rockfall. And it was something about this rockfall that my mind had pounced upon—something that at the time I must subconsciously have noted, but which my brain, in the excitement of the moment, had tucked away for consideration later.

Now, suddenly, it brought forward for consideration the fact that while the roof of the shelter had been limestone, the rockfall had not been limestone, but green shale instead. Green shale, the kind of stone that could be picked from this very stream bed, chunks of soft, smooth rock eroded from the Decorah beds that lay atop the Platteville. The shale could not have been the product of the rockfall; it had been carried there.

Incredible as it may seem, I believe that in that moment I sensed exactly what had happened—an incredible hypothesis rising full-blown out of an incredible situation.

I rebelled against it. To hell with it, I thought; I have had enough; I don't need any more. But even so, I knew I had to have a look; I would never rest until I'd had a look. Not knowing would haunt me. I hoped, I think (it's hard to remember now), that I would find the fall was limestone and not shale at all.

When I went to look, I found my subconscious had been right. The rock was shale, worn smooth by water action. And underneath the little pile of rocks were hidden two of Stefan's photographic cubes.

I squatted there and looked at them, remembering back to what Charles had said. A psychopath, he'd said. A psychopath and he did this filthy thing, then hid the cubes away so we couldn't find them.

Strangely, I couldn't be absolutely sure of the words he had used. Had he said psychopath? Had filthy been the word he had used, or some other word that was very much like it? I remembered he had said violence, but realized he had meant something more than violence, something perhaps so subtle that he could not explain it to me in terms I would understand. And that was the crux of it, of course, illustrative of the gulf between his time and mine.

I tried to imagine a twentieth-century social worker attempting to explain compassion for the poor to an aristocrat of Rome who only thought in terms of bread and circuses, then knew the analogy was a bad one, for the gulf of understanding between the social worker and the Roman would have been narrow compared to the gulf between myself and Charles.

So here, this day, I sit at the kitchen table, nearly done with writing, with the two cubes beside the pile of paper. I wonder at the blind course of circumstance that could have led me to them. And I wonder, too, rather bitterly, about the burden of knowledge that one man must carry, knowing it is true and yet unable to speak a word of it, condemned to write of it in secret for his own salvation (and I'm beginning to think it is no salvation).

I wonder, as well, why I cannot feel compassion for these people of the future, why I cannot see them as our descendants, children of our children many times removed. Why I cannot wish them well. But, no matter what I do, I can't. As if they were alien, as alien as that other people who had broadcast cylinders to the stars—aliens in time rather than space.

Now about the cubes.

One of them, I am fairly certain, although I cannot be entirely sure since I'm no historian, contains a photo of that moment on Christmas Day in the Year of Our Lord 800 when Charlemagne was crowned by Leo III as emperor of the West. Charlemagne (if it indeed is he) is a thug, a massive brute that one dislikes instinctively, while Leo is a fussy little person who seems more overwhelmed by the situation than is Charlemagne.

I cannot be sure, of course, but a number of things make me believe the photo is of Charlemagne and Leo, not the least of which is that this would be, in historic context, the one coronation that a man going into time would want to photograph. Or, rather, perhaps the coronation a man of my own time would want to photograph. I realize that with Stefan there can be no telling. If his thinking and his viewpoint were as twisted as the viewpoint of the others of his time, God knows what his reasons might have been for doing anything at all. Although he did photograph Marathon—and the thought occurs to me that his doing so may mean he did think somewhat along the lines we do and may possibly supply a clue to his so-called psychosis. Could the fact that he was believed psychotic by the people of his time mean no more than that he was a throwback?

I find small comfort in the thought. I would prefer to think he was not a throwback. Knowing he was not, I could feel more comfortable about the remaining cube.

I wish now I had taken the time to know Stefan better; as it stands, no one really knew him. He had been around for years, and all we ever did was wave at him as we went driving past. He was a difficult man, of course. Humphrey said he was the sort of man who would not even tell his name. But we, all of us, could have made a greater effort than we did.

Sitting here, I try to reconstruct him. I try to envision his sneaking down the hollow to hide his cubes. He must have been on the way to cache the Marathon cube when he met his death. Illogical as it may seem, I have even wondered if he was engaged in some ghastly joke, if he had deliberately planted an intentional clue by being killed just below the bridge to enable me, or someone else, to find the hidden cubes. Could there have been two authentic and historic cubes that were intended to lend some credence to the third? This is all insane, of course, but under stressful circumstances a man thinks insanity.

My own thinking must be going faulty; I am clutching at any evidence that will enable me to discount the third cube.

The photograph shows a crucifixion. The cross is not a tall one; the feet of the man upon it are no more than two feet or so above the ground. The wrists are nailed to the crossbar, but the ankles are tied to the post, with no support for the feet. To support the body so that the nails will not tear out, a wooden peg had been passed beneath the crotch and driven into the post. In the distance lies an ancient city. Half a dozen bored and listless soldiers—I take them to be Roman soldiers—lounge about, leaning on their spears, there apparently to prevent interference with the execution. Besides the soldiers there are only a few others, a small band of silent men and women who simply stand and watch. A dog sniffing at the post and one knows, instinctively, that in a little while he'll lift his leg against it.

There is no mocking placard nailed upon the cross. There is no crown of thorns. There are no other crosses, bearing thieves, to flank the single cross. There is no sign of glory.

And yet—and yet—and yet . . . Stefan filmed a moment out of Marathon, snatched for posterity the significance of that fargone Christmas day, proving that indeed he had a keen sense of the historical as it might be interpreted by the culture of the present. The present, not the future. If he had been so right about the other two, could he have been wrong about the third? There had been, of course, many crucifixions, the punishment reserved for slaves, for thieves, for the contemptibles. But of all of them, in the context of history, only one stands out. Could Stefan have missed that one? Much as I might like to think so, I do not believe he did.

The thing that saddens me, that leaves in me a feeling of chilling emptiness, is that nothing of importance seems to be transpiring. There is the sense of shoddy death (if death can be shoddy, and I think it often is). Here the soldiers wait for the dying to be done, so they can be off to better things. The others simply wait, with resignation on their faces; there is nothing one can do against the power of Rome.

And yet, I tell myself, if this is the way it really was, this is the way it should have stayed, this is the way the event should have been transmitted to us. Out of this sad and empty happening, Christianity might have built a greater strength than it has from all the trappings of imagined glory.

The head of the victim on the cross had fallen forward, with the chin resting on the chest. Turn the cube as I may, I cannot see the face.

If I could look upon the face, I think I would know. Not by recognizing the face, for we do not know the face—all we have is the imaginings of long-dead artists, not all of them agreeing. But from some expression on the face, from something in the eyes.

I wonder about the saddle. Could it somehow be fixed? Could it be made to function once again? Could I figure out, from scratch, how to operate it?

(Editor's note: This manuscript was found in the briefcase of Andrew Thornton, along with the notes for a book he had been writing, after Thornton's disappearance. Police theorize he may have wandered off and been killed by a bear in some densely wooded and remote area where there would be little hope of finding his body. The possibility he may have wandered off is supported by his distraught frame of mind, which the manuscript reveals. Thornton's disappearance was reported by his close friend, Neville Piper, upon his return from Greece. The saddle mentioned in the manuscript has not been found; there is some question it existed. Neither have the cubes been found. Dr. Piper, who presently is engaged in writing a book on the Battle of Marathon, setting forth some new findings, disclaims any knowledge of the so-called Marathon Photograph.)

CLIFFORD D. SIMAK, during his fifty-five-year career, produced some of the most iconic science fiction stories ever written. Born in 1904 on a farm in southwestern Wisconsin, Simak got a job at a small-town newspaper in 1929 and eventually became news editor of the *Minneapolis Star-Tribune*, writing fiction in his spare time. Simak was best known for the book *City*, a reaction to the horrors of World War II, and for his novel *Way Station*. In 1953 City was awarded the International Fantasy Award, and in following years, Simak won three Hugo Awards and a Nebula Award. In 1977 he became the third Grand Master of the Science Fiction and Fantasy Writers of America, and before his death in 1988, he was named one of three inaugural winners of the Horror Writers Association's Bram Stoker Award for Lifetime Achievement.

DAVID W. WIXON was a close friend of Clifford D. Simak's. As Simak's health declined, Wixon, already familiar with science fiction publishing, began more and more to handle such things as his friend's business correspondence and contract matters. Named literary executor of the estate after Simak's death, Wixon began a long-term project to secure the rights to all of Simak's stories and find a way to make them available to readers who, given the fifty-five-year span of Simak's writing career, might never have gotten the chance to enjoy all of his short fiction. Along the way, Wixon also read the author's surviving journals and rejected manuscripts, which made him uniquely able to provide Simak's readers with interesting and thought-provoking commentary that sheds new light on the work and thought of a great writer.

THE COMPLETE SHORT FICTION OF CLIFFORD D. SIMAK

FROM OPEN ROAD MEDIA

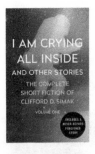
I AM CRYING ALL INSIDE AND OTHER STORIES — THE COMPLETE SHORT FICTION OF CLIFFORD D. SIMAK — VOLUME ONE — INCLUDES A NEVER-BEFORE-PUBLISHED STORY

THE BIG FRONT YARD AND OTHER STORIES — THE COMPLETE SHORT FICTION OF CLIFFORD D. SIMAK — VOLUME TWO — INCLUDES THE HUGO AWARD-WINNING TITLE STORY

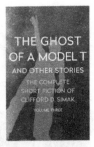
THE GHOST OF A MODEL T AND OTHER STORIES — THE COMPLETE SHORT FICTION OF CLIFFORD D. SIMAK — VOLUME THREE

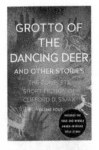
GROTTO OF THE DANCING DEER AND OTHER STORIES — THE COMPLETE SHORT FICTION OF CLIFFORD D. SIMAK — VOLUME FOUR — INCLUDES THE HUGO AND NEBULA AWARD-WINNING TITLE STORY

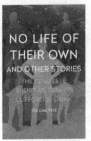
NO LIFE OF THEIR OWN AND OTHER STORIES — THE COMPLETE SHORT FICTION OF CLIFFORD D. SIMAK — VOLUME FIVE

NEW FOLKS' HOME AND OTHER STORIES — THE COMPLETE SHORT FICTION OF CLIFFORD D. SIMAK — VOLUME SIX

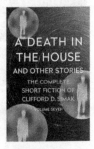
A DEATH IN THE HOUSE AND OTHER STORIES — THE COMPLETE SHORT FICTION OF CLIFFORD D. SIMAK — VOLUME SEVEN

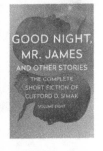
GOOD NIGHT, MR. JAMES AND OTHER STORIES — THE COMPLETE SHORT FICTION OF CLIFFORD D. SIMAK — VOLUME EIGHT

EARTH FOR INSPIRATION AND OTHER STORIES — THE COMPLETE SHORT FICTION OF CLIFFORD D. SIMAK — VOLUME NINE

THE SHIPSHAPE MIRACLE AND OTHER STORIES — THE COMPLETE SHORT FICTION OF CLIFFORD D. SIMAK — VOLUME TEN

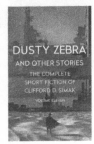
DUSTY ZEBRA AND OTHER STORIES — THE COMPLETE SHORT FICTION OF CLIFFORD D. SIMAK — VOLUME ELEVEN

THE THING IN THE STONE AND OTHER STORIES — THE COMPLETE SHORT FICTION OF CLIFFORD D. SIMAK — VOLUME TWELVE

INTEGRATED MEDIA

Find a full list of our authors and
titles at www.openroadmedia.com

FOLLOW US
@OpenRoadMedia

Printed in the USA
CPSIA information can be obtained
at www.ICGtesting.com
LVHW041323041023
759945LV00001B/9

9 781504 083119